Homecoming

A DOWNEAST NOVEL

MARIE FORCE

Homecoming
A Downeast Novel
By: Marie Force
Published by HTJB, Inc.
Copyright 2025. HTJB, Inc.
Cover Design: Kristina Brinton
Photo Credit: Marie Force
E-book Layout by The E-book Formatting Fairies
ISBN: 978-1958035931

HTJB, Inc.
PO Box 370
Portsmouth, RI 02871 USA
marie@marieforce.com

The Ballard Family

Kendra, 40, executive assistant to Chuck Ballard at Ballard Boat Works (BBW), married to Hugo, daughters Luna, 11 and Aurora, 9

Kellen, 39, chief strategy officer at BBW

Keith, 37, laborer with BBW

Kingston, 35, lobster fisherman

Kieran, 34, oversees fiberglass shop at BBW and owns local watering hole, The Trap.

Kara, 32

Kirby, 31, Kara's closest friend in the family, master craftsman and oversees anything having to do with wood accents on the boats at BBW

Kelly, 30, married to Matt Gallagher, mother of Connor

Kyle, 29, runs the paint shop at BBW

Kolby, 27, mailman

Keenan, 26, works in business development at BBW

CHAPTER

One

"Where thou art, that is home."
—Emily Dickinson

THEY RODE home from the wedding in stunned silence. After a gorgeous day celebrating their dear friends Victoria and Shannon, Kara Torrington had received a phone call from her mother.

You and Dan need to come home. Your brothers have been charged with murder.

Her parents weren't interested in getting *her* home to Maine as much as they were in *her husband*, a successful criminal defense attorney who specialized in getting wrongly accused people exonerated.

Kara wasn't sure if her brothers fell into that category. Some of them had been raising hell from the minute they were born, and she wasn't at all surprised to hear serious trouble had found them, although she was shocked to hear that Kirby was one of the two who'd been charged.

Keith? That wasn't as much of a surprise, but Kirby... He'd never been in any kind of trouble. She was fairly confident Keith would turn out to be responsible for whatever circumstances had landed them both in jail, accused of the worst possible crime. Not that she thought Keith was capable of murder. At least she hoped he couldn't have done something like that.

Kara had seven brothers and three sisters but wasn't particularly close to most of them. Not anymore. However, she talked to Kirby regularly and was truly shocked to hear he'd been arrested for anything, let alone murder.

Relocating to Gansett Island to run a division of the family business several summers ago had been the smartest move Kara could've made for herself. It had gotten her out of the hornet's nest of family drama, away from her sister Kelly, who'd casually stolen Kara's boyfriend—and then married him—and Gansett had brought Dan Torrington into her life. He was, without a doubt, the best thing to ever happen to her. And she never would've met him if Kelly—and Matt—hadn't stabbed her in the back.

While things had worked out well for Kara on Gansett, where she'd made the kind of friends that made a life complete, the thought of going home to Maine and being surrounded by the unruly Ballard family was the last thing in the world she wanted to do, especially when she was seven months pregnant.

She placed a hand on her rounded belly and gasped when the baby gave a hard kick.

"Is Bruiser playing soccer again?" Dan asked as he parked the Porsche he'd inherited from his late brother, Dylan, in the driveway.

"He's playing something."

He reached over to put his hand on top of hers. "Does it hurt?"

"No, it's just weird to have someone moving around in there."

"Wait for me." He got out of the low-slung car, came around to the passenger side and offered her a hand out.

Without his help, she wasn't sure she would've been able to

get out on her own. The pregnancy had left her feeling ungainly and off-balance.

Inside, she went straight to the bedroom and retrieved suitcases from the back of the closet.

Dan came up behind her and put his hands on her shoulders. "Babe."

"What?"

"Look at me."

She turned to face him.

"We don't have to do this."

"What do you mean?"

"We're under no obligation to go there or to deal with any of this. You're in the third trimester. We have a perfectly good reason to tell them we can't make it."

Kara stopped to consider that. She was sorely tempted to use her pregnancy as an excuse to stay put on Gansett Island. She'd worked so hard to build a life for herself separate from her family, even if she still worked for the family business.

Everything was better from a distance.

She might've stayed away if her Kirby hadn't been charged. He had to be freaking out, and there was nothing she wouldn't do for him.

"I can't let Kirby get swallowed up in whatever Keith has done. We have to go for him. He was my best friend growing up." When tears threatened, she did her best to contain the emotional overload, which was harder than usual thanks to the pregnancy.

Dan put his hand on her face and caressed her cheek with his thumb. "Then that's what we'll do, but please know that I'll throw myself in front of anything or anyone who tries to hurt you, and I won't be nice about it."

She smiled. "It'll be amazing to have someone sticking up for me for once."

"Baby, I will *always* stick up for you."

"Are we still talking about my family?"

Grinning, he leaned in to kiss her. "Of course we are. Where has your dirty mind gone?"

"Right." She rolled her eyes. "My dirty mind. You're the one who's made me this way."

"That's a slanderous accusation."

"It's not an accusation—or slander—if it's the truth. My lawyer husband taught me that."

Dan laughed. "Touché."

The friendly bickering with him helped to keep her mind off where they were going and why as they finished packing.

Kara received a text from her grandmother, Bertha. *Heard you've been summoned.*

You heard correctly.

Are you okay?

Never better.

You don't have to do this.

I wouldn't if Kirby wasn't involved.

I figured you'd say that. Text me your ETA. I'll pick you up.

I hate the reason for this, but I'm THRILLED I get to see you today.

Likewise, my love. Safe travels.

She cleaned of anything that would spoil in their absence out of the fridge and put a few things in the freezer. Stephanie McCarthy would water Kara's plants since she and her husband, Grant, who was Dan's best friend, had keys to their house.

While Dan walked the garbage out to the curb and took their bags to the car, Kara looked around at the cozy little cottage they called home, wondering how long it would be until they returned.

Soon. They'd be back soon because this was their home. It was where they belonged.

She was giving her screwed-up family a week, two at the most, and then she and Dan were coming home to Gansett.

. . .

THEIR PILOT PAL, SLIM JACKSON, HAD WARNED THEM that the climb out of Gansett Island and the flight itself would be bumpy since the atmosphere was still churned up from the recent hurricane.

Kara held Dan's hand as tightly as she could without hurting him. She hated flying on a good day, and this was most definitely not a good day.

Erin, Slim's wife and Kara's friend, looked back at Kara from the copilot seat. "Are you okay?"

"I'll be better when we land," Kara said with a grimace. Pregnancy had made her nauseated for months, and the bumpy air wasn't helping.

"Nothing to be afraid of," Slim said. "Think of it as potholes on a rough road."

Kara appreciated his attempt to defuse her anxiety, but the only thing that would relax her would be a safe landing in Maine, where a whole new reason for anxiety would present itself. This would be the first time back to Maine since leaving. Since she'd moved to Gansett to start the company's launch business in the island's Great Salt Pond, she'd found the peace and harmony that'd been sadly lacking in her life while growing up as one of eleven Ballard siblings.

The thought of going back to Maine for any reason made her sick. That her family was counting on her husband to fix a terrible situation for them only made everything worse.

Before her mother had called them home, had she given any thought whatsoever to how they'd stood by Kelly after she made off with the man Kara had planned to marry? Were they recalling the big fancy wedding they'd thrown for Kelly and Matt after their treachery? Kara would bet her life they never thought about any of that, especially at a time like this when the family name and everything it stood for faced the greatest threat yet.

The mighty Ballard Boat Works Company that employed a thousand locals and accounted for a huge chunk of the Downeast economy would take a huge hit if the Ballards' sons were convicted of murder. The charge alone might be enough to ruin three generations of hard work and sacrifice in building a successful, well-regarded business.

Her dad used to tell them that it only took one fuckup to ruin everything for all of them. He must've been having a complete meltdown with two sons charged with murder. Not that Kara believed for a second that Kirby had anything to do with such a thing. She wished she could be so certain about Keith, but she barely knew him, and what she did know of him wasn't good.

Kara tried to tell herself she didn't care what became of the business or her family, but she did. And she was angry with herself for caring after everything they'd put her through.

"Hey," Dan said, drawing her out of her thoughts. "Are you okay?"

"Sure," she said with an edge of sarcasm. "I'm on the roughest flight of my life on the way to the last place on earth I want to go so my hideous family can shamelessly use my wonderful husband to defend my brothers, one of whom could be guilty, for all I know. Sure, everything is just dandy."

"It's going to be okay, honey. I'll be right there with you, and as soon as we get this dealt with, we'll come right back to the island where we belong. I've already got my best people in LA working on getting as much info as they can about the charges, so try not to worry."

"It's hard not to worry. I don't want to be there, as you know."

"I get it, love."

"They're using you."

"You think I don't know that? The minute my name is attached to the defense, this case becomes a whole new ballgame for the prosecution."

"That's what they want, and I despise that."

"It's fine. I'll do what I can for them and be on my way."

"Nothing is ever that simple with my family."

They'd been scheduled to go to Maine a couple of years ago, after Kara stored the launches for the winter, and they'd almost made it when she'd changed her mind about taking the best thing in her life to the worst place. She hadn't wanted the Ballard stain to touch her relationship with Dan and had managed to keep contact with her family to a minimum since they'd been together. They'd canceled that trip at the last minute, so this would be the first time Dan had ever been to Maine.

Some of her family had come for the wedding. Three of her brothers had ended up in jail the night before after a bar fight. Dan thought she hadn't heard about how he'd gotten them out on the morning of the wedding and threatened them with grave consequences if they did anything to ruin her big day. Kara's friend Tiffany Taylor, wife of Gansett Police Chief Blaine Taylor, had told Kara about the trouble her brothers had gotten into and how Dan had taken care of it.

That's what he did. He took care of things. He took care of her, and he'd do that in Maine, too. She was certain of it, but if he was off dealing with the mess her brothers had made, he couldn't be with her every minute of every day while they were there, which would leave her on her own to fend them off.

The thought of dealing with her family took her right back to the years of growing up in the midst of mayhem—and not the good kind.

Kara had seen how other families functioned, especially since she'd arrived to live and work on Gansett. She'd become close to the McCarthys, a family of six siblings and numerous cousins who were the best of friends. Her family wasn't like that. Sometimes she wondered if they'd sooner stab each other in the back than share confidences.

She blamed the family business for most of the strain.

For as long as she could remember, several of her siblings

had been competing to be the one to take over for their father when he retired. Kara couldn't imagine wanting anything badly enough to fight with her own family members over it. The only thing she'd ever wanted that much was Dan, and she'd always fight for him and their relationship. Nothing else had ever meant as much to her as he did, and she was determined to keep him and their marriage as her top priority in Maine.

The business had come between multiple generations of her father's family. She had an uncle she barely knew thanks to the rift that'd led her parents to buy out her father's brother at tremendous financial pain. Once his brother was out of the picture, her father had made a huge success of the business, but at what cost? He was estranged from his brother, and now his own kids were going to end up fighting over the business.

In addition to her sister's treachery, part of the reason she'd wanted to leave Maine in the first place was because she couldn't bear to be part of the discourse on what would become of the business after their father retired or died. Even though she'd worked for the company for years, Kara wanted nothing to do with any of that, and it'd been a relief to get away from the constant drama.

The very thought of dealing with that again made her feel sicker than pregnancy and a rough flight put together. In the years she'd spent living on Gansett, she'd found a peaceful, happy life that was in stark contrast to what she'd experienced in Maine. She would protect that hard-won peace, no matter what.

Her phone chimed with a text from her cousin Renata Ballard, who was six months older than Kara and had been among her closest friends growing up, even after their fathers had fallen out.

Heard you and Dan have been called home to deal with the brothers. I'm sorry. Can only imagine how you must be feeling.

Renata and Dan had met many times over the years via Face-Time, becoming friends one call at a time.

I'm pissed to be summoned, pissed to be on the bumpiest flight ever. Generally pissed.

Don't blame you. You guys can stay with me if you need a place to crash.

That's so sweet of you, but I'm pretty sure Bertha would be crushed if we didn't stay with her.

Of course she would. No problem at all. Let me know that you're all set tho. I'm excited for some time with you and to meet your hubby in person.

Thank you for giving me a reason to look forward to this trip from hell.

There're lots of people here who love you and will be there to support you through this.

I appreciate that. I'm so worried about Kirby. There's no way he had anything to do with this.

I've been thinking the same thing.

Do you know what happened?

One of the summer residents was found dead, and Keith/Kirby were the last two people seen with her. That's all I know so far. She was 21.

OMG.

Kara went cold all over as the news settled on her along with the realization that the scandal would have all of Hancock County talking about the Ballard family and the sons who might've killed a young woman.

"Renata said the victim is a twenty-one-year-old summer resident."

"I know. I read the local news report."

Of course he was already working the case, knowing how badly she'd want to get back to Gansett as quickly as possible.

"I'll cover all the bases, babe. Don't worry."

"Are you licensed to work in Maine?"

He nodded. "We were preparing to take a case in Maine about five years ago, so I got licensed there. Unfortunately, the defendant died of cancer before his case could be heard, so this'll be my first case in Maine. I've worked in thirty other states over the years. I got licensed in Rhode Island when Grant asked me to help with Charlie's case."

That was the case that brought him to Gansett originally. Charlie was Stephanie's stepfather, and Dan helped to get him released after fourteen years in prison for a crime he didn't commit.

"Hearing the victim in the Bar Harbor case was a summer resident makes me more anxious than I already was. The summer people tend to be wealthy and keep to themselves. They usually don't mix and mingle with the locals. Often, they're long gone by this part of September, back to their real lives in New York or Connecticut or wherever they came from."

"That's good to know."

Kara's mind raced with scenarios that would've put thirty-seven-year-old Keith and thirty-one-year-old Kirby in the path of the twenty-one-year-old woman who'd been murdered.

A sense of dread overtook her as she braced herself for landing and to deal with the storm that awaited her on the ground.

CHAPTER

Two

AS THE RUGGED Maine coastline came into view, Kara tried to focus on the things she loved about her home state as she breathed through a new wave of nausea from the plane rocking and rolling its way toward a landing.

"Almost there, sweetheart." Dan leaned forward to look out the window. "The coast reminds me a bit of Gansett."

"Uh-huh."

"Doing okay?"

"I think so." She was desperately trying not to vomit. "I ate too much cake at the wedding." Shannon and Victoria's celebration already seemed like days ago rather than hours.

"There's the airport now."

Kara was at once relieved and anxious to see the familiar Hancock County-Bar Harbor Airport come into view.

"Final approach," Slim said from the cockpit. "Prepare for landing."

Their friend brought the plane in for a smooth landing five minutes later.

"Welcome to Trenton, Maine," Erin said, "where the local

time is five twenty-seven, and the temperature is a seasonable sixty-eight degrees."

"Trenton?" Dan asked.

"It's a bit north of Bar Harbor and Mount Desert Island."

"Ah, another island. I forget that Bar Harbor is on an island, too. And you pronounce it as *dessert* rather than *desert*?"

"Yep, that's the French pronunciation, and unlike Gansett, this island has a road to the mainland."

Slim brought the plane to a stop outside the terminal and cut the engine. "Sorry for the rough ride, guys."

"We blame Hurricane Ethel for that, not you," Dan said. "Thanks again for bringing us."

"No problem. We're going to spend the night up here and check it out. Neither of us has ever been. Where should we stay?"

Kara suggested a few of the local hotels. "They should have vacancies since the high season is over and leaf peeping hasn't started yet."

"Sounds good," Erin said. "I can't wait to see Bar Harbor."

"It's pretty," Kara said with a decided lack of enthusiasm for a place that'd brought her far more pain than pleasure in the last few years she'd lived there. As Slim helped them out of the plane, Kara said, "Text me if you have any questions about anything."

"We'll be fine," Slim said. "Take care of your family, and don't worry about us. And when you're ready to come home, give me a ring. I'll pick you up."

Dan shook his hand. "Thanks again."

"Any time."

They both hugged Erin and then walked together into the terminal to meet Kara's grandmother, Bertha Lively. Her face lit up with delight when she saw them coming with their friends.

Kara hugged her very best friend in the world. Her grandmother had a weather-worn, perpetually tanned face from a life-time on the water, blue eyes and short, curly white hair.

"I'd say I'm glad to see you, but not under these circumstances," Bertha said.

"Likewise." She pulled back from Bertha to let Dan hug her. They'd met once before in Boston. "These are our friends from Gansett, Slim and Erin Jackson. This is my grandmother, Bertha Lively."

Bertha shook hands with them. "Such a pleasure to meet my Kara's friends."

"For us, too," Erin said. "We've heard so much about you and your lobster boat."

"Oh shoot, it's nothing special."

"Yes, it is," Kara said. "It's very special, and so are you."

"You're already my favorite grandchild. No need to suck up."

While Dan, Slim and Erin laughed, Kara wanted to cry with relief from seeing her beloved grandmother. The scent of Jean Naté brought back a million of the best memories from her childhood.

"Slim and Erin are spending the night."

"I'd offer to drive you, but I've got the pickup," Bertha said.

"No worries," Slim said. "We're renting a car."

As they hugged their friends and said goodbye, Kara wondered when she'd see them again. This day hadn't turned out like she'd thought it would when she woke up snuggled up to Dan in bed on Gansett Island. When she'd gotten dressed for the wedding, she certainly hadn't expected to be sleeping at Bertha's house in Maine that night.

Dan put their suitcases in the back of Bertha's beat-up old Ford pickup that'd once been white but was now more rust than anything. "This truck is *sick*," Dan said. "What year is it?"

"Seventy-two and still purring like a kitten."

"Amazing."

Kara sat in the middle between them and dug around for a

seat belt that probably hadn't been used in years. As she fastened it under her baby belly, she hoped there wouldn't be any sudden stops.

When Bertha fired up the truck, Kara laughed for the first time in hours. "It's purring like a kitten with bronchitis."

Bertha barked out a laugh that was among Kara's favorite things. "She's got a few rough spots here and there."

"Renata said we can stay with her," Kara said in case it might be too much for Bertha to have guests.

"No way. I want you with me."

Kara withdrew her phone to let her cousin know she'd been claimed by Bertha.

Not surprised, Renata replied with laughing emojis. Even though she and Renata were paternal cousins, Renata loved Kara's maternal grandmother as much as Kara did. *I'll check in tomorrow.*

Can't wait to see you.

Same, girl—and to finally meet your MAN in the flesh!

Thank goodness for Bertha and Renata, who were among the people Kara had surrounded herself with when she'd lived in Maine. Her "found family," as she referred to them along with her friends, Jessie and Ellery, and her uncle Buster, who had autism and still lived with Bertha. As he was nearly fifteen years younger than Kara's mother, Buster had been more like a cousin than an uncle to her growing up, and she loved him dearly.

Kara received another text, this one from her mother. *Are you coming? When will you arrive?*

"Ugh."

"What?" Dan asked.

She showed him the text. "My mother is losing it asking when we're getting here."

"I've got this." He handed her phone back to her, took out his and started typing. A minute later, he said, "All set."

"What did you say to her?"

"I told her we've just arrived in Maine, that I'll check in tomorrow morning and that no one from the family is to contact you about your brothers' case. They're to come right to me with any questions or concerns."

"My hero," Kara said softly.

"Mine, too," Bertha said.

"Don't worry about anything. I'll take care of it."

"Have I mentioned that I really, *really* love your husband?" Bertha asked Kara.

"I do, too."

"Aw, you ladies flatter me."

"It'll go straight to his fat head," Kara said with a smile for him.

"It's already there."

Bertha laughed as she took the last turn toward the true home of Kara's heart. The large, chaotic house where she'd been raised had nothing on Bertha's tiny shack by the sea, as she called her simple six-room ranch house with one bathroom and a million-dollar view of the water.

"Here it is, home sweet home," Bertha announced as they pulled into a driveway behind a pile of lobster traps so high they nearly blocked the view of the house.

"Did you get more traps, B?" Kara asked.

"Johnny Wistcoff retired and gave me his."

"I can't believe he actually retired."

"Well, he turned ninety, and his arthritis has gotten bad."

"Ninety and still lobster fishing," Dan said. "You Mainers are studs."

"We're a hardy sort." Bertha led the way inside. "Buster! Come say hi to Kara and Dan!"

When Buster appeared out of one of the back bedrooms, holding a bowl of soup, Kara resisted the usual urge to hug him. He didn't like to be touched, so she only smiled at the familiar surge of love for her precious uncle.

"Hey," he said with warmth in his blue eyes.

His dark blond hair had gotten long, and he'd begun to grow in the winter beard that kept his face warm in the cold.

"Hey back at you. This is my husband, Dan."

Buster nodded.

"Nice to meet you, Buster."

"Uh-huh."

"Come in, make yourself at home, Dan." Bertha led the way into the tiny house that was Kara's favorite place in the world. She didn't have to be told to make herself at home in the family room that consisted of worn furniture covered with throw blankets, wood-paneled walls, framed paintings of the coast, as well as Bertha's boat, the *Big B*, the lighthouse and Acadia. Everything was exactly as it had been the last time Kara was there, which was hugely comforting. As much as everything else changed, Bertha and her home remained constant.

She sat on a love seat and patted the spot next to her, inviting Dan to join her. The gold fabric, which had once had a nubby texture, had worn smooth over decades of providing comfort to Bertha's many visitors. Kara had slept there most weekends until she was too tall to fit and then had moved to the sofa.

As he took a seat next to her, Dan looked out of place in all his refined handsomeness, but he'd proven to her many times before that he was more than capable of fitting into her life. And he was wild about Bertha.

"How about some dinner?" Bertha asked. "I made a seafood casserole earlier, and I've got salad and bread."

Dan's stomach groaned loudly, making them laugh. "You'd never know that I feasted at a wedding just a few short hours ago."

"That's a yes for Dan," Bertha said. "Kara?"

"I'm not sure I can eat yet. That flight was rough."

"You need a little something. I can make you a grilled cheese or cinnamon toast."

"With a little bit of sugar?" Kara asked with a hopeful smile.

"Of course. What do you take me for?"

Kara laughed at Bertha's sassy reply. "That'd be great. Thanks, B."

"Anything for you, love."

Just that simply, Kara felt better. Bertha's cinnamon-sugar toast had always hit the spot when she wasn't feeling well. "I had a lot of stomach issues when I was a kid," she told Dan, "and had to miss school. My mom would drop me off with Bertha so she could go to her exercise class and get her nails done. Bertha's cinnamon-sugar toast cured everything."

"She left you when you were sick to get her nails done?"

Kara shrugged. "I'd rather have been here. It was fine."

Bertha set up TV trays that'd been a wedding gift more than fifty years earlier and positioned them in front of Dan and Kara.

"Those remind me of my grandmother's house," Dan said of the tables.

"Grandmothers are required to have TV trays," Bertha said. "It's in the manual."

Dan smiled at her witty reply. "Can I help with anything?"

"Not at all. You're my guest. You have to let me take care of you."

"If you insist," he said, still grinning the way people often did in Bertha's presence.

"I insist," she said over her shoulder as she returned to the kitchen.

"Have I mentioned that I adore her?"

"And vice versa. She doesn't wait on just anyone."

Dan's phone lit up with a text.

Kara glanced at the screen and saw her mother's name.

He turned the phone so she couldn't see the message. "I got this, sweetheart. Don't give it a thought."

"It's kind of hard to think about anything else when two of my brothers are in jail facing murder charges."

"There's no way Kirby had anything to do with it." Bertha returned, carrying two plates that she put on the trays. She pulled silverware from her back pocket. "Whatever happened, Keith must've dragged him into it."

"That's what I think, too. Kirby must be freaking out."

"Put it out of your mind for now, sweetheart," Bertha said. "There's nothing you can do tonight. We'll know more in the morning when Dan gets to talk to them."

"Should I try to see them tonight?" he asked.

"It's best to wait until the morning when the police chief is there. Rushton White is a good man. I don't know any of the other current officers, but he's been with the department for decades and can be trusted."

"That's good to know."

"I wouldn't go anywhere near that place unless he's there."

"I won't. I may be running some other names past you for background as this goes forward. Is that okay?"

"Whatever you need. Many of my grandsons have a wild streak that's gotten them in trouble over the years, but I can't see any of them going so far as to murder a young woman."

"Definitely not Kirby, but who knows with Keith," Kara said.

Bertha's deep sigh said it all.

CHAPTER
Three

BERTHA'S third bedroom had a queen-sized bed and not much room for anything else, which was fine with Dan. As long as Kara could get some rest, that was all he cared about. That and keeping her far, *far* away from the unfolding nightmare within her notorious family. He snuck out of bed at first light and went to the living room to retrieve running clothes from the suitcase they'd left there the night before.

He was heading for the front door when Bertha appeared in the kitchen.

"You're off to an early start," she said as she turned on the coffee she'd prepared the night before.

"Gotta keep running so I don't have a dad bod by the time the little one shows up."

She grunted out a laugh. "You don't have an extra pound on you."

"I make sure of it."

"The act of running for fun baffles me."

"You don't need to run when you do the work of ten men on any given day. I push pencils for a living."

"Good point. Listen... I appreciate what you're doing here,

how you came running when Judith called, but I want you to know... If you feel like it's going to be too much for you—or particularly for Kara—take a pass on the whole mess and go back to your happy place on Gansett."

"That wouldn't win me any favor with my in-laws."

"Screw them. You don't owe them anything. The only one you need to be thinking about is Kara."

"I'm always thinking about her, and trust me, if this gets to be too much for her, we're out of here."

Bertha nodded. "That's good. She's worked so hard to make a life for herself away from this place. I won't see her dragged back to where she was when she left."

"I'd never let that happen."

"I know you won't." Her sweet smile took years off her lined face. "In case you haven't noticed, I'm quite fond of you. I couldn't have chosen a more perfect husband for my girl."

Moved, Dan went to her.

She met him halfway in a hug that surrounded him in a scent that reminded him of his grandmother.

"My Nana has been gone a long time. It's nice to have a grandmother again."

"That's sweet of you to say."

When they pulled back from each other, he said, "Try not to worry. I know it's deeply upsetting to have your grandsons facing serious charges, but I'll do everything I can for them."

"Keith can be an asshole."

"I know. I've had the pleasure of meeting him before. Ironically, I got him out of jail on Gansett."

"*What?*"

"Several of them got arrested after a bar fight the night before our wedding, in the island's biggest dive. Kara doesn't know that. I bailed out him, Kyle and Kieran with a warning about what I'd do to them if they ruined her big day."

Bertha shook her head and then went to pour herself a

coffee. "I blame my daughter for them turning into hooligans. She was off getting massages when her kids were running wild. I tried to warn her years ago that she'd be sorry for letting them go unsupervised, but I never could tell her anything. She's known everything from the minute she could talk. Chuck wasn't much better, but at least he had an excuse. The man works like a dog. Always has. I suspect his work ethic had as much to with avoiding his family as with building his business."

"This is all helpful information. Keep it coming."

"Go have your run. I'll leave some breakfast for you and Kara before Buster and I leave for work."

"You work on Sundays?"

"Seven days a week this time of year. It's prime lobster season."

"Ah, I see. Don't worry about cooking for us. We can take care of ourselves."

"Not in my house."

"Yes, ma'am," he said, grinning as he left with a wave.

Dan took off running down Bertha's street, which lined the water's edge where seagulls foraged for breakfast and a hint of fog clung to the surface of the placid cove. A dozen lobster boats were anchored amid skiffs, small motorboats and a few sailboats.

The houses in Bertha's neighborhood were mostly like hers, built in the '50s or '60s and beaten up by the elements of coastal living. Most had lobster traps stacked in the yard or driveway and several had boats on trailers. Some yards boasted well-tended gardens and rosebushes, while others featured old appliances and other junk that should've been carted away years ago.

He did a three-mile loop, enjoying the sights and scents. A group of busy seagulls entertained him with their morning antics, diving for fish and crabs and anything else they could scrounge from the shallow water.

It wasn't even seven o'clock when he returned to Bertha's,

sweating profusely and ready for some water and then coffee to jumpstart his day.

Bertha and Buster were long gone.

Dan wasn't looking forward to dealing with Kara's brothers, but he was more than happy to take one for the team to keep his beloved out of the scrum. He'd already figured out that her parents were using him before she said it last night. But he didn't fault them for calling him. In their position, he'd have done the same thing if he had a lawyer of his caliber in the family.

A lawyer of his caliber.

He chuckled. Kara would roll her eyes to high heaven if she heard him describe himself that way. It was true, though. If his sons stood accused of a heinous crime, he'd want someone like him, too, not that his sons would be anywhere near such a thing. People had no clue what to do when a situation blew up their lives. Often, they did the wrong thing, such as allowing the accused to speak to police without a lawyer present, which only added to the jeopardy when the wrong thing was said to the right person.

He hoped Judith had passed along his advice that Keith and Kirby not talk to anyone before they had legal representation. Although, he wouldn't put it past Keith to spout off and make everything worse.

Dan recalled his first impression of Keith: sleeve tattoos on his arms and chips on both shoulders. He'd bristled at Gansett Police Chief Blaine Taylor's order to make restitution to the Rusty Scupper, the bar they'd busted up the night before the wedding in a drunken fight. They were also ordered to stay out of trouble for the remainder of their time on the island or Chief Taylor would toss their asses on the first ferry out of town.

Kyle's attitude had been similar to Keith's, but Keiran had seemed somewhat humbled by his night in jail. Thankfully, they hadn't caused any trouble during the wedding, and as far as Dan knew, Kara had never caught wind of the incident.

He despised the way her family upset her. Bringing her here, seven months pregnant, certainly wasn't ideal. His goal for today was to quickly assess whether the situation was a matter of a local police department jumping the gun on arresting suspects without sufficient cause or whether he faced a long, drawn-out battle to defend two brothers-in-law he barely knew.

Coffee in hand, he went down the hallway to look in on Kara, who was still asleep. He picked up his phone off the bedside charger and brought it with him to the kitchen. Before he checked his phone, he lifted the lid on a pan on the stove to find eggs, potatoes and bacon. The scent made his mouth water.

He'd worry about his dad bod another day.

Sitting at Bertha's well-worn kitchen table with a second cup of coffee, he ate his breakfast and scrolled through his messages. Two from Judith already.

What time will you be seeing the boys?

What can we do to help?

Dan replied to her. *I'll be there by nine and no help needed right now. I'll check in later. Please remind every member of the family again not to talk to the media or anyone else about the case. That's critical. ALSO DO NOT contact Kara about this. That's my line in the sand, Judith. Keep her out of it, or I'm gone.*

He could see she was already replying, but it took a few minutes for her text to arrive. *I understand.*

"You'd better believe I mean it," he muttered.

"Who are you talking to?" his beloved asked when she appeared in the doorway, disheveled and rosy cheeked from sleep.

He held out his arms to her.

She sat on his lap and snuggled into his embrace.

"I was talking to myself."

"You sounded annoyed."

"Work stuff. Nothing to worry about."

"Is my mother already harassing you?"

"Define harassing."

She groaned.

"Don't sweat it, babe. I can manage her. She's not going to push me around or tell me how to do my job."

"Sexy."

"What is?"

"You. Managing my mother."

Dan choked out a laugh. "Seriously? *That's* sexy?"

"God yes. She's been pushing me around my whole life. I would've loved to have had you around to fight my battles for me back in the day."

Even though he was still sweaty, Dan tightened his hold on her. It burned his ass to hear her talk about anyone pushing her around. "No one can touch you now, sweetheart. You're older, stronger, more able to defend yourself. You wouldn't even need me to help fight your battles these days."

"Probably not, but everything is better when you're here."

God, he loved her with all his heart, and he honestly suspected he could kill anyone who tried to harm her in any way. Not that he would. Who had time for all that paperwork? But anyone who bothered his wife would have to deal with him, including her own family. Especially them.

"Bertha made breakfast for us."

"Of course she did."

"Are you hungry?"

"Not yet. Woke up nauseated as usual."

"You're in the home stretch, love. Soon enough, you'll be feeling great again."

"I hear we're going to be sleep-deprived and cranky after our precious package arrives."

"You could never be cranky, and I'll make sure you get plenty of sleep." He gave her a pat on the bum so he could get up. "I'm going to shower and head to the cop shop to see what's what, okay?"

"Thank you."

"You don't have to thank me."

"Yes, I really do. You've been dragged into this nightmare because you're married to me."

"Being married to you is the best thing to ever happen to me. If it comes with some in-law aggravation, well, then, so be it. The pros vastly outweigh the cons."

"You say that now."

"I'll say that always." He kissed her. "Don't forget that while a situation like this is new to you and your family, I handle nightmares for a living, so don't fret."

"Can't help it. This'll be your first full exposure to the special joy known as the Ballard family. What if you regret your choice of wife—"

He kissed the words off her lips. "Hush. I'll never regret my choice. I married the one person in this whole world I couldn't live without, and nothing that happens here will change that. Tell me you believe me."

"I do..."

"No buts, Kara. You and me, and little Dylan... We're forever. This is temporary." He rested his hand on the curve of her baby bump and was rewarded with a swift kick to the palm from his son. They'd chosen not to find out for sure what they were having, but they both believed the baby was a boy because of that kick. "Please don't spend one second worrying about things changing between us because of your family. I love you madly."

She wrapped her arms around his neck and kissed him. "I love you, too."

"Sorry about the coffee breath." He tried to keep that away from her when she was nauseated in the morning.

"It was worth it."

"What're you going to do while I'm gone?"

"Renata is coming to get me to go into town for a bit."

"That'll be fun."

"How're you getting to the police station?"

"I hired a guy to drive me around."

"You did what?"

"I haven't got time to be lost in the woods of Maine. I got shit to do so I can get my gorgeous wife back home before our baby is born."

"Who did you hire?"

"His name is Walter something."

"*Walter Cummings?*"

"Yeah, that's it."

Kara busted up laughing. "He's the town drunk."

"Oh."

"But supposedly, he only drinks at night."

"Well, that's comforting."

"How in the hell did you find him?"

"I googled people who drive for a living in the area while we were on the plane yesterday, and he popped up. I want to be able to say, 'Take me to this place,' and get there without a problem while I work on the way."

"We could've rented a car and used a modern convenience known as GPS, you know."

"That wouldn't give me the kind of local insight I can get from someone like Walter, who knows the score around here." Dan glanced at the clock over the stove. He had thirty minutes until Walter was due to pick him up. "Do you mind if I eat your share of breakfast?"

"Of course not. You'll need your strength to deal with my brothers, and I'll have something in town when the nausea wears off."

He grinned at her. "Your brothers don't scare me. I've seen much worse."

"Have you, though?"

"I promise you that I have. I want you to go with Renata and have a wonderful time with your cousin and not worry about anything to do with this case. You hear me?"

"Yes, dear. Tell my Kirby I love him, and I don't believe for a second he had anything to do with this."

"I'll tell him if I get the chance."

After a shower, Dan dressed in one of the two suits he'd brought with him, knotted a burgundy tie and checked his appearance in a mirror on the back of the bathroom door. He, who'd become accustomed to every luxury in life, adored this tiny house that'd been a refuge for Kara during her chaotic childhood. Every item was worn and battered from decades of use that told the story of a life well lived.

From the first second he stepped through the door, he'd felt "at home" there in a way he seldom had anywhere outside of the house where he'd been raised and the place he and Kara called home on Gansett Island. He loved his place in Malibu, too, but it'd never felt like home to him, not like Bertha's house already did.

Satisfied that he looked like the successful attorney he was, he left the bathroom and went to kiss his wife goodbye for now. "I'll be back as soon as I can."

"Text me when you're free, and I'll tell you where I am."

"Have fun with Renata."

"I always do."

"Love you."

"Love you, too. Good luck."

"Dan Torrington doesn't believe in luck. It's all skill, baby."

"God, I walked right into that."

Laughing, Dan stole one more kiss and then headed out with his work bag slung over his shoulder, containing the tools of his trade: a small recording device, notebooks, two of his favorite pens and a couple of granola bars with protein. He'd filled his water bottle with ice water and was ready to confront whatever waited for him at the police station.

CHAPTER
Four

WALTER WAS RIGHT ON TIME, pulling up in a maroon sedan that had to be at least twenty years old but shone as if it'd just been washed. He jumped out of the car and came around to shake hands with Dan.

"Good to meet you. Read a lot about you last night. Impressive stuff."

Dan was relieved that the man seemed sober. He was in his mid- to late-fifties, balding, with a reddish complexion that indicated either a history of drinking or sun exposure, possibly both. He wore a light blue dress shirt that had been badly ironed and khaki pants. "Nice to meet you, too. Thanks for doing this."

"It's my pleasure to drive the celebrity lawyer around."

The hint of New England in his words reminded Dan of Ned Saunders on Gansett. "No need to make a thing of that."

"Oh, the whole town is abuzz with the news that the Ballards brought in the big gun to defend their boys."

"The big gun, huh?"

"Yep, that's what they're calling you."

"Lovely." He laughed to himself at how Kara would make fun of him if she heard him referred to that way.

Walter held the back door for Dan, waited for him to get settled, then closed the door and ran around to the driver's seat.

Dan was amused at Walter's excitement. "I assume you know where we're going?"

"Yes, sir."

"You can call me Dan. Sir isn't necessary."

"Got it."

"What's the word around town about the case?"

Walter glanced at him in the mirror, seeming hesitant to speak his mind.

"It's okay. You can tell me."

"They're your family, so it must be strange to be dealing with something like this."

"Not really. I barely know them. My wife hasn't lived here in years, and I only met them at the wedding." He didn't add the part about bailing some of them out of jail before the wedding.

"That family is something."

"I want you to speak freely with me. I'd appreciate any insight you have."

"Don't like to gossip."

"It's not gossip if it's true, right?"

Walter shifted in his seat. "I... uh..."

"Let me put it this way. The Ballards, as a family, mean nothing to me. Their daughter Kara has my whole heart and soul. Our life together doesn't really include them, so there's nothing you could say about them that would bother me. However, it would bother me if anything we talked about in the car got around town. Does that help to clarify things?"

"It does, yes. Heard some talk about how Kara left and never came back after her sister married Matt Gallagher. People thought he was Kara's boyfriend."

"He was until he wasn't."

"Oh, damn. I wondered how that went down."

"It went down ugly, but it turned out well for Kara—and for

me. We met because she left this place to make a life for herself elsewhere. For that, I'll always be thankful to Kelly and Matt, although I'll never forgive them for the way they hurt Kara."

"That's lame."

"Totally lame. What can you tell me about Keith?"

"Honestly? He comes off as an asshole, but underneath it all, he's considered a fairly good guy. He can fix anything, and people rely on him for repairs they can't afford to have done otherwise."

"That's interesting. I didn't know that about him."

"He does it all, plumbing, electric, roofing, you name it. However, he's still an entitled asshole at times who thinks the world revolves around him. If you ask me, the parents are to blame. They let him run wild as a kid, and he was a menace."

"Was it all of them or just him?"

"Some of the others were jerks, too. Not all of them, but a few. Kyle is another one who stands out as a bit of a dick. They were spoiled as kids. The family is one of the wealthier ones in the area, and it's not like they don't give back to the community, because they do. But the kids had too much handed to them. Although, some of them turned out just fine. Strange how that happens, right?"

"It is."

"Eleven kids raised the same way. Some are awesome people, and others... Well, they're something else altogether."

"You think Keith could murder someone?"

"Oh jeez... I've been thinking about that nonstop since I heard the news, and honestly, I don't see it, but with him... Hard tellin'. Kirby, on the other hand, no freaking way. He's a sweetheart."

"That's what I've heard."

"I can't imagine how he'd be mixed up in something like this."

"Kara said the same thing. They're close."

"He's good people. Always doing something for someone else. Volunteers at the food bank and is a Big Brother to a fatherless kid in town. He doesn't have a single one of Keith's rough edges."

That, right there, was why Dan had hired a local person to drive him. Insight from someone who wasn't part of the family but was well-connected in town would be priceless. They were on a highway that took them past a variety of homes and properties, some well-kept, others not so much. Like in Bertha's neighborhood, lobster traps and boats were prevalent. "This place is big for an island."

"It's one hundred and eight square miles, fifteen miles wide and eight miles long. It's the sixth-largest island in the Lower 48 and the third-largest on the Eastern Seaboard."

"We could put a hundred Gansett Islands on one Mount Desert."

"Maybe not a hundred, but it's much bigger than your island. Plus, we have about ten thousand year-round residents."

"That's ten times what we have, plus some."

"The French voyager Samuel de Champlain visited the island in 1604 and gave it its name based on the treeless mountains. He called it Ile de Monts Deserts, which, literally translated, means island of the bare mountains. Another interesting thing to remember is that even though it's spelled Desert, we say dessert, as in Mount Dessert, which is the French pronunciation."

"My wife mentioned that and saved me from embarrassing myself with the locals." Walter was more than paying off in the first half hour. Dan wanted the lay of the land without having to ask Kara to show him around. He wanted her to rest and relax and spend time with people who filled her up and made her happy.

"I'm sure your wife would've set you straight if you got it wrong."

"She would've taken great pleasure in that."

Walter grunted out a laugh. "Don't they all?"

"Seems that way. How many towns are on the island?"

"Four: Bar Harbor, Tremont, Southwest Harbor and the town of Mount Desert. The Cranberry Isles are also part of Mount Desert."

"How do you get to them?"

"A short ferry ride."

"Ah, I see."

"The national park encompasses more than forty-eight thousand acres on the island and is well worth a visit. The highest peak is Cadillac Mountain at more than fifteen hundred feet in elevation. Have you been to Acadia before?"

"This is my first time to Maine."

"Oh, well, you're in for a treat. This time of year is the best. The tourists have cleared out, and the foliage is about to explode. Very scenic."

"Where do the rich people live?"

"Down long private roads that lead to houses you usually can't see from the main road. You get a better sense of the prime real estate around here from the water."

"Good to know."

Dan was surprised that it took more than half an hour to get to downtown Bar Harbor, with Walter pointing out items of interest along the way that gave Dan a better sense of the place. Despite the sprawling size of the island, this was small-town America at its finest. While the area was gorgeous and the scenery stunning, he also detected an undercurrent of poverty in some areas, due to the prevalence of run-down houses and buildings.

Bar Harbor itself, however, was the crown jewel. The seaside town was made up of colorful buildings. The restaurants, bars, shops and hotels would've reminded Dan of Gansett if it wasn't for the large hill that sloped down toward the water, where lobster boats and other vessels were moored.

He also noted the presence of a cruise ship and asked Walter about it.

"They're big business around here. They keep coming long after the summer tourists go home. Some people love them for the income they generate. Others hate them for the crowds they bring."

Walter turned onto Firefly Lane, pulled into the public safety complex that housed the police and fire departments and parked in a visitor spot.

"Any insight on what to expect in there?"

"They'll know who you are and might be reserved until they decide you're an okay kind of guy."

"I've gotten that reception before. My grandmother-in-law tells me Chief White is a good guy."

"He is. People like him around here. He's a straight shooter. No bullshit."

"My favorite kind of LEO."

"What's that stand for?"

"Law enforcement officer."

"Oh, duh. I should've caught that."

"Thanks for all the info. Should I text you when I'm ready for a ride back?"

"Sure, that'd work. Got a few errands I can do while I'm in town."

"I have to put this out there, so don't be insulted, okay?"

"Okay…"

"Kara told me you have a reputation for enjoying your spirits."

"Is that a fancy word for booze?"

"It is."

"Well, that *was* my reputation when she lived here. I've been sober for thirty-seven months now."

"That's amazing, Walter. Congratulations."

"Thanks. It's been a long, hard road, to say the least, but I'm sticking to it. Go to meetings and all that. Made a real mess of my life for a long time. Thankfully, my kids are the forgiving sorts. The wife? Not so much, but she hasn't left me yet, so I take that as a good sign."

"I'm sorry to bring it up, but I'm about to be a dad for the first time, so—"

"Say no more, my friend. I totally understand, and you're safe with me."

"I'll text you in a bit."

"I'll be close by. Good luck."

"Thanks." Dan had a feeling he'd need all the luck he could get.

CHAPTER
Five

INSIDE THE POLICE STATION, he was greeted by an admin with a nameplate on the desk that identified her as Linda. He asked her if he could see Chief White. He put his business card on the counter. "I'm here for Keith and Kirby Ballard."

"Detective Cosgrove is the lead investigator on that case."

"I was told to ask for the chief."

Linda lowered her voice. "You should know... Cosgrove is the type that'd be put out by you going over his head. It'd get you off on the wrong foot with him."

"Thank you for that advice. Is the detective available?"

"Let me get him for you." She started to walk away but turned back. "I want you to know that I greatly admire your work. My brother was falsely accused. It took a long time to exonerate him, but his reputation never recovered. What you do matters greatly."

"Thank you very much. I'm sorry about your brother."

"It wasn't the only trouble in his life, unfortunately, but it about broke him."

"As these things do."

Linda nodded and then went to get Cosgrove.

Dan had known his reputation would precede him, but he hadn't expected to be confronted with it at reception.

She returned a few minutes later with a man who Dan figured was about thirty-five, with close-cropped brown hair, a muscular physique and cool blue eyes. He wore a striped dress shirt with a navy blue tie and a gold badge clipped to his belt.

"Detective James Cosgrove, this is Daniel Torrington, here for the Ballards."

Cosgrove shook Dan's outstretched hand. "Good to meet you. Come in."

He was led into a conference room where Cosgrove had set up shop. "I only caught the case this morning, so I'm still getting up to speed with assistance from the Maine State Police, which responded to the scene and made the arrests over the weekend."

"What do you know so far?"

"Tanya Sorenson, age twenty-one, was in town for a bachelorette party for her future sister-in-law. They were staying at Tanya's parents' home here in Bar Harbor. The women went out for the evening and visited a number of bars. It was an unusually busy September Friday in town as the effects of Hurricane Ethel had passed by us, and people were eager to get out again. The bars were packed. The party Tanya was part of was one of about six or seven bachelorette parties moving through town Friday night."

Dan took notes on everything Cosgrove told him.

"According to statements taken from her friends by state police, Tanya was seen dancing with Keith Ballard throughout the latter part of the night at the Barnacle Lounge. They said he more or less joined their party around ten and hung out for the rest of the night. The bride-to-be, Jessa Kaul, who's engaged to Tanya's older brother, August Sorenson, expressed discomfort with Tanya hanging out with a guy who was clearly quite a bit older than her. We were told they argued about it.

"Tanya told Jessa she wasn't her sister or even her sister-in-law yet, and she needed to mind her own business. The bride backed off, and Tanya was last seen walking down Main Street, holding hands with Keith. We have video that shows them together. Tanya failed to return to the house where they were staying. The other women notified us yesterday morning that she hadn't come home or checked in with them, which they said is way out of character. They described the man she'd been last seen with, and from the video, we identified him as Keith Ballard. Tanya's body was found late Saturday morning on a remote beach by a fisherman who spotted her as he was motoring along the shore. She'd been beaten and strangled."

"How does Kirby Ballard figure into it?"

"We have an eyewitness that put Kirby on the scene with Keith and Tanya about half a mile from where the body was found."

"Your witness is credible?"

"He is."

"What other evidence do you have to tie my clients to this case?"

Cosgrove stared at him, unblinking. "They were the last ones seen with her before she was found dead."

"Understood. What else?"

"That's all I have so far. Like I said, I caught the case this morning. I'm waiting on the autopsy and other evidence gathered from the scene where the body was found."

"I'm not sure how many murder cases you've worked on in your career, Detective, but this sounds like a massive rush to judgment to me. You have no forensics tying either of the Ballard brothers to her—and even if you did, witnesses put her with Keith throughout the evening, so there's bound to be DNA that can be easily explained in court. If all you have is reports that they were seen together, that's not enough to charge murder."

"I didn't file the charges. The state police did. They felt they had enough."

"The case is circumstantial at best. Even if you get a DNA hit, I can make that go away in two seconds by conceding they were dancing and holding each other in public."

"That'll be up to the judge to determine. Like I said, I didn't make the call to arrest them, and I've only been on the case for two hours."

"Understood." Dan placed his business card on the desk. "Will you please email copies of the police and autopsy reports when you have them?"

"Okay."

"Why haven't they been arraigned yet?" That was supposed to happen within twenty-four hours of being arrested and charged.

"The judge who presides over the Superior Court in our area has the stomach flu, and there wasn't another judge available over the weekend. He expects to be back to hearing cases tomorrow."

The delay in arraignment would provide Dan with grounds to appeal if it came to that in the future. "I'd like to see my clients."

"I'll have them brought up to a room."

Ten minutes later, Cosgrove returned and asked Dan to follow him. He pointed to a closed door being guarded by a male Patrol officer.

"Thank you. I'll find you after I consult with them."

"I'll be back in the conference room."

"Got it."

Dan entered the room to find his brothers-in-law dressed in orange jumpsuits. Keith was seated at the table, while Kirby paced.

"What the hell are *you* doing here?" Keith asked in a tone dripping with disdain.

"Your parents asked me to come."

"Well, you can go back to where you came from because we don't need you."

Kirby balked. "*Are you crazy, Keith?* Of course we need him!"

"I'd rather rot in prison than have to look at his smug face."

"Great," Dan said. "My wife and I will be thrilled to head home today."

"*This* is her home," Keith said with a snarl.

Dan smiled. "Not anymore. Best of luck to you, gentlemen. From what I've seen of the case so far, you're going to need it."

"Don't go," Kirby said. "I want you to represent me."

"I don't," Keith said.

"I assume you have the resources to hire your own attorney?" Dan asked Keith.

"I'm fine. Don't worry about me."

"Great, I won't." Dan went to the door and signaled to the officer who was standing in the hallway. "Keith Ballard has declined my representation. I'd like to confer alone with Kirby Ballard."

"Let's go," the officer said to Keith.

"Be careful who you trust, little brother," Keith said to Kirby. "The slicker the lawyer, the deeper the bullshit."

"You ought to know," Kirby said.

Keith didn't like that, but he didn't say anything more as he was escorted from the room.

"Thank you for coming." Kirby fell into a seat across from Dan. He was tall and muscular like Keith, but as Walter had said, he lacked Keith's sharp edges. He had a baby face and the same golden-brown eyes and reddish-gold hair as Kara. "I know this is the last place Kara wants to be."

"She'd do anything for you. She said to tell you she loves you and knows you weren't involved with this."

"I wasn't." He leaned across the table. "I had nothing to do with her. Keith called me for a ride. I met him by the wharf where the cruise ships offload passengers and waited for him while he said good night to her. I asked him if she needed a ride, too, but he said she was all set. I didn't like leaving her there, but Keith said she was a grown woman who could get herself home."

Dan wrote down everything Kirby said. "How far was she from home?"

"I have no idea. I never spoke to her. I just saw her talking to Keith outside my truck. When he got in, I asked if he was sure we shouldn't take her somewhere, and he said he was sure. What was I supposed to do?"

"Nothing you could do, but a witness saw you two with her, and now you're caught up in this."

"I had zero contact with her. That has to count for something, doesn't it?"

"It will, for sure."

"In the meantime, this will be forever attached to my name."

"We'll see what we can do about that. Try not to worry too much. There'll be no forensic evidence tying you to her murder. I'll file a motion to dismiss the charges against you."

"How long will that take? I need to get back to work."

"The judge is out sick and supposed to be back to work tomorrow. I'm on it. I'll do everything I can for you."

"Thank you, Dan. I really appreciate it. I know how difficult it must be for Kara to be back here. Tell her I said thanks for coming."

"I will. Sit tight and don't talk to anyone unless I'm with you. You got me?"

"Yeah, I won't."

"That's really important, Kirby. They're looking to make a case against you. Don't make it easy on them."

He nodded. "I hear you, man. I gotta get out of here."

"I'll file the motion to dismiss today and will be back tomorrow to update you."

"Thanks again."

"You got it." Dan stood to leave. "Are you being held with Keith?"

"No, they have us separated."

"That's for the best. Don't talk to him either."

"I've got nothing to say to him on a good day. The only reason I went to get him when he texted me for a ride is I didn't want him getting another DUI. He's already got three, and it makes us all look like shit when he gets in trouble."

Jeez, Dan thought. *Three DUIs.* That wouldn't go over well with the judge, but Keith was no longer his problem. "I'm on it. Hang in there."

"I'm hanging by a thread."

Dan knocked on the door, which was opened by another officer. Dan was glad he could go home to Kara and tell her the case against Kirby was all but nonexistent. Hopefully, he would have it resolved within a day or two and get him out of lockup.

He returned to the conference room, where Cosgrove pored over a stack of pages. "You should know that Kirby had no contact with her at all. After Keith texted for a ride, Kirby asked if they should give her a ride home, Keith said she was all set, and that was the extent of Kirby's involvement with her. He can also attest that she was alive when he and Keith left her on the sidewalk."

"Yes, I have his statement."

"How can you hold him when you have nothing to tie him to her murder?"

"I have an eyewitness who saw them with her."

"Kirby was never *with* her."

"So he says."

"You can check his phone records to confirm that what he told you is true."

"We're working on that now."

"I'm filing an emergency motion to dismiss the charges against him."

"Knock yourself out."

Dan had nothing to say to that, so he left, determined to get the motion to dismiss filed immediately. He sent a text to Walter, letting him know he was ready for a ride.

Be there in five, boss.

While he waited outside the station, Dan texted Judith. *Keith declined representation. Met with Kirby and will file an emergency motion for dismissal today. He had no contact with the victim and was only there to pick up Keith. His case should be easily resolved —I hope. More to come.*

Keith DECLINED representation? Is he serious?

Yes, he was quite serious that he didn't want me anywhere near the case.

I'll talk to him.

Dan was happy to let Judith deal with her son—and he'd be happy if he didn't have to. Either way, he'd do whatever the family wanted. His goal was to get both brothers out of jail and see the charges dropped as soon as possible so he and Kara could go home to await the arrival of their baby.

Walter pulled up to the station's main door a few minutes later. "Where we headed, bossman?"

"How do you feel about a walk downtown? And you can call me Dan."

"I like bossman. It suits you."

"All right, then," Dan said, amused.

"I'm up for a walk. Where're we headed?"

"I want to see the bar, the sidewalk where Keith was seen with the murder victim after the bar closed and the beach where the body was found."

Walter pulled into a guest parking spot and said, "Right this way."

CHAPTER
Six

"WHAT'S THE WORD AROUND TOWN?" Dan asked as they headed toward the downtown area.

"It's all they're talking about."

"Figured that."

"No one can believe Kirby's caught up in it."

"He had no contact with her."

"Well, that's not surprising. He's a good dude. People like him. Keith, though... While many people like him and appreciate that he helps out when needed, they aren't completely sold on his innocence."

"He refused representation from me, so I'm not sure what he's going to do."

"Is he insane?"

Dan shrugged. "Hard telling. Not sure if he's got a beef with all lawyers or just me. I barely know him."

"It's probably all lawyers. He's been in trouble here and there over the years. Wouldn't surprise me if he blames the lawyers."

"Sounds about right. He was none too pleased when I showed up to get him out of jail the morning of my wedding."

Walter snorted out a laugh. "Yeah, probably pissed him off that he needed you."

"That's how it seemed then—and today."

"Well, I guess he's not your problem if he declined representation."

"Doesn't break my heart, but Judith is insisting that he *will* be represented by me. I'll let them fight that out. Incidentally, I need to remind you again... Anything we talk about is privileged."

"I thought of that, so here's a buck." He handed a one-dollar bill to Dan. "I'm retaining you as my lawyer so no one can make me tell them what you have to say."

Impressed, Dan took the bill and tucked it into his shirt pocket. "I like you, Walter."

"I like you, too, bossman. You're not the windbag I expected you to be with all that fancy success you've had."

Laughing, Dan said, "According to my wife, I'm a major windbag."

"Well, she's gotta say that to keep you humble."

"That's her primary role in my life."

"She's always been a good kid. A neighbor's son worked with her in business development at Ballard and said she was one of the good guys."

"She is that. The best I've ever known."

"How'd you meet her?"

"Went to Gansett Island to help a close friend with a case. His future father-in-law had been unjustly incarcerated. I met her through him and his family."

"Ah, I see. And you've been together ever since?"

"Not quite," Dan said with a laugh. "She led me on one hell of a chase. Can you believe she wasn't instantly smitten with me?"

Walter barked out a laugh. "Made you work for it, did she?"

"Like I've never worked for anything in my life. She was worth it, though. I knew that from the start."

"I'm glad she's made a happy life for herself away from this place and all the family drama."

"So the family drama is well known around here?"

"Oh, hell yes. You know how it goes in small towns. People talk. And with eleven kids in a family, you can't turn your head around here without running into one of them."

"I suppose that's true."

"Not to mention the business employs about a thousand locals. Everyone knows someone who works for them. The Ballard name carries a lot of weight in these parts. Sometimes good weight, other times not so much. But people are still shocked that the Ballard sons could be accused of something like murder." They approached a building close to the top of the hill that led to the waterfront. "That's the place where they were, right there."

The Barnacle Lounge had the look of a dive bar, nestled between two souvenir shops on Main Street. A second cruise ship was now anchored in the harbor, a hulking presence seeming to loom over the town. Since the bar was currently closed, Dan peered in the window to get a sense of the place. "What goes on here?"

"It's mostly a townie bar, so I'm surprised a bachelorette group ended up there. But the victim and her family spend summers here, so it might've been known to them. They have live music on the weekends. People go there to drink and dance."

The vibe reminded Dan of a few of the popular spots on Gansett Island.

They walked on, down the hill through the bustling center of Bar Harbor, passing tourists with stickers on their jackets that identified them as cruise ship passengers. There were so many of them that the sidewalk reminded Dan of Times Square in New York City, albeit on a much smaller scale.

"Damn. Lotta people."

"This town has a love-hate relationship with the cruise ships. While we love the business, the crowding is an issue. Lots of drama over that."

"I'll bet." He hoped the cruise ships never discovered Gansett. As they approached the bottom of the hill, they used the crosswalk. "What's that?" Dan asked, gesturing toward a busy wharf.

"Where the cruise passengers come and go."

"Ah, I see."

"Over this way is where the witness says he saw the brothers with the victim."

Dan looked around but didn't see any cameras in the area like there'd be in a city. "I'm surprised there aren't more cameras with all the cruise traffic coming through town."

"That's also been an issue. While people want the security, folks up here don't like being watched as they go about their business. It's a fine line, you know?"

"I get it. Why live in a small town if you're going to be watched like you'd be in a city?"

"Exactly."

"What do you know about the witness?"

"Fella named Jonah Brown."

"Is he a local?"

"Born and raised. This is where it gets interesting, though. He worked for Ballard Boat Works for years before being let go about two years ago. Never did hear why."

"Very interesting indeed." Dan felt the spark of reasonable doubt catch fire within him. Could an ex-employee with an ax to grind against the family and company be an impartial witness against two of the owner's sons? He could build a defense upon that question. But first he needed to find out why the man had left the company.

"Where was she found?"

"This way." Walter led him about a quarter of a mile from the wharf to a rocky stretch of beach that'd been roped off with yellow crime scene tape. A number of people were working the area, most of them in the jumpsuits forensic investigators wore to keep from contaminating the scene. "She was found right there." He pointed to a spot about fifty feet from the road.

"Where's the victim's house from here?"

He pointed toward the terminal. "Two miles that way."

"What do you know about the Sorenson family?"

"By all accounts, good people with nice kids, who worked in town in the summers. They weren't like some of the summer kids who think theirs doesn't stink. You know what I mean? The son bartended for years while he was in college, and the daughter taught sailing. She spent the summer here and had gone back to UConn for her senior year a few weeks ago."

"It's so terribly sad."

"Indeed."

They walked back to town and hooked a left to go up the hill to where they'd left the car.

Walter was gasping by the time they reached the top of the steep incline. "Clearly, I need to work out more if walking up a hill wrecks me."

"Run a mile a day. It'll change your life."

"Really? I'll give that some thought."

"Make sure you stretch—a lot—especially at first."

"I'll do that."

While Walter drove him back to Bertha's, Dan made notes of the things he'd learned about the case that day and plotted his next move. When Walter pulled into the driveway at Bertha's, he said, "Shoot me a text to let me know what you need, bossman."

"Will do. Thanks for today. Appreciate the ride, the conversation, the local perspective."

"My pleasure."

Dan went inside and fired up his laptop to write the motion

to dismiss the charges against Kirby, planning to submit it before the end of the day.

KARA SAT AT A SIDEWALK CAFÉ ACROSS FROM RENATA. "It's so good to see you in person." She hadn't seen her cousin since she'd left Bar Harbor almost four years ago. Her cousin hadn't come to the wedding because of the rift between their fathers. Without that, Renata would've been her maid of honor.

Renata stirred cream into her coffee. "Same. I'm thankful for FaceTime, but there's no substitute for in-person time."

"I know. It's great to see Bertha, too. I miss her so much."

"I'm sure you do. She misses you just as much. We had lunch a month or so ago on one of her rare days off. It was great to see her."

"Thank you for being so faithful to her."

"I adore her, as you know."

"Yes, I do know that." Kara took a sip of ice water she'd flavored with lemon, which would help to settle her stomach. "I hate being so far from her when she's getting on in years. She won't live forever."

"She's got twenty more years left in her, and you'll never convince me otherwise."

Kara laughed. "You're probably right."

"She'll outlive us all."

"I sure as hell hope so. I can't imagine life without her."

"I know, me either. So how are things with Dan?"

"Still wonderful," Kara said with a smile. "We're very happy together."

"That's so great. You really landed on your feet after everything that happened here."

"Leaving was the best thing I ever did for myself, but I've missed you, Jessie, Ellery, Bertha, Buster, Kirby, Kendra and the girls and a few of the others."

"You've stayed close to us while you were gone."

"I've tried, but like you said, it's not the same as seeing each other all the time." Kara took in the quaint Bar Harbor downtown, which was busy with tourists enjoying the September day. "Nothing ever changes around here."

"Except it's busier than ever. The cruise ships just keep coming, every day."

"Is that still the biggest controversy in town?"

"Sure is. It's a love-hate relationship for sure."

"I keep hoping the ships don't discover Gansett Island. It would ruin us to add that to what we already get in the summer."

"How many people live there year-round?"

"About seven hundred, but that swells to thousands in the summer. The ferries come full of cars and people almost hourly every day for months. Not to mention the people who come by boat and plane. The islanders breathe a collective sigh of relief around this time of year, when school starts up again and things return to off-season normal." Speaking of Gansett made Kara miss being there, and she'd only been gone a day.

"You really love it there, huh?"

"I do. It's become home to both of us."

"Are you going to LA this winter?"

"That's the plan. Dan likes to spend some time in his office out there, even though he's cut way back on his innocence project work. He still supports the team working on the project and likes to get some face time with them."

"What do you do while he's working?"

"I relax a bit after the insanity of the summer. It's nice to take a break."

"You're lucky you can afford to."

"And I know it. Believe me."

"I need my Dan Torrington to come along with his millions. If he's handsome, too, that'd be nice."

Kara laughed through a twinge of discomfort as Renata

reminded her of the economic disparity between them since Kara had married Dan—and all his millions.

"Sorry. I shouldn't have said that."

"It's fine. No big deal."

"It must be nice, though, to not have to worry about money anymore," Renata said as she studied the café's menu.

"Is everything okay, Ren?"

"Yeah, it's great. My rent's going up, my roommate's moving out and my boss is a pain in my ass. Other than that, all good."

"I thought Kath was working out well as a roommate."

"She was until the landlord notified us that he needs another thousand a month. She can't swing it, so she found something cheaper. She's not on the lease, which leaves me stuck with figuring out what to do."

"I'm sorry. That's got to be so stressful."

"It is, especially since I want to quit my job and tell Myles the ass pain to go eff himself with all his sweet gestures as he tries to get me to date him when I absolutely do not want to."

She worked as the general manager of a lobster wholesaler, now run by the son of the owner. Myles had been a thorn in her side since his dad retired three years ago.

"What's he done now?"

"It would take me all day to tell you the many ways that man annoys me."

"Is he still hot and single?"

"Unfortunately, yes on both fronts. I keep hoping he'll get a girlfriend and a life away from work, so I won't have to spend all day every day with him being nice to me."

"How do you stand it?"

"Shut up! I'm being serious."

Kara laughed. "I know. Have you looked around for something else?"

"I'm always looking, but it's hard to find something that

would match the salary and benefits I have now. He keeps giving me raises because I think he suspects I want to quit."

"Does that mean you could swing the apartment on your own?"

"I'd have to seriously cut back everywhere else."

Kara wanted to offer to help her, but after what Renata had said before, she didn't think it would be welcome. "The man is crazy about you. He has been since long before his father retired."

Renata recoiled. "He's my boss. I can't date him when I'm dependent upon him for a job. Remember what happened to my mother? How'd that work out for her?"

"Don't shoot the messenger. I'm just asking."

"The very thought of it makes my skin crawl."

"Even though he's smoking hot?"

"Even though. He's the most annoying human being on the *planet*. I want him to marry someone else and go away so I can do the job I used to love in peace—and quiet. He never shuts up."

Kara bit her lip to keep from laughing at the faces Renata made as she described Myles and to stop herself from saying she'd felt the same way about Dan when she first met him. What a mistake it would've been to not have given him a chance. But Renata didn't want to hear that. She'd made up her mind about Myles and wasn't likely to change it any time soon.

"Let's talk about something else. The subject of that man makes me crazy. How's pregnancy?"

"I'd like to say it's magical and all the things, but I spend most of every day dealing with nausea. It's so gross." She'd brought crackers to munch on before they ordered lunch.

"Do the crackers help?"

"Oddly enough, it helps to feed the nausea, if that makes sense. It gives my stomach something else to do but roll and roil."

"Sounds dreadful."

"I hear the end result is worth it."

Renata frowned. "Better you than me. I can barely take care of myself."

"You'd be a great mom."

"That feels like something that might happen in the way far-off future. Right now, I'm just trying to get through the day." She glanced at her watch. "Ass pain will expect me back in exactly thirty minutes and grill me about where I've been if I'm one minute late."

"What would he say if you told him to eff off?"

"I tell him that every day. He just laughs."

Kara was more certain than ever that Myles might be in love with her cousin but was possibly frustrated that he couldn't date her because she worked for him. And there was the fact that she seemed to actively despise him. It'd be funny if Kara didn't love Renata so much and want only the best for her.

Her phone lit up with a text from Dan. *Saw Kirby (Keith wasn't interested in me being his lawyer) and am working on a motion to dismiss the charges against him since he was nowhere near the woman who was killed. And according to him, she was alive when he and Keith left her on the sidewalk.*

She read the text to Renata.

"Keith is a fool to turn away a lawyer of Dan's caliber."

"He's a total fool, but that's nothing new." She wrote back to Dan. *Thank you so much for taking care of things. How is Kirby holding up?*

As well as can be expected. He's stressed but keeping it together.

My hero.

Aw, shucks. When will you be home to tend to me?

Smiling, Kara texted, *Shortly.*

Oh yay! Can't wait.

"I love the way that man makes you smile," Renata said. "You deserve that so much."

"Kara?"

She looked up and choked back a gasp at the sight of her sister Kelly holding her son, Connor, in her arms. Kelly was blonde, with fragile features and a delicate build—Kara's total opposite.

"I thought that was you. Are you home because of the boys being arrested?"

Kara owed her sister nothing, so she went with a one-word answer. "Yes."

"Matt's going to offer to help out on the case if he's needed."

"He should definitely do that." Dan would chew up and spit out the man who'd broken Kara's heart when he cheated on her with her own sister.

"You should move along, Kelly," Renata said. "Nothing to see here."

Kelly gave their cousin a foul look. "Mind your own business."

"I could say the same to you. Kara doesn't want to talk to you, and of course you know that, but you still have to come over here and interrupt our good time."

"Don't be a bitch, Renata. It'll give you wrinkles."

"What does being a lying, cheating whore do for your complexion?"

Again, Kara had to bite her lip to keep from laughing out loud. Renata was the best.

"I can't believe you'd be so rude in front of your nephew and cousin."

"We're not being rude to him," Renata said. "He can't help who his parents are."

Kelly gave them a hateful look before she stormed off to wherever she'd come from.

"Please don't ever let me get on your bad side," Kara said with a laugh. "That was magnificent."

"I was rather pleased about the complexion comment. I

usually think of something that good after the fact, but with her, it was right there in the moment."

"She inspires our inner bitches."

"I can't believe she had the nerve to come over here and act like nothing is wrong."

"It's a reminder of why I don't live here anymore. Running into her out of the blue isn't something I ever want to have happen."

"She can't touch you anymore, and she knows it. You *won*, Kara. You got the guy of guys, and she knows her little Matt can't hold a candle to Dan. That keeps her awake at night."

"She's still so freaking pretty."

"Only on the outside. The inside is a festering cauldron of nasty."

Kara sputtered with laughter at Renata's way with words. "Does it make me a bad person that I hope Matt reaches out to Dan about helping with the defense?"

"I want popcorn and beer to watch Dan deal with him."

"Me, too! I was thinking Dan would chew him up and spit him out."

"I so want to see that. I want it more than I want Myles the ass pain to go away and leave me alone."

"If there's a show to watch, I'll make sure you have a front-row seat."

"I'm so glad you're home. I've missed you so much."

"I've missed you, too."

CHAPTER
Seven

RENATA DROVE Kara home to Bertha's and then took her time getting back to work. Myles would be annoyed at her for stretching her lunch hour, but he needed her more than she needed him, so she stuck to the twenty-five-mile-per-hour speed limit as she made her way to Southwest Harbor. The boats would be pulling up to the wharves with the day's catch soon, which would keep Myles out of her hair for a few hours anyway.

She used that time without him hanging over her shoulder to get the bulk of her work done.

When she pulled into the parking lot, the first thing she saw was his bright red Ram truck with the Williams Lobsters & More logo on the side of it. He loved that stupid truck, which meant she couldn't stand it because she couldn't stand him.

And no, unlike what Kara mistakenly thought, she was *not* attracted to him in any way, shape or form.

Williams Lobsters had been founded in the 1940s by Mr. Williams's grandfather and great uncle, who'd been lobstermen first and foremost before they got into the retail and wholesale side of things. Today, their online business was booming, with lobsters and other seafood products shipped daily around the world.

Everything had been fine when Myles's father, Mr. Williams, had run the business. She'd loved working for the kindly man who'd so appreciated everything she did to keep things running smoothly. Then he'd ruined everything by retiring and turning over the business to his son with the MBA from Dartmouth who'd come in and tried to upend everything that was working just fine in an attempt to make it "better."

Renata wanted to shove that Ivy League degree up where the sun didn't shine, except that would require her to be near him when he was naked, and the thought of that made her want to vomit.

She grabbed the bag with the sandwich she'd gotten for him —on his credit card—and brought it with her into the office that visitors told her reeked of lobster. The scent was so familiar to her that it barely registered anymore. It was the scent of home to her, and unlike most people, she didn't find it repulsive.

Rather, it was comforting to work in and around the industry that'd made her home state famous.

Myles wasn't in his office. *Thank God for small favors*, she thought as she left his lunch and the receipt on his desk and went to her own desk to catch up on the calls and emails that'd come in while she was gone.

During ninety minutes away from her desk, they'd received thirty-two new orders that needed to be processed before the end of the day.

Renata got busy printing shipping labels and updating inventory. She was deep in her own groove when Myles came through the main door and made a beeline straight for her desk. While she saw him coming, she'd perfected the art of ignoring him and his wavy dark brown hair, striking blue eyes and muscular build. None of that appealed to her in the slightest.

"How was lunch?"

"Good." She'd also learned that ignoring him only made him more dogged in his attempts to get her attention. "We had a midday rush."

"I know. I saw." He was obsessed with checking their storefront to keep track of the daily revenue.

"Your lunch is on your desk."

"Thank you. How's your cousin?"

Renata never took her eyes off her screen. "She's good."

"Is her husband dealing with the brothers?"

"Yes." The less she said, the faster the conversation might end.

"The cops must've shit a brick when that guy walked in their door."

"Uh-huh."

"I can't believe your cousin is married to him. He's a rock star. He'll have them out of lockup in no time."

Go away. Please, please, go away and leave me alone. She had those thoughts repeatedly during the workday but would never say them out loud. Being mean to him would be like kicking a golden retriever puppy. Not that she'd ever kick a puppy, but she'd like to be mean to Myles so he might get the message that she didn't want to be friends or whatever else he wanted with her. While she couldn't bring herself to cross the line from annoyed to rude, it was a daily struggle to be nice.

"I'd love to meet him if I get the chance while he's in town."

Was he asking her to arrange that? She glanced up at him. "He's going to be pretty busy. They're eager to get home to Gansett as soon as they can."

"Still… If the opportunity arises, keep me in mind."

"Um, sure. I, ah, need to get these orders out."

"I'll leave you to it."

Renata wished she could bang her head against something hard, but she'd also learned that didn't help anything. She'd done that once after a particularly trying day with him and had ended up with three stitches in her forehead that she'd had to explain to him after he'd come to the ER to see if she needed anything.

She'd told him she'd hit her head getting into her car.

He'd offered to drive her anywhere she needed to go.

"Oh my God." The words were out of her mouth before she could take a single second to decide whether it was wise to say them out loud.

"You say something?" he called from his office.

"Nope."

Oh. My. God.

Kara was right. He *did* like her as more than a coworker.

No. Just no, no, nopety nope, nope, nope. Absolutely not. No.

WHEN KARA WALKED INTO THE HOUSE, SHE FOUND DAN typing away on his laptop at Bertha's kitchen table, wearing the black-framed blue-light glasses he wore whenever he used his computer. She called him Dr. Torrington when he wore them because they made him look like a college professor.

"There's my gorgeous wife. I was just wondering how long I had to wait to see you."

All these years later, he still said stuff like that to her, and it never felt like a line because she knew he meant every word. "Here I am."

He got up, removed the glasses and came to greet her with a hug and kiss. "How was the visit with Renata?"

"Good. It was nice to see her in person."

"I'm sure it was." He studied her in that intense way of his, as if he could see right through her. Sometimes she suspected he could. "How's the nausea?"

"Brutal."

Wincing, he said, "Did you eat anything?"

"Just crackers. They helped."

"Do you want me to make you some toast or eggs or anything?"

She shook her head as she tried not to gag at the thought of eating anything. "Thank you, but no. I'm okay for now."

"My baby mama cannot live on crackers alone."

"For right now, it's the only option. Hopefully, it'll pass." It usually let up by late afternoon, but some days it was a twenty-four-hour event.

He gathered her in close to him. "Do you want to lie down for a while?"

"Yeah. I can't seem to shake the exhaustion lately."

"I read that it's normal to be super tired in the third trimester. You're growing a whole human in there."

"And I hear it's supposedly the most natural thing in the world. Doesn't feel that way on days like today."

"I wish there was something I could do to make it easier for you."

"This helps," she said, snuggling into his warm embrace. She was so comfortable that she could doze off standing up. That'd happened before when he was holding her just right.

"Let's get you to bed before you fall asleep standing up again."

Kara laughed. "I was just thinking about that. It's your fault for making me so comfy."

He kept an arm around her as he directed her toward the bedroom.

She sat on the bed while he removed her sneakers. "My hero."

"Aw, shucks. It's the least I can do when I'm the one who did this to you."

"That's true."

Smiling, he raised her legs onto the bed and covered her with a soft blanket.

"How's the motion coming?"

"It's almost done. Hopefully, we can get a hearing in the next few days."

"I hate to think about my precious Kirby in jail."

"He told me to tell you not to worry. They're treating him well, and he's coping."

"He knew I'd be worried about him."

"Yes, he said that."

"What's happening with Keith?"

"I have no idea. Your mom said she'd talk to him and convince him that he needs me, but I don't see that happening."

"Someone has to defend him."

"He'd probably prefer any lawyer off the street to me."

"Who does he think he's going to get that'll be better than you?"

"Aren't you afraid a comment like that will feed my already out-of-control ego?"

"I've given up on trying to control your ego. But honestly, who's he going to get that'd do a better job than you?"

"I don't know, but I hope he gets someone who's dealt with capital offenses before."

"What does that mean? A capital offense?"

"It's a term used to describe the most serious of crimes, such as murder, which can result in the death penalty." He quickly added, "The death penalty was abolished in Maine in 1887, so that's not in play here. But life in prison with no chance of parole certainly is. Keith needs an attorney who knows how to navigate those charges."

The thought of her brothers facing that sort of fate made her feel sicker than she already did.

"Try not to worry," Dan said, tuning in to her concerns. "There're miles of road between being charged and getting convicted, and if you ask me, their case is flimsy from what I've seen so far. They have one eyewitness who says he saw them with her, and Kirby was in his truck while Keith spoke to her on the sidewalk. They asked if she wanted a ride somewhere, and she said she'd walk. Keith got into Kirby's car. She was alive when they left."

"I keep thinking about her. She came for a celebration and ended up dead."

"I know. It's very sad. I'll be interested to read the statements from her friends when they become available. That'll give me some more information about what went on that night." He leaned in to kiss her. "Enough about that for now. I've got it handled. You need to rest."

"I hate being tired and nauseated all the time. It makes me feel weak."

"You'll be back to full steam as soon as the baby arrives."

"I hope so."

"You will. Of course you will."

Kara was so tired she could barely keep her eyes open. Prepregnancy, she hadn't napped during the day in years. These days, she napped almost every day. She thought of what Renata had said about how it must be nice to not have to worry about money anymore. At times like this, it was nice, but that didn't mean she'd forgotten what it was like to have to work for everything she wanted.

Her parents had paid for college and helped out until those who went to college graduated, but after that, the Ballard kids had to fend for themselves. Despite what people thought about them being spoiled rich kids, their parents had a thing about kids being "handed" too much. At times, she'd resented them for their hard line, but she had to admit that philosophy had made her self-reliant at an early age.

She heard Dan tiptoe out of the room and tried to clear her mind so she could rest. But Renata's comment had hit her in a spot where she hadn't known she was vulnerable to criticism. If you could even call it that. Even though she and Renata had always been blunt with each other, Kara hadn't expected to feel different among the people she'd been closest to at home.

But everything was different now, and it'd taken only one day back in town for someone who truly mattered to tell her that.

DAN WAS PUTTING THE FINISHING TOUCHES ON HIS motion to dismiss the charges against Kirby when Bertha came in with grocery bags in both arms. He jumped up to take the bags from her.

"Thank you. How'd it go today?"

Buster followed her in with two more bags. He put them on the counter and disappeared down the hallway.

"Not too bad. Keith declined to be represented by me, and I'm filing a motion to dismiss the charges against Kirby."

She stopped unpacking the grocery bags and turned to him, incredulous. "Keith declined to be represented by you."

"Yes, ma'am." Dan emailed Walter, asked him print and deliver the motion to the court in Ellsworth, and closed his laptop. He rarely encountered a jurisdiction that didn't permit electronic filing these days, but Hancock County happened to be one of them.

"Keith is a goddamned fool," Bertha said.

"His mother said something to the same effect. She's going to talk to him."

"What in the world could he be thinking, turning down representation from a lawyer like you?"

"He seems to have taken an instant dislike to me from the minute we met at the rehearsal dinner."

"He's a jackass. I know a grandmother shouldn't say such things about her own grandchildren, but in this case, it's true. And you know what? He always has been. From the day he was born with a massive chip on his shoulder, he's been a trouble-maker." She glanced around the corner and then returned her gaze to Dan, lowering her voice. "He tormented Buster when he was a kid. That earned him no love from me, I'll tell you."

"What did he do?" Dan asked, intrigued by the insight into Keith.

Bertha sighed and reached for a whiskey bottle in the cabinet over the stove. Then she tipped the bottle toward him, brow raised in question.

"Yes, please."

She poured two drinks and brought them to the table to sit with him. "He was just a little bastard, always teasing Buster and poking at his limitations. The other kids loved Buster, especially Kara, and they'd defend him against Keith and his nonsense. I wanted to kick his ass into the middle of next week any time Buster came home crying because Keith was mean to him."

"What's the age difference between them?"

"Buster is ten years older than Keith, but he played with the kids when they were younger. He was a late-in-life surprise to my husband and me, but he's been nothing but a joy to me, especially as I've gotten older. That anyone could be unkind to him made me feel capable of murder, even if it was my own grandson. Judith and I nearly came to blows over it a few times when she refused to get involved. 'Boys will be boys,' she'd say, which only made me angrier. Honestly, I don't think she knew what to do with him any more than the rest of us did." She lowered her voice even further when she said, "Needless to say, it doesn't surprise me in the least that he's finally in this kind of trouble. It's been coming all his life."

"Except I don't think he had anything to do with killing her. If Kirby is to be believed, she was alive and well when they left her in town."

"Kirby doesn't lie, and he'd have no reason to protect Keith, who's been an SOB to him on more than one occasion."

"Why would Kirby take the call from Keith to pick him up in town if there's no love lost between them?"

"Because that's who he is. Keith has had DUIs in the past, and no one wants the bad publicity that goes along with that sort of thing. It's hard to articulate how important the company is to the local economy. Everyone knows someone who works there, and it's the kind of business where reputation matters. Having a Ballard in trouble isn't good for business."

Kara wandered into the kitchen, looking sleepy and adorable. "Kendra texted me that they've already had several big orders canceled since the news broke about the arrests."

Dan had to think about who Kendra was. Ah, right, the eldest Ballard, who served as Chuck's executive assistant. "Is there a group text for your family that I could hit up to ask everyone at once not to text you about the case or the fallout?"

"God no." Kara made a disgusted face. "That's the last thing I'd ever want to be part of, and besides, I like Kendra. It's okay that she texted me."

Dan reached for her hand and drew her in to sit on his lap. "I don't want you worried about the implications or fallout or whatever."

She leaned her head against his. "I'm fine. Don't worry."

"How was the nap?"

"Epic, as they all are lately."

"You're like me when I was expecting," Bertha said, smiling. "I could've slept all day every day."

"That about sums it up. And now I'm starving after being nauseated all day."

Bertha jumped up with more vigor than an eightysomething woman should've had, but she wasn't your average eightysome-thing woman. "I've got dinner coming right up."

"Let me help," Kara said.

"No need. I've got it."

"But I want to. Cooking with you is one of my favorite things to do."

"Then by all means, get your apron on."

Kara got up and went to open the bottom of four drawers where she retrieved an apron that had her name printed on it in red, childlike handwriting with red handprints.

"That's the cutest thing I've ever seen," Dan said.

"We made it when I was eight or nine," Kara said as she put on the apron that was now far too small for her, especially with the pregnancy belly.

"You were seven and had just learned to write your name. You were very proud of that."

"Adorable," Dan said. "What can I do to help?"

"Can he peel potatoes?" Bertha asked Kara.

"I believe he can."

"I can hear you two talking about me, and yes, I can peel potatoes. My mother didn't raise a fool."

"Didn't she, though?" Kara asked, smiling at him over her shoulder.

"Haha." Dan unbuttoned the cuffs of his dress shirt and rolled up the sleeves. "I'm not just a pretty face. Put me to work, ladies."

Bertha chuckled. "You two are awfully cute together. Reminds me of my Tony. If we weren't sparring, we weren't communicating."

"That about sums us up," Kara said.

"It's a fun way to be," Bertha said.

"It works for us," Dan said, smiling at his wife. "Kara's goal in life is to keep me humble."

"It's a full-time job."

"I can see how that would be," Bertha said with a twinkle in her eye for Dan.

"Hey!"

"Truth hurts, love." Kara handed him four huge potatoes to peel. "Don't nick your manicure with the peeler."

"I do not have a manicure, as you well know." Even though she was teasing him, he was thrilled to see some color back in her cheeks, which were far too pale for his liking lately. He'd peeled two potatoes when his phone rang with a call from the Bar Harbor Police Department.

"Dan Torrington."

"This is Detective Cosgrove. Your client's arraignment has been scheduled for eleven o'clock tomorrow."

"Thank you for letting me know. How are we coming on the report?"

"I'll have it to you tonight."

"Thank you. Has Keith gotten an attorney yet?"

"Not that I've heard."

"Will he be arraigned as well?"

"Yes."

"Thank you for the heads-up."

"No problem."

The line went dead.

"What was that about?" Kara asked.

"Stuff you don't need to know, love."

"I think I'd like to know, if that's okay. It's more stressful to wonder."

Dan wanted to shield her from this situation with every ounce of armor he could put between her and her family, but she was the boss. Whatever she wanted was what he'd do. "They're being arraigned in the morning."

"What does that mean exactly?"

"They appear in court to hear the charges against them, enter a plea and request bail."

"Will they get bail?" Bertha asked.

"Not likely. Because of the seriousness of the charges, they may be held without bail."

"God," Kara said. "Kirby must be so scared."

"He was holding up well when I saw him. He knows he didn't do anything, so that's keeping him calm."

"Still... It's not like they can't manufacture a case against him if they're so inclined."

"Why would they do that?" Dan asked. "What purpose would it serve?"

"Who knows what anyone's agenda is?"

"I understand your concerns, sweetheart," Bertha said, "but we have to let it play out with all our faith in Dan to get Kirby out of there as soon as possible."

"The judge may take up my motion to dismiss tomorrow as well."

"What I don't understand is how they can be charged with this when they legitimately didn't do it," Kara said. "Kirby said she was fine when they left her, right?"

"He did."

"So how can they charge them?"

"They have an eyewitness who put them with her. Someone saw them together."

"But Kirby never left his truck, you said."

"He didn't, but the witness recognized the truck as his and identified Keith as the other person there. Apparently, the state police felt the witness ID was enough to charge them since they were seen with her close to where the body was later located."

"Surely they have to have more than that to charge two people with murder," Bertha said.

"I'm waiting for the reports, but I don't want you guys to worry. The case is flimsy from what I've seen thus far. I'm hoping I can make it go away quickly."

"What if you can't?"

"Then we'll play it out and hope for the best."

CHAPTER
Eight

A KNOCK on the door interrupted their conversation.

Bertha went to answer it.

Dan held back a groan when Kara's parents walked into the house, looking oddly out of place in the home where Judith had grown up. Whereas Bertha was all down-to-earth modesty, Chuck and Judith were polished from head to toe. As he had the first time he met them, he thought of them as straight from rich people central casting. This time, however, there were dark circles under their eyes and a sense of weariness that hadn't been there on previous occasions.

He didn't miss the stricken expression that crossed Kara's face when she first realized who'd come to visit. She hadn't had time to properly prepare herself to see them and would feel off her game. Ever since they'd hosted a fancy wedding for Kelly and Matt, there'd been distance between Kara and her parents.

Despite that, Kara stood and went through the motions of hugging them both.

"Oh, look at you, sweetheart," Chuck said, smiling. "You're beautiful."

"Thank you, Dad."

"Are you feeling well?" Judith asked.

"I'm nauseous and exhausted, but other than that, I'm okay."

"I was nauseated with all of you," Judith said. "It's awful."

"Yes, it is. Not sure how you went through that eleven times."

"It was rough. I'm sorry you're dealing with it. Hopefully, it'll pass soon. I was usually much better in the third trimester."

"That's good to know."

"Thank you both for being here," Chuck said. "It means a lot to us that you came when we called."

Dan shook hands with his father-in-law and accepted an awkward hug from his mother-in-law. "Of course."

"Listen," Chuck said, "neither of you owes us anything, so we really do appreciate that you came."

"Family is family." Dan appreciated that Chuck understood the situation. Judith was probably another story.

"You're too kind," Chuck said.

"Can you sit for a minute?" Bertha asked her daughter and son-in-law.

"We don't want to interrupt your evening," Chuck said. "We just wanted to come by and say hello and thank you."

"It's okay if you want to sit for a minute," Kara said.

They settled around Bertha's scarred kitchen table, where a full lifetime of memories had been made. She opened a beer for Chuck and a bottle of wine for Judith.

"Thanks, Mom," Judith said.

"It's nice to see you," Bertha said. "It's been a while."

"Yes, it's been too long," Judith said. "Life gets busy, and the days go flying by."

"Indeed," Bertha said.

Watching the family dynamics at play was fascinating for Dan, who knew for a fact that Kara wouldn't let a single day pass without seeing Bertha if she still lived nearby. He could almost feel her judging her mother for letting so much time go by between visits with Bertha.

"Is Buster here?" Judith asked.

"He is."

"I'll have to say hello before we go."

"He'd like that."

After an awkward moment of silence, Judith said, "We've just come from seeing the boys at the police station."

"How are they?" Bertha asked.

"Keith is his usual defiant self," Chuck said, his expression grim, "while Kirby is scared shitless."

"Did you talk to Keith about pulling his head out of his ass and letting Dan represent him?" Bertha asked.

Dan bit his lip to keep from laughing out loud at the way she said that. This was the first time he'd seen them together, and the contrast between her and her daughter couldn't be more pronounced.

"We tried," Chuck said, "but he's not budging. He's asked Matt to come by in the morning."

"*Matt?*" Kara asked, astounded. "What does he know about defending a capital murder case?"

"He is a lawyer," Judith said.

"Not all lawyers are created equal," Bertha said, "and you may as well be sending a used-car salesman in to defend him."

Dan choked back a laugh at the idea of Kara's ex defending Keith. "No skin off my chin. I've submitted a motion to dismiss the charges against Kirby, which I'm hoping will be taken up during the arraignment tomorrow."

"So he might be released?" Judith asked, perking up considerably.

"I don't think it'll be that simple. They have an eyewitness that puts him and Keith with the victim shortly before she was found dead. That may be enough to keep them held without bail while the details are sorted out."

"They didn't do it!" Judith said. "She was alive when they left her. How can they possibly accuse them of such a heinous crime with no evidence they were involved?"

"I know it's a horrible situation, but we have to be patient while the system does its thing."

"While my sons rot in jail, their reputations destroyed, over something they had nothing to do with."

"I know you don't want to hear this, Judith," Bertha said, "but we're all painfully aware that Keith could be capable of something like this. We know it, and the cops know it, too."

Judith recoiled. "How can you say such a thing about your own grandson?"

Dan reached for Kara's hand and gave it a squeeze.

"Because it's true. Take your head out of the clouds for once, will you? That kid has been trouble since the day he was born."

Judith crossed her arms and gave her mother a defiant look. "I'm sure you blame us for that, when we did the best we could like all parents do."

Kara gasped.

The others glanced her way.

"Something you want to say, Kara?" Judith asked, brow raised.

"The best you could?" Her tone was incredulous. "You let him run wild his entire life, and now you're acting surprised that it's caught up to him. Not to mention he's taking Kirby down with him, who most definitely had nothing to do with this."

"I'm sure you feel better saying that about us," Judith said.

"I don't feel good about any of this," Kara replied. "A young woman is dead, and my brothers stand accused of murder. Do you honestly think I want anything other than to see them exonerated? But don't sit here and act like you had nothing to do with Keith ending up the way he is. That's *all* on you. Both of you."

Dan had never been prouder of his wife, who'd grown herself a strong backbone in the years she'd lived away from this place. The

Kara he'd first met probably wouldn't have had the stones to say that to her mother. Now she didn't give a shit, and he thought it was sexy as hell that she felt free to speak her mind to her mother.

"She's right," Chuck said. "We did let him and the rest of you 'run wild,' as you put it. We love our family, but overseeing eleven kids was a bigger job than we were equipped to do."

Bertha scoffed. "That's because you didn't even *try*, and when people like me tried to tell you trouble was coming, you didn't want to hear it."

"How long have you been waiting to say that?" Judith asked with a sneer for her mother.

"Don't, Judith," Chuck said. "She's right. She did try to tell us, and so did others. We didn't want to hear it because we had no idea what to do with him."

Judith got up and headed for the door. "Nice visit. Tell Buster I'll see him next time." She let the screen door slam behind her as she went out.

"I'm sorry about that," Chuck said.

"Don't apologize for her," Bertha said. "Her own self-absorption and inability to listen to anyone else's opinion is all on her, which you probably know better than anyone."

Chuck sighed as he stood and glanced at Dan. "Thank you again for your help. We owe you."

"No, you don't. I'm glad to help Kirby."

He gave Kara a kiss on the cheek. "It's good to see you, honey. I'm sorry it's under these circumstances."

"Me, too."

After he walked out, they sat in silence until they heard the car start outside.

"Well," Kara said, "that was fun. When can we do it again?"

"Hopefully never." Bertha got up to finish dinner. "She makes me madder than a wet hen, and she has for her entire life."

Kara went to her grandmother and hugged her from behind.

"Don't let her get to you. It's how she is, and we certainly know that by now."

"Yes, we do."

"If I could just add," Dan said, "that I was ridiculously turned on by the way my wife stood up to her mother."

"Dan! Not in front of my grandmother."

Bertha rocked with laughter as she turned to hug Kara. "I love you two."

"We love you more," Kara said. "And can we talk about Matt stepping up to defend Keith?"

The three of them laughed until they cried, and then they got on with their evening as if the visit from Kara's parents had never happened.

In the morning, Dan arrived at the courthouse in Ellsworth fifteen minutes before the eleven o'clock arraignment. He'd received the full police report late the night before and was more convinced than ever that the case against his brothers-in-law was short on the kind of hard evidence the prosecutors would need to proceed to trial.

"Let me know how it goes, bossman," Walter said. "From what people are saying, Kirby's an innocent bystander who got caught up in a mess."

"That's how it seems to me, too, but we'll see what the court has to say."

"Good luck."

"Thanks."

Inside, he went through security, then asked where he might be able to meet with his client before the proceeding.

"You'll see him in there," an officer said.

"Okay, then."

Dan went into the courtroom to await the defendants' arrival. When Kirby was led into the room, hands and feet in shackles, the first thing Dan noticed was the huge bruise on the side of his face. "What the hell happened?" he asked when Kirby was seated next to him at the defense table.

"Nothing."

"Kirby, come on. What happened?"

"I had words with my brother in the bathroom. He didn't like what I had to say."

A rustling behind them was the only warning they got that Chuck and Judith had arrived, bringing the scent of expensive perfume and cologne with them.

Judith gasped when she saw Kirby's face. "What happened?"

"Don't worry about it, Mom. It's nothing."

Keith was led in next and seated at the other end of the table.

Matt came to sit next to him. He looked over and nodded to Dan, who ignored him. He had nothing to say to the man who'd broken Kara's heart. Maybe he should take this opportunity to thank Matt for being a lying, cheating son of a bitch. Because of what Matt had done, Dan and Kara were happily married.

But first things first.

"All rise and come to order. The Honorable Judge Morton Collins presiding."

Collins had white hair and a ruddy complexion that indicated time spent outdoors. He took a quick look around the courtroom, stopping his gaze for a long second on Dan before moving on to the others.

Dan loved when his reputation preceded him.

"Who is representing these men?"

"Matt Gallagher for Keith Ballard."

"Please stand when you address the court, Counselor."

Matt shot up, nearly falling over the table in his haste. "My apologies."

"Your Honor."

"My apologies, Your Honor."

It was all Dan could do not to laugh out loud as he stood.

"Daniel Torrington for Kirby Ballard, Your Honor. We call your attention to the motion to dismiss submitted last night. Kirby Ballard was simply providing a ride for his brother and had no contact whatsoever with the victim. We request the dismissal of all charges and his immediate release."

The judge looked to the prosecutor.

"We have an eyewitness that puts both brothers with the victim shortly before she was found dead. The state is opposed to releasing either defendant at this time."

"Motion for dismissal and release is denied. Both will be held without bail until a probable cause hearing next Thursday at eleven. By then, the state will need to produce additional evidence tying both men to this murder, or the charges will be dismissed."

"Yes, Your Honor," Dan said.

"I can't stay in jail for another week," Kirby said softly, so only Dan could hear him.

"I'll ask that you be held separately from your brother."

"They are holding us separately. The punch happened in the bathroom when we had words, and he got off a cheap shot."

"I'll do everything I can to get you out of here as soon as possible. Keep the faith, okay?"

"Yeah, sure. Why would I lose faith or anything?"

"Hang in there, Kirby. Keep your head down and your mouth shut. Remember not to talk to anyone about the case unless I'm there, too."

Kirby nodded as an officer came to shackle him to take him back to jail.

Neither Kirby nor Keith looked toward their parents as they were led away.

"So, um, maybe we should work together on this, huh?" Matt said to Dan.

Matt had dark blond hair, brown eyes and a baby face. The

thought of him touching Kara made Dan's stomach turn. He wished he could punch him in the face for hurting her.

Was this guy for real? "That's not going to happen, Matt, but ballsy of you to ask. I'll give you that."

"We're on the same side here."

"Let's get one thing perfectly clear. You and I will *never* be on the same side of anything. Ever."

Matt frowned. "I hate that Kara is still so bitter toward me—and Kelly—after all this time. Kelly said she was rude to her when they saw each other yesterday."

Dan was stunned to hear that Kara had seen Kelly and not told him about it. He smiled at his so-called brother-in-law. "Kara doesn't have a bitter bone in her body. In fact, I was thinking that I should thank you for cheating on her with her sister, because that led her to Gansett, where we were lucky enough to find each other. She thinks you both did her a huge favor by being lying, backstabbing assholes, and I couldn't agree more. She's the best thing to ever happen to me, so thanks, man. Truly. And also, fuck off."

Shit, that felt good. So, so good. I can't wait to tell Kara about it.

Dan practically whistled on his way out of court, despite being disappointed that he'd been unable to spring Kirby. He wasn't giving up on that.

"Dan!"

He turned to face Chuck Ballard.

"What happens now?"

"We'll continue to gather information and make decisions accordingly. Oh, and, Chuck? You might want to find a real lawyer for Keith before that jackass mall cop does more harm than good."

"Yes, I know. I'll do that."

Dan nodded and sent a text to Walter that he was ready for a ride as he continued toward the main doors. It was time to get busy doing his own investigation into the events of the night in question so he could find the evidence he needed to get Kirby out of jail.

Before he did that, however, he needed to have a conversation with his wife about the encounter she'd had with her estranged sister—and his encounter with her husband. He was looking forward to that last part.

Even though the hearing hadn't gone exactly as he'd hoped, there had been a few positives to go with the negatives. Recalling Matt's shocked expression after Dan told him to fuck off, he laughed to himself as he went down the courthouse stairs to meet Walter.

CHAPTER
Nine

WHEN HE GOT BACK to Bertha's, he was surprised to find Kara still asleep. Before her pregnancy, she'd rarely slept past nine o'clock, even on a day off. Now, she couldn't seem to get enough sleep. He kissed her forehead and left her to rest.

"Hey."

Dan winced over having woken her and returned to stretch out next to her. "Sorry."

"Don't be. I need to get up."

"Why?"

"Because it's what people do in the morning."

"I hate to tell you it's afternoon now, and pregnant people can sleep the day away if they wish to."

"Lying around in bed makes the exhaustion worse sometimes." She reached over to link her fingers with his. "How'd it go in court?"

"Mixed bag. They were held without bail, but I'm working on that for Kirby. The good news is that Matt showed up to represent Keith and completely humiliated himself in front of the judge. I quite enjoyed that."

"He does real estate stuff mostly. He's got no business defending anyone."

"Oh, I know. That quickly became apparent. And get this, he suggested we work together because, and I quote, 'We're on the same side in this.'"

"Stop it. What'd you say? Don't leave anything out."

"I told him that he and I would *never* be on the same side of anything. Then I thanked him—and his wife—for being lying, cheating assholes because their actions sent you to Gansett, where we found each other. I told him you're the best thing to ever happen to me, and I said he can fuck off."

"I've never been hotter for you than I am right now."

"Really?"

"Oh yeah. On fire, baby."

He moved closer to her and put an arm around her. "We should do something about that."

"Not in my grandmother's home."

"She would approve."

"She probably would, but I still don't think I can."

"We should try. Just so you'll know for sure."

"You're shameless."

"My baby mama is on fire for me. What would you do if you were me?"

"I need to brush my teeth."

"Be quick about it. I'm already halfway to the finish line."

She glanced down at the bulge in his pants. "You're so easy."

"Move it or lose it."

"You say that as if it'll actually go away when we both know it won't."

He loved her sassy mouth almost as much as he adored her sharp wit, her intelligence and sexy body. Her sassiness was next level, though, and sparring with her had become his favorite activity, second only to making sweet love with her.

While she was gone, he shed the suit and stripped down to

his boxer briefs. He lay on his side, head propped on his upturned hand as he waited for her.

She returned to bed wearing only a T-shirt and a big smile on her gorgeous face, which was glowing from her morning ritual of creams and potions.

Dan held out a hand to her. "I look at you and I wonder every day what I did to get so lucky."

"You drove me crazy for weeks, bothering me until I gave in and took mercy on you."

He laughed as he wrapped his arms around her. "I was *charming* you. How quickly you forget."

"Your version of charm resembled a battering ram."

"That's not true."

"Yes, it is, but I'm thankful my prickliness never drove you away, because I would've hated to miss what we've become."

"I love you so much. All the time. But when you say things like that..." He placed her hand over his heart. "It hits me right here in all the feels."

"You really told Matt to fuck off?"

"I really did."

She slid her hand down his chest, over his abdomen and into his briefs to stroke his hard cock. "That makes me hotter for you than I've ever been."

"Is that right? Tell me all about it."

As she stroked him to the point of madness, she said, "I'm picturing him going home to Kelly and telling her how mean old Dan told him to fuck off when he suggested they work together. And then I'm picturing Kelly, thinking about you telling me what you said, and it's just the best thing ever."

"My vindictive little she-cat. You're so sexy when you're mean."

Kara laughed. "I'm never mean until their names are mentioned."

"They gave you good reason to be."

"Mmm, and you… You're my sweet revenge."

"Yes, I am, and you're mine." He kissed her as fiercely as he ever did these days, always mindful of her pregnancy. She told him she didn't want him to be careful with her, but he couldn't help it. She was the most precious thing in the world to him, and he'd never be anything other than careful with her.

He loved the sound that came from the back of her throat when he removed her T-shirt and sucked on her ultrasensitive nipple. Would it be weird to ask her to record that particular sound so he could listen to it any time he wanted? Probably. Instead, he committed it to memory, so he'd never forget the way she responded to him.

They'd always been hot together, but pregnancy had made it even better. He wouldn't have thought that was possible until she showed him.

"We need to be quick in case Bertha and Buster take a half day."

"When was the last time they did that?"

"Never, but there's always a first time."

"You're so cute when you're worried about your grand-mother catching you having sex with your husband."

"In *her* house!"

"She loves me. She'd want you to get your groove on with me as often as you can, even in her house."

"Whatever you say, stud. You'd better get on with it before I change my mind."

He held himself up on his arms so he wouldn't put weight on the baby bump and pushed into her, loving the way her eyes rolled back in her head when he filled her. "You're not going to change your mind."

"No, I'm not, but I still want to hurry up. I feel like a teenager sneaking around with my boyfriend."

"Don't talk about him while your husband is inside you."

She started to laugh and couldn't stop.

"And don't laugh when I'm inside you either!"

That only made her laugh harder.

This called for emergency measures, he thought as he picked up the pace and redirected her attention to the task at hand.

When the laughter stopped and her fingers dug into the muscles of his back, he wanted to let out a victory whoop but knew better than to interrupt the "flow" of things a second time.

The thought nearly made him laugh, but he held it back and doubled down until she cried out from the orgasm that hit her like a bolt of lightning. That was new with her pregnancy—the slow climb had become a far more intense flash point that finished him off every time.

"Holy crap, woman," he said, panting as he crashed down next to her on the bed. He missed snuggling on top of her afterward and looked forward to the day they could do that again.

She curled up to him, arms and legs around him, smothering him with her sweetness and love.

How had he lived before he'd had her? He could barely remember a time without her. It was like she'd blotted out most of his life before her and given him a fresh new start that he'd badly needed after catching his fiancée in bed with his best man the night before the wedding that hadn't happened. He rarely thought of either of them now that he had everything with Kara.

"I can't stop thinking about Kelly hearing you told Matt to fuck off."

"Maybe he won't tell her because he's too humiliated."

"Oh, he'll tell her. He records every little slight and never forgets it."

"Why didn't you tell me you saw her yesterday?"

"Honestly? I never gave it another thought after it happened. It was no big deal."

"Are you sure?"

"Yep. Renata handed her her ass, and it was spectacular."

"Tell me everything. Leave nothing out."

As she recited the play-by-play of the encounter with Kelly, her eyes danced with glee when they would've been dull with pain only a few years earlier.

He thought she ought to know that, so he told her.

"I really look different when I talk about her?"

"Night and day, babe. You're full of glee for the retribution rather than aching from the treachery."

"I feel like a bitch for enjoying the retribution so much."

"Don't do that. You deserve every delicious bit of retribution you can find with her."

"Connor is a cutie. I felt bad acting that way in front of him."

"You didn't cause this. His mother did, and he'll find that out one day and understand why you are the way you are."

"I'd like to have a relationship with him if it can be separate from his parents. He's an innocent bystander."

"Maybe when he's older, he can come visit us on his own."

"That'd be fun."

"He'll know you. Don't worry."

"I want him to know his cousin, too. And speaking of cousins, my sister Kendra invited us to dinner. I'd like to see her and my nieces, if you don't mind."

"I'm with you, babe. Whatever you want to do is fine with me."

"I'll tell her we're in."

"I'm looking forward to meeting her."

"She was so bummed she couldn't come the wedding because both girls were sick."

"I remember how bummed you were."

"She's always been good to me."

"What's the age difference between you again?"

"Eight years. She was more like a second mom to me than a sister."

"Is she close with Kelly?"

"Not really. Kendra was furious about what Kelly and Matt did. There's no love lost there."

"I hope it was worth it to Kelly to have Matt after everything she had to give up."

"She'd never admit that it was anything other than worth it."

"I told your dad he needs to get Keith a real lawyer before that 'mall cop' does more harm than good."

"You called him a mall cop?" she asked, raising her head off his chest to smile at him.

"I did. That might be giving him too much credit."

"Just when I think I can't love you more than I already do…"

"That's all I gotta do?"

She returned her head to his chest. "That's it."

"I'll see what other ways I can come up with to describe him while we're here."

"I look forward to hearing all of them."

"Dogcatcher?"

"That's an insult to dogs."

They laughed—hard.

"I'm so glad you don't hurt over them anymore," Dan said. "They don't deserve it."

"No, they don't. I'm not proud of my vindictive streak where they're concerned, but it is what it is."

"While they don't deserve your hurt, they *do* deserve every bit of vindictiveness we can come up with.

"They sure do."

RENATA GOT TO WORK TWENTY MINUTES LATE, HOPING that would be enough to annoy Myles to the point that he'd keep their interactions to a minimum that day.

No such luck.

When he heard her arrive, he came out of his office, smiling at her with a tall Americano in hand that he placed on her desk.

She didn't have to check to know it'd been made to her exacting specifications with oat milk and frothing.

"Thank you."

"Everything okay? You're never late."

"Sorry."

"Don't be. It happens."

"You're supposed to be pissed when I'm late. Be a normal boss, would you?"

"Why would I get pissed at my most productive, effective employee? The one who keeps the wheels from coming off the bus every day? I don't care if you're late."

"Don't say that! I'll take advantage of you."

His Adam's apple bobbed in his throat as he swallowed hard.

Renata instantly regretted her choice of words, since it seemed he might enjoy that.

"You, um, you wouldn't do that."

"Yes, I would, Myles. Quit acting like I'm not capable of bad things."

"What bad things are you capable of?"

"The same things as anyone else. If my boss tells me he doesn't care that I'm late, it might become a habit."

"No, it won't."

"You can also quit acting like you know me so well, because you don't."

"Yes, I do."

"Shut up and go to work."

"I have a favor to ask of you, but I'm kind of scared of you right now."

Renata bared her teeth at him.

The jerk laughed.

"What favor?"

"You can say no if you want to. In fact, I wouldn't blame you if you did."

"Spit it out, Myles. I have shit to do and so do you."

"My, um... My cousin is getting married next month, and the RSVP deadline is coming up. I'm under tremendous pressure to bring a date. In fact, it'd be good to have a date, so I won't have to answer questions about why I'm not dating anyone... And, um, I thought if you weren't doing anything, you might, you know..."

Renata stared at him, shocked to realize he was asking her out in an awkward, bumbling, roundabout sort of way.

"Will you be my plus-one to this wedding, so I can enjoy it without being hassled by large groups of aunts and uncles, who won't be happy until we're all married with four kids each?"

Both families were woven into the fabric of the area. Everyone knew his mother was one of fourteen and his father one of eleven. Myles had sixty-two first cousins. She knew that because one of them, Ellery, was her friend. It was hard to find anyone who wasn't connected to one of them in some way or another.

"Renata?"

She'd zoned out on him while he waited, twisting in the wind, for her to reply to his invitation to attend his cousin's wedding. Ellery had told her that their cousin Nathan's wedding would be an extravaganza, with the entire family invited.

"Yes, Myles?" Why did her mouth feel so dry, while the palms of her hands were sweaty? Neither of those things ever happened to her.

He grimaced. "Are you trying to torment me by any chance?"

"Why would I do that?"

"I, um, I don't know, but it'd be nice if you'd just say, 'Yes, Myles, I'll go to the wedding with you,' or 'No, thank you, Myles, I can't make it.'"

"*If* I said yes, and that's a very big *if*, it'd be a one-time thing as a favor. Nothing more. Am I clear?"

"Yes."

"And you wouldn't tell anyone that we're dating or blow it up to be more than it actually is."

"Right."

"You have to swear to God you won't tell anyone I'm your girlfriend."

"I swear to God I won't do that."

"No matter how many aunts pressure you for details, you won't share any because there are none to share."

His lips quivered with the start of laughter.

"What's so funny?"

"You are."

If she asked him to elaborate, that'd be encouraging the continuation of an excruciating conversation that she desperately wanted out of. However, she was too curious not to ask, "Why am I funny?"

"You're terrified of anyone thinking we might be a real couple."

"Because we're *not* a real couple."

"Yes, I know. Any other conditions?"

"There'd be absolutely no dating privileges of any kind."

He sat on the corner of her desk, settling in, which wouldn't do at all.

"Don't you have work to do?" she asked. "If you don't, I do."

"We both do, so let's complete this negotiation and get on with our day."

"I haven't said I'd go with you yet."

"I'm aware of your lack of confirmation."

The son of a bitch was enjoying this a little too much. *So are you*, her brain said. *Shut up. No, you shut up.*

"Renata?"

Startled out of the fight with herself, she glanced at him and saw that he was watching her with a warm, affectionate look on his face. She didn't want to encourage that.

"I don't think I can go with you, but thanks for asking."

His smile quickly transformed to a frown that reminded her of a little boy who'd dropped his ice cream on the sidewalk.

"Don't be that way," she said.

"What way?"

"All sad and pouty. You had to know I was a huge long shot on this favor."

"I did know that, but I was still hopeful you might remember that time I drove more than an hour—in a snowstorm—to pick you up when your car broke down, or that other time when I fixed the roof on your house when it was raining inside, or that one time when I—"

"You've made your point." Clearly, she needed to stop calling him when she found herself in a jam. "What's the dress code for this thing?"

"Formal."

"Of course it is. Fine. I'll go. But we are *not* dating, you will not tell anyone we are, and there'll be no romantic shit of any kind. Am I clear?"

"Crystal." He was smiling brightly again. "Thank you for doing this for me. You're saving my life with the aunts."

As he walked away, whistling, Renata dropped her head into her hands as she wondered when exactly she'd lost control of that so-called negotiation. It'd been more like bribery. Whatever. She'd go with him to the wedding, keep her distance while they were there and get things back on track afterward by being nothing more than coworkers.

That was all they would ever be, even if he hadn't figured that out yet.

CHAPTER
Ten

KENDRA and her family lived in a restored farmhouse in Trenton, just north of Mount Desert Island. Kara had seen photos of the renovation but was looking forward to seeing it in person for the first time since the project had been completed more than three years ago. In another life, her sister might've followed her keen interest in architecture and interior design into a different career.

But in this life, she worked as their dad's executive assistant at Ballard Boat Works and kept things running smoothly for the entire company.

That was the role Kendra had always played in their family— the organizer, the peacemaker, the surrogate mother and chauffeur.

"How long does it take to get used to the smell of dead fish?" Dan asked as he drove Buster's truck to Kendra's with the windows down.

Kara laughed. "I'm smell blind to it, so I can't say, but it probably takes a while for you flatlanders to become accustomed."

"It's incredibly disgusting."

"It's the smell of home."

"Yummy. So give me the backstory on Kendra again. You were close to her growing up, right?"

"As much as we could be with eight years between us, but more so now that we're both adults. I spent far more time with her growing up than I did with my mother, so for a time, she was just another authority figure. Now she's a friend. We refer to her as Switzerland because she tries to keep an open line of communication with all of us, even though she and Kellen, the second-oldest and the chief strategy officer, have had a lot of arguments over the company's direction. They didn't speak for a couple of years."

"Don't they work together?"

"In offices across the hall from each other."

"That must've been interesting."

"It was terrible, and only because Kendra finally said enough is enough did they start speaking again. From what I hear, though, there's a lot of tension between them to this day, and in some ways, my dad fosters that as he tries to figure out which one of them he's going to put in charge when he retires."

"That sounds awful."

"It is, but Kendra goes out of her way to try to keep it peaceful now that they've sort of kissed and made up."

"Sounds like the eldest child. You could be describing my oldest sister, Barb. Very similar."

"With hindsight, I can see that Kendra was instrumental to me getting through school and childhood, but at the time, I resented having to do what she told me to."

"I feel that. Barb was bossy with me and Dylan. We mostly ignored her."

"Kendra is the kindest person you'll ever meet. She'd get so hurt when we were mean to her, so that ruined our fun somewhat."

"What'd she have to say about what Kelly did?"

"Other than the shit with Kellen at work, it's the only time

I've ever known her to be on the outs with any of us. I guess they've patched things up since then, but Kendra has told Kelly that she doesn't approve of what she did or how I was treated."

"That's something, anyway."

"I don't expect others to hold a grudge forever on my behalf."

"Just so you know... I always will."

"Well, you have to."

Dan laughed as he pulled into Kendra's driveway. "Trust me, it's no problem." He took in the large white house with black-framed windows, a huge front porch and festive window boxes full of pumpkins and fall color. "Beautiful house."

"Yes, it is. Kendra designed and decorated it."

"Amazing."

Two barefoot young girls came running out of the house.

Kara got out of the truck to greet her nieces with hugs and kisses. "You guys are huge!"

"You knew that, Aunt Kara," Luna, the eleven-year-old, said. "You've seen pictures."

"I still didn't realize how tall you'd gotten."

Luna had the same reddish-blonde hair and golden-brown eyes that Kendra and Kara had, while nine-year-old Aurora had her father's dark hair and eyes.

Both girls hugged her a second time, which tugged at Kara's heart. Staying gone had kept her away from the nieces she'd been close to while living in Maine.

"You guys know my husband, Dan," Kara said, keeping her arms around the girls.

"He's cute," Aurora said with a giggle.

"He's okay."

Smiling, Dan said, "It's very nice to finally meet you ladies in person."

"Mom says you're famous," Luna said.

"Not that famous."

"Don't tell him he's famous," Kara said. "It goes right to his head."

The girls laughed and led the way to the porch, where Kendra waited to greet them with hugs.

"The house is a showstopper," Kara said, oddly emotional to see her eldest sibling for the first time in years.

"Aw, thanks. We like it."

"This is Dan, as you know."

Kendra shook his hand. "Nice to finally meet you in person."

"Likewise. Your girls are even more adorable than they are on FaceTime."

"We've decided to keep them if they get inside right now and finish setting the table."

The girls ran into the house, the screen door slamming behind them.

"How'd you do that?" Kara asked her sister.

"Do what?"

"Make them hop to with just a certain look and tone."

"It's built in. You'll see. It'll be there when you need it."

"I sure hope so. I fear I'm going to let this little one get away with murder."

"We most certainly will not be doing that," Dan said.

"Poor choice of words in light of current events," Kara said as Kendra led them inside.

"Nah, it was funny," Kendra said.

"Oh, Ken, it's gorgeous." Kara had seen it through photos and FaceTime, but none of that had done justice to her sister's talent for putting together a warm, cozy space. "I love it all, but the fireplace is incredible."

The stonework around the fireplace extended all the way to the ceiling, making it the focal point of the large, open-concept first floor.

"Come see the kitchen. It's my favorite part."

The gourmet kitchen ran the length of the far wall and was

fronted by the largest island Kara had ever seen. "It's stunning. I can see why it's your favorite part."

"Can you design and decorate a house for us?" Dan asked. "When we're ready, that is."

"I'd love to," Kendra said, seeming pleased by the request.

"It's her favorite thing," Luna said. "She's obsessed with decorating."

"You and your sister are my favorite things," Kendra said. "I'm obsessed with raising you to be decent human beings, which is harder than it seems."

"Kids are not *things*, Mother," Luna replied.

"We're all things occupying space in the universe," Kendra said. "God save me from the preteen know-it-all."

"Great says you were just like me at my age," Luna said.

"Great?" Dan asked.

"That's what they call Bertha," Kendra said.

"Oh, I love that. It's so fitting."

"Isn't it? She must be thrilled to have you guys staying with her."

"She is." Kara dipped a carrot stick in the bowl of ranch dressing that Kendra had put out for her, knowing how much she loved it. "She's got a crush on my husband."

"I've got one on her, too, so that works out well," Dan said.

"She sings your praises because you've made our Kara so happy."

Dan smiled at Kara. "Works both ways. She saved me from myself."

"I do that every day. It's a big job."

Kendra laughed as she opened a Sam Adams for Dan and put a glass of ice water in front of Kara. "I wasn't sure what to expect with your fancy reputation preceding you."

"No way. You've gotten to know me through FaceTime and stuff."

"It's not the same as being in person."

"No, it isn't," Dan said. "I'm glad we finally got to fix that, even if the reason we're here isn't the greatest."

After they finished setting the table, the girls surrounded Kara once again. When she noticed Aurora looking at her pregnant belly, Kara said, "You want to feel the baby? He or she is usually busy this time of day."

"Can I?"

"Of course. Put your hand right here." Kara laid the child's hand flat against the right side, where she usually felt the strongest kicks. "It might take a second."

"Oh! I feel it! That's so cool. And creepy that you have a whole person in there."

"I know, right?"

"Can I try?" Luna asked.

"Absolutely."

Both girls got to feel some strong kicks that delighted them.

"I can't believe that's our cousin in there," Luna said.

"Pretty cool, right?" Kara asked.

"Yeah, it is," Luna said. "How come you don't know if it's a boy or a girl? Don't most people find that out and do those stupid gender-reveal things? We went to one last year for the neighbors. They shot off a cannon that exploded in pink."

"Dan made a good point when he said so few things in life are a surprise, and it'd be fun to find out when he or she arrives."

"I wouldn't be able to stand waiting," Aurora said.

Kendra laughed. "Because you have no patience."

"Mom says she was born without patience," Luna said.

"Always in a rush, our Aurora is."

"I got stuff to do."

"I'm impatient, too," Dan said. "I want what I want when I want it."

"See, Mom? He's like me, and he's famous."

"She's going to be a lawyer," Kendra said. "I swear."

Dan gave Aurora a fist bump. "That's the way to be."

"What are you going to name the baby?" Luna asked.

"Dylan. That was Dan's late brother's name."

"He died?" Aurora asked, wide-eyed.

"That's what late means, dummy," Luna retorted.

"No name-calling in this house, Luna. We're very sorry you lost your brother, Dan. I love that you're going to name the baby after him."

"That was all Kara's idea, and I love it."

"Can Dylan be a name for a boy or a girl?"

"Yep," Dan said. "It's versatile that way."

"That's cool," Luna said.

"She doesn't give that compliment to just anyone," Kendra said with a smile for her daughter. "Congratulations, guys. Your baby's name has the Luna seal of approval."

"We're very honored," Kara said.

"You should be," Luna replied, grinning.

"Daddy's home," a male voice called from the mudroom. Hugo came into the kitchen, looking hopeful. "They used to come running." He was tall, with dark hair and blue eyes. He wore a dress shirt with a fleece vest over it.

"Five years ago," Luna said.

Hugo kissed the tops of his daughters' heads. "And yet, I still hope. Every night."

He hugged and kissed Kara. "So good to see you, sis."

"You, too, bro. It's been too long."

"Way too long." He extended a hand to Dan. "Nice to meet you in person."

"Same, man. Your house is gorgeous."

"That's all thanks to my beautiful, talented wife." He kissed Kendra's cheek and peeked into a pot on the stove. "Oh yum. Mama made my favorite beef stew."

"How was your day, dear?"

"Outstanding. We got a big new order that'll keep us busy for the next few months."

Hugo owned an apparel company that provided branded clothing and merchandise to yachts, sailing teams and marine-related companies, including BBW.

"That's great, hon. Congratulations."

"Thanks."

"Glad to hear the business is doing well, Hugo," Kara said.

He opened a Sam Adams for himself and put a new one on the counter in front of Dan. "We're having our best year ever. Took a minute to get it off the ground, but it's finally cruising."

"You've worked so hard," Kara said. "You deserve all the success."

"Aw, thanks. It's been fun to build it from nothing and see it take off. Don't look now, but we're in the running to provide sweatshirts to the US Olympic Team."

"Come on!" Kendra said. "When did that happen?"

"A couple of weeks ago. I didn't want to say anything until I knew more."

"That's very cool," Dan said. "Congrats."

"Thanks. We're excited and nervous, too. It's a big order. We'll be hiring more people to make it happen, which is always scary."

"You've got this, Daddy," Aurora said.

"Thanks, pumpkin. How do you feel about coming to work for me?"

"As soon as I finish third grade," she said with a giggle.

To Dan and Kara, Hugo said, "I was thinking on the way home that you two can use my Jeep while you're in town, if you'd like. I've got a company truck these days and have been thinking about selling the Jeep. I never use it, and it's all yours if it'd help you out."

Kara looked at Dan. "The Jeep is way nicer than Buster's truck and doesn't smell like dead fish."

"I'm sold," Dan said. "We were planning to rent a car if it turned out we're staying awhile."

Hugo went to a hook by the back door and brought them the keys. "No sense paying for a car when I've got one that's not being used. Keep it as long as you need it."

"Thank you, Hugo," Kara said. "You're the best."

"Yes, thanks," Dan added. "We appreciate it."

"I'll drive Buster's stinky truck home," Kara said with a smile for Dan. "You can have the smell-free Jeep."

"Oh thank you, Jesus."

"Poor Dan can't stand the smell of dead fish," Kara told her sister and brother-in-law.

"Whereas it barely registers with us," Kendra said.

"That's what I said, too! Smell blind."

Kendra served up the stew, and they migrated to the dining room table that the girls had set. When the girls finished their meal, Kendra sent them to finish their homework and take showers. As soon as they'd left the room, Kendra zeroed in on Dan. "What happened in court today?"

Dan gave her a thorough analysis, including Matt's fumbling attempt to represent Keith.

"I can't believe Keith was stupid enough to turn you away," Kendra said.

"You can't?" Kara asked. "It's just like him to think he knows better than everyone about everything."

"Yeah, that's true. His own arrogance is going to be the end of him. I just hope he doesn't take the rest of us down with him."

"What do you mean?" Dan asked.

"We had two big orders cancel since they were arrested, worth about two-point-two million in revenue."

"Oh my God," Kara said. "Dad must be having a meltdown."

"He's very upset about all of it."

"Kirby said the victim was standing on the sidewalk when they drove off, after offering her a ride home," Dan said.

"Then how can they charge them?" Kendra asked.

"They have an eyewitness that puts them with her close to

the time of death. Tomorrow, I'm going to work on finding a good local private investigator who can help me figure out what really happened. Do you guys know anyone?"

"A guy I went to high school with does that," Hugo said. "Mostly for divorce cases, but he's got a reputation for being fair and thorough."

"I'd love to have his help if he's up for it."

"I'll text him."

"I'm so scared for Kirby," Kendra said. "Whatever happened sure as hell had nothing to do with him."

"I know," Kara said. "I've been saying the same thing. I can't bear to think about him sitting in jail when all he did was come when Keith called him."

"Which is way more than Keith deserved after the way he's treated Kirby all his life."

"No kidding."

"How has he treated Kirby?" Dan asked.

"He's never missed a chance to take a shot at him," Kendra said, "to poke at him, to belittle him. Keith is a fucking bully. He always has been, but he took perverse pleasure in picking on Kirby for some unknown reason."

"It was because Kirby didn't fight back," Kara said. "He couldn't be bothered with Keith or his bullshit, so he just ignored him, which made Keith more determined to get to Kirby. It was sick."

"What did your parents say about it?" Dan asked.

The sisters laughed.

"They acted like it wasn't happening right in front of them," Kendra said. "I got in Keith's face about it more than they did. Not that it did any good."

"So if Keith was a dick to Kirby, why would Kirby pick him up after a night out?"

"That's who Kirby is," Kendra said with a sigh. "He's the one who comes when no one else will because that's what he does.

Keith knew if he called Kirby, Kirby would come. So of course he took full advantage of him."

"Is it okay to say I really, really admire Kirby, and I'd like to punch Keith in the face?" Dan asked.

Kendra raised her wineglass in a toast to Dan. "Welcome to our world."

CHAPTER
Eleven

THE NEXT DAY, Kara met Renata and their friends Ellery and Jessie for lunch in town. Since it was another bright, sunny autumn day, they took advantage of the opportunity to eat outside.

"I need a lobster roll," Kara said. "I've yet to have one that's as good as the ones here."

"Is lobster safe during pregnancy?" Jessie asked. Her curly brown hair was piled into a messy bun, and her enviably long lashes were fully mascaraed, as always. Jessie said she felt naked without her mascara.

"Yes, thankfully. It's actually good for me and the baby."

"I ate it when I was pregnant," Ellery said. "It's hard to avoid around here. I heard someone say it's like chicken is in other places," Ellery added with a laugh as she tucked a strand of shoulder-length blonde hair behind her ear. Her infectious laughter had been one of the best things about Kara's childhood.

"That's funny and true," Renata said. "Look at how many people we know who make a living off of lobster."

Ellery raised her hand. "Half of our income."

Renata raised her hand. "All of mine."

"Representing my grandmother, uncle and brother." Kara raised both hands to register her vote. "I need a foot, too."

"Don't attempt that while you're seven months pregnant," Renata said.

"Yeah, good call. I'd end up in the ER."

"You're a very cute prego," Ellery said.

"I feel like a beached whale."

"Nah, you're slaying it, as always," Jessie said. "You're unfairly adorable."

"I forgot how good you guys are for my ego," Kara said.

"We're always here," Ellery said. "That's never changed."

"I know, and I'm sorry I've been gone so long. I hope you guys know it had nothing to do with you."

"You did the right thing for you, but we've missed you," Ellery said.

Despite her friend saying the right things, Kara picked up an undertone of... something. "I've missed you, too. I wanted to be here for you after Pete's accident." Her husband, a lobsterman, lost a finger on the job a few years ago. "Before now, that was the closest I've gotten to saying to hell with it and coming home."

"I felt your support from afar. Feels like a long time ago now that he's gotten used to it. The hardest part afterward was that he sort of lost his nerve for the job for a while."

"It must've been hard for him to go back to it after such a terrible injury."

"It was, but it's all he knows, so what choice did he have?"

The waitress came to take their order. Kara and Renata ordered lobster rolls, while the other two got salads.

"How're things at the inn?"

Ellery shrugged. "We're still open, so that's something, I guess."

She'd struggled for years to make her bed-and-breakfast business profitable.

"I had to hire a part-time person to handle the breakfast and checkout so I could get the kids to school."

"How're the kids?"

"They're getting so big. Annabelle is obsessed with cheerleading, and Keaton is all about soccer. They keep us busy."

"Keaton scored two goals last weekend," Jessie said.

"That's amazing! Dan and I want to come see him play while we're home."

"How long will you be here?" Ellery asked.

"I'm not sure yet. It depends on what happens in the next week or so."

"The whole situation is so shocking," Jessie said. "No one knows what to think."

"I sure as hell hope they know Kirby had nothing to do with whatever happened to that woman," Renata said.

"A friend of mine was at the bar they were at Friday night," Jessie said. "They saw Keith dancing with her and said he had his hands all over her. The cops talked to her and took her statement."

"Dancing isn't the same as murder," Renata said.

"I never said it was," Jessie retorted in a sharp tone that took Kara by surprise. "I'm sorry. I know he's your cousin and brother, and you guys don't want to think he's capable of something like this."

"He's an asshole, not a murderer," Renata said.

Kara had never experienced such an uncomfortable moment with her three closest childhood friends, who'd also been close to one another.

"How's my cousin?" Ellery asked Renata.

"He's fine."

"Heard a rumor that you're his plus-one to Nate's wedding."

"It's just as a favor so people won't drive him crazy asking why he's not dating anyone."

"So you want them to think he's dating you?"

"No! Not at all. We're just friends or whatever."

"Right," Ellery said skeptically. "Does he know that?"

"Yes, I told him it's just a favor. Nothing else."

"Poor Myles," Ellery said. "He's crazy about Renata, and everyone knows it but her."

"He is not crazy about me," Renata said, sounding panicked. "That's ridiculous."

"No, it isn't," Ellery said. "He's a nice guy, and for some reason, he's decided you're the one he wants."

"'For some reason'? What the fuck does that mean?"

Ellery shrugged. "Take it however you want."

Renata glared at Ellery. For a second, Kara worried her cousin might reach across the table to smack their friend.

"Kara? Is that you?"

Kara looked up to see her brother Kolby in his post office uniform, mailbag slung across his chest. She got up to hug him.

"I thought that was you. Spotted you from across the street. How's it going, ladies?"

"Good," Renata said with a forced smile that Kara noticed but Kolby wouldn't. "Nice to see you, cousin."

"You, too. Been too long." He looked at Kara. "How long are you here?"

"Depends on what happens with the brothers."

Kolby grimaced. "It's all anyone wants to talk about. I wish I could do my route in disguise, so I don't have to deal with all the questions."

"Sorry you're caught in the crossfire."

He shrugged. "Nothing new there, right?"

"Yeah, for sure."

"You did the right thing getting out of here. I hope you don't have to stay for long."

"Despite the circumstances, it's good to see people like you and the girls. I've missed you."

"Missed you, too, sis. You look cute as a prego."

"Right. I look like a water buffalo."

"It's not quite that bad. Yet."

Kara gave him a friendly punch to the arm. "Watch it, mister."

"Let's get together while you're here. I'd like to meet Dan."

"We'll do it. Somewhere far from here where no one knows us."

"Perfect. Call me."

"I will."

He surprised her with a kiss on the cheek. "Really have missed you."

Kara hadn't realized how much she'd missed him until now. "Same, Kolbs." She returned to her seat and took a sip of her ice water.

"Must be weird not to see your brother for years," Jessie said.

"It is. I've missed him and some of the others." Eager to change that subject and the one they'd been on before Kolby spotted them, Kara said, "How's Doug doing?" Jessie's longtime boyfriend had struggled with opioid addiction.

"He's great. Three years sober, and it seems to be sticking this time."

"I'm so glad to hear that. You must be so happy."

"I am," she said. After a long silence, she said, "Did you find out what you're having?"

"No, we decided to let it be a surprise."

"You'd deny us our right to the cheesy gender-reveal party?" Ellery asked, smiling.

"God yes. I'm trying to picture Dan at a gender-reveal party. He'd be mocking the entire thing the way I did the engagement party Judith insisted on throwing us." Kara shuddered. "That day turned into a disaster, so we're all set with parties like that."

"Was that the day the disgruntled lawyer guy slashed Dan's hand with the knife?" Renata asked.

"Yes, that's the one. Ironically, that man just died in the

hurricane. He decided to ride it out on a boat with another guy. They were both killed."

"That's really sad," Ellery said.

"It was. He has a young daughter, so it's been rough on her and their family."

The waitress arrived with their food as well as ketchup and vinegar for their french fries.

"I was surprised when you said you guys were going to stay on Gansett." Jessie poked at her salad as if she wasn't that interested in eating. "I figured Dan would want to be back in LA."

"He'd tired of LA long before we met. He loves Gansett as much as I do."

"What goes on there?" Ellery asked.

"Nothing and everything. We have the most amazing group of friends, most of whom are related to each other in some way. There's one family of siblings and cousins, the McCarthys. Their family owns a marina, a hotel and a couple of event venues. Their son Grant is Dan's best friend, which is how he ended up on Gansett."

"Is it dead in the winter?" Renata asked.

"Yeah, it's slow, but we stay busy. There's always something going on. Birthday parties and celebrations of some sort or another." Kara took a bite of delicious lobster while noticing the others were barely touching their lunches. She wanted to ask them what was wrong but was afraid of what they might say. Finally, the tension got the best of her.

"What's going on, you guys?" Kara asked. "Why are you all so tense?"

"You've been gone a long time," Jessie said without looking away from Ellery, who glared right back at her. "Things change."

"What's changed?"

"*Everything*, Kara," Jessie said. "Wake up. You don't get to come home after years away and act like nothing happened here while you were gone."

Stung by the sharp comment, Kara said, "I'm not acting like anything."

"You've found a whole new life that doesn't include us," Ellery said gently. "That kind of hurts."

"That's not true! You guys know why I left. You're the ones who told me to go!"

"It never occurred to us that you'd never come back," Jessie said.

Kara sat back against her chair, her heart aching with the realization that her actions had hurt her closest friends at home. "I... I'm sorry. I just... I couldn't come back here. I just couldn't."

"There's a lot more here than Kelly and Matt," Ellery said.

"I know that."

"You guys," Renata said, "lighten up. She did what was needed to get through a tough situation."

"That was ages ago," Jessie said. "She's happily married now to a rock-star lawyer and has been for years. It's just a little hurtful that we haven't seen you in all this time."

Kara was too stunned to speak. She'd gone out of her way to stay in close touch with all three of them, texting, calling and FaceTiming regularly. In fact, she'd done most of the heavy lifting in their relationships while she was away. If she didn't reach out, she didn't hear much from Jessie or Ellery. She'd chalked it up to everyone being busy. It had never occurred to her that they resented her for being gone so long.

They picked at their lunches and coexisted in awkward silence until the waitress returned with their check, which Renata grabbed.

"I've got this," she said.

"Thank you," the others said.

Kara stood. "It was really nice to see you guys. I'm sorry if I hurt you by staying away. Take care." She walked away with her head held high even as her heart ached with sadness but not regret. There'd never be regrets for doing what it took to survive the betrayal of her sister and boyfriend, not to mention her parents, who threw the pair a big fancy wedding, as if Kara's feelings didn't matter in the least.

Only when she was in Buster's truck did she allow the tears to spill down her cheeks.

Renata knocked on the passenger door window. "Open up."

Kara didn't want to, but she leaned over anyway to flip the manual lock on the old truck.

Renata got in and shut the door. "I'm sorry about that."

"Don't be."

"They shouldn't have made you feel guilty for surviving the ultimate betrayal and finding a new life for yourself."

Kara looked over at her cousin. "Do you feel the same way they do? That I let you down by leaving and never coming back?"

"Not really. I mean, it's not like you left because of me or them. You haven't seen much of Bertha either. It's not just us."

"I didn't have much chance to prepare myself for this trip home, to think about how things would've changed while I was away."

"Be honest, you rarely think about this place. Why would you? You've got a whole new life with a great guy who worships the ground you walk on. What good will looking backward do you at this point?"

"It pains me to think the three of you ever thought you weren't still important to me, especially you."

"I've always known where I stood with you, but I've missed you like hell since you left."

"I've missed you, too."

"There's so much bullshit in this place for both of us. I mean, if our fathers saw us sitting here together, they'd be pissed. How fucked up is that? You'd think two brothers would be thrilled to see their daughters as best friends, but not our fathers."

"We've never let that get in our way."

"No, we haven't, but it's no surprise to me that you checked out of here and never looked back. I'd do the same thing if I could."

"Why can't you?"

Renata leaned her head back against the seat. "Because I'm not brave like you are. I couldn't just pick up and move somewhere I've never been the way you did."

Kara laughed. "I was freaking out about every aspect of that move, but as scary as it was to leave everything familiar, staying wasn't an option. I couldn't bear to live anywhere near them, to risk running into them every time I went somewhere. It was worse for me to stay than to go, and not for nothing, already having a job made everything possible."

"I understand everything you did and why you did it. Don't let Jessie and Ellery have you second-guessing anything. They're just butt-hurt that you got to leave here, and they never did."

"I didn't think they wanted to. What's up with Jessie and Doug? She didn't seem too thrilled that he's doing well."

"She is thrilled about that, believe me, but I wonder sometimes if she wants out of the relationship and is afraid she'll set back his recovery if she makes a move."

"Whoa. Really? I can't imagine one of them without the other."

"I know. They've been together for fourteen years. Since senior year of high school."

"Why does she want out?"

"I mean I could be reading it all wrong, but the addiction years took a heavy toll on both of them, but it was super hard on her to remember why she loved him so much when he was basically destroying everything they'd worked so hard to have. They have two mortgages on their house that they'll be lucky to ever pay off, and he's different after the long struggle."

"How so?"

"He's very focused on helping other people kick their addictions and less focused on her and their life together. She says he has far more time for his addict friends than he does for her."

"Has she said anything to him?"

"They've been in therapy for years. If you ask me, she was done with him five years ago but hasn't had the heart to end it. Imagine what it'd be like for her if he relapsed after she breaks up with him."

"That's an awful burden for her to carry."

"It is, and we've suggested having the therapist there for the discussion, and she's considered that but can't seem to bring herself to make it happen."

"How do you even begin a conversation like that?"

"I don't know, but it's not getting easier as more time goes by."

"Would it be a total surprise to him?"

"I think so. I saw him about a month ago, and he didn't say anything to me about her being unhappy. I think he would if he sensed it, because he has before."

"Which means she's gotten really good at hiding it."

"Yeah, exactly, or he's so tuned out he's not seeing the forest for the trees right in front of him."

"It's made more complicated by the fact that they bought her parents' house when her parents retired to Florida. She can't afford to buy him out, so they'd have to sell it if they break up, and she's done a ton of work to it."

"Wow, I had no idea she was dealing with all that."

"I think despite everything, she still loves him like she always did, so who knows? Maybe they'll work it out."

"I hope whatever happens makes her happy, and I'm sorry I wasn't here for her during a rough time."

Renata looked over at her. "I know you've made a solid attempt to stay in touch, but they're right when they say a lot of real life went on since you left, and things are different now."

"Of course I expected that."

"But you didn't think it would be weird with us."

"No, I didn't," Kara said, sighing. "I feel like I've let you all down or something without meaning to."

"Don't take that on. It's possible there's a hint of jealousy running through it. Not only did you find a whole new life for yourself, but you also landed yourself a hotshot husband."

"I don't think of him that way."

"Well, the rest of the world does. His career has been the stuff of legend. Everyone knows who he is."

"I'm incredibly proud of all his accomplishments, but to me, he's just Dan, the love of my life."

"Which is wonderful. I greatly enjoyed picturing Kelly's reaction to hearing you were with him and going to marry him."

Kara snorted out a laugh. "You vindictive bitch."

"Oh, come on. Don't act like you didn't enjoy that just as much."

"Maybe just a little."

"Liar."

"You gotta hear what went down between him and Matt in court yesterday."

"Do tell."

They laughed like fools after Kara told her the story.

Kara looked over at her beloved cousin. "I'm really sorry if my absence made you or the girls think I don't care about you all as much as I always have."

"We know that. People change. They grow up and move on. It happens. You shouldn't ever apologize or feel bad for doing what was best for you. Jessie and Ellery probably feel a bit stuck. To them, you've been off on a grand adventure, while everything stayed the same for them. Of course, that has nothing at all to do with you."

"It sure felt like it did back at the restaurant."

"Nah, you're just a symptom of a larger problem for them."

"Isn't Ellery happy with Pete and the kids?"

"His injury has been a lot. It took a long time for him to get back up to speed, and they took a huge financial hit while he was out of work. They're still digging out of that hole, and the inn is a constant source of strain for them. I've suggested she sell it, but it was her grandmother's home, so there's a lot of emotion attached to that decision."

"I hate that everything is so hard for them."

"I do, too, but they've got to figure it out. Try not to be hurt by what they said. You're not the source of their unhappiness."

"Thank you for coming after me and providing that perspective."

"No problem."

"So you're really going to that wedding with Myles?"

"Don't remind me."

CHAPTER
Twelve

DAN MET with Hugo's investigator friend, Carter Smith, at a lunch place on Route 102. Walter dropped him off with the usual instructions to text when he was ready to go home.

Carter was a big dude with thinning gray hair and a matching goatee. He shook Dan's hand and gestured for him to have a seat.

"Thanks for seeing me," Dan said.

"Got to admit I was a bit curious about the fancy lawyer."

"I'm not so fancy."

"Whatever you say. Your boys are in a world of trouble."

"What're you hearing?"

"Keith's DNA is all over her."

"He doesn't deny they were together. Eyewitness reports have them dancing together for hours."

"That's not all they did."

That was the first Dan had heard of proof Keith had sex with the victim. "Where're they saying that happened?"

"In the bathroom at the bar." Carter put a grainy photo on the table that showed Keith and a young woman wrapped up in each other outside the restrooms.

"Where'd you get that?"

"Got a buddy that works at the bar."

If Carter had it, the cops did, too.

"Keith's a regular there. Not the first time he's been in trouble over stuff that's gone on there."

"What else has happened?"

"A few women complaining that he couldn't take no for an answer when he'd been drinking. Bouncers removed him in those cases. He's been in two fights there and was one fight away from being banned for life." Carter leaned in, his expression earnest. "The thing is, they like him there. Everyone says when he's not drunk, he's the nicest guy you'll ever meet."

"Charming."

"It's true, though. I know him a little bit. He's got a reputation for being the guy you call when your plumbing craps out, no pun intended, and you can't afford a plumber. He can fix anything, and he's willing to help anyone who needs it. A lot of people who wouldn't be able to afford repairs otherwise rely on him."

"I've heard he has some redeeming qualities."

"He has a lot of them, but he comes across rough around the edges, and the booze situation has gotten worse in recent years."

"The police report stated the victim, Tanya Sorenson, was found on a beach near town, beaten and strangled."

"That's the info I received as well. A local guy named Horace Gordon fishes off that beach every morning. He's the one who spotted her and called it in around eleven the next morning. From what I've heard, he's pretty broken up about it. Has a granddaughter around the same age and is taking it hard. The 911 call came in about five minutes after the cops got a call from the women she'd been with the night before, reporting that she hadn't come home."

"How soon after that did they pick up Keith and Kirby?"

"Two hours later."

"Which means they didn't do any kind of real investigation before they arrested them and charged them with murder."

"That's my take as well. They had a few people tell them she'd been seen with Keith, had video of her walking in town with him after last call and an eyewitness that put Keith with her near the beach, and Kirby's truck there as well."

"It sure as hell sounds like they jumped the gun arresting them."

"Since he'd been reportedly 'all over her' in the bar, they felt they had probable cause to arrest and charge Keith, which is a huge stretch. Kirby was an even bigger stretch."

"I'd like to start with the women she was with and go from there," Dan said.

"That'd be my first move, as well. But here's the thing, man... And don't take this the wrong way, but I think you should let me work on my own. Mainers are weird about outsiders poking around in their business, especially the fancy, made-for-Hollywood sort of outsider."

"Ouch," Dan said, grinning.

Carter shrugged. "Just calling it like I see it, but don't take that as an insult. I'm wildly impressed by the work you've done to free unjustly incarcerated people."

"Thank you, and I understand where you're coming from. I brought you in to get your advice on how to go forward, so I'll let you do your thing."

"I think that's for the best. I'll get right on it and keep you informed of every development."

"That works for me. If you bill me weekly, I'll get it taken care of right away."

"It's going to add up fast."

"Believe me," Dan said, "I know."

. . .

AFTER CARTER LEFT TO GET TO WORK, DAN CALLED HIS father-in-law.

"Hey, Dan, how's it going?"

"I've hired a private investigator, a friend of Hugo's named Carter Smith. He'll dig into the case and see what he can find that'll help."

"I'll pay for that."

Dan had hoped he'd say that. Not that he couldn't or wouldn't foot the bill if he had no other choice, but he preferred that Chuck paid the expenses.

"What do you know about a man named Jonah Brown?"

"How do you know of him?"

"He's the eyewitness who ID'd your sons with the victim the night she was murdered."

"Are you shitting me?"

"Nope."

"Oh my God."

"What?"

"We fired him two years ago after he'd failed multiple drug tests. He sued us, saying the firing was unjust because he has an illness. We've refused to settle, and he's demanding at least two hundred fifty thousand to make it go away. We're fighting him because he was fired for cause—and we can prove it. It goes to trial in December."

"Isn't that interesting?"

"Sure is. He's certainly no friend of ours."

"We can introduce the family's history with him at trial, if it goes that far."

"Do you really think it'll go to trial?" Chuck asked. "It's already affecting our business. We've had multiple orders worth millions canceled since the news broke, not to mention the damage to my sons' reputations. So much for innocent until proven guilty."

"My goal is to present as much evidence as I can at the

preliminary hearing, to poke enough holes in the prosecutor's case to get the judge to dismiss the charges. That's our best shot of getting this dealt with quickly, but there're never any guarantees the judge will rule in our favor."

"I appreciate what you're doing. Make sure you're tracking your time so we can pay you."

"There's no charge for my time."

"Come on, Dan. This could be a long haul. You can't do that for free. You certainly don't owe us anything."

"No, I don't, but I owe your daughter everything. That makes you, Keith and Kirby family to me, and my time is free to you."

"Thank you. That's very generous of you."

"I want this situation resolved as quickly as possible so I can take my wife home."

"I understand, and it was good of you both to come in light of, well, everything."

"Yes, it was good of her to come when she sure as hell had good reason to stay away."

"I've said it before, but it bears repeating. We handled the situation with Matt and Kelly badly, and we regret hurting Kara."

"It means a lot to her that you've owned that, but those kinds of hurts don't just scab over. They fester a bit. Just because she's here, and just because I'm here, doesn't mean she's forgiven and forgotten what went on."

"I understand."

"I'm not trying to be a dick, Chuck. I swear that's not the case. But what was done to Kara is somewhat unforgivable."

"Yes, it is. I've made a lot of mistakes in my life, but that was the biggest one, and I deeply regret the role I played in hurting her."

"That's why we're here, because she knows that, and she believed you when you told her so."

"I'm glad to hear that."

"Her mother, however, is another story."

"Yes, she certainly is, and if it makes you feel any better to know this, we've had some of the worst arguments of our married life over Kelly and Matt and what they did to Kara."

"Kara would tell you she's better off for their deception. We're incredibly happy together. But that doesn't negate the deep pain that was caused by two people she loved and trusted."

"We agree on that, and I've said as much to Kelly and Matt, too. All this strife in the family is painful to me. It's been too much a part of my life. Beginning with my brother and now among my kids. I wouldn't wish it on anyone."

"Nor would I. I lost my only brother far too soon, and there's almost nothing I wouldn't give to have one more day with him."

Chuck's deep sigh echoed through the phone.

"You should patch things up with your brother, Chuck. Life's too short to carry around grudges."

"That's very true, but some grudges are insurmountable."

"I refuse to believe that. There's nothing that can't be fixed if everyone involved wants it to be."

"That's the rub. He doesn't want anything to do with me."

"It's been a long time. He might surprise you."

"I'll give that some consideration when I can think about anything other than my sons being charged with murder."

"Understood. I'll be in touch."

"Thank you, Dan, for everything. We owe you."

"No problem."

"Sure it is, but you came anyway. We'll remember that."

"Take care, Chuck." He ended that call and made another to Carter. "I just talked to Chuck Ballard. The eyewitness, Jonah Brown, was let go from BBW a couple of years ago after multiple failed drug tests. They're locked up in litigation over it, and BBW is refusing to settle. It's due to go to trial in December."

"In that case, he must've taken great pleasure in pointing the finger at Ballard's sons."

"That's my thinking. Can you dig into him, talk to his

friends, see what he's had to say about Keith, the company, the family in general?"

"Yep. I'm on it."

"Thanks, man."

"You got it."

With Kara out to lunch with her friends and Carter on the case, Dan decided to go for a run. He took the same route as last time, along the scenic road that curled around the southern part of Mount Desert Island. He was eager to check out Acadia National Park and looked forward to getting out on the boat with Bertha and Buster to learn more about the lobstering business.

He felt a little disloyal to Kara for liking her hometown so much. The rugged natural beauty reminded him of Gansett Island as well as Malibu. As he jogged along, he thought through everything he knew so far about the case, the things he'd learned about Keith and Kirby and other members of Kara's family. He'd enjoyed seeing Kendra, Hugo and their sweet girls last night and had bonded with Hugo over their shared interest in football, baseball and hockey.

After not being sure what to expect, it'd been a relief to find people within Kara's immediate family whom he truly liked. She assured him there were others he'd like, too, and he looked forward to meeting them.

His phone buzzed with a text that he stopped to read, only because of Kara's brothers being in lockup. Otherwise, he would've let it wait for later.

This is Matt. I know you said you don't want to work together, but I've got some info you might be interested in. Give me a call.

Dan groaned. Matt was the last freaking person on the planet he wanted to talk to. He put his phone back in his jacket pocket and continued on his way. Yes, he wanted to know what Matt had, but he sure as hell wasn't going to jump right on it and call him back.

Freaking Matt. Didn't he have any pride? Why would he be

kissing up to Kara's husband after the way he'd treated her? Was he hoping to make a friend of Dan so he might smooth things over between Kara and Kelly? If so, he was going to be disappointed. Dan would never be part of suggesting that Kara make up with the sister who'd stabbed her in the back—and the heart.

Despite what he'd said to Chuck about him and his brother, the rift between Kara and her sister was the sort of thing that probably couldn't—and shouldn't—be fixed.

He was completing the third mile of his run when his phone rang. He kept moving as he pulled out the phone, stopping when he saw Kara's name on the screen. "Hey, babe. How was lunch?"

"Dan, it's Renata. I'm with Kara at the ER. She's having some pain."

His heart nearly stopped beating. He immediately turned around and headed back to Bertha's, sprinting now. "What's wrong?" He could barely get the words out over the panic.

"They're not sure yet, but she's on a monitor, and the baby's heartbeat is strong. She asked me to call you."

If she was fine, why hadn't she called him herself?

"How far is Bertha's from where you are?"

"About thirty minutes."

He'd die if it took that long to get to her. "I'm coming. Tell her... Tell her I'm on the way."

"Try not to freak out. The doctors aren't."

"Take care of her until I get there."

"I will."

Dan pressed the red button and then called Walter. "I need a ride to the hospital right away. My wife is there. I'm sending you my location."

"I'm coming, boss."

"Hurry, Walter. Please hurry."

CHAPTER
Thirteen

KARA WAS TRYING NOT to panic. That's why she'd asked Renata to call Dan. He'd hear it in her voice, and whatever meltdown he was having would be made worse. At first, she'd thought it was gas after lunch, but when the pain got sharper and more regular, she'd had no choice but to tell Renata, who'd insisted on driving her to Mount Desert Island Hospital.

They'd taken her straight back to a cubicle and put a monitor on the baby, whose strong heartbeat was the best sound Kara had ever heard.

If the baby was okay, where was the pain coming from? She wished she'd read more about the things that could go wrong so she would know the potential complications. But she hadn't wanted to think about anything other than a smooth pregnancy followed by the arrival of a perfectly healthy baby.

Any other outcome was unimaginable.

With Kara stable and in good hands, Renata had reluctantly returned to work to get out a huge order that'd come in that morning. She'd promised to check on Kara later.

"Your blood pressure is up a bit," the nurse, Debbie, said. "Has it been high during your pregnancy?"

"No, not at all. My midwife has said it was right where it should be."

"Who should I contact to request your records?"

"Victoria Stevens, nurse practitioner-midwife at the Gansett Island clinic." Kara retrieved Vic's number from her phone and gave it to the nurse, thankful that Vic and Shannon hadn't left yet on their honeymoon trip.

"I love Gansett. I spent summers there with my grandparents when I was a kid."

If the nurse was making conversation, there was no need for panic, right?

"We love it there, too. It's home for us."

"What brings you to Maine?"

"My... um... my family's here."

"Ah, I see."

"Am I losing my baby?" Kara asked softly.

"Oh, I don't think so, sweetie, but let's wait to see what the doctor says when she arrives. We called in the OB. She'll be here soon." Debbie patted Kara's arm. "Try not to worry. That won't help anything."

"I'm trying." And failing. If something happened to the baby... *No, don't go there. Think positively.* Tears slid down her cheeks as every emotion she'd ever felt seemed to overwhelm her all at once—especially fear, grief, heartbreak and love. So much love for this little being she hadn't even met yet.

Thankfully, the baby was moving as much as it ever did, which brought a measure of comfort.

Half an hour later, Dan rushed into the room, wild-eyed, hair standing on end the way it did after he went for a run. He came right over to her and gathered her into his sweaty embrace. Whereas she normally might've balked at being held against his damp T-shirt, he was all she wanted at this moment.

"What're they saying?"

"We're waiting for the doctor, but the nurse said everything looks good. The baby's heartbeat is strong, and he—or she—is moving around a lot."

Dan placed a hand on her belly so he could feel the baby moving. "So where's the pain coming from?"

"I'm not sure."

"Could be Braxton Hicks contractions," Debbie said when she returned. "They can mimic labor pains and are often quite uncomfortable."

"I read about them," Kara said. "I thought they weren't painful."

"Everyone has a different experience. Some moms report finding them painful, while others say it's more like a tightening sensation."

"I've had that, the tightening. This is my husband, Dan."

"Nice to meet you," Debbie said.

"You, too," Dan said. "When will the doctor be here?"

"In about fifteen minutes. We're going to start an IV to get some fluid into you since you're slightly dehydrated, which can also cause Braxton Hicks contractions, if that's what this is. I'll be right back."

Dan dropped his head to her chest. "Scared the hell out of me."

Kara ran her fingers through his hair. "Scared me, too."

"This kid of ours is already putting us through the paces."

"Seriously." Kara grimaced when another of the odd pains rippled through her midsection.

"Hey, kid, it's me, your dad. Let me tell you something... Your mom is pretty awesome, and she can't wait to meet you. Neither of us can. But if you could just go a little easier on her until it's time to make your debut, we'd sure appreciate that."

When he looked up at her, heart in his eyes, she smiled.

"Thanks for coming running when Renata called."

"I'll always come running to you and the peanut."

. . .

KARA WAS RELEASED AT AROUND NINE O'CLOCK THAT
evening after a thorough exam and numerous tests had ruled out
any serious concerns with the baby and her blood pressure had
stabilized. The pains were determined to be Braxton Hicks
contractions.

"I feel stupid for panicking over something normal," she said
as Walter drove them back to Bertha's.

"Don't feel stupid. I'd rather you panic than have something
happen to either of you."

"Still... much ado about nothing."

"It's not nothing if you're in pain. And besides, the last few
days have been stressful."

She hadn't gotten a chance to fully process the odd vibe
coming from her friends at lunch before the pain had required
all her attention.

Now that she was feeling better, she picked over the things
that Jessie and Ellery had said and tried to figure out how she
felt about them. On the one hand, she understood where they
were coming from. On the other, however, she made no apologies for doing what was best for herself. But she hated that her
friends had been hurt by her long absence.

"Thanks for everything, Walter," Dan said when he delivered
them to Bertha's.

"No problem, bossman, and nice to see your missus."

"Thank you, Walter," Kara said.

"Take good care of yourself."

"Will do."

Bertha was waiting at the door to greet them with hugs. "I'm
so glad everything is okay, sweetheart."

Kara clung to her grandmother. "Me, too."

"And they say pregnancy is the most natural thing in the
world, right?"

Kara laughed. "Is it, though?"

"Not if you ask me. I had four chaotic pregnancies followed by four easy deliveries."

"I hope I get the easy delivery."

"You will. I'm sure of it. Are you hungry?"

"I could eat something."

"I made a huge pot of chicken noodle soup earlier. How does that sound?"

"Perfect."

"Dan?"

"Yes, please. Thank you, Bertha."

"My pleasure."

Bertha served bowls of soup with crusty bread and sat with them, sipping from a bottle of Miller High Life while they ate.

"I thought you were a Manhattan kind of gal," Dan said.

"Only on the weekends, never on school nights."

"Ah, I see. I used to drink Miller High Life in high school."

"That's a scandal. You weren't old enough to drink beer then."

He grinned. "Don't tell my mother."

"What's it worth to you, pal?"

"A lot. She'd smack me upside the head even now."

"I think I'll like this mother of yours."

"She's great," Kara said. "I love his whole family."

"Nice when that happens."

"Did you like Grandpa's family?" Kara asked Bertha. "I don't remember you saying much about them."

"They didn't like me. They thought I was too rough around the edges for their refined son. His mother suggested I give up lobstering after I married so I could be a more traditional wife."

Kara nearly choked on her soup at the thought of anyone saying such a thing to fiercely independent Bertha. "She did not say that!"

Bertha chuckled. "She sure did, along with pointing out that being a lobster fisherwoman isn't very ladylike."

"Wow. Did she know how lucky she was that you didn't punch her in the face?"

"I don't think she ever realized that, but my sweetie did. Tony held my hand to keep me from overreacting."

"What did he say?"

"I'll never forget it," Bertha said with a smile. "He said, 'Mother, I know exactly who I married, and she's everything I want, so leave her alone, or you won't be seeing much of me.'"

"Whoa," Kara said. "That's hot."

"Sure was, and he was richly rewarded for that when we got home."

"Ack! Stop!"

Bertha cackled with laughter. "As if you're not doing the same thing every chance you get."

Kara sent a guilty look Dan's way.

"She has a point, babe."

"You be quiet."

Bertha laughed even harder at the face Kara made at her husband.

A loud knock on the door startled them.

"Who the heck is that at this hour?" Bertha asked as she got up to answer the door.

A young police officer stood at the door, holding a large white envelope. "Package for Dan Torrington. Can you sign here, please?"

"I've got this, Bertha," Dan said. "Who's it from?"

"Detective Cosgrove asked me to drop this off to you earlier. I got called to an MVA... That's a motor vehicle accident."

"I'm familiar with the term."

"Oh right. Of course you'd know that. Sorry. Anyway, he asked me to drop this off to you. Sorry to come by so late."

Dan took the package from the young man and signed the receipt.

"You all have a nice evening."

"You do the same."

"What is it?" Kara asked after Dan opened the envelope and examined the contents.

"Final police and autopsy reports."

"Ah, some light bedtime reading," Bertha said, grimacing.

Dan set the documents on the counter and returned to the table.

"How do you bear it?" Bertha asked. "The details of a case like this."

"It's never easy, that's for sure, but I try to focus on the facts and remind myself of the job I need to do."

"Do you ever start to hate your clients?"

"I have, many times, grown to despise them, especially when I realized they were full of shit and every word out of their mouth was a lie. It's harder to put up a full-throated defense of someone like that, which is why these days I only take clients who I believe are innocent. Everyone deserves a robust defense, but not everyone deserves that from me. Not anymore."

Bertha nodded. "I like that."

"It's easier to be picky at this point in my career. In the beginning, I didn't have the luxury of saying no to the true scumbags who deserved to be locked up for the rest of their lives. I always did my best for them, but it didn't break my heart to see them convicted and sent away."

"Did you ever get someone off who should've been convicted?"

Dan's expression was as serious as Kara had ever seen it. "A few times, which truly sucks because you're sure they'll reoffend. Most of them do before too long. The system isn't perfect, but it's the only one we've got."

"What's your first move in a case like this?" Bertha asked.

"I'll take a look at the reports while the investigator I hired talks to the women she was with that night and others who saw her and Keith together at the bar."

"You hired an investigator," Kara said.

"Yeah, that's pretty standard in a capital case. There's a lot of ground to cover."

"Who'd you get?" Bertha asked.

"Carter Smith. Hugo recommended him."

Bertha nodded. "The Smiths are good people. His grandfather was a lobsterman. Knew him well back in the day."

"Who's paying for that?" Kara asked.

"Your dad said he would. We need all hands on deck to come up with as much info as we can to hopefully get the charges tossed at the preliminary hearing."

"Is that even possible?"

"It's not *im*possible, but it's a long shot. We'd have to produce irrefutable evidence that it wasn't them, so that's the goal. To find something that gives the judge enough doubt to toss the charges."

"And you trust this investigator to be on the right side of this case?" Kara asked.

"He had a lot of nice things to say about Keith."

"Really?" Bertha asked, her left brow raised.

"Yeah. He talked about how Keith can fix everything, and people who can't afford a plumber, for example, call on him because he'll take care of the issue for a minimal charge. When he's not drinking, Carter said, people like him a lot."

"That's true," Kara said. "He's always been able to fix anything. I remember my dad asking him to fix a leak in the kitchen sink when he was in high school, and he did it in like an hour. They rarely called anyone to fix things at the house after that. He's got a ton of friends, too, a lot of them going back to childhood."

"The drinking has gotten bad in the last few years," Bertha said. "He was loaded every time I've seen him."

"Being a drinker doesn't make him a murderer," Dan said.

"No, it sure doesn't," Bertha said.

"I mean... we've never been close at all," Kara said. "I barely know him, if I'm being honest. He was in trouble a lot, fighting in school and stuff like that. But I can't see that escalating to murder."

"Not to mention," Bertha said, "the ladies *love* him."

"Oh, for sure. He's had them flocking around him all his life."

"This is all helpful information," Dan said. "We need to get you to bed, love, after the day you've had."

He didn't even know the rest of what'd happened. "I'm ready."

They got up and took their bowls to the dishwasher.

Kara bent to hug her grandmother, who was still seated at the table. "Thanks for the soup. It was delicious."

"You're welcome, sweetheart. Sleep well."

"Love you."

"Love you more."

"No way."

Bertha smiled up at her. "I'll fight you on that. Night, Dan."

"Night, Bertha. Thanks for dinner."

"Very happy to have you both here."

After Kara changed into pajamas and brushed her teeth, Dan tucked her into bed. "I'm going to review the reports and do a bit of work. I'll be in soon."

"Don't stay up too late. I need you to keep my feet warm."

"Is that all I'm good for around here?"

"Yep," she said with a laugh. "That's it."

"I see how it is." He leaned in to kiss her. "I'm so glad you and baby Dylan are okay."

"Me, too. That was scary."

"This is why Mac put a ban on all future pregnancies on Gansett Island."

"Mac is ridiculous, and his wife defied him by having twins."

"And his sister-in-law by having quads. He's lost control of things."

"He never had control, despite what he thinks."

Dan smiled and kissed her again. "Smart men know who runs the world, and it ain't us."

"That's right."

"I can't wait to get home to Gansett."

"Me, too. I want to go home with my brothers cleared of all charges, so I can get back to enjoying my life without having to think about what's going on here."

"I'll do everything I can to make that happen as quickly as possible."

"Thank you for all you're doing. It's more than my family deserves."

"It's all for you, my love. Anything for you."

CHAPTER
Fourteen

WHEN DAN CAME to bed an hour later, Kara reached for him and held on tight to her true love.

"We never got to talk about your lunch with the girls. Was it great to see them?"

"Yeah."

He pulled back so he could see her face. "That doesn't sound very enthusiastic. You were so excited to see them."

"Apparently, I stayed away too long."

"What do you mean?"

"They expressed their displeasure with my long absence."

"For real?"

"Yes. Renata says I shouldn't take it personally. They're taking out frustrations with their own lives on me, but it felt pretty freaking personal."

"They know why you left—and why you stayed gone."

"I think they felt it was unfair to punish them for what other people did."

"But you talked to them all the time. Text, FaceTime, photos back and forth."

"I guess there's no substitute for friends who are physically present."

"I'm so sorry they made you feel that way, hon. You don't deserve that."

"In a way, I do."

"How so?"

"When things blew up with Kelly—and Matt—I disengaged from everything. I went to work, came home and stayed away from everyone—except Bertha. I still saw her regularly. But I stopped everything else because I couldn't bear to see people looking at me like I was the most pathetic person they knew."

"Aw, babe. You were never pathetic. Matt and Kelly were the pathetic ones."

"Do you know what it's like to live in a place like this, where everyone knows everyone, and the whole town is talking about the sisters feuding over a man?"

"I can't say that I do."

"It was brutal. Then they got engaged, and my parents stepped up to help them plan a wedding, and I had to get out of here. I couldn't take it for another second. I left without even saying goodbye to the girls. I got in my car and drove out of town and never looked back."

"You did what you needed to for yourself and your own sanity."

"I was only thinking of myself. I didn't give a thought to what my sudden departure would mean for them. They were my real family here, you know?"

"I do know that. You've always said that about them."

"They deserved better from me."

"You're being super hard on yourself, when yourself doesn't deserve that. They might've done the same thing if it'd happened to them."

"They couldn't have left like I did. They wouldn't have been able to afford to just up and leave their whole life the way I did."

"I'm sure you used your own money to pay for the move."

"Nope. I made the company pay for it as part of my punishment of my parents. Not that I took a lot of stuff, but they paid for what I did take, and the girls know that because I told them I stuck it to my dad and made him pay for the move. They don't have a Ballard Boat Works to turn to when times get hard."

"I'll bet that's the only time you ever turned to the company or your parents for that kind of help."

"It is, but they—"

"Kara, you didn't do anything wrong. Companies pay to relocate employees all the time."

"I know it's common practice, but the success of my father's business had separated me from my friends long before this happened. I swear they never believed he wasn't fully supporting me since I had a nice apartment in town and a car I bought new, but I paid for that myself while the three of them struggled financially much more than I ever did. Coming back here has reminded me of things I'd forgotten about while I was gone."

"You made different choices for your life than they did. Ellery got married young and bought the inn. Jessie's chosen to stick it out with Doug, for now anyway. Renata keeps working for Williams when she might've moved on to something that paid better. They own their choices just like you own your decision to leave here when it became impossible for you to stay."

"I guess."

"It's true, love. You're still the same person you were the day we met."

"No, I'm not."

"You are. What do you mean?"

"I'm different now."

"How?"

"For one thing, I never, ever, *ever* worry about money anymore. I can't remember the last time I gave a thought to how I was going to pay for something."

"So your marriage to the wildly successful, devastatingly handsome and fiercely sexy lawyer hasn't helped the situation?"

Kara burst out laughing. She laughed so hard, she feared she might wet the bed. By the time she caught her breath, she had tears in her eyes and a smile on her face.

"Was it something I said?"

"Don't make me laugh like that again unless you want to sleep in a wet bed. Your huge baby is camped out on my bladder."

"I can't help it if I'm devilishly funny on top of all my other endearing qualities."

She pinched his lips closed. "Stop talking."

He twisted free of her grip. "That takes me right back to our glorious early days together when you were forever trying to get me to shut up."

"I never have succeeded in that."

"Others before you have tried and failed." When she raised a brow, he quickly added, "Parents, teachers, coaches, bosses, professors, law firm partners."

"Nice save, Counselor."

"Phew, that was a close one."

"You're always a heartbeat away from big trouble."

"I like to live dangerously." He tenderly brushed her hair back from her face. "I feel bad that your time with your friends was upsetting."

"It is what it is, but I'm hoping to have more time with them while we're here to work things out. If that doesn't happen, it'll be okay because I have you and Dylan and Bertha and Buster and your family and all our family on Gansett Island. Our chosen family."

"I'm sorry if being with me has made a tough situation worse for you, though."

"Being with you has made my whole life complete. Despite

your overinflated ego, you're the best thing to ever happen to me, and you make me deliriously happy most of the time."

He gave her the side-eye. "Only most of the time?"

"Take the victories where you can get them."

"Yes, dear. So I'm the best thing to ever happen to you, huh?"

"Go away, Dan."

"But you just said you loved me more than anything!"

"When did I say that?"

"I heard it. I swear I did."

"I'm going to sleep now."

"Kiss me good night."

"I already did."

"Do it again."

She reached for him and kissed his face off, until he was panting like a teenager in the throes of first lust. "Good?"

"Um, well, I seem to have a whole other problem now."

"You can work that one out on your own. Your child and I are going to sleep."

"Wow, that's super mean. I never knew you were so mean."

Kara fell asleep smiling, the way she did every night since Dan Torrington had given her no choice but to fall madly in love with him.

WIDE AWAKE IN EVERY POSSIBLE WAY AFTER THAT KISS from his wife, Dan set up shop on the kitchen table. He helped himself to one of Bertha's Millers and then got busy digging into the police and autopsy reports.

He was thoroughly engrossed when he sensed a presence behind him. When he turned, he found Buster hovering in the doorway as if he wasn't sure if it was okay to come into the room.

"Hey, Buster. Hope I didn't disturb you."

"No."

He went to the fridge, withdrew a Miller and twisted the cap off. "Kara?"

"She's okay and so's the baby, thankfully."

Buster nodded as he took a sip of beer. "They didn't kill that girl."

"I know."

"Keith's a dick, not a murderer."

Dan nodded, intrigued by Buster's take since Kara had once described her uncle as the keenest observer of people she'd ever met. "That's what I hear from others."

"Can you fix it?"

"I'm trying like hell."

"Good." He took his beer and headed for the door, dropping a newspaper on the table as he went.

"Night, Buster."

"Night."

Dan picked up the copy of the *Mount Desert Islander* and glanced at the front page, which bore a banner headline that said BALLARD SONS ARRESTED IN WEEKEND MURDER.

BAR HARBOR — Keith and Kirby Ballard, sons of Ballard Boat Works owners Chuck and Judith Ballard, were arrested on Saturday in connection with the murder of Tanya Sorenson, 21, who was in town for a bachelorette party. She was the daughter of Mitchell and Deborah Sorenson, longtime summer residents of Bar Harbor. The party was for Jessa Kaul, the fiancée of Tanya's brother, August Sorenson.

Sources tell the Islander that Keith Ballard, 37, had been seen with Ms. Sorenson at the Barnacle Lounge during the evening. According to onlookers, Ballard and Sorenson danced for most of the evening and disappeared together for about forty-five minutes before returning for last call.

The wedding party was staying at the Sorenson home on West

Street. Ms. Kaul and August Sorenson are due to be married at the Sorenson home in October.

Keith Ballard, who's well known to local police, works as a laborer at Ballard Boat Works. He attended Mount Desert High School, but there's no record of his graduation. His brother Kirby, 30, is also employed by BBW, as a master craftsman. He's a graduate of Mount Desert High School and Colby College.

The Sorenson and Kaul families have requested privacy at this difficult time. Calls to the Ballard family went unreturned at press time. Celebrated defense attorney Daniel Torrington, brother-in-law to the Ballards, is representing Kirby Ballard. Torrington is married to the former Kara Ballard, and the two reside on Gansett Island in Rhode Island. Another brother-in-law, local attorney Matthew Gallagher, represented Keith Ballard at today's arraignment at which the brothers were held without bail pending a preliminary hearing next week.

Dan had no sooner read the article than his phone rang with a call from the *Mount Desert Islander.*

"Dan Torrington."

"This is Elias Young with the *Mount Desert Islander.* I apologize for calling so late, but I have a couple of questions after today's court appearance. Do you have a minute?"

"I do."

"You're listed as representing Kirby Ballard. Who's representing Keith?"

"I'm not sure."

"Why are you not representing both of them?"

"Because Keith chose not to retain my services."

"For real?"

"Yes."

"Does Keith know who you are?"

"Probably. I've been married to his sister for a couple of years now, but I've only met him once before at our wedding."

"Huh, personally, I'd jump at the chance to have you on my team if I were in his shoes."

"I can't speak for him. He's not my client."

"What can you tell me about Kirby's whereabouts on the night in question?"

"He spent the evening at home and left only to pick up Keith in town to give him a ride home. He had no contact with the victim, except to ask his brother if she wanted a ride somewhere. Keith said she was all set. When they left, Ms. Sorenson waved to them from the sidewalk. I believe the place where she was staying was close to where they were."

"The eyewitness report puts both brothers on the sidewalk with her."

"Kirby never got out of his vehicle."

"That's something I hadn't heard before now. Why do you suppose he was charged?"

"You'd have to ask the state police and attorney general about that."

"Is there anything else you can tell me?"

"My client is an innocent man. He should never have been charged in this case."

"Thank you for your time."

"No problem."

Dan ended the call, hoping he hadn't made anything worse for Kirby by being blunt with the reporter.

Next, he dove into the police report, which laid out the timeline of events, including statements from witnesses that confirmed Keith and Tanya had danced for more than an hour, disappeared for a time together and then returned for last call. After that, they were seen leaving the bar hand in hand. Security cameras in town had recorded them walking down the hill toward the waterfront.

The eyewitness claimed that he'd seen Keith and Kirby

standing on the sidewalk next to Kirby's vehicle, talking to Tanya, yet Kirby claimed to have never left the vehicle. So how did this so-called witness see him on the sidewalk?

The autopsy report was next and detailed a blood alcohol level of 0.19%. He used his laptop to search for the legal limit in Maine, which was 0.08%, so Tanya was significantly over the legal limit for intoxication. She'd died from a blow to the head, but police hadn't determined the weapon used. DNA found on her body and in her vagina had matched with the sample taken from Keith Ballard after he was arrested, which meant they'd had sex when they snuck off together.

His next move was to find Tanya on social media. He located an active Instagram account full of photos with friends and family, including her brother and his fiancée taken at an engagement party for the couple earlier in the summer.

Tanya had long blonde hair, blue eyes and a gorgeous smile.

Had Keith realized she was only twenty-one? He wouldn't have known that just by looking at her because Dan would've guessed her to be in her mid-twenties at least.

His heart ached for her family as he read some of the tributes to her that'd been posted.

My baby sister is gone, August had written along with photos he'd posted of them together from the time they were young children. Judging by those early pictures, he was about five or six years older than her. *Tanya's smile lit up our world. She filled our lives with joy and laughter and a childlike sense of wonder that she never outgrew. We're forever changed by this loss and will do everything in our power to get justice for our Tanya. Sleep in peace, sweet girl.*

The post had generated an outpouring of sympathy for August and his parents as well as their extended family.

He clicked on the link to Tanya's Instagram account and scrolled through a year's worth of posts, looking for insight into her life. She'd graduated from high school in Madison, Connecticut, and had attended the University of Connecticut. She was a proud Huskie, often posing in UConn sweatshirts and other clothing, due to graduate in May.

She'd loved spending summers in Bar Harbor, where she worked as a sailing instructor at the Northeast Harbor Sailing School.

Dan fell into a social media rabbit hole as he read through posts and comments. One of the posts from May caught his attention. She'd posted a selfie in which she looked reflective. *Sometimes things don't work out the way you hoped they would. People show you who they really are, and that can be super disappointing. Thankful to all my sweet friends who are there for me when I need them.*

The comments were equally revealing.

He didn't deserve you. I never thought so.

You're better off without him.

You won't be single for long, girlfriend.

We're here for you! Glad you threw out the trash!

Dan sent an email to Clarissa, one of the female investigators who worked for his innocence project in Los Angeles. She was young and hip and understood social media at a level he never would. He sent her the link to the post that had piqued his interest. *How can we find out who the guy was?*

As a defense attorney, his goal was to introduce reasonable doubt into a case, to show the jury that the murder could've been committed by someone else who had a motive. Tanya's ex was a possible avenue in that direction. Was it a long shot? Sure, but it was a place to start.

Clarissa emailed him back a short time later. *Hey! Let me dig in. I'll get back to you tomorrow. How's Maine?*

Thank you. Maine is interesting. Lots of family dynamics at play—and not all of them the good kind. Appreciate the assist.

Happy to help.

Dan continued to read through Tanya's posts until his eyes

were crossing from exhaustion. Yawning, he closed his laptop and got up to stretch out the kinks. He did a double take when he saw the clock on the stove, which read 2:10 a.m.

He moved quietly through the house, got ready for bed and snuggled up to Kara's warm body, his thoughts full of another young woman, whose life had been taken from her far too soon.

CHAPTER
Fifteen

KARA WOKE EARLY when she heard Bertha and Buster moving around, getting ready to go to work. With a burst of energy she hadn't experienced in months, she got up to see them before they left.

"You're up with the chickens," Bertha said when Kara appeared in the kitchen.

Kara kissed her grandmother's cheek and breathed in the scent of the Jean Naté that would forever remind her of her beloved Bertha. "Don't you mean I'm up with the lobster people?"

"That, too."

She went toward Buster, arms extended in question. He gave a brief nod, giving her permission to give him a light hug, which he tolerated from her even though he didn't like to be touched. He'd told her once that he'd welcome hugs from her as long as they weren't tight ones.

He patted her shoulder as she rested her head on his chest. "How you feeling?"

"Better today."

"Glad to hear it. Don't do that again."

She laughed at his way of saying he'd been worried about her. "I'll try not to."

"You want to come out with us today, hon?" Bertha asked.

"I'd love to, but I want to wait until Dan can come, too. He'd love to see you guys in action."

"He'll get his hands dirty," Buster said with the grunt that was the closest he came to laughter.

Kara smiled up at him. "That'll be funny to see."

"Fancy pants."

"Not really, though. Get to know him. I think you'll like him."

"Buster will love him because you do," Bertha said.

"We'll see," Buster said, reserving judgment, as he did with new people. They had to earn their way into his life. He'd had too many people disappoint him over the years not to be cautious.

One of Kara's first memories was of Keith and Kyle teasing Buster. Even though she was younger than both of them, she'd intervened then and every time after that. No one picked on Buster when she was around.

Dan came out from the bedroom, looking scruffy and sleepy, which was one of her favorite looks for him because she was usually the only one who ever saw him that way. To everyone else, he was the pressed and polished LA lawyer. But to her, he was her love, her soul mate, her everything.

Kara stepped away from Buster to greet him with a kiss. "Morning. How late were you up?"

"Too late. Is there coffee?"

"Sure is," Bertha said. "We're fueled by it around here."

"Bless you."

"Bertha invited us to go fishing with her," Kara said.

"I'd love to do that."

"You want to come today?" Bertha asked.

Dan glanced at Kara. "Do you feel up to it?"

"I'd love to go. It's my favorite thing ever."

"Then let's do it."

"Don't you have work?"

"I'm waiting on a few things, so I have time."

"Go get ready," Bertha said. "I'll make some breakfast sandwiches to go while you get dressed."

Kara felt giddy at the thought of a day on the *Big B*, her grandmother's lobster boat, where some of her favorite childhood memories had been made.

"Are you sure this is okay?" Dan asked when they were in their room getting ready. "You were in the hospital yesterday."

"With fake labor pains. I'm fine. I feel so much better since I had that IV. I'm not even nauseated this morning."

"Wow, that's a great development."

"Sure is, and I'm excited to go on the boat. It's been way too long."

"I can't wait to see how it all happens."

"Bring a sweatshirt. It can get chilly on the water this time of year."

"Yes, ma'am." He was in the living room looking for a sweatshirt when his phone rang with a call from the *Los Angeles Times*. What the hell did they want? "Torrington."

"This is Kent Thomas with the *LA Times*."

"What can I do for you, Mr. Thomas?"

"Word on the street is that you're defending your brothers-in-law on murder charges in Maine. Any truth to that?"

"Depends on why you want to know."

"Really? The famous defense attorney takes on a murder in the family. How's that not news?"

"It's not my family. It's my wife's family, and I barely know them."

"So it's true that two of her brothers have been charged with murder?"

"If I tell you what you want to know, will I be reading some sort of sensationalized version in your paper?"

"I'm not planning to sensationalize anything. I heard you'd caught a new case and that it was family, thus the interest."

"My wife Kara's two brothers, Keith and Kirby Ballard, were charged by the Maine State Police with the murder of twenty-one-year-old Tanya Sorenson, a summer resident in town for a bachelorette party. They're being held at the Bar Harbor jail. We believe the facts of the case, when presented in court, will result in the charges being dropped."

"I read that there's an eyewitness who puts the brothers with the victim in the early hours of the morning she was found dead."

"Keith Ballard was with her during the evening and into the next day. Kirby picked up his brother in town. They offered Ms. Sorenson a ride home, which she declined. She was alive and well when they left her."

"Are you representing both of them?"

"Just Kirby."

"Why not the other one?"

"You'd have to ask him that."

"Ah, I see."

"You don't see anything, Mr. Thomas. Please don't publish half-truths or innuendo. I've told you what I can. I hope you'll be responsible about what you do with it."

"Thank you for your time, Mr. Torrington."

"What was that about?" Kara asked when she came to find him.

"A call from the *LA Times*. Apparently, word's out that I'm defending your brothers on murder charges."

His phone rang again with a call from the *Mount Desert Islander*. He turned the phone so Kara could see who it was. "Dan Torrington."

"This is Elias Young again from the *Mount Desert Islander*."

"What can I do for you, Mr. Young?"

"I wondered if you might be available for a longer interview to discuss the case against your brothers-in-law and how you plan to proceed with their defense."

"As much as I'd like to meet with you, I prefer to keep my strategy under wraps until we go to court."

"Can you confirm that you're still only representing Kirby Ballard?"

"Yes, that's true."

"Is Matthew Gallagher representing Keith?"

"You'd have to ask him that."

"Your wife has some history with Mr. Gallagher."

"If you're planning to drag my wife through the mud, I won't take your calls, Mr. Young. Do we understand each other?"

"Of course. I was just referring to—"

"Have a good day."

Dan ended the call and put a hand on Kara's shoulder.

She crossed her arms, looking madly vulnerable, which pissed him off. "I suppose it was too much to hope that my past with Matt wouldn't somehow end up part of this story."

"That's not going to happen, or his paper won't get another word out of me. I don't want you to worry about that coming to light."

"What? Me worry?"

Dan moved her arms so he could hug her. As he held on tight to the love of his life, he silently vowed to do anything it took to protect her from the ugliness of this situation. "Let's go fishing."

KARA COULDN'T SHAKE THE FEELING OF DREAD THAT came from the local paper asking about her past with Matt. Being back in town had resurrected a lot of feelings she'd thought she'd disposed of a long time ago. Recalling what it'd been like to be the subject of gossip was like having acid running through her veins. She'd carried that burning sensation—a combination of shame, heartbreak and outrage—around with her for months before she decided to leave and start over on Gansett Island.

"Talk to me." Dan drove them to the wharf in the Jeep, following Bertha and Buster in her truck. "What're you thinking?"

"That I haven't missed the way it felt to be the subject of intense gossip."

"You're not the subject of any gossip. One reporter made one comment."

"That's how it starts. Come on, you know that's all it takes."

"I shut him down. They're going to want me as a source as this case unfolds, and now he knows if he makes you part of the story, he's dead to me. He heard me loud and clear on that."

"Did he, though?" She looked over at him. "I can't go through that again. I just can't."

"If that becomes part of the story, we're going home to Gansett immediately. Your family can hire another attorney to deal with the case." He gripped the wheel tightly, and a muscle in his cheek pulsed the way it did when he was stressed. It'd been a while, she realized, since she'd seen that happen. "I should've passed on this from the get-go."

"No, I needed to come back here. I survived that situation a long time ago. My friends are right. It's time to come home once in a while and stop acting like Kelly and Matt ruined my life, because they didn't. They led me to my life."

"In the shittiest way possible."

"Totally, but how glad am I that I moved to Gansett?"

"How glad am *I* that you moved to Gansett?"

She leaned across the console, which wasn't easy to do with her pregnant belly, and kissed his cheek. "We're so, so glad for all of it."

"That said, I don't want anyone hassling you, even people you love."

"It wasn't a hassle so much as a wake-up call. Ellery's kids are growing up fast and barely know me. Same with my nieces."

"Your nieces know you. You've made sure of that with weekly FaceTime calls and letters back and forth. You're always sending them something."

"There's no substitute for being here with them, though. I realized that the other night. They're already so grown-up. I don't want to miss everything with them."

"We should have them to the island for a couple of weeks next summer. They'd love it, and they can help us with baby Dylan."

"That'd be awesome. Great idea."

She directed him to the wharf where Bertha kept the dinghy that delivered them to the boat on a mooring in the cove.

"Where should we park?"

"Behind Bertha is fine and leave the keys. No one takes their keys on the boats."

"They don't worry about their vehicles getting stolen?"

"Nah, no one would dare touch them. They all know each other."

In a small inflatable boat with a ten-horsepower outboard motor on the back, Buster delivered his mother and then came back for Dan and Kara.

Kara turned her face into the breeze and closed her eyes as a million memories of days on the water reminded her of who she was and where she came from. When she opened her eyes, Dan was watching her with a curious look on his face.

"What?"

"I was thinking it's a bit of a revelation to see you here in this place you're from."

"A big part of me still lives here, which is what I've come to see since I've been back."

"They say you can't go home again..."

"Which simply isn't true."

"I'm glad you're here," Buster said.

Though she still felt apprehension about the possibility of being the subject of local gossip, Kara smiled at her beloved uncle. "So am I."

DAN WAS UNSETTLED BY THE INQUIRY FROM THE reporter and Kara's friends' criticism of her. While he understood where she was coming from by feeling guilty over their hurt feelings, he also remembered in vivid detail the closed-off, shattered person she'd been when they first met. He'd had a front-row seat to the courage and resilience she'd shown in forging a whole new life for herself. She bore no resemblance to that version of herself these days, and it pained him to hear that others were hassling her for doing what she'd needed to at the time.

As Buster delivered them to the *Big B*, Dan was determined to make sure Kara had a great time doing one of her favorite things. There'd be time later to stew over the other stuff. For now, he wanted to learn about lobster fishing.

"Tell me everything. Don't leave anything out."

Bertha laughed as she fired up the boat's engine and turned on a series of electronic devices, including a VHF radio that came to life with chatter from others out fishing.

"Diesel or gas?" Dan asked.

"Diesel for the win," Bertha said.

Dan stood back and watched as she and Buster went through an obviously well-practiced routine of casting off the mooring line and steaming out of the harbor.

"We're getting a late start today because of the fog," Bertha said.

"It's seven o'clock," Dan said.

"We're about two hours late, but we were also waiting on the slack."

"Between tides," Kara asked. "The Downeast coast of Maine has some of the most intense tides you'll see anywhere. They're so strong that they pull the buoys underwater, making it impossible to spot them. You'll hear lobster people refer to 'hauling a slack' or 'heading out for a slack.'"

"Ah, okay. So um… How long does it take for the fog to lift?" After being in a serious boating accident in dense fog, he had a serious aversion to being on the water in a low-visibility situation.

Kara tuned right into his distress. "The last of it will burn off fast now that the sun's peeking through."

"Good."

She sent him a warm smile. "Nothing to worry about. I promise."

Comforted by her assurances, he said, "Two more questions. How can you tell which buoys are yours, and what does Downeast mean?"

Bertha glanced at Kara, brow raised. "You got this, my love?"

"You'll let me know if I get anything wrong?"

"As if there's any doubt."

As Kara smiled at her grandmother, Dan enjoyed the glow in his wife's eyes at doing one of her favorite things with two of her favorite people. "Everyone has their own color palette for their buoys. Ours are orange with two white stripes. If you see an orange one with three white stripes, that's not ours."

"They're also marked with an official government tag that identifies them as ours," Bertha added, "and we repaint them every winter."

"You don't fish in the winter?"

"Not anymore. I used to go out a couple days a week, but lately, I'd rather stay home and paint buoys and repair the traps."

"That's still a lot of work."

"It's easy, and we can do it inside where it's warm."

"She likes to supervise me from her recliner," Buster said, making them laugh.

"She gets a lot done from that chair," Kara said.

"And how," Buster replied.

"It's my command post," Bertha said.

"Anyway," Kara said, "the term Downeast comes from direction versus an actual location. Back in the day, when people would sail from Boston to Maine, they'd sail downwind to get to the east coast of Maine, which is where the Downeast name came from."

"So is all of the eastern coast of Maine considered Downeast?"

"Depends on who you ask," Bertha said. "It includes all of Washington and Hancock Counties and scores of fishing villages. Everyone has a different definition of what counts as Downeast."

"How many lobster fisher-people are there in this area?"

"What's the latest number from the DELA, Buster?" Bertha asked.

"Around three thousand are Downeast, but more than four thousand statewide."

"What's the DELA?"

"Downeast Lobstermen's Association," Bertha said.

"Um, that's not gender neutral," Dan said.

"Believe me, I've raised that point with them repeatedly over the years. A lot of us are women these days."

"What's the best time of year for lobstering?" Dan asked.

"Right about now," Bertha said.

Buster went down below and came back a few minutes later wearing gear with a Grundéns label on it.

As they got farther out from the harbor, the seas became choppier, and a queasy feeling set into Dan's gut. He glanced at Kara, seated across from Bertha, and saw that she was handling the movement of the sea better than he was. Of course she was. She'd been born into this.

When Bertha brought the boat alongside one of her distinctive buoys, Buster got to work on the hydraulic lift that brought the trap to the surface.

Bertha left the helm to head to the stern to assist Buster in retrieving the lobsters, measuring them, returning a few to the water and putting bands on the claws of the ones they were keeping.

They were like a well-oiled machine, going about their task without a single word passing between them.

"How do they decide which ones go back?" Dan asked.

"If they're pregnant females or undersize—or even oversized."

"They can be too big?"

"Often, the bigger ones are breeders," Kara said, "so we always return them to keep the stock healthy. Maine lobstering is among the most conservation-forward industries, and where a lot of fisheries have suffered from overfishing, our lobster industry is robust because of things done on boats like this one to preserve and protect the stock."

"That's awesome."

"I heard one of Bertha's friends say once that the goal is to not cut off our noses to spite our faces."

"Makes sense."

"Lobstering is a family tradition for most of these people." She gestured to other boats they could see in the distance. "They want to leave a legacy they can hand down to their children and grandchildren."

"Where're you putting the ones you're keeping?" Dan asked Bertha.

"Into a holding tank for now. Buster will move them to those plastic crates over there when we get back to port. They're sold by weight, and everyone uses the same crates because they're a standard weight. Makes things easier on the other end."

"How many pounds will you bring in on an average day?"

"This time of year?" Buster said. "A couple hundred. Other times, we're lucky to get fifty."

"Every day is different," Bertha said.

"My mom can't bring herself to cook a lobster because you have to boil them alive," Dan said, "and she can't bear it."

"We hear that a lot," Bertha said. "There's considerable debate about whether they can feel pain. I tend to think not, but others will disagree."

"Ah, I see."

"You want to try the banding, Dan?"

"I'd love to."

"Are you a lefty or a righty?"

"Righty."

"Okay, so you'll grasp the lobster with your left hand. Then take the pliers with your right hand, grab a band and slide it onto the claw, like this."

Easy enough, he thought, following her directions. With the lobster in hand, he reached for the pliers, managed to scoop up a band and had it heading for the lobster's right claw when it flew off the pliers, causing Buster to duck lest he get hit in the face by it. "Whoops."

While the other three laughed, he tried again, losing two more bands before he finally got one on the claw. That's when he discovered that removing the pliers without taking the band off, too, was as much of a trick as getting it on in the first place.

"That's much harder than it looks," he said as he handed over the pliers to Bertha, since they didn't have all day to wait on him.

He watched in amazement as she did six more claws in the time it'd taken him to do one.

"Tell him about the penises, Ma," Buster said.

"What's this you say?" Dan asked.

"Kara, why don't you do the honors?" Bertha asked, smiling at her granddaughter.

CHAPTER
Sixteen

"MALE LOBSTERS HAVE TWO PENISES," Kara said, giggling when Dan waggled his brows.

"The better to love their ladies with."

"Except they get things done in about eight seconds," Bertha said.

"That's no way to keep the ladies happy," Dan said. "Although, if I had two—"

"Do *not* finish that thought in front of my grandmother and uncle."

Buster released a genuine laugh that pleased Dan no end. "Typical guy."

"You know it," Kara said.

"She loves the one I do have. Just thought I'd mention that."

"You need to quit before you get grounded, Torrington."

Buster opened the door to a compartment, and a foul smell hit Dan the likes of which he'd never experienced—and never wanted to again. "What in the *actual hell* is that?"

"Bait," Buster said, his lips twisting into his version of a grin.

"Oh my God." It was all he could do not to heave over the

side as Buster brought a fetid-smelling bait bag to his mother so she could put it in the trap.

Dan looked back at Kara, who was laughing her ass off. "You could've warned me!"

"And missed you turning green? No way."

It took a Herculean effort not to embarrass himself by tossing his cookies as the smell mixed with the motion of the ocean turned his stomach and threatened to bring the delicious egg sandwich Bertha had made for him right back up. He focused on the sight of eightysomething Bertha hauling a heavy lobster trap like it was weightless as Buster prepared to return it to the water.

"Stand back," Bertha said. "This is the dangerous part."

As the trap was sent back to the deep, Dan saw why it was hazardous as the whole thing happened in a whir of movement.

"The most injuries and deaths happen with setting traps," Bertha said. "We lose someone every couple of years."

"That's how Ellery's husband, Pete, lost a finger. Got it stuck in the rigging at the worst possible time."

Dan winced as he imagined such a gruesome injury.

"He's doing much better these days," Bertha said. "Saw him just a few days ago on the water."

"Ellery said he's doing great."

"It took him some time to figure out how to work without the index finger on his dominant hand, but he's got it now," Bertha said.

"I'm so relieved for them. She was afraid for a time that he wouldn't be able to go back to work at all."

"You should have the girls and their families over for dinner while you're home," Bertha said as she returned to the helm to move on to the next trap. "We can do a lobster bake in the yard."

"Oh, that'd be fun. I want them to meet Dan in person. I found out they're kind of annoyed with me for staying away so long."

"Seriously?" Bertha asked, eyes wide.

"That was my question, too," Dan said.

Bertha frowned. "They were there. They know exactly why you stayed gone. I can't believe they'd hold that against you. I sure as hell don't."

"Well, maybe you should, because they're right that I let two people who did me dirty keep me away from all the other people I love."

"That's not what happened," Bertha said fiercely. "You ventured into the world, found yourself a whole new life and went out of your way to keep in close touch with all of us here. You don't owe anyone anything, Kara, so don't let them lay a guilt trip on you."

"I couldn't agree more," Dan said.

"While I appreciate both of you," Kara said, "I'm going to come home more often to see my loved ones here. And I want all of you to visit us, too."

"Good luck getting her to leave Maine," Buster said.

"I left Maine to meet them in Boston," Bertha said.

"Once in fifteen years."

She made a face at her son, and he made the same face back at her.

Dan laughed as the boat heaved while it steamed along the coast. As long as they kept that bait bin closed, he was thoroughly enjoying this.

AT LUNCHTIME, BERTHA PRODUCED A COOLER FULL OF sandwiches, fruit, chips, drinks and cookies.

Bertha's tuna salad brought back a thousand memories of the best days of Kara's young life. She'd gone fishing with Bertha and Buster as often as she could, often doing homework while they fished.

"When did you make this amazing lunch?" Dan asked as he

ate standing up. He was beginning to get his sea legs, but since the bait bin was still a problem, he ate tentatively.

"I was up at four thirty, like every other day. I was hoping to convince you two to come along, so I made extra."

The pace of their day was relentless. Even between stops, Buster never stopped working while Bertha navigated the tricky coastline, pointing out rocks that would tear the bottom out of the boat if you didn't know they were there.

Bertha told Dan that the steady stream of VHF chatter from others out fishing was indicative of a good day on the water. "The radio tends to go quiet on the not-so-good days."

"I'm in awe of you two and how hard you work. Being a lawyer is easy compared to this."

Bertha let out a bark of laughter. "Any job is easy compared to this, but we all have our lanes."

"Do you ever think about retiring?"

Bertha glanced at Kara, who filled him in. "That's a swear word in her world."

"I'd be bored senseless," Bertha said. "I hope I go to my final reward sitting right here at the helm of the boat that was custom-built just for me with one of the few heads you'll find on a lobster boat. A girl has her needs."

"They don't have bathrooms on them?" Dan asked.

"Nah," Kara said. "Guys can use their one penis to go off the side. Women often use a bucket."

"That's what I did on my father's boat," Bertha said. "I hated that, so when I commissioned this boat, I insisted on a head."

Dan's phone rang with a call from a TV station. "Dan Torrington."

"This is Kate Bannister from WLBZ, the NBC affiliate in Bangor."

"What can I do for you, Ms. Bannister?"

"We're doing a story about the Ballard sons being arrested for murder and wondered if you'd be willing to provide an on-camera interview to go with our story."

"I'm currently on a lobster boat. When were you looking to do it?"

"By four at the latest, to make our six o'clock newscast."

"Hang on a second." He put the phone aside. "What time will we be back in?"

"You tell me when you need to be, and we'll make it happen."

"Three thirty?"

"Done."

Into the phone, he said, "I can talk at four if you send me a link to connect." He gave her his email address.

"Talk to you then. Thank you."

"No problem."

"Is my baby gonna be on TV?" Kara asked.

"Yep. Does that make you hot?"

"No."

"She's ruthless," Dan said to Bertha.

"She has to be around you."

"I'm glad you see what I deal with, B."

"I see it."

"I hope you also see how blissfully happy I make her, and with just one penis, no less."

Bertha cackled with laughter.

"Please don't laugh at him. You'll just encourage him."

"I'm funny as well as sexy."

"And not at all full of yourself," Bertha said with an affectionate smile.

It meant everything to Kara that Bertha liked Dan so much that she teased him the way she would one of her own kids or grandkids.

"Not one bit."

Buster opened the bait bin, and Dan's expression shifted

immediately from pleased with himself to a shade of green that would make the Grinch envious.

"Uh-oh," Kara said as Dan rushed to the side of the boat to barf.

She glanced at Bertha, who was trying hard to contain her laughter.

"At least he's puking instead of me," Kara said as she took another bite of her sandwich. She felt a thousand times better since she'd been rehydrated at the hospital.

"Poor guy," Bertha said. "That smell isn't for the faint of heart."

"No, it isn't, but it's funny how it has no impact on me."

"You're smell blind to it like we are. People from away can't handle it."

"Away?" Dan asked when he returned, looking pale but no longer green. "Is that where I'm from?"

"Anyone who isn't from the Downeast coast is from away," Kara said.

"Even if they're from another part of Maine?"

"Especially then," Bertha said with a laugh.

WORK WAS SO BUSY THAT RENATA HAD HAD NO TIME TO fret about the disturbing new vibe with Myles since she'd agreed to attend the wedding with him. Judging by the dopey grins he directed her way every chance he got, that'd been a huge mistake. When she'd arrived that morning, a coffee fixed the way she liked it with oat milk and froth had been waiting for her, along with the lemon Danish she'd once described as her kryptonite.

Damn him.

She made the Danish last all morning, taking little bites as she fulfilled orders, fielded calls from customers and suppliers and printed postage labels.

If she kept super busy, maybe she'd think about something other than having to find a dress for the wedding or how she needed a haircut and style to look her best. Not that she cared about looking her best for him, but there'd be other people she knew at the wedding. The least she could do for them was get a manicure, for crying out loud.

But what if he thought she'd gone to all that trouble for him?

A searing pain sliced through her finger as she suffered yet another paper cut from the stiff parchment used for the company brochures. She hated those things.

"*Son of a bitch!*"

She was bleeding all over the place.

Myles rushed out of his office to check on her. "What's wrong?"

"Those goddamned brochures you like so much got me again. I'm going to make a workers' comp claim."

He led her to the sink in the bathroom and held her finger under the cold water.

She stood there like a stooge for a full minute before she realized he was holding her hand and standing very close to her. "That's okay." Withdrawing her hand, she added, "I'm fine."

"Do you need the ER?"

"Har-har. That's the third time this week I've been lacerated by those stupid brochures. I want to throw them all away."

He retrieved a first aid kit from one of the cabinets over the work area where she processed shipments and wrapped a bandage around her index finger. "We'll use different paper when we reprint them. We can't have you getting injured on the job."

"Thank you."

"You're welcome."

"Do you need to go home?"

"Stop passive-aggressively making fun of me while also being nice."

He sputtered with laughter. "What the hell does that mean?"

In a singsong voice, she said, "'Do you need the ER? Do you need to go home?'"

"Those were very serious questions."

"Right."

"Paper cuts can be deadly if sepsis sets in."

She glared at him and went back to her desk. "Bite me."

"When and where?"

"Shut up, Myles, and go back to work."

"Yes, dear."

"Don't call me that."

"Sorry, dear."

Renata was more annoyed than ever as she took another bite of the delicious pastry and then cleaned up the bloody mess on her desk. As she got back to what she'd been doing before the lacerating event, she was furious with him and herself most of all. She never should've agreed to that wedding. It had given him hope for something that wasn't going to happen between them no matter how much he wanted it to.

There was still time to back out, she thought.

Coward.

What? My own brain is not allowed to call me names!

What're you afraid of? A good time with a nice guy who treats you well?

Who also happens to be my boss and a source of daily irritation.

He's a nice guy who's always been good to you.

That doesn't mean I want to date him!

With all those other prospects you've got knocking down the door.

SHUT UP. I don't want prospects. I like being alone.

Do you, though? What were you thinking the other night after you saw Kara glowing with happiness and pregnancy? That maybe you've missed out on something.

I did not think that!

Now you're going to lie to yourself? What's the point of that?

I hate you.

No, you don't.

I really do.

"Renata!"

She nearly jumped out of her skin at the sound of Myles's louder-than-usual voice. "What?"

"The phone's ringing. Do you want me to get it?"

"No, sorry. I've got it."

"Jeez, where were you checked out to?"

"Nowhere." She picked up the desk extension and helped the customer place an online order. Their older clients struggled with the technology, so she had regulars who called in their orders. When she ended the call, Myles was still there.

"Are you sure you're okay? I didn't mean to make fun of your injury."

"Yes, you did, but I'm fine. And PS, I'd make fun of you if you freaked out over a paper cut."

"That's good to know."

"What goes around comes around."

He flashed a warm grin that she would've found sexy on anyone else. "I look forward to you doing your worst."

"Don't do that."

"Do what?"

"Enjoy me being a bitch to you."

"Your bitchiness has become my favorite part of the day."

"What level of masochist does that make you?"

"Highest level, baby. Highest level."

With that astonishing statement, he turned and went back to his office, whistling as he went.

Renata stood there for a full minute, staring at his office door, before she snapped out of it with one thought front and center in her mind: She had to find a way out of going to that wedding with him.

CHAPTER
Seventeen

BY THE TIME they steamed into the harbor, Dan had received four more calls from reporters. He'd put them off with promises to return their calls later in the day. As he fielded the calls, a plan came into focus that he'd implement as soon as they got back to shore.

Kara took him by the hand and brought him to the stern, which had been thoroughly cleaned by Buster as they made their way home.

"Close your eyes and smell," she said.

Dan did as she directed. "What am I smelling?"

"The pine trees. That's how we know we're home. Do you smell them?"

"I do."

"The closer we get to land, the better the scent becomes."

He put his arms around her from behind and held her as they watched the shoreline come into view. "I love you here. I love you there. I love you everywhere."

"Aww, now you're quoting Dr. Seuss?"

"If I am, that's not intentional. It's just the truth. I'm seeing a whole new version of you here, and I like it. Today was amazing."

"Even the puking?"

"You're never going to let me live that down, are you?"

"Not in this or the next lifetime."

He kissed her neck, and damn if she didn't go a little weak in the knees. So naturally, he did it again.

"No canoodling on the boat," Bertha said with a guffaw. "This is a place of business."

"Frisky business," Dan whispered in Kara's ear.

"Stand down, Counselor."

"Will you make it up to me later?"

"Don't I always?"

"Best wife I ever had."

She laughed. "Don't forget it, mister."

"As if I ever could."

Before they returned to the mooring, they stopped at a wharf to drop off their catch and take on fuel and bait that Buster stuffed into bags in preparation for the next day. The combined odors of the bait and the fuel had Dan turning green again.

"Breathe through your mouth," Kara said.

"That doesn't help. I can taste it."

Kara laughed again. "Stick your head over the side. Just in case. Buster will be pissed if you mess up his clean deck."

"I'm glad you're enjoying this so much."

"Let's get off here. We can walk back to the Jeep. It's not far."

"Are you sure that's okay?"

"Of course. They've got this down to a science." She turned to Bertha. "We're going to bug out here. Dan has some work to tend to. Thank you for a magical day."

"My pleasure, honey. I hope you enjoyed it, too, Dan."

"It was fascinating. I have all-new respect for you and everyone who does this for a living—and I'll never look at a lobster the same way again."

"Then we've succeeded in our mission," Bertha said. "I'll see you at home."

"I'm making dinner," Kara said. "We'll hit the grocery store on the way. Any special requests?"

"You still make that pasta thing?" Buster asked.

"The chicken tortellini?"

"Yeah, that. I love it."

"I love it, too," Dan said.

Kara smiled at her uncle. "I'll get right on that."

"Only if you feel up to it, honey," Bertha said. "Don't do too much."

"I feel great, and I want to cook for you."

"Then I won't say no to that. See you soon."

AFTER A QUICK STOP AT THE GROCERY STORE, DAN AND Kara arrived back at Bertha's to find the street lined with news trucks and other vehicles that nearly blocked their path to the house.

"What the hell?" Dan muttered.

"Looks like they've figured out where the celebrity attorney is staying."

"Awesome."

Dan drove around the people and vehicles to pull into the driveway. "Text Bertha and Buster to warn them about what they're coming home to and then go inside and stay there. I don't want you anywhere near this."

"Will you be all right?"

"Of course. I'll give them what they want and send them on their way."

"What do they want?" Kara asked with a tentative glance at the gaggle of reporters.

"Something they can use in their stories. Don't worry, love. I know how to manage them, and when we're done here, I'll ask them to move along. Can you handle the groceries?"

"Yeah, I got it."

"Don't worry. Everything's fine. This is actually an opportunity."

"For what?"

"To start introducing some reasonable doubt." He smiled. "Go on in. As soon as you're safely inside, I'll go deal with them."

"In case I've forgotten to say it today, thank you."

"Anything for you, love. Anything at all."

"You didn't sign on for this…"

"It's fine. I live for this shit. It's all good."

"Don't get shot or stabbed or anything else like that, you hear me?"

He laughed. "I hear you."

Kara got out of the car, retrieved the two grocery bags from the back seat and went into the house as the reporters called out questions to her about her brothers.

That wouldn't do.

When the inside door closed behind her, Dan got out of the car to face the same barrage of questions.

"Simmer down, and I'll give you a statement." He waited for them to go quiet. "First of all, hear me on this… My wife has nothing to do with the case against her brothers. If y'all start hassling her, reporting about her or anything else with her, you won't get another word out of me. Are we clear on that?"

A murmur of agreement went through the twenty or so reporters. Half were TV reporters holding cameras, while the other half looked like they'd just rolled out of bed. He tagged them as newspaper people.

"My wife is off-limits. We're here because my in-laws asked me to represent their sons. Keith has declined representation, so I'm focused entirely on Kirby's case."

"Why did Keith decline?"

"You'd have to ask him that. I believe this entire case is a rush to judgment based on the fact that Keith was seen with the victim during the evening preceding her death. Kirby's only involvement was responding to a call from his brother asking for a ride home. Kirby never spoke with Tanya Sorenson. All he did was ask Keith if she needed a ride home. She declined the offer and was alive and well when they left her standing on the sidewalk in town. Those are the facts of this case, and we believe the police have arrested the wrong men and should be considering other suspects."

"What about reports that Keith's DNA was found on the victim?"

"He doesn't deny having had contact with her. He danced with her. He didn't murder her, and Kirby has never met her or exchanged a single word with her."

"What about the eyewitness who claims to have seen the brothers with her?"

"Have you looked into his history with the Ballard family? If not, you should."

"Can you elaborate?"

"Do your own research. You'll find an interesting story there. Also, I'm wondering if the police have looked into the difficult breakup Tanya had with a boyfriend last winter. It's documented on her Instagram account. Something about the guy not being able to move on from her. I'd imagine that's an angle that'd be worth investigating as well."

As he watched the reporters take furious notes, he was pleased with how he'd managed to take control of the narrative and looked forward to seeing the headlines in tomorrow's papers and on the news that night.

"Will you continue to represent Kirby Ballard if the case goes to trial?"

"We're a long way from a trial, but I'll be here for as long as Kirby needs me. That's all for now. Do me a favor and clear the street. People live here, and they need to be able to get to their homes. Please don't come back here again."

Dan turned and walked toward the house.

"What's in this for you, Torrington?"

Surprised by the rancor in the man's tone, Dan schooled his expression and turned back to address the question. "Excuse me?"

"You heard me. What's in it for you?"

"Nothing other than stepping up for a family member who needs me and being there for my wife during this difficult time."

"Your wife is estranged from her family, is she not?"

"We're here, aren't we?"

"Hasn't it been years since she was here?"

"As I said at the outset, my wife isn't part of this story, and anyone who makes her part of it won't get another word from me. Thanks for coming by. I'd appreciate you clearing out now."

Dan was muttering under his breath when he stepped into the kitchen to find Kara standing next to an open window that she leaned in to close now that the show was over.

"Still my hero," she said.

"Some of them are such bottom-feeders."

"Thank you for not giving them anything to chew on, and well done on the introduction of reasonable doubt. I'm starting to see how this works."

"We'll be hammering home the alternative scenarios until these bogus charges are dropped." His phone rang with a call from the Bar Harbor Police Department. "Dan Torrington."

"I saw your little presser and the not-so-subtle dig at the investigation."

"Was it subtle, Detective? I didn't intend it to be. The investigation has been nonexistent, or you'd know that your eyewitness has been looking for retribution from the Ballard family and their business in court for years and has yet to see a dime of the money he thinks they owe him after he was fired for cause. Were you aware that there's a civil trial pending in December?"

"I was not aware of that."

"Well, now you are. Did you know Tanya was having trouble getting rid of a boyfriend she broke up with months ago?"

"Her parents mentioned that."

"And you're looking into where he was last Friday night?"

"I'm working my way through a number of things, and that's one of them."

"I want my client released on bail pending the preliminary hearing."

"That's not my call. It's up to the AG's office."

"If you recommend he be released on bail due to the incomplete investigation, I'm sure that'll carry some weight."

"I'll talk to them, but I can't promise anything. It's also up to the judge. In the meantime, if you could refrain from undermining my investigation—"

"I'm sorry, but I can't do that. An innocent man has been charged with murder. He's never met the victim or had any direct contact with her. I'm sure you and the state police thought you had an open-and-shut case here, but that's not at all what I'm finding."

"You've made your point, Counselor. I'll speak to the AG's office. That's all I can do."

"Thank you. I'll look forward to hearing from you or them ASAP. Have a good evening."

"You, too."

"Well, you just made his day," Kara said, smiling widely. "That was a master class you just put on there. That detective didn't stand a chance against you."

"He's overworked and understaffed, like many small-town departments are. I don't blame the state police for jumping on eyewitness testimony along with other witnesses confirming she'd been with Keith that evening. There's also the matter of his

DNA being found on the body. It'll be a stretch for them to let him out, but hopefully, we'll get somewhere with Kirby."

Kara linked her arms around his neck and went up on tiptoes to kiss him. "Thank you so much for everything you're doing. I feel so much better knowing you're on the case."

"We've still got a long way to go, but I like our chances a little better than I did at first." He glanced at the clock on the stove. "And now I've got to go meet with that other reporter to sow more reasonable doubt."

"I want you to know... I've always been impressed by your career. Not too impressed, mind you, because your ego is always a concern."

"Of course," he said, smiling.

"But seeing you work up close has been a real revelation. I'm wildly impressed."

"Wildly, you say?"

"Mmm, extremely wildly."

"That's a double adverb."

"Focus, Counselor."

"I'm focused entirely on you, so much so I'm going to miss the interview if you don't release me immediately."

Kara kissed him. "Go get 'em, tiger."

"Please remember that wildly thing at bedtime," he said over his shoulder as he went into the living room to handle the interview.

CHAPTER

Eighteen

DAN PUT in his ear buds and clicked on the link Kate Bannister had sent. While he waited for her to join the Zoom meeting, he texted Walter. *The press have figured out where I'm staying. Do you think we need security for Bertha's?*

I don't think so. Saw you on the news just now.

They ambushed me in the driveway, thus my worries about security.

I think you're okay around here. It's not like the big city.

Thanks for the gut check.

Any time, boss.

Kate Bannister began their meeting a few minutes later.

"Sorry for the delay," she said. "I got called into another meeting that just ended."

"No worries."

"I caught part of your presser. What can you tell me about the eyewitness and his beef with the Ballard family?"

"He was fired for cause and filed suit, demanding a cash settlement that the company has refused to pay. The matter goes to trial in December."

"What was the cause of his firing?"

"I'm not at liberty to divulge those details. I believe you'll find them in the countersuit filed in court by the company, but in my opinion, this information puts his motivations into question. I've requested bail for my client until a full investigation can be completed."

"Keith Ballard has a criminal record."

"I'm not representing Keith, and Kirby has never been arrested."

"But you can acknowledge Keith's criminal record?"

"I have no comment on him. He's not my client." After a pause, he added, "I will say, however, that prior arrests for DUI or fighting don't mean someone committed murder. It's a huge leap from bar fighting to murder."

"You have a reputation for introducing alternative scenarios in your cases. Do you intend to do that this time, too?"

"Absolutely. Think about the crime of murder. It takes a tremendous amount of anger, passion and evil to take a life. Where was any of that in this case? By all accounts, Keith and Tanya had a fun evening at the bar. They had some drinks, they danced, maybe they fooled around in the restroom. It happens between consenting adults. Kirby was nowhere near any of that until he arrived to give Keith a ride home. Where's the motive for murder here? I'll help you with that. Neither of these men had a motive to harm Tanya."

Dan was walking a fine line speaking for Keith, but the facts of his case affected Kirby's. "The only mistake, if you want to call it that, Kirby made was responding to a call from his brother for a ride home."

"Keith has been charged with three DUIs."

"How is that relevant other than to explain why he called his brother for a ride home?"

"I'm simply stating that he's been charged."

"It's not relevant to the facts of this case, but points to how he had a system for when he needed a ride. Kirby had made himself available to Keith, and this is the thanks he gets."

"A source informed me that your wife has been estranged from her family—"

"That's not true, and as I stated to the other reporters I spoke with earlier, my wife is off-limits. If you want to be able to use me as a source, leave her out of the reporting."

"Can you confirm an estrangement, though?"

"Thanks for your time. Talk to you later."

Dan left the meeting before she could respond. Despite the warnings he'd levied against the reporters he'd spoken with, he still feared that Kara's family history could come to light due to his involvement in the case. The very thought of that happening gave him a sick feeling in his stomach that wasn't all that different from how the stinky bait had made him feel on the boat.

Kara came into the living room with a beer that she'd opened for him.

"Thanks, love."

"How'd it go?"

"Pretty good."

She stood next to him, running her fingers through his hair. "What's wrong?"

"We need to talk about something that's becoming a concern."

"What's that?"

"In both interviews just now, I was asked about your estrangement from the family."

Her whole body went tense in one heartbeat. "What'd you say?"

"That anyone who reported on you in the context of this case would never get another word out of me."

"Do you think that shut it down?"

"I'm not sure, which is what has me worried. The idea of shit from the past being resurrected simply because I'm the one your parents called to defend your brothers makes me a little sick, to be honest."

"Me, too. What can we do?"

"That's the thing... There's no way we can stop anyone from reporting on that, if they decide it's a story."

"How in the world would that be a story?"

Dan rarely had regrets about anything in his life. He didn't believe in them. But he was beginning to regret the high-profile career that made him—and his wife—a story due to his past. "It's just that... Because of my work..."

"You're a story separate of why you're here."

"Something like that. And please know, I don't want anything to do with that. You have to believe me—"

She leaned in to kiss him. "I know that. You can't help that your reputation precedes you."

"If my reputation causes pain for you, I'll never forgive myself."

"And my friends wonder why I stayed away for all that time."

He put his arms around her and drew her in close to him, resting his cheek against their baby. "They know why."

"If they report on me, so be it. I've got nothing to hide, and PS, I didn't do anything wrong. I was the one deceived by people I thought I loved and people I thought loved me. If someone tells you they're doing a story about me and my family, you can say that on the record. 'My wife has nothing to hide. She's not the one who deceived and betrayed a loved one. That was her sister and now brother-in-law. My wife would tell you she's now very happily married and in close contact with most of her family—and has been all along.'"

"So you only *thought* you loved Matt?"

Kara tugged hard on a handful of his hair. "Focus."

"I'm sorry... you were saying?"

"You heard everything I said, and if it comes to that, you've got your comment."

"Are you sure?"

"Very sure. If they're going to make the story about us, that's what we have to say about it."

He cupped her ass and gave it a squeeze, loving the lush, sexy curves of her pregnant body. "You're one tough cookie, Mrs. Torrington. I wouldn't want to eff with you."

"You love to eff with me."

"That's true. Now that you mention it, what're you doing right now?"

"Cooking dinner for my grandmother and uncle, who'll be famished when they get home."

He groaned. "All right. Go on if you must."

"I must but thank you for always thinking of what's best for me. It means everything to me."

"You mean everything to me."

"And you make me feel that every single day."

"Do you two ever take a break?" Buster muttered when he saw them in an embrace.

"Leave them alone, Buster," Bertha said. "They're in *love*."

"Whatever."

Kara laughed, kissed Dan and went to finish dinner.

Despite what she'd said, he'd still move heaven and earth to make sure no one dragged her through the mud in the pursuit of a story.

Renata was in her pajamas with a moisturizing mask on her face, a glass of wine in hand and the *Real Housewives of Orange County* on TV. She could finally exhale after a day of extra attention from Myles after her "injury."

Maybe she'd made too big of a deal about a paper cut...

A teaser for the eleven o'clock news featured a sound bite

from Kara's sexy husband, telling the media to leave her out of their quest for salacious details about the Ballard family, or he'd stop talking to them about the case.

Seeing Dan stick up for her cousin that way made her like him more than she already did.

She put down her wine to compose a text to Kara. *Hot AF seeing your hubby go to bat for you, babe.*

You saw that, huh? It is pretty hot! The thought of all that garbage being resurrected gives me vapors, but if it happens, so be it. It was a long time ago, and I'm not the one who'll look like an asshole.

TRUE THAT.

Renata had never liked Kelly. She'd been a sneaky bitch even when they were little kids. Somehow, the rest of them usually ended up in trouble while she skated through free and clear, the freaking tattletale.

She deserved to be stuck with Matt Gallagher for the rest of her life.

Renata would never admit to anyone that she'd been relieved when Kara and Matt broke up. She'd never thought he was good enough for Kara, but he was perfect for that snake Kelly. The two of them deserved each other.

When her doorbell rang, she went completely still. Who the hell could that be at this hour?

Maybe it was the coffee she'd ordered from Amazon. They'd been delivering at all hours lately.

She threw open the door and shrieked when she saw Myles standing there with a big dopey grin on his face that faded when he got a good look at her.

Then she remembered the mask and screamed again.

"What're you doing here?"

At the same time, he said, "What's on your face?"

"Never mind that!"

"I... uh... brought you one of those mocha milkshakes you

like, because you're injured."

Renata was stunned speechless, which didn't happen very often. She did love her a mocha milkshake, but not when she had a mask on her face and no bra on! "Um, thank you." She opened the screen door to take it from him.

"How's your finger?"

"It's fine."

"No sign of festering or sepsis?"

He was totally making fun of her, but to his credit, he kept a straight face. "Not yet, but it's early days."

"Well, keep me posted."

"I'll do that. I might need a sick day tomorrow to keep it from getting infected."

"That might be wise. Do you need me to put a new bandage on it? You don't want to take any chances."

Renata didn't want to encourage his obvious interest in her, but he'd been nice enough to bring her the shake, so she went along with his foolish pretense to get inside her house. "I could use some help with that." She stepped back to let him in. "I'll, ah, just be right back. Make yourself comfortable."

She went into the bathroom and washed off the mask, which left her face looking red and puffy from the aggressive scrubbing required to remove it. Then she slathered on some moisturizer, brushed her hair and put her bra back on before gathering the bandages and antibacterial ointment needed to treat her "wound."

Tomorrow, she'd probably find it funny that he'd used her paper cut as an excuse to bring her a treat and was now seated on her sofa, seemingly engrossed in the Housewives' never-ending drama.

"Who are these women, and how can I never see them again?"

Renata laughed at the face he made. "They're an acquired taste."

"You like them?"

She poked the straw through the lid on the shake and took a deep drink, nearly moaning from the taste that exploded in her mouth. The mocha shake was her all-time-favorite treat, but she limited herself to one a month when she wanted one daily. "'Like' is a strong word. I watch them to feel better about my own life."

He frowned. "What's wrong with your life?"

"Nothing. Really. But when you watch them, you realize that whatever's bugging you is nothing compared to the crap they're dealing with, most of it probably fake to juice the ratings."

"That's bizarre logic. You realize that, don't you?"

"I never said it was logical, but it helps me de-stress to wallow in other people's chaos for an hour."

He reached for the bandages and ointment and got to work on her finger. "Why are you stressed?"

"Everyone is stressed."

"I'm not."

"Sure you are."

"No, I'm really not."

"How can you not be stressed with everything you have to do in a day?"

"I love what I get to do every day. Sure, it's busy, but that's a good thing. Keeps us in business." He gently dabbed ointment on the angry-looking paper cut and applied a new bandage. "I don't want you stressed out by work. My grandfather used to say, 'We're not curing cancer here. We're shipping lobster.'"

"I suppose that's true."

"Work is supposed to be fun."

"Says who?"

"Me, and I'm the boss."

"Yes, you are."

"If I say no stress at work, then no stress at work. You hear me?"

"I hear you. It's this thing with my cousins, too."

"I'm sure that's the most stressful thing for everyone. Are you close to them?"

"I was close to Kirby when we were kids, but not so much now. It was hard with our dads on the outs and all that."

"Why was that, anyway?"

"Fighting over the family business."

"Ah, right. I think I heard something about that."

She nudged him. "You already knew."

"I didn't want you to think I'd been gossiping about your family or anything."

"Everyone's gossiping about the Ballards these days."

"I saw your cousin's husband on the news earlier. Sounds like they've got the right guy defending them."

"He's only defending Kirby. Keith declined his services."

"Why'd he do that?"

"Because he's a fool. He's always been like that, thinking he knows better than everyone else."

"I don't know him at all, but people say he's rough around the edges."

"He is that, but there's no way he murdered that woman. He's more likely to break someone's heart than hurt them. What possible reason would he have had to kill her?"

"It's hard telling what really happened, but I'm sure it's tough to deal with all the speculation."

"Yeah, it's a tough time to have the Ballard last name around here."

"I hadn't thought of that. I'm sorry."

She shrugged. "Don't be sorry. It's no big deal. Just a few stares here and there at the coffee shop and grocery store. I'll survive."

All at once, she tuned in to the fact that he was sitting rather close to her on the sofa, with his arm across the back cushions and his body turned toward her. She had his full attention and wasn't at all sure how she felt about that.

Bad. You feel bad about it.

But it's kind of nice to have someone who gives a shit about me, especially right now with everything going on in the family.

Except that it's MYLES. Your BOSS. Who drives you crazy. Remember that?

Her conscience was being a total bitch, and for once, she decided to ignore her better judgment and enjoy a bit of the Housewives along with her shake and her *boss*, who was still sitting far too close for comfort.

"Can I ask you something?"

Renata looked over at him. "I guess..."

"Did I do something to make you dislike me so much?"

CHAPTER
Nineteen

HOLY SHIT. Renata hadn't expected that. "I don't dislike you."

"Oh. You don't?"

"Of course I don't."

"Huh, well, I thought you did."

Now she felt like a total asshole for making him think that. "It's not you. It's me."

He groaned. "If I had a dollar for every time I've heard that one."

"People say that to you?"

"*Women* say that to me. Along with, 'You're a really nice guy, but you're not the nice guy for me.' Inevitably, they end up with some douchebag who treats them like shit, and they lap up every bit of the unending drama for some reason I can't fathom." He gestured to the TV where the Housewives were engaged in yet another bitter dispute. "Why do people want to live that way?"

"I... uh... I don't know, but I'm sorry you've been treated like that."

"It's fine. I'd rather be dismissed for being a nice guy than loved for being an asshole, you know?"

She nodded, intrigued by the insight and... Oh crap, was she *attracted* to him? No way. That wasn't possible. Was it?

"I know what our problem is."

She took a sip of the shake, trying to buy herself a minute to formulate a reply. "I wasn't aware we had a problem."

"We do have one."

Why did her stomach suddenly feel weird? It was probably the lactose. What else could it be? "Are you going to fill me in on what that is?"

"I want to know why you're so different toward me since my dad retired and I took over. Before he left, I thought we were friends and maybe on the way to being more than that, but now you treat me like I'm radioactive or something."

"I do not!"

"Yes, you do, Renata. We're not friends like we used to be."

"When we'd sneak off for a liquid lunch when we were supposed to be doing deliveries?"

"Among other things. I thought we had something going, or the start of something anyway, but now... I miss my friend."

"We're still friends."

"No, we're not. Tell me something..."

"What?"

"Am I different since I took over for my dad? Am I an asshole boss or something?"

"No. Not at all."

"Then why do you treat me so differently now?"

"Because you're my boss now."

"So what? We can still do liquid lunches and doughnut Fridays and happy hour and all the other stuff we used to do."

"No, we can't."

"Why not?"

Renata sipped the delicious shake while trying to decide how much she wanted to share with him. "Do you know why my parents got divorced?"

"No, I don't."

"My dad was a partner at Ballard Boat Works before he and my uncle had their big falling-out. I'm sure you know about that. Everyone does."

"Yeah, I've heard about it."

"Well, my mom… She was my dad's executive assistant at the company. That's how they met. They dated in secret for years before they shocked everyone by getting married. In fact, that's where the trouble with my uncle began. He had an issue with his brother dating one of the assistants and keeping it a secret for years. He thought it made them look bad to the other employees. Needless to say, my dad didn't appreciate my uncle's input, but he took it to heart. My mother felt that when the brothers had their falling-out, he secretly blamed her for being the root cause. She said nothing was ever the same between her and my dad after that. They limped along for another ten years before he left when I was in high school."

"That must've been really tough for you."

"By then, I was relieved. It wasn't easy to live with them and all their dysfunction, but my mom… She was heartbroken over it all. She felt wronged. She still does, which is why they can't even be in the same room. She might claw his eyes out."

"And she ties all that heartache back to marrying her boss, right?"

"Something like that."

"I see."

"What do you see?"

"Why you feel like we can't be friends like we used to be or date or anything like that. You're afraid you'll end up in a similar situation to your mom."

"I'm not afraid of any such thing! I'm nothing like her."

"Then you're okay with us dating?"

"I never said that."

"I'd better go. Got an early breakfast tomorrow with the Lobstermen's Association."

He was the treasurer of the organization and rarely missed a meeting.

"Oh, um, sure." Renata felt oddly deflated by the sudden end to a conversation that'd gone places she hadn't expected. "Thank you again for the shake and for coming by to check on me."

"No problem. We take on-the-job injuries very seriously at Williams Lobsters & More."

Renata laughed. "This barely counts as an injury."

"It counts. I appreciate everything you do to make things run so smoothly. I hope you know how essential you are to the company—and to me."

"I, uh... That's nice to hear. Thanks."

"Don't tell me you didn't already know that."

"I knew, but it's still nice to hear."

"I'll have to tell you more often, then." He got up, zipped the jacket he'd never removed and headed for the door. "I'll see you tomorrow."

Renata walked him to the door, tightening the belt of her robe as she went. She felt upside down and inside out. "Myles..."

He turned. "Yes, Renata?"

"You shouldn't let anyone make you feel shitty for being a nice guy."

"Well, it's not like I *let* them. It just kind of happens. Nice guys finish last, right?"

"Not always." All at once, it was urgent to her that he know there was nothing wrong with being nice. "Sometimes they come out on top." The words were no sooner out of her mouth than the double meaning registered.

The slight lift of his lips indicated that hadn't gotten by him.

"That'd be nice. Someday maybe. Sleep well and call me if you need anything. Any time."

Renata only nodded because he'd rendered her speechless with the way he looked at her as he said those words.

She watched him walk to his truck as every cell in her body seemed fully tuned in to... something.

Him.

She was tuned in to him, and judging by the tingling in some important places, she was definitely attracted to him.

To *Myles*.

Her *boss*.

Shit.

KARA HAD SETTLED INTO BED TO READ WHILE DAN finished working.

Her phone buzzed with a text from Renata. *PROBLEM. I think I might be attracted to Myles—MY BOSS—and I'm freaking the F out over here.*

Kara called her. "What happened?"

Renata told her about the visit from Myles.

"Has he come over before?"

"Never! I didn't even think he knew where I lived."

"Well, he'd have that info through work, no?"

"I guess so, but it's definitely unprecedented for him to come by here unannounced."

"And all because of a paper cut. That's so cute, Ren."

"It was one hell of a paper cut. I lost a lot of blood."

"And he brought you a mocha shake."

"Yeah."

"I mean... What an asshole."

"Shut up! You're supposed to be telling me all the reasons why this is a terrible idea. When do women *ever* benefit from dating their bosses or anyone at work?"

"This isn't exactly a corporate monolith you're talking about. It's a small family business, and no one would think anything of you dating him."

"Right. Everyone would be talking about it, which would freak me out."

"One thing I learned after everything that happened to me was the opinions of other people are none of my business."

"Huh, well, that's rather profound."

"It's true, and once you start to live by that principle, life becomes a lot simpler. You strive to make yourself and your loved ones happy and don't worry about the ones who were never going to be your people anyway."

"When did you get so wise?"

"After life kicked me in the teeth and forced me to wise up. People will talk. That's their problem, not yours. The big question is, do you like him?"

"I don't want to like him."

"That's not an answer."

Renata's moan made Kara laugh.

"This reminds me of when I first realized Dan was seriously interested in me. I did everything I could to pretend it wasn't happening."

"And look at where that got you—married and knocked up."

"Don't forget blissfully happy."

"Why did you try to fend him off?"

"I told you how overwhelming he was to me at first, right? Because I wasn't in a good headspace to even consider being with someone else after everything here. But there he was, insistent and funny and handsome and incorrigible."

Dan came to the bedroom door. "Are you talking about me, love?"

"Go away. I'm talking to my cousin."

Rather than go, he came in and stretched out next to her on the bed. "Please, carry on. We were just getting to the good stuff."

Renata laughed. "He is funny, I'll give him that."

"The worst thing you can do is tell him that."

"What'd she say? That I'm a sexy devil or funny as hell or—"

Kara used her favorite tactic to shut him up and pinched his lips closed.

"Sounds like you've got your hands full over there."

"What're you going to do about Myles?"

"I don't know, but what you said helped, about other people and their opinions. Sometimes I dream about getting out of here and going somewhere where I could be totally anonymous. I could do whatever I wanted, and no one would care."

"You can do that here, Ren. You just have to decide you don't give a flying fuck what anyone thinks of you. Give it a try. It's very liberating."

Dan waggled his brows and fanned his face. "Hot as *F*."

"On that note," Renata said, laughing, "I'm going to bed. I've got the usual sugar headache from the shake, but it was *so* worth it."

"That's been your favorite thing for as long as I can remember. I think it's so sweet that Myles brought you one."

"It was sweet."

"Be nice to him. If you're not feeling it, let him down easy."

"That's the problem. I might be feeling it, and I have no idea what to do about that."

"Ever since you and Chris broke up, I've been hoping you might find someone who appreciates what a special, wonderful person you are. It sounds to me as if Myles might be that person."

"I'm not sure I can bear to go down that road again with anyone. The last time was so brutal."

"Yes, it was, but to hold Myles or anyone else accountable for what someone else did is super unfair to him and to yourself. Not everyone is a Chris or a Matt. Sometimes there's a Dan or a Myles in the mix who show you a different way."

Dan put his hand on top of hers and gave it a squeeze.

"You're right. Of course you are, but isn't it just easier to be alone than to risk all that bullshit happening again?"

Kara looked at Dan as she said, "It's easier, but it's not better. When it's the right person, it's well worth the risk."

"Thanks for listening. I appreciate you."

"Love you, kid."

"Love you, too."

Kara put her phone back on the charger.

"Let's keep talking about all the ways you're ridiculously happy after taking a chance on a handsome rogue who drove you to drink with his sexy wit and handsome face."

"Do you ever get tired of listening to the sound of your own voice?"

He thought about that for a second. "Nope."

Kara laughed. "Windbag."

"You love me."

"For some strange reason, I do."

"Thank goodness for that." He leaned in to kiss her. "I heard from Walter, who heard from a friend of a friend that the *Islander* is writing a big story about your family."

Kara grimaced.

"I wasn't sure if I should tell you that before bedtime, but I figured you'd want to know."

"Yeah, I do want to know. Did you tell my dad?"

"He already knew. They called him for a comment, but he chose not to participate."

"When is it going to be published?"

"Online in the morning and in this week's paper."

"I suppose we shouldn't be surprised. It's big news around here that two of the Ballard Boat Works sons are being held on murder charges. Anything our family does is big news due to how many people the company employs."

"I'd like to see the company if we get the chance. I'm curious as to what it looks like."

"We can go by there."

"I'd also like to see the house where you were raised, meet your other siblings and check out Acadia."

"All of which is doable." Kara gnawed on her bottom lip. "Do you think the Kelly and Matt saga will be part of this story?"

"Could be, but I really hope not."

"I keep telling myself I did nothing wrong, but it feels so sordid to have that come up again when it happened years ago."

"I heard you say something to Renata about other people's opinions..." He held out his arm to bring her closer. "Get over here. I miss you."

"I'm right here."

"Closer."

Kara snuggled up to him, resting her head on his chest and listening to the strong, steady beat of his heart, which always brought her comfort. That heart beat only for her, and knowing that, believing in it, had changed everything for her. "I meant what I said to Renata. It was worth all the risk. You know that, right?"

"Despite your forked tongue and jabs at my overinflated ego, I do know that."

Kara snorted with laughter. "Those are just my attempts to keep you somewhat humble."

"No one can humble me like you do, and I wouldn't have it any other way."

"I like to think about those early days on Gansett when you were driving me mad, showing up every day in those ridiculous loafers, paying me for rides in the launch just so you could hang out with me."

"That was one of my better strategies. You were madder than a wet hen over me wanting to just ride around on the boat with no destination in mind."

"Because that's not how it works. I'm supposed to take you somewhere."

"You took me somewhere, all right. Remember that day Kelly and Matt showed up on the island, and you took me *all the way* to paradise right there in the middle of the Great Salt Pond?"

"Shush. The walls are thin. Bertha will hear you."

He rocked with silent laughter.

"That was the day I fell in love with you, when you came running to warn me that they were there and intended to ambush me."

"I couldn't let that happen."

"You know what the best part of that day was?"

"It wasn't sex on the boat?"

"That was the second-best part."

"Huh. That's kind of insulting."

"Hush up and listen. The best part was having time to prepare myself to tell her off."

"And you did so—*epically*, I might add."

"I would've frozen up if I hadn't had that time to figure out how to handle her. You bought me time, and that made all the difference. Any time I'm forced to think about her or Matt or what they did, I think about that day and instantly feel better about it all. You made that possible for me."

"Don't forget I also gave you the opportunity for her to realize —every day of her life—that you married a *far* superior lawyer to the schmo she ended up with."

Kara giggled. "That, too. I can't believe there was a time that I thought my life was over because Matt Gallagher decided he loved Kelly and not me."

"My lucky day."

"It was mine, too. I didn't see that at the time, but I sure as hell see it now."

"Same thing with the day I caught my fiancée doing it with the best man right before the wedding that didn't happen. It's so funny how I thought I was going to spend my whole life with her, and now she never crosses my mind."

"Because you're too busy thinking about me and baby Dylan."

"That's right. You two are my whole heart and soul." He rested his hand on her belly. "I can't wait for him to get here."

"I can't either. Two more months."

"I hope we're out of here long before then. I want you home where you belong before the baby comes."

"I hope so, too."

"I'm doing everything I can to make that happen."

"I know, and I appreciate it. We all do."

"Anything for you, my love. Anything at all."

CHAPTER
Twenty

DAN WAS UP EARLY to check the headlines. The story about the Ballard family was front and center on the *Islander* home page with a headline that read BALLARD FAMILY DRAMA IS NOTHING NEW and a subhead that said, WITH TWO SONS CHARGED WITH MURDER, THE FAMILY FACES ITS MOST DIFFICULT CHALLENGE YET.

BAR HARBOR — Shannon's Sunrise Café in town was doing a bustling business early Monday morning as the usual cast of locals gathered for coffee, eggs and news after a weekend that saw the area's first murder in four years. The body of 21-year-old summer resident Tanya Sorenson was found by a fisherman on Saturday on the Bar Harbor Shore Path, shortly after her companions reported her missing following a night out. In town for her future sister-in-law's bachelorette party weekend, Sorenson was seen at several local establishments during Friday night's festivities, ending the evening at the Barnacle Lounge.

Later on Saturday, police had arrested local brothers Keith and Kirby Ballard, who were seen with Sorenson by an eyewitness shortly before the time of death established by the Office of the Chief Medical Examiner.

"It's unbelievable," said one patron at Shannon's who asked not to be identified due to his employment at Ballard Boat Works. "The whole town is reeling since the news broke of their arrest."

When asked if he suspected the brothers had committed the murder, he would only say, "I have no idea."

Other patrons defended Kirby Ballard, in particular, known around town as a genuinely nice guy.

"The thing is, despite his rough reputation," one man said, "Keith is a good guy, too. If something breaks in my house, he's my first call. There's nothing he can't fix, and he charges next to nothing for a house call. A lot of people appreciate him for that around here."

Numerous witnesses placed the victim with Keith Ballard during the evening, in which they were seen drinking, dancing and kissing at the Barnacle Lounge. Witnesses reported they disappeared together for a time before returning for last call. Security cameras in town show the pair leaving the Barnacle shortly after the bar closed, walking hand in hand down Main Street toward the waterfront. According to an eyewitness report, Kirby was seen with Keith and Tanya by the water.

Sorenson, a senior at the University of Connecticut, was the daughter of Mitchell and Deborah Sorenson. She was celebrating her brother August's fiancée, Jessa Kaul, with a weekend of festivities planned at the family's Bar Harbor residence. Police would only say that Sorenson had died from a blow to the head and that Keith Ballard's DNA was found on the body. Other tests, including toxicology, are pending.

Keith Ballard, 37, is well known to local law enforcement after a string of bar fights and DUIs. His brother Kirby, 31, has no previous criminal record. Both brothers are employed by their family business, Keith as a laborer and Kirby as a master craftsman specializing in the wood accents that distinguish Ballard Boats from all other brands.

The arrest of the brothers sent shockwaves through Bar Harbor,

Mount Desert Island and Hancock County. Their parents, Chuck and Judith Ballard, called in their son-in-law Daniel Torrington, a nationally renowned defense attorney known for his work with a Los Angeles-based Innocence Project, which has helped to free more than 60 wrongly incarcerated individuals over the last 15 years.

Torrington is married to Kara Ballard, who runs the BBW's Gansett Island launch service. She left Bar Harbor almost four years ago after her sister Kelly married Kara's ex-boyfriend, local attorney Matt Gallagher.

"Motherfucker," Dan muttered as he read that last paragraph. "They couldn't resist including that salacious tidbit."

The Ballards are one of the region's largest employers and own one of its longest-standing businesses, making their name synonymous with Downeast Maine. You'll rarely meet a local resident who doesn't know one of the 11 Ballard siblings. Most know someone who works for Ballard Boat Works. The family and its business are baked into the DNA of this area, and with two of the family's sons now accused of murder, the family—and the business—faces yet another perilous phase in its long history.

Founded in 1942 by Horace Ballard, Ballard Boat Works has withstood the test of time, producing a wide range of vessels that includes luxury yachts, work boats and everything in between. The family's Downeaster picnic-style boat has become a fixture in harbors throughout New England and around the world. Ballard Boats are known for quality workmanship and one-of-a-kind designs, and it's easy to spot one due to the distinctive markings and burgundy canvas that identify it as having been designed and built right here in Maine.

Recent estimates put the current workforce at roughly 1,000 employees, covering design, woodworking, sales and marketing, diesel engine mechanics and fiberglass experts.

Chief Executive Officer and President Charles "Chuck" Ballard is a grandson of Horace, who, along with his brother Horace the third, inherited the business from their father, Horace Jr. But the partnership between the brothers encountered rough waters 18 years ago, leading to a contentious breakup that resulted in a permanent rift between their two families.

By all accounts, the brothers haven't spoken since Horace forced Chuck to either buy him out or sell the company to outsiders. Chuck Ballard has been quoted as saying the thought of the company belonging to anyone other than a member of Horace Ballard Sr.'s family was unthinkable to him—but apparently not to his brother, who harbored no such sentiment toward the company that'd employed three generations of their family.

"I mortgaged everything I owned to buy out my brother," Chuck said at the time. "I hope he enjoys his retirement. I've got work to do."

The company has grown exponentially under Chuck's leadership, expanding from a $20 million-dollar-a-year business to upward of $200 million annually. In addition to its luxury boat lines, BBW holds contracts to build boats for the U.S. federal government as well as the governments of Canada, the United Kingdom and Germany.

Now in its third generation, BBW has continued to be a family affair. Seven of Chuck and Judith's children work for the company in capacities that range from the C-suite to the paint shop to the fiberglass team to business development.

Kellen Ballard, 39, the company's chief strategy officer, issued a statement on Sunday on behalf of the family and the company that said, in part, "On behalf of my parents, siblings and the entire Ballard Boat Works team, we expect my brothers to be proven innocent of this heinous crime and to be fully exonerated. In the meantime, Ballard Boat Works will continue to fulfill its many obligations to our employees, customers and the Downeast Maine community. The Ballard family will have no further comment on the case pending against Keith and Kirby, and we ask that you respect the family's privacy at this difficult time. Questions about the case can be directed to our attorney, Daniel Torrington."

Dan wondered how Kara would feel about being included as one of the siblings attached to the statement. As far as he knew, no one had consulted her about whether she approved of it.

"I feel for that poor girl who came to celebrate such a wonderful event and lost her life," said local resident Darcy Warner, a waitress at Shannon's. "No one deserves what happened to her."

DAN SENT A TEXT TO ELIAS YOUNG THAT SAID, HAVE YOU looked into the eyewitness who said he saw the Ballard brothers with the victim shortly before her death? He definitely has his own agenda in this situation, and I'm not seeing much being said about that aspect of the story.

He'd sent the message when Kara wrapped herself around him from behind. "How's it going?"

"Just ducky."

"How bad is the Islander story?"

"Not terrible, but Kellen released a statement on behalf of his parents, siblings and the company."

"It said that? Siblings?"

"Yep."

"Nice of him to speak for all of us," Kara said.

"I wondered if you'd say that. It mentioned that your sister married your ex-boyfriend."

"Okay..."

"And also went into the beef between your dad and uncle."

"Of course. Any time something happens with the company or the family, all that is resurfaced. The local media never tires of the rifts in the Ballard family."

Kara's phone buzzed with a text that she stood up to read. "My brother Kingston, the lobster fisherman who has nothing to do with the company, feels the same way I do. He said he's going to text Kellen and tell him not to speak for all of us."

"You should do the same if you feel strongly about it."

"It just would've been nice to be asked or even given a heads-up that they were issuing a statement on our behalf. I get that it's all PR to protect the company, but it's kind of nervy not to even tell us they're speaking for us."

"Sure is."

"I'm going to text my dad, Kendra and Kellen and tell them that."

"I don't blame you."

Kara stood to the side of him and typed up her message.

Dan couldn't resist slipping an arm around her or resting his head on the baby bump. He was greeted with a sound thump to the cheek. "Dylan is busy this morning."

"He had a rager all night long. He gets that from your people."

"Um, my people are not all-night partiers like some of the Ballards are."

"Don't use the current situation against me. That wouldn't be wise."

Dan grunted out a laugh.

"How does this sound: 'I don't appreciate being included as one of the siblings in a statement I was neither consulted on nor warned about before it went public. I'm sure I'm not alone in feeling this way. Please don't speak for me without my knowl-edge or consent. Thank you.'"

"I'm extremely turned on by assertive, no-bullshit Kara."

"Shut up. I'm being serious."

"As am I."

"Do you agree with the statement?"

"It's your statement to make. Doesn't matter if I agree, but on a scale of one flame to five, I give it ten."

"Your scale is skewed where I'm concerned."

"That's right. You're ten flames every day, all day for me."

"Since you're of no help to me whatsoever, I'm going to send this message and get on with my day."

Dan let his hand fall to cup her ass. "The fisher-people are long gone for the day. You know what that means?"

"I can't imagine."

"We have the house all to ourselves for hours and hours. What do you say we take a day off and spend some time together?"

"We spend every day together."

"But we're not naked on those days like we could be today due to the aforementioned aloneness."

"You're shameless, Torrington."

"Point of order, you knew that about me before you said, 'I do.'"

"Indeed I did, and don't legal-speak me."

"Can't help it. It's in my DNA, and you love my DNA. You regularly wallow in my DNA, in fact."

"Now you're just being gross."

"Nothing gross about it, babe. What say you? Shall we declare this a naked day in the land?"

"How about a naked half day? I've got a few things I want to do today."

"I can live with a half day as long as it's the first half. In fact, I've already gotten things started just thinking about it."

Her laughter was his favorite thing in the whole world.

"You're nothing if not predictable."

"Which is one of the many reasons you love me." Dan moved her gently to the side so he could stand, wrap his arms around her and direct her backward into the bedroom. If they'd been at home on Gansett, the closest horizontal surface would've sufficed, but here, in her grandmother's home, he wanted a door they could close.

As soon as they were both inside the tiny bedroom, he kicked the door closed and reached back to lock it, just to be safe.

"I love being here with Bertha and Buster and seeing more of your life here, but I really miss being completely alone with you at home."

"Me, too. I miss that a lot, but it's been nice to have some time with Bertha and Buster. I love this house as much as I love our place on the island."

"I can see why."

"It's funny when you think about it. I grew up in a freaking palace that had every amenity, but this ramshackle house by the shore... This is my home."

"That's because Bertha lives here. She's your person."

"She was my *first* person. I have another one now."

"Who is he? I'll freaking run him through the heart with the longest sword—"

Kara kissed him. "Shut it."

"Yes, dear." Never one to talk his way out of a sure thing, Dan kissed her and helped her out of her clothes while she did the same for him. "I *love* naked day." He kissed her neck and nuzzled her soft skin. "It's my favorite day of the whole week."

"Mmm, it's usually a good day."

Dan pulled back, frowning, and said, "Usually?"

Once again, she laughed. "Less talk. More action."

"Mmm, I like how you think." He eased her back onto the bed and came down next to her, propping his head on one hand while he used his other hand to touch every soft inch of her curvy body.

"I can't believe you still want me like you do when I'm bigger than a house."

Dan froze, shocked to his core that she'd say such a thing. "You can't believe I still want you this way when you're gorgeous and sexy and pregnant with our baby? Really?"

"I just feel ridiculous, with my big belly and disgustingly huge boobs."

Dan cupped one of them and teased her nipple into standing up straight as she shivered from the sensations. "Don't you let me hear you say anything mean about my favorite boobs ever."

"Reminder that they'll go back to normal after this."

"Not that there's anything at all wrong with your version of normal, but I plan to fully enjoy these beauties while they last."

"Would you tell me if you thought I was kinda... I don't know... ungainly or whatever?"

"Kara, sweetheart, love of my life, there's nothing about you that isn't beautiful and desirable to me."

"And you're not just saying that because you did this to me?"

"God no. I thought you were the most beautiful girl in the world before you were pregnant, and now..." He closed his eyes and rested his forehead on her chest. "Now I think you're a fucking goddess."

"You were already going to get very lucky."

"I mean it. In fact, the goddesses have nothing on my wife."

"Kara? Are you here? Kara?"

They froze.

"Oh my God. My mother."

"No," Dan said with a groan. "Way to kill a perfectly good boner."

"Let me up. I wouldn't put it past her to come in here looking for me."

He moved to let her up. "And you wondered why I locked the door?"

"I didn't wonder." Kara put on a robe she'd stolen from Buster and tied it tight around her waist. "Hold that thought."

"Mmm, sure. No problem."

After she left the room, closing the door behind her, Dan buried his face in a pillow and groaned.

CHAPTER
Twenty~One

"HEY," Kara said to her mother, who was helping herself to coffee.

When Judith turned to face her, Kara noted that every blonde hair was in place, her makeup had been artfully applied to shave ten years off her face, and she wore the latest in fitness attire that put her perfect body on full display. Her mother took one look at Kara's disheveled appearance and frowned. "Were you still in bed?"

"I was. I had a rough night." She placed a hand on the baby bump. "The heartburn is brutal."

"Oh it is. I had the worst time with that, too."

"I still can't imagine doing this eleven times."

Judith's smile had a brittleness to it that was new. "Is Dan here?"

"Yes, he's resting, though. He was up with me during the night."

"I'm sorry to disturb you. I just wanted…" Holding her coffee mug, she leaned back against the counter and sighed. "I need someone to tell me this is going to work out. My sons didn't kill that woman. They couldn't have."

"Dan is doing everything he can for Kirby. He's hoping for a dismissal of the charges or at least another bail hearing."

"I'm so worried about Kirby. Keith knows how to handle himself in tough situations, but Kirby..." She shook her head. "I can't picture him in jail."

Kara's heart went out to Judith, which was an odd feeling since she was usually inclined to keep her distance from her remote, emotionally unavailable mother. "I'm sure he's hanging in there. He's a survivor."

"Is he, though? What if someone hurts him..."

"He's in the town jail, not the state prison. He'll be okay. Hopefully, Dan will get him out of there sooner rather than later."

"We're very thankful for all he's doing."

"We're glad he could help. I know it's hard not to worry, but from what Dan says, the case against them is flimsy at best. He thinks it was a massive rush to judgment before a full investigation could take place."

"Daddy said that detestable Jonah Brown is their so-called eyewitness. He's cost us a fortune fending off his ridiculous lawsuit."

"According to Dan, the police didn't know about the lawsuit until he told them. That's included in the motion he filed."

"Listen to you," Judith said with a warm smile. "Talking like a lawyer."

"He's taught me well."

"I want you to know..."

Kara waited, eager to hear what her mother had to say, which was also a first.

Judith took a deep breath and looked up at her, seeming more emotional than Kara had ever seen her. "I'm just thrilled that you're so happy with Dan. He's a remarkable guy and obviously head over heels in love with you. You deserve that, Kara."

"Thank you. He's made me very happy indeed."

"I also want you to know that I'm... I'm sorry about what happened with Kelly and Matt. We never should've supported her the way we did. They hurt you, *we* hurt you, and I deeply regret that."

Kara stared at her in amazement after hearing the words she'd never expected to hear. "Oh. Well. Thank you."

"Being a mother is difficult, as you'll soon learn, but there're times when you have to take sides. I should've taken your side, and I'll always regret that I didn't. I wanted you to know that."

Kara went to her aloof, untouchable mother and hugged her. "Thank you. That means a lot to me."

"I hate this terrible rift between you girls, but I understand why you'll never forgive her."

"I forgave her a long time ago. I couldn't hold on to that level of outrage and live a healthy life. But I'm never letting her fully into my life again. I hope you understand. When someone shows you who they really are..."

"You have to believe them."

"Exactly."

"In case you're wondering, she's very much aware of my disapproval of her choices and the way she and Matt treated you. I put it to the side for Connor's sake, but she knows."

"I'm strangely thankful to her because without what they did, I never would've met Dan, and that would've been truly tragic."

"Yes, it would have, but it never should've happened the way it did."

"No, it shouldn't have. Thank you for what you said. It means a lot to me to know how you really feel about it."

"I should've told you this a long time ago."

"Doesn't matter. Now I know."

"I was jealous, you know?"

"Of what?"

"Your tight bond with my mother, a bond I never had with her—or with you."

"I never thought you wanted that with me—or her."

"I'm not like you and her. You two have a warmth about you that people gravitate toward. I've never had that. I love you all so very much but have the worst time showing that for some reason. I wish I was more like you and my mother."

Kara was incredibly moved by the unprecedented confession from a woman who'd never once displayed an ounce of insecurity or introspection. "All you have to do, Mom, is tell the people you love how you feel. Show them with your words and actions. Be kind and available. That's all I've ever wanted from you—your time, your attention, your affection."

"I sucked at all that. I'm trying to do better."

"It's never too late to make a change."

"I hope that's true. I feel so disconnected from you and the others…"

"Take us one at a time. I'm fairly confident everyone will appreciate the overture—as long as it's followed up by action."

"It will be. I promise, Kara. I want to be a good grandmother to your baby. I want to be part of your life. I want to get texts from you with pictures and funny stories like my friends get from their kids. I can't change the past as much as I wish I could, but I'm trying to change the future."

"For what it's worth, I'm proud of you. It's not easy to admit failings and try to fix them."

"I've been in therapy for a while now. It's helped me to see some things a little differently. And just so you know, it's worth a lot to me that you're proud. I'm proud of you, too, and the life you've built for yourself on Gansett with Dan. It's obvious that you're both very well loved there."

"We've found a beautiful life there."

"I hope this is resolved soon so you can go home. But in the meantime, Daddy and I would love to have you two over for dinner, with Mom and Buster, too, of course."

"We'd like that."

"I'll text you to make a date."

"Thanks for coming by, Mom. It means a lot to me to hear the things you said."

"I'm sorry again that it took so long."

Kara shrugged. "Better late than never."

Her mother initiated the hug this time. "Love you, sweet girl."

"Love you, too."

Kara waved to her mother as she drove off in her silver Mercedes sedan. Then she went into the bedroom to find Dan sitting up in bed, scrolling through his phone.

"What was that about?"

"You won't believe it." His eyes went wide as she conveyed the gist of the conversation with her mother. "She actually apologized for how she handled the Kelly and Matt disaster."

"Wow, that must've been nice to hear."

Kara stretched out on the bed next to him. "It was rather shocking, but also vindicating in many ways. She told me she wishes she was more like Bertha and me. She said she's always been envious of our tight bond and easy way with people."

"How do you feel about that?"

"Amazed. I had no idea she felt that way. I always thought my tight bond with Bertha annoyed her because I preferred being here to being home."

"Your mother could learn a lot about how to be from both of you."

"She said she's been in therapy for some time now, and it's been revealing."

"I'm happy for you that she made that kind of effort."

"Yeah, it was pretty cool after wishing for so long that she could be different."

"Just proceed with caution. A tiger's stripes don't change overnight. I don't want you hurt by her again."

"I hear you, but this feels legit to me. She said she wants me to text her with pictures and funny stories about the baby. I never would've done that if she hadn't said she wants me to."

"This is great news all around."

"It is, but I hear you about proceeding with caution. She wants us to come to dinner. I told her we'd like to do that."

"Sure, whatever you want is fine with me."

"Thank you for not holding her past transgressions against her."

"When did I say I wasn't doing that?"

Kara laughed and snuggled up to him.

He put his arms around her. "I'll never forget the way they treated you, and I'll never forgive them for hurting you. But that said… If you want to have a closer relationship with them, I'm cautiously optimistic for you—and for them. It seems they've learned a few valuable lessons later in life."

"Yes, I told her better late than never."

"As long as it sticks."

"Right."

"Now, about what we were doing before we were so rudely interrupted." Dan tugged at the belt to her robe. "Naked day, take two."

He'd no sooner gotten a hand inside her robe than his phone rang. "Goddamn it."

Kara laughed at the agonized expression on his face.

"I can't take all these *highs* and *lows*."

She glanced at the tent in the covers caused by his erection.

"Don't look! That makes it worse."

She was shaking with laughter when he answered the phone with a gruffly spoken, "Torrington."

He listened for a second. "As in one o'clock today?" Another pause. "I'll be there. Thanks for letting me know."

"What's up?"

"The judge has asked to see counsel in chambers at one."

"Is that unusual?"

"Highly, which means the motion has moved him to act. This is very good news."

"Can I go with you the next time you go to court?"

"Are you sure that's a good idea?"

She nodded. "I want to see my sexy husband at work."

"Then we'll make that happen." He glanced at his watch. "I've got some work to do right here before I have to leave, so hurry up and get naked."

Kara giggled at the face he made. "Yes, dear."

DAN WAS COMING OUT OF THE SHOWER WHEN HIS PHONE rang. He groaned when he saw his mother-in-law's name on the caller ID.

"Good morning, Judith."

"Good morning. I spoke to Keith just now, and he's asked if you can come by as soon as possible."

"He's not my client, Judith."

"I believe that's what he wishes to discuss."

"I'll get over there shortly."

"Thank you, Dan."

"No problem."

"Is there anything you can tell me that'll give me some hope?"

"The judge has scheduled a meeting with the attorneys today, which I'm taking as a hopeful sign. I'm working the case from every angle and hoping for more information shortly. I know it has to be so hard, but you have to be patient. This could be a marathon, not a sprint."

"I feel like I'm coming out of my skin. My sons... accused of *murder*. My God in heaven... There's just no way they'd ever hurt a woman. We might've failed them in many ways as parents, but they were taught to respect others, to protect women and children… They couldn't have done this, Dan."

"I'm doing everything I can, so try to stay calm. We have to take this one step at a time."

"Okay," she said with a sigh. "Okay."

"The best thing you can do for them is to not talk to the media or anyone else who's looking for juicy details or something they can use to make everything worse."

"Understood."

"I'll be in touch after the hearing."

"Thank you again, Dan."

"You're welcome."

Dan texted Walter and asked him to pick him up in thirty minutes. He'd missed his run, but an extra hour in bed with his gorgeous wife beat a run any day.

Kara brought a mug of steaming coffee to the bedroom. Her cheeks were flushed from their lovemaking, and her eyes were bright with happiness and contentment. It was imperative to him that they stay that way. "Who were you talking to?"

Dan took the mug from her. "Your mother."

Kara sat next to him on the bed. "Oh jeez. Is she driving you crazy? I can tell her to back off."

"Don't worry about it. I took care of it."

"I'm sorry. I hate this."

"It's fine. She's having a very hard time with this whole thing, which is totally understandable. She said Keith asked to see me."

"Oh really? Is he figuring out that Matt isn't the attorney he needs?"

Dan smiled at the catty tone. "Perhaps."

"Are you going to see him?"

"Of course. I have no beef with him. If he wants my help, he'll have it."

"You're too good for this family."

"Nah, I'm only too good for you. Wait. That came out wrong."

Kara laughed. "Shockingly, I knew what you meant."

He slipped an arm around her. "I'm so lucky you put up with me."

"Yes, you are. I can't wait to see my man in action."

"I'll be so nervous if you're there."

"Shut up. You will not."

Dan laughed. "Can't get anything by you."

"Why do you still try?"

"Because it's always so much fun. Everything with you is fun."

"Even defending my brothers on murder charges?"

"That's not so fun but being here with you is. Spending time with Bertha is fun."

"Renata wants to do dinner tonight. Are you up for that?"

"Absolutely."

A toot from outside told him Walter had arrived. "That's my ride."

"I still can't believe you hired a driver."

"I'm getting a lot of good info from him, and I can work from the car. Well worth the investment."

"Keep me posted."

"I will." He left a lingering kiss on her sweet lips. "Love you."

"Love you, too."

On the way to Bar Harbor, he took a call from Carter, the investigator. "Hey, man. How's it going?"

"Making some progress on tracking down the ex-boyfriend. A guy named Billy Norton. They dated in high school and for a couple of years while she was in college. From what your team found on social media it looks like they broke it off over the holidays last year. She never mentioned him again after that. Friends were reaching out with messages of concern that went unanswered publicly."

"Where's he located?"

"Lives in Madison, Connecticut, where they grew up and works as a plumber. I'm going there today to do some more digging and talking to people in town to get a handle on him and them as a couple. I'm also trying to figure out where he was last weekend. I should have more for you later today."

"This is great, Carter. Thank you. We've got the probable cause hearing on Thursday."

"I'm on this full time."

"Thanks again."

"You got it."

"Making some progress, bossman?" Walter asked.

"Maybe."

Dan spent the rest of the ride poring over an updated police report that he'd received from Detective Cosgrove in his email earlier that morning. The only thing that had changed was two more eyewitnesses asserting that they'd seen Keith with Tanya after the bar closed, which wasn't really relevant as far as Dan was concerned. He was fairly confident that Keith would be willing to concede that he'd walked with Tanya to the wharf area on the waterfront, where they parted company.

Walter pulled into the public safety complex a short time later, and Dan gathered his things. "I've got to be in Ellsworth by one."

"No problem. I'll wait for you right here."

"Thanks, Walter."

Inside, he asked to see Keith Ballard and was ushered through a security check and into a small airless room like hundreds of others Dan had been in during his career.

Keith was brought in a few minutes later.

Dan barely knew him, but at first glance, it looked as if Keith hadn't slept in days. In some ways, he was glad to realize the ordeal was taking a toll on Keith. A little less arrogance and defiance would be helpful to his cause. His hair, which was standing on end, was more of a dark blond than Kara's reddish blonde. He had blue eyes that were bloodshot and a ruddy complexion.

"Thanks for coming in," he said when he sat across from Dan.

"Sure. What can I do for you?"

"I… Well, I need your help."

"Okay."

He finally made eye contact with Dan. "That simple? I ask, and you say okay?"

Dan shrugged. "That's why I'm here. To help you and Kirby get out of this mess, but Kirby would have to approve me representing you as he's my client."

"Matt has no fucking clue what he's doing."

"And that surprises you?"

"Not so much. I'm sorry I was a dick the other day, but I'm kind of in shock that I find myself in need of your services."

"I'll do whatever I can for you, pending Kirby's approval."

CHAPTER
Twenty~Two

KEITH LEANED ACROSS THE TABLE, his expression fierce. "Even if Kirby doesn't agree, and he might not, we didn't do *anything* to Tanya. I need you to believe me when I tell you she was fine when we left her."

"I do believe you."

"Really?"

"Why wouldn't I?"

"You haven't had the best impression of me so far. And I'm sure you've heard an earful from people in town and my own family."

"I've heard that a lot of people rely on you for repairs to their homes they wouldn't be able to afford otherwise."

"They said that?"

"Quite a few people said that."

"I figured they'd lead with the multiple DUIs, the bar fights, the numerous relationships that ended badly, among other things."

"I've heard some of that, too, but the other thing was mentioned more often."

Keith ran his hand roughly over the stubble on his jaw. "It's nice to hear they had something good to say."

"They did for sure. The eyewitness that put you and Kirby with her is Jonah Brown."

Keith's face lost all expression. "Are you fucking kidding me? That guy has a stick up his ass for our family."

"So I've heard."

"That's just great."

"The good news is that I can easily discredit him at the probable cause hearing due to his ongoing litigation against your family."

"That's good news?"

"It's very good news. It goes to him having an ulterior motive in pointing the finger at you and your brother."

"Kirby didn't do anything other than answer my call and give me a ride. He never even talked to her."

"How'd he end up with a black eye?"

"He was mouthing off to me in the bathroom about how this was all my fault, and it pissed me off. He knows as well as I do that I had nothing to do with any of this."

"Punching him isn't going to help anything. You have to keep your anger in check around here, Keith. You don't want to be giving them anything else to hold against you."

"I know. I feel bad about it. None of this is Kirby's fault, that's for sure."

"I want you to take me through everything that happened, from the minute you first met up with Tanya until the minute you and Kirby drove away in his truck. Don't leave out a single detail as all of it could be relevant."

Keith sighed deeply and sat back in his seat. "I'd met her before that night."

"What? When?"

"Over the summer. She was here working at the sailing camp and had just turned twenty-one, so she was enjoying the bar scene for the first time. I saw her around a few times, and we ended up talking one night. She told me how she'd recently gotten out of a long-term relationship and was looking to have some fun."

"When was this?"

"Maybe June? It was early in the season."

"What happened then?"

"We danced a little, had a few drinks, some laughs, a few kisses. Nothing major. I didn't see her again for a couple of weeks. We ran into each other again after the Fourth of July and started to hang out more regularly after that."

"Define 'hang out.'"

"We'd have a few drinks in town, watch some live music and end up at my place after."

Dan wanted to moan at the idea of the cops finding out Tanya had been at his house and getting a search warrant. Her DNA would probably be found in the house, which could complicate things.

"She was quite a bit younger than you."

"Yes, and I felt guilty about that, but she dismissed it from the start. She said she was a full-grown adult woman allowed to decide who she wanted to spend time with, and anyone who had a problem with it could fuck off."

As Dan took copious notes, he ached for the strong, fearless woman whose life had been cut tragically short.

"Did her parents and friends know you guys were hanging out?"

"One of her friends did. A girl named Lauren Rogers. She'd tell her parents she was staying with Lauren when she was with me."

"Do you know where I'd find Lauren?"

"She's local. She worked with Tanya at the sailing camp. I'm not sure what she does the rest of the year."

"I'll find her."

"Why do you need to talk to her?"

"She may have information that'll help, like she could tell the court how Tanya liked you, trusted you, never had anything bad to say about you. That kind of thing. If, of course, she never had anything bad to say about you."

"Not sure why she would've. We were all fun and no drama. We both knew this wasn't a forever kind of thing, but it was fun for the time it lasted. She left to go back to school, and I didn't hear from her again until the day before she came back to town for the future sister-in-law's bachelorette party."

"What did she say when she contacted you?"

"That she'd be in town for the weekend and wanted to get together. I told her I'd be at the Barnacle Friday night and to stop by if she was near there."

This was excellent new information that would be useful to him. Knowing Keith had a preestablished, casual relationship with Tanya and that there was someone who could confirm that would help to show he would've had no reason to kill her.

"Tell me about Friday night."

"She came in with her girls around ten. We had to act like we were just meeting because none of them knew about us. Her parents would've flipped out about her hanging out with an older guy, especially one with an arrest record, so we kept it on the DL. I bought a round of drinks for her and the others, and we danced the rest of the night. At one point, we snuck into the ladies' room to fuck."

"Did you use a condom?" Dan asked, though he already knew.

He shook his head. "She's on long-term birth control, and neither of us had been with anyone since the last time we were together."

"You realize that puts your DNA in her vagina, among the other places you touched her."

"That's all I can think about, but I didn't hurt her. I'd never hurt her. She was the cutest, sweetest, funniest girl."

"Call her a woman when you refer to her."

"Right. Sorry. She was a great person, and I'm crushed that someone killed her."

"Did you get to talk to her at all during the night?"

"Here and there. It was loud and crowded, but she said her semester was going well so far, but it was hard to get back in the groove of studying after the summer."

"Was there anything else she said or did that might help us?"

"There was one thing that happened, but it didn't stand out to me at the time..." He continued to rub at the stubble on his jaw. "She got really upset at one point."

"Did she say why?"

"She said she thought she'd seen her ex in the crowd, but that wasn't possible because he was in Connecticut."

Dan's heart began to beat faster when he heard that. "Did she look for him?"

"No, but after she thought she saw him, her whole disposition changed. She wanted to get out of there and asked me to walk with her for a bit to make sure she wasn't followed."

"Where were her friends at this point?"

"I forgot that part. She argued with the future SIL because she wanted to stay at the Barnacle when the rest of them were going back to her parents' house. They didn't want to leave her alone with me. She told them she was fine and could do what she wanted. I didn't hear what they said to each other, but the others left, and she was wound up from fighting with them. She did a couple of shots and wanted to dance, so that's what we did."

"Did she say anything more about the guy?"

"No, but she'd told me before that he hadn't given up on them getting back together, but she'd moved on. He had no interest in leaving the town they grew up in, and she wanted a bigger life than that. Apparently, he'd shown up on campus a few times since she went back to school, and she'd told him to get lost. He didn't like it, but he left after accusing her of wanting other guys more than she wanted a bigger life. I guess it got a little ugly a few times."

"This is great info, Keith. What do you know about where she lived at UConn?"

"I think she was in an off-campus apartment in Storrs."

"If we need it, I'll try to track down her friends and room-mates to get some more info about what happened with him."

"Do you think it was him she saw?"

"I'm going to check the security footage from the bar and see if we can ID him as being there. If we can, that could be enough to get the heat off you and Kirby. You had no motive. He did."

"What if you can't prove he killed her?"

"I don't have to. I just have to show it's likely that someone other than you two did it. If I introduce enough evidence to provide reasonable doubt of your involvement, it'll never get to trial."

"What if it's not enough, and they still think we did it?"

"Let's take it one day at a time. I'll do everything I can to get you out of this."

"And what happens then when I have to live the rest of my life as someone who was accused of murdering a woman?"

"Being charged isn't the same as being convicted."

"Isn't it, though? Won't there always be people who think it might've been me?"

"Not if someone else is eventually convicted." Dan leaned in. "Look, Keith... I know this is excruciating, but you didn't do it. You just have to be patient while we gather information that we can use to exonerate you. I've got good people working this from all angles."

"You had them working on it before today?"

"Yes, I've had them working on it since about one minute after your mother called me Saturday afternoon."

"You really are good at this, aren't you?"

"That's what I hear."

"I know we didn't get off on the best foot… but I want you to know… Kara's a good kid who doesn't suffer fools. If she thinks you're okay, you probably are."

Dan laughed. "For some strange reason that makes me the luckiest guy in the world, she approves of me."

Keith held out his hand across the table.

Dan reached out to meet him halfway and shook his hand.

"Thank you, Dan."

"You're welcome."

DAN NEXT ASKED TO SEE KIRBY, AND WHEN HIS BROTHER-in-law was seated across from him, he noted that Kirby couldn't stay still. His fingers were tapping on the table, and his leg bounced so hard that his entire body moved with it. "Are you sleeping at all?"

"Not really."

"Do you need anything?"

"I need to get the hell out of here before I lose my mind."

"I have some good news for you. Keith asked for a meeting and has signed on to be represented by me, pending your approval."

"Why do you need my approval?"

"Because you're my client, first and foremost, so my allegiance is to you, but if you're okay with me also representing him, I can mount a joint defense, provided you both sign conflict-of-interest waivers."

Kirby thought about that for a second. "Normally, I'd want nothing to do with being on the same team as Keith, but he didn't do this. I don't want to see him railroaded because of his past problems. I've seen him trying to turn things around. He needs a good lawyer, and Matt Gallagher is *not* a good lawyer."

"In that case, I'm happy to represent you both. Keith gave me a ton of very useful information about the victim and his prior involvement with her as well as her difficult split with a long-time boyfriend. I've got people working on this, with a goal of discrediting the investigation and getting the charges dropped at the preliminary hearing."

"That's days from now. I'll never make it."

"The judge has asked for a meeting today as well. Not sure what that's about, but it's good news that he asked to see us."

"None of this is good news until I'm out of here."

"You didn't do this, so give me a chance to prove that, and it'll go away."

"It's just unreal, you know? To be living your life, minding your own business, and then get caught up in something like this." He sent a hesitant look Dan's way. "When I first heard about what you do, your innocence project, I admit I was a bit skeptical. Like, are you out there getting criminals out of jail? I mean, who doesn't say they're innocent of whatever they're charged with? Now I get it."

"It happens far too often, which is why I've made it my life's work."

"Thank God there're people like you protecting people like me."

"It's possible you could end up with a nice big settlement from the state at the end of it."

"I don't care about that. I care about my good name, my reputation, my life."

"There hasn't been a person I've spoken to who hasn't said what a good guy you are and how there's no way you had anything to do with this."

"Well, that's nice to hear. I've had far too much time to think while I was in here and to imagine what's being said."

"I know it's hard to believe from in here, but I honestly think you'll be going home very soon. I'm taking advantage of every opportunity I get to say you had nothing to do with any of this. I'll say it again when I meet with the judge today."

"Thank you, Dan. Thank you so much."

"I'm glad I could be here to help. Don't lose hope, okay?"

"Yeah, I'll try not to."

"I'll be back soon."

"How's Kara doing? It can't be easy for her to be back here."

"She's holding up as long as you are."

"Tell her I'm okay and not to worry."

"I will. She'll be glad to hear it."

After he left Kirby, he went to speak to Detective Cosgrove. "Please tell me you're starting to realize you have no case against my clients."

"We have additional witnesses that can put Keith with Tanya before last weekend."

"He fully admits to having dated her during the summer."

Judging by his surprised expression, the detective hadn't expected Dan to concede so quickly.

"You know what I've found to be true when you're dealing with innocent people improperly charged with crimes?"

"I'm sure you're going to enlighten me whether I want you to or not."

"The common denominator is that innocent people have nothing to hide. If you want to know about Keith's prior relationship with Tanya, we could get you in the room with him to clear up any remaining questions."

Cosgrove thought that over. "I'd be interested in talking to him, but not today. I've got other things to take care of."

"I hope your other things are related to this case as my clients are innocent and being held on serious charges. They're going to have one hell of a civil case when all is said and done."

Cosgrove frowned. "Unfortunately, theirs is not my only case, and while I'm sure you're used to dealing with much bigger departments, we're stretched thin here."

"Understood. Well, I'll let you get back to work. All of this will come out in court if not before."

"What's that supposed to mean?"

"Just what I said. We're under no obligation to refrain from sharing what we know before the hearing. You have a good day, Detective."

CHAPTER
Twenty-Three

WALTER DROVE Dan to Ellsworth for the meeting the judge had called in his chambers.

In the outer office, Dan met an attorney who handed him her card. "Assistant Attorney General Cori Brooks for the state." She was tall, with brown skin and long, braided hair. Her handshake was firm and her expression no-nonsense. She wore a sharp-looking red suit and sky-high black heels.

He handed her his card. "Daniel Torrington for the defense."

"Duh."

"Just being polite."

Cori smiled. "Despite being on opposite sides of this one, I've admired your career."

"Thank you."

An admin ushered them into the judge's chambers.

Judge Collins sat behind a desk covered in a stack of files, other papers and a half-eaten salad. He had his shirtsleeves rolled up and reading glasses propped on the end of his nose. He stood to shake hands with both of them. "Thanks for coming in."

"No problem," Dan said.

They sat in his visitor chairs.

"I have signed conflict-of-interest waivers from both Ballard brothers, who wish to be represented jointly."

The judge took the forms from him and added them to the pile on his desk. "I've thoroughly reviewed the reports on this case, and you have a problem, Counselor." This was directed toward the prosecutor. "Your case is weak."

Dan wanted to stand up and cheer.

"I'm aware of that, Your Honor, and the police are working to gather more information."

"As are we, Your Honor," Dan said. "So far, we've learned that the eyewitness is locked in a wrongful-termination lawsuit with Ballard Boat Works, which he's probably going to lose because he was fired for cause after failing numerous drug tests. In addition, Keith Ballard had known Tanya Sorenson for months before the night in question and had a relationship with her over the summer. She reached out to let him know she'd be in town and wanted to see him. They had a fun evening together that included sex in the ladies' room. She thought she spotted her ex-boyfriend in the crowd at the Barnacle, so when the bar closed, she asked Keith to walk her down the hill, away from the bar. She said she was sure she was seeing things at the bar and was fine to walk the rest of the way home."

The judge frowned at Cori. "If it wasn't for the seriousness of this crime and Keith's criminal record, I'd immediately order the charges dropped."

"Kirby Ballard never met Tanya or ever had anything to do with her. You have my motion to immediately dismiss the charges against Kirby or at least release him on bail."

Collins sighed deeply. To Cori, he said, "I'm giving you until Thursday's hearing to produce evidence that ties these men to this murder, or they'll be released with the charges dropped."

"Yes, Your Honor."

The judge directed his intimidating gaze at the prosecutor. "Find out where the ex-boyfriend was the night in question."

"We're working on that, sir."

"Work faster."

"Yes, sir."

Dan walked out with Cori.

"I suppose it's too much to ask you to stay out of the press with your commentary about our case."

"Yes, it is too much to ask. My clients are innocent men charged with the worst possible crime. I'll do whatever it takes to see them exonerated."

"Fair enough."

Dan got into the back seat of Walter's car. "I need to visit the offices of the *Mount Desert Islander*."

"That's right around the corner."

"I need to do a few things before I go in there."

"Whatever you need, Boss."

Dan made notes about his meeting with Keith. He texted Judith and Chuck to let them know he was now officially representing Keith and that the judge had given the prosecution until Thursday to produce compelling evidence, or the charges would be dropped. He wondered who'd break the news to Matt that he'd been replaced and chuckled to himself when he imagined Matt finding out that he'd been replaced by Dan. He hoped it was as humiliating as possible for Matt.

It was funny because rarely in his life would Dan ever have described himself as petty. But mention Kelly or Matt to him, and all his inner pettiness came roaring to the surface.

He sent a text to Kara to update her as well.

That all sounds promising.

To me as well. I'm optimistic it'll be over soon.

God, I hope so. Are you on the way home?

Not yet. Will be home in an hour or two.

I'll be here.

Counting on that.

Dan sent a text to Carter. *I need video from inside the Barnacle that night. Is that something you can help me get?*

He wouldn't get full discovery info until the case was bound over for trial, so he had to use his own network in the meantime.

On it, Carter replied five minutes later.

Dan next texted Clarissa in his LA office to ask for photos of Tanya's ex so he could look for him on the video from the bar.

"This shouldn't take long," Dan said to Walter when they parked outside the *Mount Desert Islander* offices.

"Take your time. I'll grab a coffee."

"Sounds good." Inside, he asked for Elias Young and was shown to his cubicle.

The young reporter's eyes bugged when he realized who'd come to see him. He jumped up so fast that his desk chair smacked against the wall. "I, um, wasn't expecting you."

Dan extended a hand to the man he guessed to be in his mid-twenties. He was medium height with brown hair and eyes. "Dan Torrington."

"Um, yes, I know. Ah, I'm Elias Young."

"I was wondering if there's somewhere we can talk."

"Um, sure, we can use the conference room. Let me just get my stuff."

Dan stepped back to give him some room and noticed that all eyes in the newsroom were trained on him. He gave a little wave to the others.

"Right this way," Elias said. "Can I get you anything? I think we have some water in the kitchen. There might be some coffee left, too."

"I'm fine, thanks."

Elias closed the door to the conference room and set up across from Dan with a notebook, pen and digital recorder. "Do you mind if I record this?"

"Knock yourself out."

"Okay... so what's this about?"

"I wanted to bring you up to speed on what we're learning about the case."

While Elias took furious notes, Dan told him about Keith having dated Tanya during the previous summer, how she'd texted to let him know she'd be in town for the weekend and that they'd planned to meet up at the Barnacle. While they were together, she shared with Keith how her ex-boyfriend wasn't going away and feared for a second that she'd seen him in the crowd inside the bar. She asked him to walk her out of downtown because she was afraid of running into him.

"If she was afraid, why do you suppose she didn't accept the ride home the Ballard brothers supposedly offered her?"

"I honestly don't know that. I can only assume she didn't want Keith taking her to her parents' home for some reason. Maybe because of the fight with the future sister-in-law over him earlier?"

"It seems like an odd choice."

"To me as well, but the one thing I can assure you and your readers is that Keith and Kirby Ballard had nothing to do with her murder. In fact, I'm shocked they were charged based on the evidence I've seen thus far. There's no way the AG has a case they can take to trial."

"I'm allowed to quote you on all this?"

"I wish you would, and as soon as possible."

That gave him pause. "Are you using me to stick it to the cops?"

Yes, Dan wanted to say, but instead, he said, "Not at all. I thought you'd be interested in an update on the case, but if you're not, I can take it to another outlet."

"That won't be necessary."

"How soon can you publish a story?"

"Later today online."

"I'll look forward to reading it. Call me if you have any additional questions." He got up to leave and then stopped to look back at the reporter. "I've told you how their eyewitness is locked in litigation with Ballard Boat Works and the Ballard family. Have you looked into how he was fired for failing drug tests and is suing them."

"I'm working on that."

"Have a great rest of your day."

"You do the same."

"Oh, I will."

Dan texted Walter as he left the offices, satisfied that he'd begun to sow the reasonable doubt that would soon exonerate his brothers-in-law and clear them of any involvement in Tanya's murder.

He asked Walter to take him back to Bar Harbor to meet with his clients.

"This could all be over soon, so keep the faith," he said to the brothers.

"We're trying," Keith said for both of them.

On the way out of the police station, he smiled as he took a call from Kara. "Hey, love. How's it going?"

"All good here. How about with you?"

He got into Walter's back seat. "I'm on my way back to the house now."

"Are you working all afternoon?"

"Depends on whether I get a better offer."

"I thought I might show you Acadia if you have time."

"That definitely counts as a better offer. I'd love to see it with you."

"And how do you feel about dinner at my parents' house afterward?"

"I thought we were seeing Renata tonight."

"My mom told me to invite her, which is a very big deal in light of the rift with her father."

"Wow, that's cool. If you're sure that's what you want to do, then that's fine with me."

"I'm not sure of anything, but after what my mom said, I want to give them the benefit of the doubt, even if they probably don't deserve it."

"I get it, babe."

"It's so strange to be back here and plunged back into everything that goes with this place, but a funny thing has happened since I left here devastated and demoralized."

"What's that?"

"Other than falling for a dark-haired, sexy, egotistical attorney…"

"Where is this stud? I'll have him killed."

She snorted with laughter. "Other than that, I seem to have discovered my backbone and my ability to dictate the terms of who I let in and what I put up with. They no longer have the power to hurt me the way they once did."

"Good for you, love. That makes me so fucking proud of you."

"It was a long road to get here, made significantly easier by having my very own person to lean on through it all."

"Your person loves when you lean on him."

"He never lets me down."

"And he never will."

"Are you going to get my brothers out of jail?"

"You can bet on it."

"I love you."

Dan closed his eyes and sighed. Those words from her made his entire life worth living. "Love you more."

"No way."

"We'll have this fight when I get home."

"I can't wait."

KARA SHOWED HIM THUNDER HOLE AND SAND BEACH before directing him to drive the Jeep up Cadillac Mountain.

She'd forgotten how incredible the view was from the top of the mountain and loved watching Dan experience it for the first time.

"This is really something." He made a slow circle to get the full effect. "And the drive up was cool, too."

"It's funny how you take something for granted when it's just there your whole life, but then you come back and see it differently."

"That's true. I feel that way about LA when I've been away for a while. I notice things I used to drive right by without seeing them." He put his arm around her and brought her in closer to him to snap a selfie. "We need to come to Maine more often going forward."

"Yes, we do. I want to spend as much time with Bertha as I can while I can."

"I do, too. I just love being around her. She's one of the most incredible people I've ever met."

"Thank you for seeing that. Matt used to phone it in with her, and of course she could see right through that."

"His loss, babe. She's worth taking the time to get to know."

"Tell me about how it went with Keith."

"I had a nice chat with him earlier. He gave me a lot of useful information."

"You know what the best part of that is?"

"What's that?"

"He dumped Matt for you."

Dan roared with laughter. "He did indeed, my vindictive little she-cat."

"Me? Vindictive? Never. But I hope he went home and told Kelly all about how my brother threw him over for the much more successful—not to mention sexier—"

"Not to mention..."

"Dan Torrington, Esquire. This is truly a moment to relish."

"I want you to enjoy every freaking minute of it."

"Oh, I will. Don't you worry about that. Did you see Kirby, too?"

"I did."

"How is he?"

"Not great, but he promised he's hanging in there and keeping the faith."

Her deep sigh said it all. "I hate this for him. He'll never get over being accused of such a thing."

"He will. In time. I've seen people convicted of heinous crimes come back to live productive lives after being exonerated. It doesn't happen overnight, but it can and does happen. And he's not going to get anywhere near a conviction."

"Are you sure of that?"

"As sure as I can be about an unpredictable system."

"Those words 'unpredictable system' make my stomach hurt."

"Don't think about it. We're doing everything we possibly can to get them out of there, and I'm confident that we'll introduce enough doubt at the hearing to get the charges thrown out."

"How does this happen? How do two innocent people get charged with murder?"

"Happens all the time. Family members of victims are agonized, the community is anxious, law enforcement is under tremendous pressure to make an arrest... Sometimes there'll be just enough evidence to justify an arrest, and then a case is made around that evidence that's sold to a jury, and an innocent person is convicted and sent to prison. Often, the accused don't have the resources to hire top-level defense attorneys with investigators who can uncover the truth. It's a very imperfect system, but it's the only one we've got."

"That's terrifying."

"It is."

A gust of wind had Kara shivering and zipping her coat.

"Let's get you out of this chill."

They drove down the mountain and through the lush forest that made up Acadia.

"Are Bertha and Buster coming to dinner?"

"She took a pass. She said she's having a rough day with the arthritis."

"I hate to hear that."

"As do I. The thought of anything being wrong with her is beyond me."

"She's strong as an ox. You know that."

"I do, but she's still in her eighties and working full time."

"She's doing exactly what she wants."

"Yeah, definitely."

"You're sure you're okay about going to your parents' house?"

"Will you be there with me?"

"There's nowhere else I'd rather be than with you."

She covered his hand with hers. "Then I'll be just fine."

CHAPTER
Twenty-Four

AFTER THEY LEFT THE PARK, Kara directed him toward Bar Harbor and the home where she was raised. She received a text from Renata that she couldn't make it to dinner but would catch up with Kara later. When they got to town, she told Dan to take a right. A few more miles passed before she said to slow down and prepare to take a left turn.

"I wouldn't have even seen a place to turn there if you hadn't shown me," Dan said.

"When I was first driving, I'd go by it more times than not until I started to recognize the landmarks."

As Dan drove down the winding dirt lane that led to Sea Swept, the Ballard home, Kara's anxiety spiked the way it always did when she went there. "This road... I remember having to steel myself for whatever would be happening here when I arrived. It rarely had anything to do with me, but it was always something."

"Are you sure it's a good idea to come here now?"

"It's fine. None of it has the same power over me that it once did. I've moved on from here in every possible way. And in some ways, I've moved too far past here, which I've been reminded of on more than one occasion."

"Did you talk to your friends about the clambake Bertha suggested?"

"Yes, and we're hoping to squeeze it in soon."

"I'm looking forward to meeting them all in person."

"They said the same. I think you're the reason they were all so quick to agree to come."

"That's not true, Kara. Quit being hard on yourself over them. You've been great about staying in close touch with all of them, and visiting works both ways, you know? It's not like they didn't know where to find you."

"True, but I walked away and never looked back."

"No, you didn't. That's not what happened. You left and stayed gone because it was in your best interest, and I can't bear to see you apologize to anyone for doing what was best for you."

She reached across the console for his hand. "Thank you for being my best friend."

"Thank you for being mine."

"You really are the best friend I've ever had. Right up there with Bertha and Buster and Renata."

"That's a lofty bit of praise right there, knowing what they mean to you."

"As much as I love them, and I love them fiercely, you're in a whole other category all by yourself. I hope you know that."

"When I think of how hard you tried to run me off..."

Kara laughed. "Shut up about that! I'm being serious."

"As am I. You were savage in your contempt for me." He drove the Jeep around the last bend before the house revealed itself, and then he braked, coming to a full stop. "Shut. The. Hell. *Up.*"

"Welcome to Sea Swept. It's quite something, right?"

"It sure is. Wow. *This* is where you grew up?"

"Bertha's house was my real home."

"I know, but this... Wow."

"Did you think Chuck and Judith would live in a regular sort of house?"

"I guess not, but still..."

Like everything else in Maine, the house looked different to her with the perspective of time. The gray shingles were more weathered than they'd been, the landscaping a bit overgrown and the roof worn from battling the coastal elements for more than forty years.

They drove past the tennis court and the fenced inground pool before pulling up to the house.

"Park over there," Kara said, pointing to the right. "That's the door we use."

As they were getting out of the car, Kendra pulled up in her Volvo SUV. She put the window down. "Heard you were coming, so we crashed."

The girls were out of the back seat before the car had fully stopped and ran over to hug Kara.

"Mom says it's called crashing when you invite yourself somewhere," Luna said.

Kara laughed. "It's not technically crashing when it's your grandparents' house."

"That's what I said," Aurora replied. "How can we crash at Gram's house when she always wants us to come over?"

"Exactly."

Dan came around the car to greet the others. "Ladies."

"Hi, Uncle Dan," Aurora said with a shy smile.

"How was school today?"

"I'd rather not discuss it."

"Math test gone wrong," Kendra said.

"That happened a lot to me, but I still got into Stanford Law. Don't despair."

"Wait, you went to law school, and you sucked at math?" Luna asked.

"Don't say 'sucked,' Luna," Kendra said, earning an eye roll from her daughter.

"That doesn't count as a swear, Mom."

"I did stink at math, and I still went to a top law school," Dan said as he and Luna followed the others into the mudroom.

"That's impressive," Luna said.

"Don't tell him he's impressive," Kara said. "It makes his head swell."

The girls giggled at the scowl Dan directed her way. "That is not true."

"Yes, it is."

"What are we arguing about already?" Judith asked when they entered the gourmet kitchen that'd been redone since Kara was last there.

"Aunt Kara is saying that Uncle Dan's head swells when someone says he's impressive," Luna reported.

"And Uncle Dan says that's not true," Dan added.

"Isn't it, though?" Judith asked with a smile and subtle tilt of her head.

Kara laughed, surprised by the playful teasing from her usually uptight mother. "See? It's not just me who sees it."

"I can't catch a break around here," Dan said, accepting a Sam Adams from Chuck and taking a deep swig.

"I found out I can go to law school even if I *stink* at math," Luna said.

Dan winked at her. "You go, girl."

"Kolby and Keenan said they might come by after the gym," Judith said to Kara. "I hope that's okay."

"Of course. I'd love to see them." Her two youngest brothers were roommates and best friends who did just about everything together when they weren't working. "I saw Kolby for a second the other day."

"He said he was glad to see you."

"I was glad to see him, too." Kara helped herself to a carrot

stick and some ranch dip, touched that her mother remembered that she loved that snack. "The kitchen looks beautiful,
Mom."

"You think so? I'm so happy with it. I did exactly what I
wanted this time, rather than what the so-called kitchen
designers suggested the first time around."

She'd gone with navy blue lower cabinets, white uppers and a
white countertop that had replaced darker cabinets and counter-
tops. A huge island with barstools was the centerpiece.

"I really love it," Kara said. "Especially the backsplash."

The painted tiles above the stove featured sailboats with spin-
nakers with the sailing theme carried through the smaller
spaces, too. What would've been overdone in a smaller kitchen
worked perfectly in this one.

"I do, too," Judith said with a warm smile for Kendra. "My
favorite designer helped me choose everything."

"You're definitely designing our house when we're ready,"
Kara said to Kendra.

"Sign me up," Kendra said.

"This house is amazing," Dan said. "Did you guys build it?"

"We did," Chuck said. "About forty years ago, when it cost a
fraction of what it would today."

"He did a lot of it himself on nights and weekends for years,"
Judith added. "We thought it would never be finished."

"And they kept having kids until they filled all the
bedrooms," Kendra said, making everyone laugh.

"That wasn't exactly the plan," Judith said. "It just worked
out that way."

"And we're thankful for every one of them—and their partners," Chuck said. "Especially lately."

"We're so relieved that you're representing Keith now, too,"
Judith said to Dan.

"We're on it, so try not to worry."

"That's easier said than done. Our family has been through

some things over the years, lots of ups and downs, but this..."
Judith shook her head as tears filled her eyes.

Chuck put an arm around her. "We'll get through this the same way we've gotten through everything else. One step at a time."

Judith nodded, wiped away her tears and forced a smile. "Of course we will. I made my famous stuffies. Who wants one?"

Luna and Aurora, who were seated at the island to be closer to the snacks, raised their hands.

"Me!" Kara said. "With Tabasco, please."

"Remind me what's in these so-called stuffies," Dan said.

"Magic," Kara said. "That's what's in them."

"Along with some clams and chorizo and other yummy things," Kendra said.

"He'll have one," Kara said. "He's like a seagull. He eats everything."

The girls giggled at the face Dan made.

"Is that true, Uncle Dan?" Aurora asked. "Are you like a seagull?"

"I've never gone dumpster diving, if that's what you're asking, but I do like to eat."

As the girls giggled their heads off, Kara felt more at home in the house where she'd been raised than she ever had before, thanks in no small part to the presence of her beloved husband.

He made everything better.

AFTER DINNER, THEY LINGERED OVER THE CHOCOLATE cake her mother had made from scratch and served with vanilla ice cream. Dan kept looking at Kara for signs that she was ready to go, but she seemed relaxed and happy in the presence of her family members. He was so happy for her to have this time with them to make new memories, despite their worries for Keith and Kirby.

Kolby and Keenan had kept them entertained with funny stories from their group of friends at the gym and the people Kolby saw daily on his mail route.

"Are you going to come by the office while you're here, Kara?" Keenan had taken her place as the director of business development. "Everyone would love to see you. They've been abuzz over you bringing your hotshot husband home to deal with the current troubles."

"I'd love to see everyone," Kara said.

"And I'd love to see this company I've heard so much about," Dan added.

"Come by tomorrow," Chuck said. "I'll give you the full tour."

Kara glanced at Dan. "Do you have time for that?"

"I should. I'm waiting for others to get me info and have done what I can personally at this point."

"I know we said we wouldn't talk about it tonight," Judith said, sounding almost tearful, "but how do you think it's going to go, Dan?"

"We have a very strong case for dismissal. I believe it'll turn out to be a severe overreach by the state police in charging them before they had all the facts."

"Oh God," Chuck said. "I hope so."

"I don't want to get your hopes up quite yet, but I'm feeling increasingly confident that they'll never get the case to trial. Just keep anything we talk about between us, if you would."

"None of us will say a word," Chuck said with a stern look for the rest of the group.

"It's still so shocking that Kirby was arrested," Kolby said. "He's literally never hurt a fly. Remember how he'd capture them and take them back outside?"

"Yes," Kendra said with a soft smile. "He would say it wasn't the fly's fault that he ended up in the house."

Judith used a napkin to dab at her eyes. "I can't bear to think of him locked up in a cage. I worry this will break him."

"It won't," Kara said forcefully. "We won't let it. Tomorrow, I want to see him."

"I'll take you," Dan said. "I think it'll help him to see you."

"After that, we'll swing by the office," Kara said.

"I'll take you both to lunch after a tour of BBW," Chuck said.

"Only if I can go, too," Judith said.

Everyone looked at Kara, awaiting her verdict.

"Of course," she said. "That sounds great. But only if we can go to the Travelin Lobster."

"Whatever you want, sweetheart," Chuck said.

"WANT TO SEE MY OLD ROOM?" KARA ASKED DAN AFTER they'd cleared the table and helped with the dishes.

"I'd love to."

"Right this way."

"No funny business with my daughter up there," Chuck said sternly.

Dan and Kara laughed.

She placed a hand on her baby belly. "A little late for those warnings, Dad."

Chuck scowled. "Don't remind me."

"I promise to be on best behavior, Chuck," Dan said, holding up crossed fingers.

Kara smiled as she took his hand and led him upstairs to the room she'd once shared with Kelly. That felt like a million years ago now that she'd barely spoken to her sister in years. Their room was the third one on the left. "That was the bathroom I shared with Kelly and Kendra when we all lived at home. The boys had their own bathroom that we stayed far, far away from. All the rest of the bedrooms were theirs. My parents' room is on the main floor."

"Eleven kids overhead. Unfathomable."

"We weren't all here for long. There's fourteen years between

Kendra and Keenan. By the time he was in kindergarten, she was off to college. Kellen went to college the following year. It was only super crazy in the summer while they were home. Kingston moved out the day he turned eighteen and never looked back."

"He's the lobsterman, right?"

"Yes, he worked with Bertha for years before he got his own boat when he was twenty."

"That's pretty cool."

"I can't imagine him doing anything else." She showed Dan into the room where two twin beds remained along with her childhood treasures. Everything of Kelly's had been removed, leaving her side of the room all but empty other than the bed. On the shelves over Kara's old desk were some of her favorite books, including Nancy Drew mysteries and a few Agatha Christie novels that Bertha had given her after she'd expressed an interest in the genre.

Dan picked up the trophy she'd won at a summer tennis camp when she was fourteen. "I had no idea I was married to a champion."

"First place for the whole camp that year. I used to play a lot of tennis, but I haven't played in years. We had tournaments on the court outside when we were kids."

"That sounds fun."

"It was. Kirby always beat me, though. I don't think I ever won a match against him. Kendra was really good back in the day, too. She played on the high school team."

"You didn't play in high school?"

"I'd moved on to lacrosse by then."

"I never have understood that game."

"Most people don't unless they play or have a kid who plays. I was pretty good at it once upon a time." She held up the letter she'd earned playing varsity lacrosse.

Dan took the letter from her and examined it. "That's very sexy."

She rolled her eyes. "Honestly..."

"I'm being honest. It's sexy to picture you running down a field with your golden ponytail flying behind you as you whip the ball around and score goals." He shuddered dramatically. "Very hot."

Kara sat on the bed that still had the quilt she'd picked out when they redecorated the room. She'd gone with flowers, while Kelly had gotten an ugly black thing that Kara had found depressing. Her mother had gotten rid of that at some point, or Kelly had taken it.

"What're you thinking?" Dan asked when he sat next to her.

"How I used to share this room with Kelly and tell her all my secrets that she then used against me when it suited her purposes."

"That had to be devastating."

"It was, but I wasn't as surprised as I should've been. She'd had a mean streak, for lack of a better term, her whole life. You never knew when it would show up. Part of me has always thought that her pursuit of Matt was more about hurting me than it was about having feelings for him."

"If that's true, then she sure is stuck with him now."

"They deserve each other."

"Indeed."

"Anyway," Kara said, forcing a smile, "this is my old room."

"I'm very happy to be your new roommate."

She leaned in to kiss him. "You're the best roommate I ever had."

Dan put his arm around her. "Let's get going back to Bertha's. I want to snuggle my baby mama."

"Your baby mama would love that."

CHAPTER
Twenty~Five

"THAT WAS SURPRISINGLY FUN," Kara said when they were on their way back to Bertha's with a box of leftovers Judith had sent to her mother and brother, along with another piece of cake for Dan to have before bed because he'd loved it so much.

"It was a very nice evening. I was glad to get the chance to see Kolby and Keenan, too. Who's left for me to meet?"

"You'll meet Kellen tomorrow. He's second-in-command to my dad and Kendra at BBW."

"So your dad and Kendra are like one person?"

"More or less. She speaks for him, and everyone knows that. She doesn't want to be CEO or COO or anything like that. She wants to go to work, do her job and go home to her girls and family. But she and Kellen often disagree on the direction of the company. She didn't want the government contracts, for instance. She thought they were taking on too much. Kellen argued that it was reliable money, and they couldn't turn them down."

"I can sort of see both sides of that."

"I could, too, but it got bad between them for a while. Kendra says she doesn't want to be the big boss, but she kind of is anyway."

"Where was Hugo tonight?"

"He had a meeting with a new client in Boston and is staying overnight."

"Okay, so who else is left?"

"Kingston. I'll text him to see if we can see him at some point. You'll also see Kyle, who runs the paint shop at BBW, and Kieran, who's in charge of fiberglass, but you met them at the wedding. And then that'll be everyone. Not that you've officially met Kelly…"

"I'm good with the limited exposure I've had to her. And by the way, eleven kids are *a lot.*"

Kara howled with laughter. "*Ya think?*"

"We can't have that many. I don't care how much you beg and plead for my seed, I ain't doing it."

"Eww, and don't worry. That's not going to be an issue. Number one, I will never 'plead for your seed,' and number two, I want to be able to give our children all the love and attention they need. That's hard to do when the pot is split eleven ways."

"I'm so glad you had Bertha, Buster, Kirby, Renata and the friends who meant so much to you."

"I'm grateful to all of them every day for the roles they played in my childhood."

"I have to say… I love seeing you having peaceful, happy, fun times with your family, though. I've wished for that for you for almost as long as I've known you."

"I've been afraid to admit that I hoped for it, too. Coming home has been good for me. It reminded me that not everything here was terrible."

"We'll come here any time you want now that the seal has been broken."

"Is it weird to be low-key relieved that my brothers gave us a reason to come home?"

"Yes, it's weird," he said with a laugh, "because the reason we're here is terrible."

"Don't tell anyone I said that, but I'm glad we had a reason that couldn't be ignored no matter how much I wanted to at first. And that it wasn't some health crisis for Bertha or someone else."

"Good point, but I won't tell anyone you're glad your brothers got arrested."

"I never said that!"

She loved to make him laugh like that.

"Whatever you say, babe. I heard what I heard."

"Stop trying to make me mad when I'm in a good mood."

"How good of a mood are we talking about?"

"The best kind of mood."

"Does the good mood extend to me?"

"It did until you started spewing fiction over there."

"I'm very sorry. I take it all back."

"Don't ever let anyone say you're not a shameless opportunist."

"Guilty as charged."

He pulled into Bertha's driveway and parked to the far right so the Jeep wouldn't block in Bertha's truck. "Does that give them enough room?"

"Plenty," Kara said.

Inside, Bertha was spiking a cup of tea with a shot of bourbon, which she said was good for her aching joints after a long day on the water. She smiled when Kara went right over to hug her as Dan went to change his clothes.

"How was dinner, love?"

"Surprisingly lovely. Judith went all out with homemade stuffies, seafood casserole and her chocolate cake, which someone—mentioning no names—had two pieces of and brought another home for later."

"Her chocolate cake is to die for," Bertha said.

"She sent you and Buster some, along with enough leftovers for dinner tomorrow."

"That was nice of her."

Kara had already filled in her grandmother on Judith's visit and their conversation. "She seems to be really trying to be different."

"I see that, too. I just hope it lasts."

"I guess we'll find out."

"Who else came to dinner?"

"Kendra and the girls, Kolby and Keenan. It was a nice time. Dad invited us to come by the office tomorrow so Dan can check it out, and we're going to lunch after."

"I'm happy for you, sweetheart. I've long hoped to see you reconcile with them in a meaningful way. Estrangements are exhausting. Just ask your father about that."

"Yeah, they are exhausting, and I'm glad, too."

Dan returned to the kitchen. "Where'd you put that cake, hon?"

"I hid it from you."

"I'll find it. I can sniff out cake like a dog with a bone."

Bertha laughed. "Take pity on him, Kara. He's a growing boy."

"Please, Kara. I need my cake."

She rolled her eyes at him and went to get it from the hiding spot in Bertha's bread box.

"Yesss!"

Bertha handed him a fork.

"Don't moan to me that you're getting a dad bod," Kara said as she fixed herself a glass of ice water.

"You like when I moan to you," he said around a mouthful of cake.

Kara gave him her sternest look. "Not in front of Bertha."

Bertha rocked with silent laughter. "Oh, how I love you two."

"We love you, too," Kara said. "We're coming up here more

often going forward. I don't want to go months and months without seeing you."

"Don't do anything on my account, love. I know you worry about me running out of years, but I'm not going anywhere. I've got a lot of living left to do." She placed her hand gently on Kara's baby belly. "And another great-grandchild to raise and teach our way of life."

Overwhelmed with love for the woman who'd been her true north her entire life, Kara hugged her and blinked back tears. "You'd better be sticking around. I can't raise this kiddo without you."

"You won't have to, love. I promise."

"DID YOU KNOW THAT CAKE MAKES ME HORNY?" DAN whispered in the dark when they were tucked into bed.

"Hush. That's not happening with my grandmother and uncle across the hall."

"We can be so quiet."

"You've never been quiet a second in your life."

"That's not true. I can be silent when needed."

"I don't trust you, especially when you're hopped up on sugar."

"You may be right, but let's be honest. I'm not the weak link when it comes to being quiet during sex..."

Kara pinched his lips shut, which only silenced him for a second.

He wriggled free, like he always did. "If this situation drags on, we're going to need our own place so we can get back to business as usual around here."

"It's not going to drag on, because my husband will tell you he's an amazing lawyer who knows how to get things done."

"That is true, but even he isn't Superman."

"Isn't he? According to him—"

Dan kissed her, making her laugh.

"The truth hurts, doesn't it?"

"Shhh, I'm kissing my wife. I can't hear you." His hand slid up her leg, ducked under her T-shirt and over her baby belly to cup her breast before she could recall that she'd told him this wasn't happening.

Though she was sure Bertha and Buster were dead asleep by now, she still couldn't get past them being right across the hall in the tiny house. "Dan…"

"Hmm?"

"I can't."

"You can. Just relax and trust me."

"I trust you to be loud."

"I'll be so quiet, you won't even know I'm here."

The thought of that was so preposterous that she started laughing and couldn't stop, until he gently pinched her super-sensitive nipple and made her gasp.

"Shhh."

How did he change her mind, which had been resolute a few minutes ago, with only a few kisses and caresses that set her on fire for more? Resisting him was futile when she wanted him desperately. He was a master at getting clothes off with a minimum of fuss and was inside her so quickly, she could barely prepare before he was kissing her to keep her quiet.

He was right. She was the weak link when it came to being noisy during sex.

His lips curved into a smile against her lips as he moved in her, making the bed creak and her heart race. How did he do that to her every time? Even when she'd planned to say no? Even when her grandmother and uncle were—*hopefully*—sleeping across the hall?

Ugh, the very thought of them close by was almost enough to ruin her chances of making it to the big finish but leave it to Dan to get her there. Every. Single. Time.

He muffled the sounds she made with another deep kiss as he joined her, panting and clinging to each other.

"Weak link," he muttered as he nestled into the curve of her neck.

"Shut up."

"Just sayin'..."

"Go to sleep, Dan."

"Yes, ma'am. But first, I need to tell you that I love you more than anything in this whole wide world."

"You're forgiven."

Kara fell asleep with her arms around her love and a smile on her face.

DAN'S FIRST ORDER OF BUSINESS—AFTER A RUN AND A cup of coffee—was to check in with Carter about where he was with getting video footage from the bar.

"I was just going to call you," Carter said. "I've got the security film and am reviewing it now."

"And you know who we're looking for?"

"Yep, I got the photo Clarissa sent."

"Great job. Thank you."

"I'll call you in a bit with an update. I also spoke with Tanya's parents and brother yesterday afternoon, and they confirmed that the ex-boyfriend didn't go quietly. They said she was handling it and there was no way he could ever have harmed her. They'd been together for years, he loved her so much, etcetera. Tanya and her parents had chosen not to involve the police because their two families are friends."

Dan groaned. "That might've been a big mistake."

"Your thinking matches mine."

"If we can put him in that bar where she was dancing and kissing another man, this could be game over."

"I agree. For what it's worth, Tanya had never mentioned Keith to them or indicated concerns with anyone else in her life."

"Keith said she didn't mention him to them because they wouldn't have approved of her seeing a much older man. Send me everything you have on the ex-boyfriend. I'll get some people in my office looking into his whereabouts last weekend."

"Texting it to you now."

"Thanks, Carter."

"No problem. I'm also talking to Tanya's local friend Lauren this morning, to confirm that she was happy seeing Keith over the summer. I'll be back to you as soon as I have you can use."

"Great. Thanks again."

The information Carter conveyed, combined with what they already knew and no new information from the prosecution, had Dan feeling optimistic about Thursday's hearing. He sent a text to Chuck and Judith, updating them. At the end, he added, *Please ask everyone to be there in support of Keith and Kirby. This is a time for a united front, and having the entire family there will send a message that you're all behind them and believe in them.*

Chuck wrote back right away. *We'll make sure everyone is there. Thanks for all you're doing. I feel much better after reading your update.*

Hang in there.

Thank you, Dan, Judith said. *We'll never forget what you've done for us.*

Happy to help.

He got up, stretched the muscles that'd gone rigid while he was sitting and went to check on his sleeping beauty.

With her hands together under her cheeks, she looked like an angel.

Dan stretched out next to her and ran a hand over her bare arm.

"Mmm. Is that my husband or some random guy who's come to ravish me?"

"Is that a fantasy or something?"

She opened her laughing eyes. "Wouldn't you like to know?"

"Yes, I actually would like to know."

"Don't start your foolishness first thing in the morning."

"It's almost noon. I've been up for hours."

She sat straight up. "It's *noon*?"

"Nah," he said, chuckling. "Just a little after nine."

She walloped him with a closed fist to the shoulder.

"Ow."

"That was a mean thing to do to your pregnant wife."

"It was kind of funny."

"Not even a little bit funny."

He pinched his fingers together. "Little tiny bit."

"We're in a fight as of right now."

She got up and left the room, slamming the bathroom door.

Dan would have to do some groveling to come back from this, but that was okay. Groveling with her—anything with her—was more fun than anything he'd ever done before. His phone rang with a call from Kendall James, the attorney covering for him on Gansett Island.

"Hey, Kendall."

"Hi, Dan. How's it going up there?"

"We're making some progress and hoping for good news at the preliminary hearing on Thursday."

"Keep us posted. Everyone here is asking after you and Kara."

"That's nice to hear."

They reviewed a number of pending cases that Kendall was handling in his absence, including the estate of Jim Sturgil, who'd died during the hurricane.

"I heard you had some history with him," Kendall said.

"You could say that. He stabbed me at my engagement party."

"So I heard."

"He was pissed that I took over his practice after people quit him for being a dick to his ex-wife and daughter. It was one of those reap-what-you-sow things. He showed up at the engagement party drunk and looking for trouble, and he found it."

"Damn, where'd he get you?"

"He sliced my palm wide open with a carving knife."

Kara returned to the bedroom as he said those words. Her eyes went wide with questions.

"Oh my God! Was he disbarred?"

"No, because no one involved in the incident wanted that, including me. We just wanted him to leave us alone, which he mostly did after he returned to the island following a few months in jail while the legalities played out."

"Wow, and here I thought nothing much of anything went on out here."

"A lot goes on there."

"That's what I'm finding."

"How are your sons settling in?"

"They love it so far and have made some friends at school. We've agreed to give it this year to see what we think, and then we'll decide if we want to stay."

"Watch out for Gansett. It gets under your skin very quickly. I never thought I'd permanently relocate to a tiny island off the Rhode Island coast, but it's home now."

"My brothers love it here, and I like living near them again. We'll see what happens."

"Thank you for covering the practice for me while I'm away. You showed up right on time."

"Happy to help. I'll update you by email in the next day or two."

"Perfect. Have a great day."

"You do the same, and good luck in court."

"Thanks."

"Who were you talking to about Jim Sturgil and the butcher knife?" Kara asked.

"Kendall James. She hadn't heard the whole story."

"I hate that story."

Dan glanced at the thin white line across his palm. "Ancient history."

"Not ancient enough for me." She shuddered. "I'll never forget that day."

"I remember the good things. The way you tended to me and kissed it better was the part I recall."

She brushed her reddish-blonde hair until it was a shiny waterfall down her back. "You would remember that."

"Let's get some breakfast into you, and then I'll take you to see Kirby before we meet your dad at the office. I'm looking forward to seeing this company I've heard so much about."

"Yes, me, too."

"Why do you sound less than enthusiastic about a visit to the company?"

"Do I?"

"Uh-huh." He put his hands on her shoulders and gave her a gentle massage, startled by the tension he felt in her rigid muscles. "What's wrong, sweetheart?"

"Nothing. I'm fine. Really..."

He turned her to face him. "Talk to me."

"There're a lot of emotions tied up in the company—some good, some bad, some truly awful."

"We don't have to go there if it's too much for you."

"I want to show it to you. It was a big part of my life here. It's definitely something you should see."

"Not if it causes you pain."

"I'm okay. I promise, and I'd like to see everyone there. It's been a minute."

"If you're sure." He kissed her and tucked a strand of silky hair behind her ear. "I'm going to grab a shower while you have something to eat. Bertha left you an egg sandwich if you feel up to it."

"That sounds good. I can't believe how much better I've felt since I had that IV."

"I'm so glad about that. I hate to see you suffering."

"It's a small price to pay for our little miracle."

"I hope she looks just like her gorgeous mama."

"I think he is going to look just like his handsome daddy, and he's going to talk as much as you do, if not more. In fact, I may need to invest in earplugs to survive you two."

"You really think we're having a boy?"

"I honestly don't know, but it's just a feeling I have. And the desire for earplugs has been growing along with the baby."

"You think you're so funny with that, don't you?"

"I only speak the truth, my love."

Dan smiled. "If my son is one-tenth the orator that I am, he'll have a very successful life."

Kara rolled her eyes. "God help me."

CHAPTER
Twenty-Six

KARA THOUGHT she was prepared to see Kirby in jail. She was dead wrong about that. The sight of him in an orange jumpsuit broke her heart and had tears rolling down her face. "Can I hug him?" she asked the guard.

"For a second."

Kara went to her brother and held on tight for as long as she could, until the guard said, "That's enough."

She wiped her face as she sat next to Dan, across a table from Kirby. "I'm sorry to be so emotional."

"It's all right. I'm glad to see you, even if I hate that it's happening here." He looked exhausted and hadn't shaved in days, which was jarring. She'd never seen him with stubble or a beard, as he was always meticulously groomed when he wasn't at work.

Kara reached across the table for hands roughened by hard work. "Everyone knows you had nothing to do with this. It's all anyone is talking about."

"Keith didn't either. I was there when we drove away from her. I dropped him off at home. He said he was exhausted and heading straight to bed. I might've checked his location a little later to make sure he stayed put. He did."

"That's good info, Kirby," Dan said. "I'll be sure to mention it at the hearing."

"How do you think that'll go?"

"I'm cautiously optimistic. We've got a few things to introduce that'll take the prosecution by surprise and should give the judge enough reason to dismiss the charges, but that's never a guarantee."

"I'm going crazy in here. You've got to get me out."

"I'm doing everything in my power to make that happen. You have to stay strong, no matter how this goes. The truth is on your side."

"Why do I feel like that doesn't matter at all?"

"It does. Of course it does."

"But you've made a career out of exonerating wrongly accused prisoners. Don't act like there's no chance I'll be convicted even though there isn't a shred of evidence connecting me to her."

Dan sighed as he sat back in his seat. "I'm not going to lie to you. It happens. More often than it should, but there're almost always extenuating circumstances, just enough for prosecutors to create a convincing narrative. There's nothing like that in your case."

"But there is for Keith?"

"His situation is trickier. He was with her and had sex with her in the bathroom at the bar. He'd been seeing her over the summer."

"I knew that."

"He also knew how she'd gone through a rough breakup with her high school boyfriend, Billy Norton, who wasn't taking it well. Tanya swore she saw Billy in the Barnacle Friday night. We're reviewing video as we speak to look for him. If we can show he was there, then we've got someone with an actual motive for murder. Maybe he was outraged to see her carrying on with Keith. Maybe she'd agreed to meet him after she parted with you and Keith, and that's why she didn't want a ride home. These are all possibilities that can be introduced to create reasonable doubt about your involvement and Keith's. What reason would he have to kill her when she hung out with him willingly many times before?"

"Wow," Kirby said. "Hearing that makes me feel a lot better."

"Please don't give up hope," Kara said. "Dan will never stop fighting for you no matter what happens at the hearing."

"Thank you," Kirby said to Dan before shifting his gaze to her. "And you, for coming back here when it's the last place you want to be."

"It's been good for me to come home. I hate that it was because of this, but it's been nice to be here."

"Have you seen Kelly?"

"Once, for a minute, but it was no big deal."

"Good. Keep your distance. She hasn't changed one bit after everything."

"I wouldn't expect her to change at this point, but I'd like to know Connor at some point."

"When he's older and can decide for himself."

"That's the plan."

"When are you due?"

"November."

"Do you know what you're having?"

"We chose not to find out for sure, but I think it's a boy."

"What will his name be?"

"Dylan—either way—after Dan's late brother."

Kirby looked at Dan. "I didn't know. I'm sorry."

"Thanks."

"What happened to him?"

"He died years ago in Afghanistan."

"Oh wow. I really am sorry."

"Me, too." Dan put his arm around Kara. "I'm looking forward to meeting Dylan Torrington the second."

"I'm not sure the world is ready for Dan Torrington's offspring," Kara said.

Kirby laughed, which pleased her. "I'm sure he'll be great, just like his dad."

"Time's up," the guard said in a jarring reminder of where they were and what was at stake.

Kirby stood and leaned in to hug Kara again before they were told not to.

"I love you," Kara said. "I'll never give up on you, and neither will Dan."

"Means everything. Love you, too."

After Kirby was led away, Kara broke down into sobs.

Dan held her, stroking her back and telling her it was going to be okay.

"You were right. I wasn't prepared to see him in here." Kara used her sleeve to wipe the tears off her face. "I'd like to see Keith, too."

"I'll let them know."

WHILE HE WAS GONE, KARA BLEW HER NOSE AND TRIED to pull herself together, knowing her brusque older brother would be put off by her tears. Even though she wasn't close to Keith, seeing him in an orange jumpsuit put a new lump in her throat.

"Fancy meeting you here," Keith said with a crooked grin for his sister.

"Are you doing okay?"

"I'm just great. Never thought I'd see you in these parts again."

"Funny how a single phone call can change everything."

"Thanks for coming even though you had no good reason to."

"I had two good reasons to come, and I'm glad I did. Other than this, of course, it's been good for me to be back here. It's been too long."

"Well, I, for one, wouldn't have blamed you if you'd told us to fuck off after everything that went down."

"I'd never do that."

"You're a better person than I am."

"Duh."

Keith barked out a laugh that softened his rough exterior. "Good one."

"Kirby just told me something interesting," Dan said, filling Keith in on how his brother had checked his location after he dropped him off.

"He's such a fucking mother hen."

"Who keeps you out of trouble," Kara said.

"Yeah, he does, and I feel sick that he's gotten caught up in this bullshit." He gave Kara an intense stare. "You know it's bullshit, right? I may be an asshole at times, but I'm not a murderer."

"I know that, Keith."

"That's the worst part of this whole thing, you know? That people could think I'd hurt a woman. I've had my share of fights and scrapes, but always with someone who could fight back. Never with a woman."

"That's good to know," Dan said. "We can resist their efforts to introduce your past charges by saying you've only ever fought with men. Never with a woman."

"Never, ever, *ever*. If they say otherwise, it's a fucking lie."

"I'll fight for you. I promise."

"Thank you. I'm sorry again if I was a dick…"

"It's okay."

"Nah, it really isn't. I took it out on you—both times—and it wasn't and isn't your fault. You're trying to help and sitting here with nothing but time on my hands, I've come to recognize that."

Kara was impressed by Keith's insight and felt her heart go

out to him in a way it never had before. She'd tended to avoid him, sensing the potential peril that accompanied him and his rough attitude.

"Thanks for coming, you guys. We appreciate you putting your own lives on hold to help us."

"Let us know if you need anything," Kara said.

"Mom's been bringing me stuff. I'm okay."

Kara gave her brother a quick hug before the guard led him away.

"Are you okay?" Dan asked.

"As okay as I can be after seeing my brothers in jail." She followed him through a door he knocked on to have opened for them. "What did he mean about both times?"

"Uhhh, well..."

"Must've been the time you got them out of jail on the morning of our wedding."

Dan stopped short and turned to her. "You know about that?"

Kara patted him on the face. "Dan, honey, wives know *everything*. For someone so smart, I would've expected you to figure that out by now."

"Seriously, though, how'd you find out?"

Kara headed for the main entrance, eager to get out of there. "I'll never tell."

EVERYTHING HAD BEEN WEIRD AT WORK SINCE THE night Myles had stopped by Renata's house. She kept waiting for him to say something about their conversation that night, but he didn't. In fact, he didn't say much about anything over the next couple of days. Rather, he kept to himself in his office, with his head down, getting more work done in a day than he normally did in a week, or so it seemed to her.

There was no chitchat, no teasing banter about her paper cut or random coffees showing up on her desk along with the lemon Danish he knew she loved.

Damn it all to hell, she missed him.

And that infuriated her. What the hell was wrong with her? She'd told him exactly why she could never date her boss, and apparently, he'd respected her thoughts on the matter by backing off.

So why did she feel like absolute shit?

Renata grabbed her phone and took it outside for a break. Not that she'd done a damned thing to deserve a break, but she was taking one, nonetheless.

She called Kara, thankful to have her best friend close by for once. Until Kara came home, she hadn't realized how much she'd truly missed having her around.

"Hey! How's it going?"

"Awesome."

"What's wrong?"

"Tell me what you're up to first." She wanted to be respectful of why Kara was in town. The arrests of Keith and Kirby counted as real problems compared to her manufactured situation.

"Dan and I just came from seeing Keith and Kirby."

"How're they holding up?"

"Okay, I guess. We're all hopeful for the preliminary hearing on Thursday."

"What's the plan for that?"

"I'm not really supposed to say anything about it, but Dan has a strategy that he's hoping will work."

"I'll hope and pray that it does."

"Me, too. Now, why are you sarcastically awesome?"

"Because I told Myles to back off, and he did."

"Ummm... Isn't that what you wanted?"

"I thought it was until he actually did it."

Kara laughed. "Can you see how ridiculous that is?"

"Yes! I know it is, but it was the right thing to tell him how my parents' marriage was eventually ruined because of work-place drama."

"You're not your mother, and he's not your father."

"It's a similar situation, though."

"How so? He owns the company outright. It's not like he has a brother-partner who's going to be pissed about him secretly dating an employee for *years* before marrying her."

"You're supposed to tell me the many reasons why I absolutely shouldn't date my boss, not give me permission."

"If you'd like to send me a script, I'll follow it to the letter, and then I'll tell you you're making a mountain out of what doesn't even count as a molehill."

"That's not in the script!"

Kara, that bitch, laughed again. "You're being ridiculous. You liked Myles—a lot, as I recall—before he was your boss. In fact, I thought you were on your way to dating him then."

"The same thing stopped me. He wasn't technically my boss, but I knew he would be someday soon."

"Here's a novel idea. Get another job. Then you'll be free and clear to date the man you've wanted for quite some time but couldn't allow yourself to have because of the job."

"I like this job."

"Do you like him more than the job?"

"How the hell do I know?"

"You know, Renata, which is why you're all tied up in knots over this. You like him. A lot. You have for a long time. Do you have any idea how often his name comes up when we chat? Myles said this, Myles said that, Myles brought me a mocha shake, Myles did the funniest thing..."

"That isn't true. I don't talk about him like that."

"You do, pal, and you have for years. I've been wondering when something was going to come of that. And you admitted, just the other night, that you're attracted to him."

Renata moaned. "I hate you since you married that goddamned lawyer."

Kara cackled with laughter.

"It's not funny. Your argumentativeness has gotten much worse."

Kara just continued to laugh and laugh.

"I really do hate you."

"You do not, so shut your face. I'm telling you the truth, which you say you don't want to hear, but you really *do* because you want to date Myles. Among other things."

"Stop!"

"Not going to stop. Listen, Ren, there's absolutely no reason you can't be with Myles if you want to be. If you can't deal with him being your technical boss, even if he never acts like he has power over you, then leave the job. But don't turn your back on someone who could become your forever."

Renata groaned at the word *forever*, but Kara pressed on, undeterred.

"Take it from me, I tried that, and thankfully, all my efforts to hold Dan at arm's length failed. It would've been a big mistake to turn my back on him simply because of some obstacles that were easily overcome once I decided to take the risk."

"My mother would never forgive me for dating my boss."

"Your mother's life and mistakes aren't your burden to carry. Her regrets aren't going to become yours simply because the situation is similar."

"I hate you even more when you're right."

"You're making me laugh harder than Dan does, and that's not easy to do. Are we still on for dinner tonight, or are we in the biggest fight?"

"We're on for dinner, but you'd better not be smug about being right for the first time ever."

"*Whatever.* Why don't you ask Myles to join us? I'd love to meet him."

"That's not going to happen."

"Why not?"

"Because."

"Renata... You're being ridiculous."

"I'm not. It's just, you know..."

"Chris was a long, *long* time ago."

"Believe me. I know."

Hearing his name was enough to make Renata want to crawl into the fetal position with a week's worth of mocha shakes and Netflix for days and days.

"It's really hard to take that kind of chance again, after what happened to both of us with our first loves. I can't tell you how hard I resisted what was happening with Dan, and you know what I realize now?"

"What's that?"

"How much time I wasted that could've been spent being happy."

"I've never been gutsy like you are."

"Shut all the way up with that shit! You're the badass I've always wanted to be! Remember when that awful girl in school was hassling me, and you punched her in the face?"

"And got suspended and spent six weeks with my broken hand in plaster?"

"That was the coolest thing I'd ever seen, and it's still right up there in my all-time top ten. Please don't tell me you don't have the fortitude to at least try to see if this thing with Myles is the real deal."

"I thought I had the real deal before."

"That was nowhere close to the real deal. He was a boy pretending to be a man, and he didn't deserve you."

"And Myles does?"

"Myles is a full-grown man with a good job, and he's nice to you, which is already three thousand steps above what's-his-name. I like him, and I haven't even met him yet. Bring him to dinner, and I'll give you a more thorough assessment after."

"If I ask him to do something, it'll give him hope."

"I'm starting to wonder if maybe *you* don't deserve *him*."

"That's rude. You're supposed to be on my side at all times."

"I am, Ren. You know I am. Give this guy a chance. I want to dance at your wedding."

"Shut up before you jinx me, and PS, just because you're all blissfully married doesn't mean I want to be."

"Fair enough, but you deserve to be happy. You just need to give yourself permission to let it happen."

Normally, if she was gone this long, Myles would come looking for her. That he didn't even poke his head out the door made her feel oddly sad at having lost something she'd never really had in the first place.

"Should I make the reservation for four?"

"I'll let you know." She checked her phone after she received a text. "Hey, Ellery texted to say her kids are playing soccer this afternoon if we want to swing by to watch the game. We could do dinner after that."

"I'd love to. Send me the info."

"Will do. She'll be thrilled if you come."

"I'm looking forward to seeing the kids."

"You won't believe how big they are."

"I'm excited."

"I'm texting you the info she sent now. Can't wait to see you."

"Who can't you wait to see?" Myles asked from behind her. "Are you seeing someone else? Is that the real reason you won't go out with me?"

Renata took a deep breath to calm herself before she turned to him, flashing a big smile. "That was my cousin Kara, who has absolutely no interest in dating me." She brushed by him as she headed back to the office, working up a good head of steam as she went. How dare he eavesdrop on her conversation and then jump to conclusions?

And no, she didn't find his obvious jealousy appealing. At all.

Well, maybe it was a *little* appealing...

No. No, it wasn't.

Myles appeared next to her desk. "I'm sorry. I had no business listening to your call and then acting like a jackass."

"No, you didn't. And for the record, I'm not seeing anyone, which you know because you're with me every day, and if I was seeing someone, you'd probably be aware of it."

"Can you come into the office for a second?"

"Uh, yeah. I guess." *What the hell is this about?* she wondered as she followed him.

CHAPTER
Twenty~Seven

"HAVE A SEAT," Myles said as he settled behind the desk that had been his grandfather's and father's before him.

Renata sat in his visitor chair.

"I talked to my dad about the future of the company, and we want to make you an offer."

She eyed him warily. "What kind of offer?"

"We agree that your contributions can't be easily summarized or given a value because, quite frankly, we'd be screwed without you. I'm sure you've been thinking it'd be easier to get another job than to deal with whatever's going on between the two of us—and don't say there's nothing going on."

"Okay, I won't," Renata said with a small smile as an oddly warm feeling overtook her before a slightly horrifying thought occurred to her. "Did you tell your dad there's something going on between us?" she asked in a high, squeaky voice that had her clearing the panic from her throat. She'd die of embarrassment if the delightful Mr. Williams ever thought she was anything other than professional at work.

"Not in so many words, but I told him I thought it was high

time we made you a partner in the business—and he completely agreed."

Renata was stunned speechless, which didn't happen very often. A partner in the company. Had she heard him correctly?

"Are... are you doing this for the right reasons, Myles?"

"What would be the right reasons?"

"Because I truly deserve it and not because you want to sleep with me."

The minute she asked the question, she regretted it because he looked like she'd slapped him across the face.

"You truly deserve it, and you know you do. You've been the heart and soul of this place for going on a decade. We value and appreciate your contributions, and we wish to reward you by making you a partner." He handed over a sheet of paper that outlined the offer, including the significant increase in pay as well as a paragraph about profit sharing that made her eyes bug out when she saw what the number would've been for the previous year, which had been given as an example.

"As you know, this year has been better than last, so you can expect quite a bit more than what it would've been in that example. We're prepared to make this offer retroactive to last January first, so you'd benefit from your hard work this year, which has been our busiest one yet."

Renata's mind raced with a million thoughts that overwhelmed her all at once, one in particular—that he'd said the exact right thing after she foolishly questioned his motives in making the offer.

"What do you think?"

"It's... um... a very generous offer, and I appreciate the recognition."

"You've earned it, Renata. My dad and I agree completely on that."

"Could I think about it?"

The question clearly surprised him. "Of course. Take as much time as you need."

"Thank you for this. It means a lot to me."

"Thank you for everything you do to keep things running so smoothly here. Much of our success is due to your hard work."

Renata needed to get out of there before she embarrassed herself by breaking down. She got up and took the offer letter with her when she left his office. She was through the door when she turned back to him. "Would you like to go to a soccer game and dinner with my cousin and her husband later this afternoon?"

"Are you going to be there, too?" he asked, smiling as his eyes danced with amusement.

Renata sighed with exasperation. "Yes."

"Then I'd like that very much."

She nodded and returned to her desk, where she sat for a long moment to gather herself and process what'd just happened.

They'd offered her a partnership.

She'd asked Myles out on what could only be considered a date.

Holy shit.

DAN WAS ASTOUNDED BY THE SHEER SCOPE AND SIZE OF the Ballard Boat Works campus. He'd seen pictures online, but they didn't do justice to the vast enterprise he saw before him. Spanning about twenty acres, the yard included multiple large white buildings bearing the maroon company logo, as well as a full marina and a mechanism that Kara called a travel lift, which was used to haul boats out of the water and put them back in.

He watched as a huge sailboat was slowly moved to another location.

"We call this 'the hard,'" Kara said of the asphalt area where boats were lined up on stands and blocks. "You're either in the water or on the hard."

At the far end of the complex, a two-story white building with the BBW logo housed the executive offices.

"Do some of your brothers still oversee the launch services in other harbors?"

"They do that from here, with managers running the business locally. I'm the only one who's onsite and also works as a driver."

"Ah, I see." He knew how much she loved being on the water, driving the launches.

Outside the main doors were barrels containing red geraniums still in bloom in the bright autumn sunshine.

"This is incredible, Kara. It's way more than I imagined."

"It's a lot," she said with a dry chuckle as she led him into the office building.

An older woman working the reception desk let out a cry of excitement as she got up to greet Kara with a hug. "It's so good to see you!"

"You, too. This is my husband, Dan. Dan, meet Marilee, the one who holds the whole operation together."

"I wouldn't go that far." Marilee's cheeks turned pink with embarrassment. "And it's lovely to finally meet Kara's esteemed husband. We've heard so much about you."

Dan shook her hand. "Nice to meet you, too."

"I've followed your impressive career."

"Thank you."

"Is Dad in?" Kara asked.

"He's waiting for you in his office and couldn't be more excited for your visit."

"This way," Kara said, leading Dan toward a staircase to the second floor.

As they walked down a long hallway, people called out hellos to Kara. She stopped at the second-to-last office on the right.

"Hey, sis! I heard you were coming in today." He got up, came around his desk and hugged her.

"Dan, meet my oldest brother, Kellen, the company's chief strategy officer."

The two men shook hands. Kellen, who was about six feet tall, with blue eyes and the same reddish-blond hair Kara had, looked like a more refined version of Keith.

"Glad to finally meet you," Kellen said. "Your reputation precedes you."

"We don't say much about that," Kara said. "Goes straight to his fat head."

Kellen laughed while Dan gave his wife a playful scowl.

"It's really good to see you, Kara."

"You, too. Been too long."

"Sure has, and of course, we all hate the reason you had to come home."

"It hasn't been all bad."

"I'm glad to hear that. Dad is looking forward to showing Dan around and having you guys visit."

"Is Kendra here?"

"She had to take Luna to the dentist, but she'll be back in a bit."

"Ah, okay. Hopefully, we'll catch her before we leave. Can you join us for lunch, Kell?"

"I'd love to, but I'm up to my eyeballs today. Rain check?"

"Absolutely. Let's go see Dad."

The door to Chuck's office, located at the end of the hallway, was propped open, but Kara knocked anyway. "Anyone home?"

"Come in!" Chuck came around the desk to greet them both with hugs. "I'm so glad to see you here, sweetheart."

"It's nice to be here."

Dan could tell by her expression that she meant that, and she wouldn't have felt that way a week ago. That was a big relief to him. He'd feared the visit home would set her back, but he should've known better. His Kara was resilient and thrilled to see the people she loved and far more able now to rise above the people who'd hurt her than she'd been when she left this place.

"Let's go on a tour and then grab some lunch," Chuck said as he donned a maroon BBW jacket with a white logo on the chest. "I'm starving."

"You're always starving," Kara said.

"Some things never change," Chuck replied with a chuckle. "Keenan is in your old office."

Kara ducked her head in to say hello to the youngest Ballard sibling, who looked ridiculously grown-up sitting behind the desk that'd once been hers.

"Is Dad taking you to lunch? Can I go?"

"No, you can't go," Chuck said. "This is Kara's day, and you've soaked me for lunch twice this week already."

"Fine," Keenan said with an exaggerated pout. "Would it kill you to bring me something back?"

"We'll see," Chuck said. "He's a bottomless pit, as always."

"Like father, like son," Kara said.

"I can't even deny that."

She greeted several other employees and introduced Dan.

All of them commented on his career and expressed their thanks for him helping Keith and Kirby.

Chuck led the way downstairs. "I'll be back in a bit, Marilee."

"Have a nice lunch. So great to see you, Kara and Dan."

"You, too, Marilee."

"We'll start in the fabrication shop." Chuck led them into one of the cavernous white buildings where hulls of a wide variety of shapes and sizes were under construction. "Over here, we have several of the open-air launches like Kara has on the island, moving into our thirty-two-foot, thirty-eight-foot and forty-four-foot picnic boats, which have become our most popular products. We can't make them fast enough to meet the demand."

"Sounds like a good problem to have," Dan said.

"It is, most of the time. We've had a few cancellations since the boys were arrested, which is worrisome."

A man with gray hair and wearing a BBW fleece jacket approached them. "Hey, Kara. It's nice to see you."

"Hi, Mark. This is my husband, Dan. Mark is one of our designers."

Dan shook hands with him. "The boats are gorgeous."

"Thanks. We're proud of them."

Everyone working in the shop—or so it seemed to Dan—came over to say hi to Kara and meet her husband, some of them hugging her like the old friends they were. The same thing happened in the wood shop, where Kirby's coworkers said how much he was missed and that they hoped he'd be released soon, and again in the paint shop, her brother Kyle's domain.

He gave Kara a quick hug and an even quicker nod to Dan, who'd last seen him at their wedding—including when he'd bailed him, Keith and Kieran out of the Gansett Island jail.

"How long are you here for?" Kyle asked Kara.

She glanced at Dan. "Depends on how long the court stuff takes."

"We're hoping to get it resolved soon," Dan said.

"That'd be good. The charges are bogus."

"We're doing everything we can," Dan said.

"Well, it was good of you guys to come. We all appreciate it."

"You'll be in court on Thursday?" Chuck asked his son.

Kyle nodded. "I got the text. I'll be there."

"See you then," Kara said.

"It's nice to see you, sis."

"You, too."

They continued their tour through the fiberglass department, where Kieran was in charge. He was the blondest of all the siblings, with sleeve tattoos that extended to his neck and black gauges affixed to his earlobes. He gave Dan a quick overview of how a design became a boat and discussed the various techniques they employed to make their boats distinctive.

"Every part of this is so interesting to me," Dan said. "I've never given much thought to how boats are built."

"They go from us to paint and then to wood with Kirby," Kieran said. "Then it's finish work on the interiors."

"Thanks for taking the time to show me your corner of it," Dan said.

"No problem."

"How's things at The Trap?" Kara asked of the bar her brother owned.

"Business is brisk, as always."

"Glad to hear it."

"Stop by for a drink anytime. Just give me a heads up so I can warn the natives that my sister is coming by."

Kara patted her pregnant belly. "I'll take you up on that after the baby is born."

"Sounds good." Kieran gave Kara a hug. "Don't be a stranger around here. We miss you."

"Miss you, too. Thanks for the tour."

"Any time."

Next, they checked out the fabric shop, where the distinctive maroon-and-white-striped cushions were made along with pillows, canopies and other accessories, before ending up at the marina office, which was still doing brisk business in late September.

"This is our in-between season," Chuck said. "We still have transients coming into the marina while others are starting to haul for the winter. By late October, we'll be hauling twenty to thirty boats a day."

"I couldn't be more impressed by your operation," Dan said.

"Thank you. We're proud of what we've built. When I came into the business, it was a marina with a small sideline building one line of boats. We've grown it exponentially in the last forty-odd years. But like anything worth having, it hasn't been without its challenges."

"I can only imagine."

"Let's have some lunch, shall we? Mom is meeting us in town."

THEY WERE HALFWAY THROUGH AN ENJOYABLE LUNCH with her parents when Dan received a text that had him excusing himself to make a call.

"What do you suppose that's about?" Chuck asked anxiously as he watched Dan walk away, phone pressed to his ear.

"He was waiting for some updates from the investigators he has working on the case," Kara said. "Hopefully, that's what it is."

"The tension is going to kill me," Judith said bluntly.

"Don't be dramatic," Chuck said.

"I'm not. We come here all the time." Judith gave a tentative look at the crowded restaurant beyond their table. "And yet, I feel the judgment of everyone in here. They're wondering if my sons are capable of killing a woman."

"I know it's awful, Mom," Kara said. "But Dan is working the case hard, even when it doesn't appear that anything is happening. He's doing everything he can."

"And we appreciate him—and you—so much," Chuck said. "I don't know what we would've done without him."

Kara and her parents picked at their food while they waited for Dan to return. Her stomach was in knots. She couldn't begin to know how her parents must feel.

More than fifteen minutes later, Dan returned, smiling as he came toward them. "Good news. We're able to put the victim's ex-boyfriend in the Barnacle at the same time she was there with Keith and her friends."

Judith exhaled an audible sigh of relief. "Will that exonerate Keith and Kirby?"

"I can't say for sure, but it gives us the opportunity to introduce another suspect, one who'd have true motive. Often, that's enough to get the charges tossed or at least get them released on bail while the police investigate further."

"God, I hope so," Judith said, giving voice to what they were all thinking.

After they parted company with her parents, they went back to Bertha's so Dan could do some work and Kara could rest up before their next outing. She stretched out on the sofa and listened to him on the phone, talking to the people he employed locally and in California, who were working on her brothers' case.

On the drive back to Bertha's, Dan had told her repeatedly how blown away he'd been by the company and how he hadn't expected it to be such a massive complex. "Even seeing the photos online couldn't have prepared me."

Now it was her turn to be impressed as she listened to him at work, asking questions, probing for details and beginning to form the argument he'd use at the hearing on Thursday when so much would be decided.

Kara felt for her parents as well as her brothers and hoped the situation would be resolved sooner rather than later. She couldn't fathom it dragging on indefinitely. What if it did, though? Would Dan stay involved for the long haul? The thought of that, with a baby due in eight weeks, exhausted her.

Hopefully, they'd be long gone back to Gansett by the time the baby arrived.

The next thing she knew, Dan was kissing her awake. "Hey, Sleeping Beauty. What time is the soccer game?"

"Four thirty."

"How far is it from here?"

"About twenty minutes."

"We should get going, then."

Kara stretched her arms over her head. "That was the best nap ever."

"You were out cold."

"For how long?"

"About ninety minutes."

"Holy crap."

He placed his hand on her baby belly. "You and the tiny human need your rest." The baby responded with a dropkick to Dan's palm that made him laugh. "He's going to be a handful."

"Like his daddy."

"I'll give you a handful, baby."

"Not in my grandmother's living room," she said primly.

"That prickly tone turns me on."

She gave his chest a gentle push. "Let me up, Counselor. I've got a game to get to."

CHAPTER
Twenty-Eight

KARA WOULDN'T ADMIT to anyone, even Dan, that she was nervous about seeing Ellery and Jessie again after their recent lunch had devolved into an indictment of Kara's choices after the Kelly and Matt debacle.

She hoped they could move on from past hurts, but if they couldn't, Kara wasn't about to grovel. As Dan and others had said, she'd done what she needed to in order to survive something she'd thought for a time might break her. It hadn't broken her, but it had made her stronger and more resilient than she'd been before.

"I remember bringing chairs when we went to my niece's game," Dan said.

"Oh right! Good thinking. Bertha probably still has some around here from when we were playing sports." Kara poked around in the garage and found two stadium chairs covered in dust that made her cough and then sneeze. "Found 'em!"

Dan laughed and pulled a strand of cobweb out of her hair.

"There's no spider with that, is there?"

"I don't think so, but I'll keep an eye out."

He banged the dust off the chairs and tossed them into the

back of the Jeep. When they were on their way to Trenton, Dan reached for her hand and gave it a squeeze. "I'm looking forward to meeting your friends in person."

"I'm glad that's finally happening."

"Are you excited to see them?"

"I'm more nervous than excited. The last time didn't go so well."

"I refuse to let you feel guilty about anything."

"Thank you for the reminder."

"It's easy to look back, with the benefit of hindsight, and soften the razor-sharp edges of heartbreak and make the villains a little less villainous. But they don't deserve to be redeemed or forgiven or given a pass of any kind. What Kelly and Matt did, what my ex did, what my so-called best man did, was monstrous. We're under no obligation to forgive and forget."

"You're absolutely right, and that was very well said about how time softens the sharp edges."

"I read somewhere, after Dylan died, that the human spirit is naturally resilient and how it's almost impossible to remain mired in a state of intense grief and heartbreak indefinitely. We simply can't sustain that initial level long term. I remember the first time I laughed after he died, and how bad I felt afterward. Like how can I find something funny when he's gone forever? But it was just proof that life goes on, whether we want it to or not, and there's nothing wrong with laughter, joy or happiness after a great loss. The person we're grieving wouldn't want us to be sad forever."

Kara wrapped her free hand around their joined hands. "Sometimes I feel like we don't pay enough attention, on a daily basis, to the loss of Dylan, and I'm sorry if days go by without us mentioning him."

"Please don't be. He's always with me, and like I said, I can't dwell in that space all the time. He'd be so happy you and I found each other, and he'd adore you. I know he would. He was never that fond of *her,* which should've been a sign to me. He liked everyone, except people who didn't deserve it."

"I wish I could've known him."

"I do, too. Having him around is the only thing that could make my already perfect life better."

"Your point is well taken about the march of time and how it changes things, though."

"It's inevitable, I suppose, that we can't hang on to that level of distress forever, even if it's always a part of us going forward."

"Very true."

They pulled into the parking lot at the elementary school where the rec league game was being played.

"Damn, that's a lot of cars."

"Kendra was thrilled when the girls gave up soccer for dance. She said youth soccer was the craziest thing she was ever involved in, and the games were horrible. If you looked away for one second, you'd miss the only goal of the game."

"That sounds about right. My sisters hated it when their kids played, too."

"Is this what's in store for us in a few short years?" Kara asked as Dan grabbed their chairs from the back of the Jeep and tucked them under his arm. They walked toward the field, holding hands.

"Maybe we can steer Dylan toward baseball instead. It's not quite as unhinged as soccer."

"Do we have youth soccer on the island?" Kara had never paid much attention to such things.

"Of course we do. All the kids play."

"Yay."

Dan laughed as he dropped her hand to put an arm around her.

Renata spotted them and came over to greet them. "Um, so don't shoot the messenger, but Matt's nephew is on the opposing team, and they're here."

"Awesome," Kara said through gritted teeth.

"I didn't know. I feel bad."

"Don't worry about it. It's a big field."

"Can I hug you now that I'm finally meeting you in person?" Renata asked Dan.

He put down their chairs and held out his arms to her.

Seeing the two of them hugging each other made Kara emotional as a good-looking man joined them.

"Um, this is Myles. My cousin Kara and her husband, Dan."

"Heard a lot about you both," Myles said as he shook hands with them.

"Likewise," Kara said, earning a glare from her cousin.

"Is that right?" Myles asked. "What does she say about me?"

"Please," Renata said disdainfully. "I never mention your name. Let's go watch the game."

Myles and Kara laughed as they followed Renata to where Ellery and Pete had set up camp for their family and friends.

Her friends greeted Kara with hugs and excitement to meet Dan.

Kara received hugs from Ellery's parents and her sister, who were also thrilled to see her and meet her husband.

Jessie and her boyfriend, Doug, arrived a few minutes later, and more hugs were exchanged.

"You look wonderful, Doug," Kara said when she hugged her old friend.

"Thanks. It's been a journey."

Their group formed a loud cheering squad for Ellery and Pete's son, Keaton, who scored two goals for his team's winning effort.

"Pizza's on us tonight," Pete said as they prepared to leave.

"Kara."

She turned to find Matt's sister-in-law, Hallie, who'd been her friend once upon a time. She was married to Matt's brother. "Oh, hey, Hallie. How are you?"

"I'm good. You?"

"Doing well."

"You look great."

"Thanks, so do you. Um, this is my husband, Dan. Dan, this is Hallie Gallagher."

As this was awkward enough already, she hoped he'd deduce who she was without her having to fill in the blanks for him.

"I've missed you these last few years," Hallie said.

"Me, too. How're the kids?" Kara kept her gaze fixed on Hallie as she prayed she wouldn't be ambushed by Kelly and Matt.

"Getting big. Josh just started eighth grade, and Noah is in sixth. Our youngest, Luke, is in fourth grade. He's the soccer player."

"Hey, Kara," Hallie's husband, Joe, said.

"Hi, Joe. It's nice to see you."

"You, too."

Kara introduced him to Dan, who shook his hand.

"Are you guys coming?" Pete asked.

Kara wanted to kiss him for giving her a reason to say goodbye to people who would've been her in-laws in another life. "It was great to see you guys. Give your parents my best," she said to Joe.

"Will do."

They were on their way to a clean getaway when Kelly and Matt, carrying their son, Connor, approached.

Kara cast her sister a warning look that had her backing off as they left with their friends.

"You're not even going to say hello?" Kelly called after her. "Don't you want to see your nephew?"

"Keep walking," Renata said as she turned to deal with Kelly. "Go away, Kelly, and leave her alone. That's what you wanted, right? Well, be careful what you wish for."

"I never wanted this! For her to act like she doesn't know me when we see each other!"

"What did you think was going to happen?" Renata asked. "You made your choices, and now you get to live with them. I hope he was worth it."

"Let's go, Renata," Myles said gently. "The others are waiting for us."

Kara hated that her hands were shaking. Why did that happen when she hadn't done anything wrong?

Dan kept his arm wrapped tightly around her as they walked with their group toward the parking lot.

"She has some fucking nerve," Renata muttered.

"In case I forget to tell you later," Dan said, "that was well done, cousin."

"Very well done," Ellery said. "I can't believe her."

"I can," Jessie said. "Same old Kelly she's always been, doing what she wants without giving a shit how it affects anyone else and then acting all surprised when people are pissed at her."

Kara listened to what they were saying as outrage bubbled up inside her. She stopped walking, which meant the others stopped, too.

"Are you okay?" Dan asked.

"Yes, I'm fine. Give me just a second, will you?"

"Kara..."

"I'm okay. I swear." She turned back toward her sister, who hadn't moved since they walked away.

She knew Dan would follow her, but she kept her gaze on her targets.

Matt saw her coming and alerted Kelly.

"What do you want?" Kelly asked.

"That's what I wanted to ask you. What is it that you want from me? When you ambush me in public, what're you expecting to happen?"

Kelly, who was a petite blonde with gorgeous blue eyes and

flawless skin that Kara had envied all their lives, seemed uncertain of how to reply.

So Kara waited.

"I guess I just wish we could fix what's broken between us."

"Let me ask you this... If I'd done to you what you did to me, would you be looking for reconciliation?"

Kelly had the good sense to at least squirm a little. "I don't know."

"Yes, you do. You never would've spoken to me again, so you've already gotten more from me than I would've gotten from you if the roles had been reversed. But let me make one thing crystal clear... I don't give either of you an ounce of thought. I've moved on from what you did to me. I have a rich, beautiful life full of people who build me up rather than knock me down. I choose to focus on them rather than on painful things from the past. I'm sure you can understand that."

"I'm sorry. Is that what you want to hear?"

Kara tipped her head, intrigued to receive an actual apology from her sister, who'd never apologized to anyone for anything in the past. "What is it, exactly, that you're sorry for?"

"That you were hurt by what we did."

"Did you think I wouldn't be? When you started seeing each other behind my back, how'd you think that would turn out?" When Kelly didn't reply, Kara continued. "You didn't think about me, did you? You saw what you wanted, and you took it, like you always had before with clothes, shoes, dolls, toys. It didn't matter what I had, you wanted it, and you took it."

"It wasn't like that."

"Wasn't it?"

"We... we should go, Kelly," Matt said, seeming distressed.

"Why?" Kara asked him. "Is it uncomfortable to witness the destroyed relationship between two sisters that you helped to cause?"

"I... um..."

As Kara stood before them, she realized that at some point, they'd lost the power to hurt her and wondered when exactly that'd happened.

"Look, we all have better things to do than rehash the past. Hopefully, you've learned that actions have consequences. There's no reason we can't be civil with each other for the sake of our children, but please don't think things will ever be the same between us. Because they won't. You've both shown me who you really are. I've chosen to believe you, and as such, I'll be keeping my distance. I hope you understand. Have a great day."

Kara turned to walk away and found Dan watching her with unmistakable pride.

"Kara! Wait!" Kelly moved quickly to close the distance between them. "I'll always be sorry that I hurt you."

"Thank you for saying so. It matters."

"If I could just... I'd like to introduce you..." Her gaze encompassed Dan. "Both of you... to your nephew."

"Of course," Kara said.

Kelly gestured for Matt to come closer. "Connor, this is your aunt Kara and uncle Dan. Can you say hi?"

The adorable blond boy buried his face in his father's coat as he said a soft hello.

Kara smiled and ducked her head to waggle her fingers at him. "It's nice to meet you, Connor."

He smiled and so did she, because how could she not?

"Thank you," Kelly said tearfully.

Kara nodded, hooked her arm through Dan's and walked away from them, feeling as if a massive weight had been lifted that she hadn't even known she was still carrying.

"Un-fucking-*believable*," Dan said in a low, gravelly tone. "That's what you are."

Kara laughed. "Who, me?"

"I'm so incredibly proud of you. That was gutsy and ballsy and all the things."

"Thanks. It felt pretty good to put it out there, and I'm glad we got to officially meet Connor."

"Just when I think I've seen all the sides of my beautiful wife, she goes and shows me something new."

"I like to keep you guessing."

"You do that so well. How do you feel?"

"Relieved. I can run into them now, and it won't be a big deal. And our children can grow up knowing each other, even if they won't be close. That's something anyway."

"That's everything."

In the parking lot, they joined the others, who were eagerly awaiting an update.

"All good," Kara said.

"Tell me you didn't forgive them," Renata said.

"No, I didn't. But it felt good to say a few things and to meet Connor."

"She was *magnificent*," Dan said.

"He has to say that," Kara replied, smiling at him.

"No, I don't. It's the truth."

"I was prepared to call 911 if it came to blows," Renata said.

Kara laughed. "No chance of that when I'm seven months pregnant."

"You're my hero," Renata said. "The way you went marching back there to confront them. Amazing."

"I'm tired of the fighting. It's exhausting carrying around all that outrage. Now she knows where we stand, and I got to officially meet my nephew. It's over and done with as far as I'm concerned. In other news, I'm starving and ready for dinner."

"How does pizza with the others sound?" Renata asked.

Kara glanced at Dan, who nodded. "That sounds perfect."

CHAPTER
Twenty-Nine

AFTER DINNER at a local pizza restaurant, Renata invited everyone back to her house for a drink and dessert since it was still early.

Kara ended up with Ellery's daughter, Annabelle, on her lap. She snuggled the little girl, breathing in the sweet scent of her hair, thankful that Ellery's kids hadn't treated her like a stranger after so many years away. The time Kara had spent with them on FaceTime had paid off with a warm reception from the children.

Pete sat next to them on the sofa. "It's so great to see you, K. We've missed you around here." He had the burly build that came from years of tending traps and hauling lobsters. His brown hair was streaked with blond from the summer, and his golden-brown eyes were filled with warmth and affection. He and Ellery had been together since high school, and he'd also been one of Kara's closest friends.

"I've missed you guys. It's nice to be with you all again."

"I like your hubby. I wasn't sure what to expect with the fancy reputation, but he's good people."

Kara gazed at Dan, talking to Doug and Myles in the kitchen. "Yes, he is."

"I shouldn't have doubted you," he said with a warm smile.

"Haha. I got lucky, and I know it."

"It wasn't luck. You deserved it." He lowered his voice to add, "Never thought much of what's-his-name."

"Why didn't you say so then?"

"Would you have wanted to hear it?"

"Probably not," she conceded.

"Never expected him to turn out to be such an AH, though."

"I know what that stands for," Annabelle said.

"Button that lip, missy," her dad said. "She loves all the naughty words."

"And where does she hear these naughty words?" Ellery asked as she joined them.

"I can't imagine," Pete said with a wink for his daughter.

"It's you, Daddy. Mommy says you need your mouth washed out with soap."

Kara snorted with laughter at the face Pete made.

"That's gross," Pete said as Annabelle giggled.

"I've tried it," Ellery said. "Doesn't work."

"I love you guys," Kara said, suddenly tearful. "So, so much, and I promise it won't be long before you see me again."

"About that," Ellery said tentatively. "I feel bad about what I said the other day. Travel works two ways, and you're not so far away that we couldn't come see you, too. I'm sorry if I made you feel guilty. I don't blame you at all for staying gone when you left."

"Thank you for saying that, but I don't want you to feel bad about what you said. Being here again has made me see that running away from everyone I love because of what two people did wasn't the right thing to do."

"You did what you had to at the time," Ellery said. "No one should hold that against you, least of all us."

Jessie sat on the floor by Ellery. "What she said. We felt awful about the other day, and I hope she told you how sorry we are."

"Please don't be. As I said to her, I've learned that it makes no sense to stay away from everyone else I love because of what those two did. Other than my brothers being charged with murder and all that, it's been nice to be home."

Renata and the other guys ended up seated on pillows next to Jessie.

"We want to come visit this island of yours," Ellery said. "Maybe next summer?"

"We'd love that. Even though it's crowded with tourists, that's the time to come. It's very quiet the rest of the year."

"Quieter than here in the winter?" Pete asked.

"Gansett is like a church compared to here."

"Yikes," Doug said. "Not sure I could deal with that."

"It's kind of nice after the summer madness," Dan said. "We've become very fond of Gansett's quiet off-season."

"Not that it's ever totally quiet," Kara added. "We have a great group of friends who keep us very busy. There's always something going on."

"Do you ever get stir-crazy knowing you can't jump in the car and go somewhere else?" Jessie asked.

"Not really," Dan said. "We have friends at the ferry company, so we can get a car onboard more or less whenever we want. And we spend part of the winter in Southern California, which gives us a break from being isolated."

"I never feel confined there," Kara said. "It's a very peaceful place to be marooned."

"I can't wait to see it," Renata said. "After hearing about it for so many years."

"Let's plan something for the summer," Dan said. "We'll rent a big house so we can all stay together."

"That'd be awesome," Jessie said. "Yay, something fun to look forward to."

"We have something else to look forward to," Doug reminded his partner. "Do you want to tell them?"

Jessie hesitated, but only for a second. "Doug asked me to marry him, and I said yes."

Kara was briefly stunned, as were Renata and Ellery, but they all rallied to hug their friends and congratulate them.

"I know what you're all thinking," Doug said. "That Jessie needs to move on from me after everything I've put her through, but I've worked really hard—and we've worked very hard as a couple. I'm optimistic that the bad stuff is behind us now." He glanced at Jessie when he added, "There's no one else I want to share the good stuff with than the one person who never gave up on me."

Kara was surprised by the tears that filled her eyes. "I'm so happy for you guys. And so proud of you both for what you've worked through together."

"We all are," Ellery added, dabbing at her own eyes. "When's the big day?"

"We're hoping for next fall," Jessie said. "You guys will be my bridesmaids, right?"

"Try and stop us," Renata said for all of them.

AFTER JESSIE AND ELLERY AND THE OTHERS LEFT, DAN and Kara hung out to help clean up. "This was really fun," Kara said to Renata. "Thanks for organizing it."

Myles rolled up his sleeves to wash the dishes.

Kara gave Renata an impressed look that had her cousin shrugging. "Can I borrow that sweater we talked about?"

"What?"

Kara tipped her head toward Renata's bedroom.

"Oh," Renata said with big eyes that nearly made Kara laugh. "Yeah, sure, come with me to try it on."

Kara followed her into the bedroom. "You used to be quicker on the uptake."

"No shit, right? It's Myles. He scrambles my brain."

"He'd doing the dishes. Without being asked."

"I noticed that."

"He's very cute."

"I noticed that, too." Renata crossed her arms in a protective gesture that tugged at Kara's heart. "He offered me a partnership in the company."

Kara's mouth fell open in surprise. "Oh my God, Ren. That's huge."

"Believe me, I know."

"Do you understand why he did it?"

"Of course I do. He wants in my pants."

"Renata... Come on. He's offering you a piece of the company his grandfather founded. That's got nothing to do with what's in your pants."

"It's easier for me to make it about that than to look at the bigger picture."

"You mean the picture that shows he's in love with you and wants to be partners with you in every way?"

Renata scowled. "Why you gotta say it like that?"

Kara sputtered with laughter. "Because it's the truth?"

"He's not in love with me."

"Renata... He offered you a piece of his family's business because he wants you to be his equal, not his employee." She stepped closer to her cousin. "He's doing the dishes... *without being asked.*"

"They all do that stuff at the beginning."

"Dan washes all the dishes in our house. I cook. He cleans up."

"I can't picture him doing dishes."

"Well, he does. He also does the laundry and cleans the bathroom and anything else that needs to be done."

"We all know you got a unicorn. Doesn't mean the rest of us will."

"Why're you trying so hard to deny what's right in front of you?"

Renata's bullish expression would've been funny if Kara didn't know everything there was to know about her lifelong best friend.

She placed her hands on Renata's shoulders. "Can I say something?"

"Can I stop you?"

"Haha. Nope. If you turn your back on Myles because of something someone else did years ago, who benefits from that?"

"Sometimes it's just easier not to bother."

"Yeah, it is, but what if you'd be missing out on the best thing to ever happen to you? Like I said before, I shouldn't have waited so long to give Dan a chance. And I'll tell you something else you can never repeat to anyone... I'm glad Kelly and Matt did what they did."

"Really?"

"Yep. What they did led me to the best thing ever, and that's worth all the hell and heartache that came before. He's worth it all, and I have a feeling your Myles will be, too."

"He's not my Myles."

"Isn't he?"

"Why you gotta be such a bitch?"

Kara laughed so hard that she had tears in her eyes when she came up for air. "You're ridiculous. Go put that man out of his misery, will you, please?"

"I'll think about it."

"You do that. I promise you, Ren, if he's the real deal... you'll never regret taking the leap."

"I never thought I'd ever see you this happy after what went down here. Dan's really great, and you deserve that."

"So do you. And thank you. I agree. He's the best. I want you to have that. I want you to have it all."

Renata hugged her. "Thank you. I love having you home. Come back more often, will you?"

"I will. I promise. One other thing... About that partnership he offered you... Please tell me you know that you've earned that a thousand times over."

"I do know it. I'm the one who keeps that place running smoothly."

"And they *know it*. They know it, Ren. You deserve it. You've earned it, and if nothing else, I hope you'll take a minute to wallow in that accomplishment."

"Thank you for saying that. It means a lot."

"How do we feel about Jessie and Doug?"

"She told me they had a long, long talk before he proposed, and he made her realize that everything they had before is still there in the aftermath of his addiction, only they appreciate it more than they ever did in the past because they know how close they came to losing it."

"That's an incredible point."

"She thought so, too. When he proposed, he promised her that no one would ever love her more than he does."

"What else is there?" Kara asked, thrilled for her friends.

"Indeed."

"Go get that for yourself," Kara said.

Renata smiled. "Love you."

"Love you more."

"No way."

"Want to bet?"

"I CAN FINISH THOSE," RENATA SAID TO MYLES AFTER Dan and Kara had left. Why was she suddenly nervous to be alone with him after this day in which everything had changed?

"I don't mind doing it." He glanced at her, standing next to him, glass of wine in hand. "This was fun. I love your friends—and your cousin. Her husband isn't what I expected."

"He's very normal despite his massive success."

"Yes, exactly. Thanks for including me."

"It was fun."

"No one seemed surprised to find a new guy in their midst." He wiped his hands on a dishtowel as he turned to her. "Does that mean you've told them about me?"

"I might've mentioned your name once. Maybe twice."

"Maybe twice," he said with a laugh. "I see how it is."

"Do you?"

"I think so." He stepped toward her, making her heart do a funny twisting thing that she feared might be unhealthy, and tucked a strand of hair behind her ear. "I see a beautiful, funny, smart, sarcastic, cautious woman who's so afraid of getting hurt that she'd rather stay on the sidelines than dive into everything life has to offer."

Renata was shocked speechless by his insight. She cleared her throat and forced herself to speak. "What would this diving in entail exactly?"

"Well..." He stepped even closer, took her wineglass and placed it on the counter. "It might start out like this." He kissed her as softly and as gently as she'd ever been kissed in her life. "But I expect it'll quickly escalate into something more like this." There was nothing soft or gentle about the second kiss. It made her knees go weak and her heart rate accelerate into the danger zone.

She'd kissed her share of guys, but never had a kiss transported her out of the here and now to somewhere she'd never been before. His tongue brushed against hers as he pulled her tighter against him. By the time he raised his head and gazed down at her in stunned amazement, Renata had grabbed handfuls of his shirt to hold on for dear life.

That amazed her. When had she ever felt the need to hold on for dear life during a kiss? Never. Not once. Ever.

He looked as undone as she felt.

"So, um, that happened," he said.

"Yeah, it did."

"Is this when you push me away and kick me out?"

"I don't seem to be doing either of those things."

"I noticed. I'm not sure what to make of it."

"Are you making fun of me, by any chance?"

"Would I do that?"

"Yes, I believe you would."

"Do you want me to go?"

Renata was well aware that this was one of those moments upon which a life could go in one of two directions. If she asked him to leave, he would. If she asked him to stay, he would, and that would be that.

"It's okay if you're still not sure," he said as he started to pull back from her.

Renata tightened her hold on his shirt.

He froze.

"Don't go."

"Are you sure?"

She laughed as she shook her head. "Not at all sure of anything, except that I don't want you to go."

"If you give me a chance, I promise I'll do everything in my power to make you happy."

"Why me?"

He huffed out a laugh. "I've asked myself that a thousand times during the last few torturous years in which I realized that my ascension to the boss's office had ruined any chance I had with you."

"Wait. The last few *years* have been *torturous* for you?"

"God yes. Before my dad retired, I felt like you and I were on the way to this, and that stopped when I became the boss. We were still friends, but not like we were before. I've missed that for all this time. I've missed you."

"You see me every day."

"I've missed the you I was friends with before I became your boss on paper."

"On paper? You own the company. It's more than on paper."

"It's very much on paper because we all know who runs that place, and it's not me."

"It is you."

"It's *us*, Renata. You and me, but mostly you. We're a team at work, and we could be so much more than that outside of work. You asked why you, and all I can tell you is that it's always been you for me. From the beginning. Do you know how often I've wished I made it official with you before my dad retired and changed the dynamic? I thought we had time, but he surprised me with an early retirement, and then it was too late. Or so I thought."

"The beginning" had been close to a decade ago. And in that time, she'd never known him to date anyone else.

"Have I finally rendered you speechless?"

"Not quite, but close."

"Never thought I'd see that happen."

She flattened her hands against his chest and smoothed out the wrinkles she'd made in his shirt, making another interesting discovery. "When did you get all these muscles?"

"Had to do something to deal with the frustration."

"What frustration?"

He looked her dead in the eyes. "The frustration that came from being madly, deeply, completely, torturously and permanently in love with my coworker."

Once again, she was rendered speechless. And when she recovered enough to form words, they were halting. "You..."

"I love you, Renata."

"Oh." In a voice several octaves higher than usual, she said, "You do?"

"Yes, I do."

"Is... is that why you asked me to be a partner in the business?"

He shook his head. "I asked you to be my partner because you've earned it by your hard work that's helped to grow our business exponentially. But that's only a small part of the overall equation. If I had my way, you'd be my partner in all things... life and business. And love. Mostly love."

Renata stared up at him, as if seeing him for the first time. Now that she knew how he felt, she could see it in the way he looked at her so tenderly, as if she was everything he'd ever wanted. "I feel stupid."

"What? Why?"

"Because I didn't know you felt that way."

"Sure you did. You just weren't ready to acknowledge it. I hope you are now."

Was she? How did one know if one was ready for something like this? "I'm kind of messy... What if I screw it up?"

"I won't let you. And PS, you're not messy. You're perfectly yourself, and yours is the best self I've ever known. All I want is to spend as much time with you as I possibly can. That's all I've wanted for as long as I've known you." He ran his finger lightly over her cheek, setting off a wildfire of sensation she felt everywhere. "If you give me the chance, Renata, I'll make you happy. I promise."

He was offering her everything he had to give, and she had a choice to make. Dive in headfirst and hope for the best or continue to keep him at arm's length in an effort to protect herself from ever being hurt again.

Her heart, it seemed, was working way ahead of her brain as she slipped her arms around his waist and rested her head against his chest.

He put his arms around her and held her tightly.

She fit perfectly in his arms, with his chin resting on top of her head, like two pieces of a puzzle.

"What're you thinking? I'm kind of dying over here, out on the biggest limb I've ever been on, dangling over the edge of the abyss."

Renata laughed at his dramatics. "I think," she said, "it might be safe to come in off the limb."

"What are you saying?"

"It's possible that the reason I've been so freaked out about this is because I love you, too, and I wasn't sure what to do about it."

"I have a few suggestions if you're interested."

Smiling, she looked up at him, feeling as if she'd come home in the last few minutes to the person she'd always been meant to find, the one who'd been there all along, patiently waiting for her to be ready for him.

He cradled her face in his hands. "Do you think you could say that one thing again, when you're looking at me this time?"

"I love you, Myles."

"I love you, too, Renata."

When he kissed her again, he held nothing back.

When he lifted her off her feet, she wrapped her arms and legs around him and held on tight.

"We need a bed, and we need it now. Which way?"

"Down the hall to the left."

"Are you sure, Renata?"

When it felt right, she discovered, there were no doubts or fears or anything other than the kind of joy she'd never experienced before. She nodded. "I'm very sure."

CHAPTER
Thirty

KARA WOKE up alone in bed the next morning, groaning when she saw that it was after nine o'clock. She'd rarely slept past seven before she was pregnant. Now, she spent more time in bed than out, or so it seemed. She reached for her phone on the bedside table and found a text from Dan.

Gone into town to meet with my investigator. Will be back in a bit. Left you some breakfast. Text if you need anything. Love you.

Even when he wasn't there, he could still make her smile. After all this time, she was still amazed that they'd found each other in this great big world. Only through a series of unfortunate events for both of them had they ended up on a remote island off the coast of Rhode Island at the same time. She would never stop marveling at the miracle of him and them.

Under the text from Dan was one from Renata.

I have news.

Kara responded with question marks.

This requires a call.

Kara's phone rang a minute later.

"You're sleeping late these days, Mama."

"What's the news?"

Renata laughed. "There were a couple of... developments... with Myles last night."

"What kind of developments?"

"Um, the I-love-you and multiple-orgasm type of developments."

Kara let out a shriek that had the baby kicking hard in protest of the disruption.

"Jeez, split my eardrum, why don't you?"

"Can you say that one more time, slowly this time?"

"You heard me right the first time."

"Ren..."

"I know. It's pretty crazy, right?"

"It's amazing. How do you feel?"

"A little sore from the workout and tired from the lack of sleep, but otherwise... I feel pretty great."

"I love this so much, more than I've loved anything in, well, ever."

"Stop."

"I won't stop. This is the best news, Renata. I think he's amazing, and I told Dan last night that he's in love with you. He never takes his eyes off you, but not in a creepy way. It's more like he-can't-bear-to-look-at-anything-else-when-you're-in-the-room kind of way."

"I can't believe you noticed that."

"I was watching because I wanted to get a read on him, and I liked what I saw."

"That means everything to me, as you know."

"I'm happy for you, Ren. Are you happy for you?"

"Shockingly, I am. Normally, I'd be anticipating disaster from the get-go, but I don't think I need to do that this time."

"I don't think so either. This is the best thing ever. I couldn't be happier for you."

"Thanks. I want to tell you something..."

"I'm listening."

"Seeing you living your happily ever after with Dan after everything you went through before... It, well... You gave me the courage to take the leap with Myles, so thank you for that."

"Oh my God! You're making me cry."

"It's true. You showed me what's possible and made me want that for myself, so when he was standing right in front of me, saying all the things I never expected to hear, it was easier for me to believe him than it would've been without you two showing me the way."

"Renata... I'm seriously weeping."

"Thank you for that."

"I'm so honored that we helped you in some way."

"You really did. You helped me realize I'm not my mother, and I'm not living her life. I'm living my own life, and this feels right to me. He feels right. He feels like home."

"I'm a literal puddle over here. This has made my year, and that you're excited about it rather than trying to wiggle out is the best news of all."

"He blew my mind in every possible way last night."

"Girl..."

"I had no idea it could be like that."

"I'm tempted to shriek again, but the baby didn't like it the last time."

Renata laughed.

"There's nothing quite like finding that one person you were meant to spend your life with. I'm so, so happy for you."

"Thanks. I'm pretty happy for me, too."

"Are you at work?"

"You're going to laugh... I took the day off because I was too tired from messing around with my boss all night."

"That is *fabulous*."

"He said I'm going to be a partner, and if I want a day off, I should take a day off. So I sent him to work and took a day off."

"I love it."

"I think I might treat myself to a massage later."

"You go, girl. Love you so much."

"Love you, too. Thanks again for showing me what's possible."

"I can't wait to tell Dan we inspired you."

"Tell him I love him, too, for making my girl so happy."

"I'll do that the minute he gets home. Call me later?"

"If I'm not busy."

They hung up laughing, and Kara used a tissue to mop up her tears. Imagine being one half of such an incredible love story that you inspired others to take a chance on love so they could have what you have. It was unbelievable and amazing at the same time.

She hoped Dan would be home soon so she could tell him all about it.

DAN MET CARTER IN THE SAME COFFEE SHOP WHERE they held their initial meeting. Carter used an iPad to show Dan the footage from the Barnacle in which Tanya's ex-boyfriend was clearly present.

"I matched this image to his Snapchat account and went back through his Twitter—I refuse to call it by that stupid new name—and found a bunch of rants about how no one is loyal anymore, how you can give someone everything you've got to give and it's still not enough."

Dan perused the increasingly unhinged tweets that showed how bitter Billy was about the breakup with Tanya. "What else do we have on him?"

Carter pushed another sheet of paper across the table. "Charged with domestic assault two years ago, but the charges were dropped when the victim refused to cooperate."

"Do we know who the victim was?"

"We do." He produced another page that showed the initial

complaint that was filed by Tanya, alleging he'd knocked her around when she tried to leave his apartment. "When the rubber met the road, she was unwilling to testify against him in court."

Dan winced. That decision might've ended up costing her her life.

"I poked around with some of their friends and learned that after the domestic incident, he begged for forgiveness and convinced her to give him another chance, even with everyone in her life pleading with her to end it with him for good. The second chance lasted about six months, after which time she told him they were done and to leave her alone."

"And did he?"

"Nope." Carter produced a copy of a restraining order filed in Storrs, Connecticut, that had required Billy to be at least one thousand feet from Tanya.

"I heard her parents hadn't wanted to involve the police because their families were friends."

"All of this happened in Storrs. I'm not sure her parents knew about it. He violated the order by being in the Barnacle that night."

"That's enough for the cops to pick him up."

"Your thinking matches mine."

"Great work, Carter. Seriously... This is everything we need to introduce enough reasonable doubt to get my clients released."

"They should drop the charges against them, too."

"One step at a time. I'll take this to the detective on the case and see what he can do immediately."

"Keep me posted? I'm invested."

"Of course." Dan reached across the table to shake his hand. "Appreciate it."

"Are you kidding? Getting to work with you is the best thing to ever happen to my career."

"You'll hear from me again. A good investigator is hard to find."

"Really?"

"Absolutely."

"Wow. That's great. Thank you."

"Thank you on behalf of the entire Ballard family."

Dan tossed a twenty on the table to cover their coffee and breakfast sandwiches and went out to the car, where Walter was waiting for him.

"How'd it go, bossman?"

"Pay dirt. I need to see the detective on the case."

As Walter drove him to Bar Harbor, Dan felt his heart beat fast with the kick of adrenaline that came with blowing a case wide open. There was nothing more thrilling for him than to find something concrete that would exonerate his clients, especially when they were his beloved wife's brothers.

Speaking of his beloved, he put through a call to her, hoping she was awake.

"Morning," she said, yawning.

"It's almost afternoon. Did I wake you?"

"No, I've been up for a while. Guess what?"

"What?" he asked, smiling because he always did when he talked to her.

"Renata and Myles are in love, they did the dirty and she says it's all thanks to us."

"Wait. *What?*"

Her laughter was one of his favorite things in this life. "She said we inspired her to want what we have and to take a chance on Myles."

"Well, that's quite a compliment."

"It made me weepy when she said it."

"I'll bet it did, but I'm not surprised. We are kind of epic, after all."

"Yes, we are. I'm so, so happy for her. I worried for a while that she might never take another chance after her last relationship ended badly."

"This is great news. I really like Myles. He seems like a great guy."

"He is a great guy, and she already knows that for sure because they've been friends and coworkers for years."

"I'm glad you were in town when this happened."

"Me, too. Where are you?"

"On my way into Bar Harbor with some new information for the police that should bode well for your brothers."

"Oh wow, really?"

"Yep. I'll update you when I know more."

"This day is turning out awesome. Thank you for all you're doing."

"You got it. See you soon. Love you."

"Love you, too."

"Y'all are too cute," Walter said, smiling in the mirror.

"She's the best thing in my life."

"As long as you know that, you'll always treat it with the respect it deserves. Messed that up a bit for a time myself, but we're getting back on track. She no longer hates the sight of me, so I take that as progress."

Dan laughed.

"Gave her a lot of reasons to hate me over the years. Regret that terribly and will spend the rest of my life making amends for those hurts."

"You're doing the hard work. I'm sure that matters to her and your kids."

"I think it does. Rome wasn't built in a day, and this won't be either. But I'm determined to see it through."

"Good for you, Walter. It would've been easier not to bother."

"That's for damned sure."

"Says a lot about who you are that you're bothering."

"Either that, or it says I'm really a masochist at heart."

Dan grunted out a laugh. "Maybe a little of both. Got a few friends in recovery. It's a tough road but seems worth the effort in the end."

"I sure hope so. No matter what happens long term, it beats the way I was living before."

"I'm happy for you, man. Truly."

"Thanks. Means a lot coming from you."

They pulled up to the public safety complex a few minutes later.

"Not sure how long this'll take."

"I'm not in any rush. Take your time. I'll grab some lunch."

"I'll update you in a bit."

"Sounds good."

Inside, Dan asked to see Detective Cosgrove and was shown to the same conference room where they'd met before. The table was covered with folders, papers, discarded coffee cups and take-out wrappers.

Cosgrove stood and shook his hand.

"Thanks for seeing me. How's it going?"

"Slowly. We're stretched thin with people on vacation after the tourist season ended."

"I told you about Tanya's breakup with Billy Norton and how he hadn't taken it well."

"Yes, and you also told the media that, and they've been up my ass about it ever since."

"Sorry, but it's an angle that requires pursuit."

"I've been looking into it, but I haven't gotten very far."

"I may have some info that could help." Dan laid out the pages Carter had produced and took Cosgrove through the sequence of events that'd led up to Tanya's breakup with Billy and everything that'd followed.

"Holy shit," Cosgrove said as he reviewed the police report on the assault in Storrs and the subsequent restraining order.

Next, Dan used his phone to show the detective pictures of

the young man from his social media accounts as well as the film from the Barnacle that put him in the crowd at the bar the night Tanya was killed.

"I'm not saying Billy Norton killed her," Dan said, "but I think you'll agree that this information would demolish any case you might be building against my clients."

Cosgrove reviewed each document and then watched the video twice, his face expressionless. Then he stood. "I'll be right back. Do you mind if I borrow your phone for a second?"

"Be my guest."

While the detective was gone, Dan used the time to write a draft of the motion to dismiss that he'd file with the court that afternoon if the prosecutors didn't move to dismiss based on this new information. He'd learned to be prepared for any scenario.

Cosgrove returned twenty minutes later with an older man whom he introduced as Chief of Police Rushton White.

Dan stood to shake the man's hand as Cosgrove put Dan's phone on the table. "Nice to meet you, sir," Dan said. "My grand-mother-in-law speaks highly of you."

"Bertha is good people."

"She says you are, too."

"That's nice to hear. Detective Cosgrove has shown me the information you produced, and we agree, after consulting with the AG and the judge, that all charges against your brothers-in-law should be dropped immediately, with our apologies for the ordeal."

Dan wanted to give a shout and a fist pump. He maintained his professional demeanor, but it wasn't easy. "When will they be released?"

He looked at Cosgrove. "Immediately."

"I'll need a copy of that video," Cosgrove said, "and I assume I can keep the other documents you provided?"

"They're all yours."

The detective nodded and left the room to see to the chief's order.

"Thank you very much."

"I regret that this happened, but I'm sure you understand how things work in situations like this. The state police had an eyewitness who put them with her shortly before her time of death..."

"I understand, and I appreciate you doing the right thing when new information came to light."

"I wish we'd met under different circumstances," White said. "I've admired your work for many years."

"Thank you. Most LEOs probably think of me on the same level they'd put the plague."

"Only the ones who don't play by the rules. The rest of us are far more concerned with making sure we charge the right people than we are with charging *someone*."

Dan deeply respected the sentiment behind that statement. Justice at any cost had made him a celebrity, but he wished his services had never been needed by any of his wrongly accused clients.

"You'll want to come with me to greet your family members," White said.

"Lead the way."

CHAPTER
Thirty-One

DAN WAS WAITING outside the building when Keith and Kirby emerged in street clothes, both grinning from ear to ear as they approached him.

"What the fuck happened?" Keith asked as he hugged Dan so hard, he nearly cracked his ribs.

"We produced evidence that showed it was possible someone else had motive to kill Tanya, and he was in the area on Friday night."

Kirby hugged Dan, as tears streamed down his face. "They really dropped all the charges?"

"They really did, and they're going to issue a statement that'll fully exonerate you of any involvement in Tanya's murder."

"Thank fucking God," Keith said. "I don't know how you did it, but damn, man. We owe you everything."

"What he said," Kirby said. "Thank you so much, Dan. We'll never have the words..."

"I'm glad I could help." He produced his phone. "I assume yours are dead. Could you please call your mother to tell her the good news?"

Kirby took the phone from him. "With pleasure." He dialed his mother's number and put the call on speaker.

"Hi, Dan. How's it going? Please tell me you have some news."

"Hey, Mom, it's me, Kirby."

Keith leaned in. "And me, Keith. We're out—and all the charges have been dropped."

Judith's scream was so loud that people on the sidewalk turned to see what was happening.

The three men grinned like fools.

"Kara married her magician," Keith said. "I don't know what he did, and I don't really care, but we're free and clear, and it's all thanks to him."

"Thank God," Judith said. "I'm going to go call Dad and text the others. We'll have a celebration dinner here tonight. Is that okay?"

Kirby glanced at Keith, who nodded.

"That'd be great, Mom. Tell everyone we can't wait to see them."

"They can't wait to see you, too. This is the best news ever. Thank you so, so much, Dan. You have our eternal gratitude."

"Glad I was able to help."

After they ended the call, he took back the phone and texted Kara. *The boys have been sprung. All charges dropped. Will call you shortly.*

She didn't respond, which meant she was either sleeping or doing something away from her phone.

"Where can we drop you guys?" Dan asked.

"I want to go home and take a real shower," Kirby said.

"Me, too," Keith said.

Dan held the back door to Walter's car for them to get in and then went to the passenger seat.

"Hey, Walter," Keith said. "How'd you get hooked up with this guy?"

"He was looking for a driver to get him around. He said he does his best work in the car."

"Do you need directions?" Dan asked Walter.

"Nah, I know where they live." He glanced up at the mirror. "Real glad to see you guys outta that place."

"You and us both," Keith said.

"Had the window down, so I heard all the charges are dropped, too."

"That's right," Kirby said.

"Thank goodness."

"Will it always stick to us, though?" Kirby asked. "That we were charged in the first place?"

"I trust Chief White to release a statement that'll take care of any doubt," Dan said.

"That'd be good," Kirby said. "It's gonna take a long time to get past this, no matter what he says."

Dan turned so he could see him. "That's true, but you *will* get past it. I've known a lot of people who were tried, convicted and served hard time who were later exonerated and able to put their lives back together. It doesn't happen overnight, but it does happen eventually in most cases."

"Only in most cases?" Keith asked.

"Some are so damaged by what they endured that they struggle on the outside and sometimes end up in pretty dire straits. We do what we can for them, but we're not always successful in helping them turn things around. People like them… They're the reason I do this work."

"Thank God you do this work—and thank God you married our sister," Kirby said. "Who knows what might've become of us without you on the case?"

"I'm confident that the police would've eventually realized they had the wrong guys, but it might've taken a while. I don't believe there was any malice involved here, despite how it might seem to you."

"Felt pretty malicious to me," Keith said. "I haven't been a Boy Scout, so the minute they heard I was with her, they jumped to all kinds of conclusions."

"Which is what you'd probably have done in their shoes," Dan said.

"Are you defending them?" Keith asked, sounding incredulous.

"Hardly. I'm merely stating that human nature is such that when something seems obvious, you tend to follow that path until you have reason not to."

"Well, I might've been a bit of a degenerate at times, but I hate to think it would be obvious to anyone that I was capable of killing that beautiful young woman—or anyone else, for that matter."

They dropped the brothers at their respective homes, and then Walter drove Dan back to Bertha's.

"Congratulations, bossman. You must be feeling pretty good right about now."

"I'm relieved that the family can put this behind them and get back to normal."

"I suppose this means you and the missus will be heading back to your little island."

"As soon as we possibly can. It's been great to be here, to see everyone, to deal with everything that needed to be done, but Gansett is home for us."

"I get it, man. Once you find that special place, that's where you want to be most of the time."

"Yes, exactly. And autumn on the island is my favorite time of year. The tourists are gone, and Gansett becomes ours again while the weather is still fantastic. You should come visit sometime."

"I'd love to. When is your little one due?"

"Late November."

"That'll be here before you know it."

"All the more reason to get home."

Dan sent a text to Slim Jackson. *The Ballard boys are out of lockup with all charges dropped, so Kara and I will need a ride home in the next few days.*

Say the word, and we'll be there. And congratulations. Feel a little sorry for the folks up there. They didn't know what was about to hit them when Dan T. came to town.

LOL. Thanks, friend. Can't wait to see everyone.

You've been missed around here.

That's nice to hear. We've missed you guys, too.

He also texted Kendall to let her know he'd be returning soon, to update her on the successful outcome with Kara's brothers and to thank her for covering for him. *If you're interested in continuing to work a bit, I can keep you busy. Got a baby arriving in a few short months, and I'll take all the help I can get.*

I'm around for anything you need and happy to stay busy. Congratulations on the brothers. Must be a big relief.

HUGE relief. I'll touch base when we get back to the island.

Safe travels.

Walter pulled up to Bertha's and parked in the driveway, leaving the engine running as he got out to shake Dan's hand. "Been a real kick getting to know you, Counselor. Hope you'll touch base the next time you're up this way. I'll buy you a lobster roll."

"I'll definitely take you up on that. Thank you for everything. You made it easier for me here, and I appreciate it."

"Pleasure's all mine, my friend. Keep in touch."

"Will do."

Dan waved as Walter drove off and then went inside to find his wife.

BERTHA AND BUSTER HAD TAKEN A RARE DAY OFF FOR Bertha's dreaded annual physical that she said was pointless because she felt fine, but she went because everyone who loved her made her do it.

Buster had appeared in the doorway to Kara's room, while she was still in bed.

"Let's fish."

"Um, okay. Give me a minute to open my eyes."

"Hurry up."

She'd laughed at the brusque tone that'd been such a big part of her childhood memories. Buster had been one of her very best friends as a child, being as he was only ten years older than her and always around when she visited Bertha's. He'd taught her to fish, to catch crabs, to repair traps and to tie all the fanciest knots.

They'd rarely exchanged a word because he preferred quiet to chatter, and she'd respected his boundaries on that, which had made her one of his favorite companions. Kelly, who'd been a certified blabbermouth as a child, didn't cut it with Buster.

Kara had been ridiculously honored then to make his inner circle, and as she brushed her teeth and hair and washed her face, she couldn't wait to spend time with him. It didn't matter what they did, because it was always fun.

She pulled on yoga pants and Dan's favorite Stanford sweatshirt before grabbing a granola bar and a bottle of water to take with her.

Ever since the IV at the hospital, she'd felt a thousand times better. That was good to know for future pregnancies if she was plagued by nonstop nausea again.

Future pregnancies... Ha! She needed to see how this delivery went before she thought about another baby. Truth be told, the delivery part of the program was terrifying to her. Not that she'd admitted that to anyone, even Dan. Women had been giving birth for centuries. She refused to make a big deal out of it. Besides, if that wimp Kelly could do it, she'd have no problem.

That thought made her chuckle to herself as she walked

across the backyard to the water's edge, where Buster had set them up with chairs and poles.

"Did you do the bait?"

He gave her a what-do-you-take-me-for look that made her laugh.

"Sorry."

"Some things don't change."

"No, they don't. Worms still freak me out."

"Baby."

She stuck her tongue out at him and got the slightest lift of his face in response.

Kara hadn't fished since the last time she did it with Buster. She'd forgotten how relaxing it was to cast, reel and repeat until she felt the telltale tug of a fish on the hook. Then it got exciting as she engaged every muscle, or so it seemed, to land her catch.

"Nice one," Buster said as he freed the fish and returned it to the water.

Kara was glad he remembered that she didn't like to touch the fish either.

They'd caught two each when they heard car doors closing in the driveway.

Kara turned to see Dan give Walter a bro hug and a handshake. Her heart gave a happy lift at the sight of him coming toward her with a big smile on his face.

"Did you get my text?" he asked.

She stood to greet him with a kiss. "Haven't looked at my phone in a couple of hours. Someone wanted to fish first thing."

"First thing," Buster said disdainfully. "Right."

"Your brothers are out of lockup, and all charges have been dropped."

Kara let out a whoop, dropped her pole and launched herself into Dan's arms. "You did it!"

"With some very excellent help."

She hugged him tightly. "Thank you so much."

"Anything for you, love."

"Good job," Buster said to Dan. "Charges were bullshit."

As Kara hugged her love, she realized this meant they'd be going home to Gansett soon. She was surprised to feel a pang of sadness to be leaving Maine and the people she loved there.

"We need to celebrate."

"Your mom is way ahead of you. She invited the whole family to dinner tonight. You probably have a text from her."

"I need to go grab my phone. Want to take a turn with the pole?"

"I'd love to."

"Show him the ropes, Buster."

"Yep."

Kara walked inside, deeply relieved that the dark cloud over their family had lifted and her brothers were free men. She hoped there'd be a public statement to remove the stain on their reputations.

She had twenty-two unread texts, including one from her mother asking whether Kelly and Matt should be invited to the celebration dinner.

Fine by me, she replied. *Happy to hear the great news.*

We owe Dan everything. Thank you for bringing him into our lives. You chose a very fine man, in more ways than one.

Kara laughed at the double meaning in her mother's words. *He's the best.*

Bertha announced her arrival when her old truck backfired as she killed the engine.

Smiling, Kara went out to meet her. "How was the doctor?"

"Fine. Nothing new."

"Did you hear the big news?"

"What big news? I was in a rush to get home. Never looked at my phone."

"The boys are out, and all charges are dropped."

"Oh thank you, Jesus. And Dan. Mostly Dan."

Kara laughed as she hugged her grandmother. "Mom's having a celebration dinner at the house tonight. Everyone's invited."

"That's a party I want to attend."

"I was hoping you'd say that." Kara pulled back from her, sad to think about leaving her beloved grandmother.

"What's with the frown?"

"I guess we'll be heading home soon."

"That should make you happy, not sad."

"I am happy, but I wish I could bring you with me."

"You know I'd be miserable anywhere but right here, where I'll be the next time you come home to visit. And I'll come to see your little one when he arrives. That's a promise."

"Really? You'll leave Maine for me?"

"Try and keep me away."

Kara hugged her again. "I love you so, so much. More than just about anything."

"Same goes, love. All the way around the world and back again."

THE DINNER AT HER PARENTS' HOUSE THAT EVENING WAS the first time in years Kara could recall all eleven Ballard siblings being in the same place at the same time. Kirby and Keith had greeted Kara with warm hugs and thanks for everything Dan had done for them. Even Kingston, who rarely had anything to do with the family, was there with a big hug for Kara.

Kingston had reddish-blond hair, a matching beard and piercing blue eyes. "Heard your hubby is the man of the hour."

"We're so thankful it's resolved. For us, anyway. I hope they catch the person who killed Tanya."

"I heard something on the radio on the way over here that they've got a suspect," Kingston said.

"I feel for her family. What a terrible thing."

"Indeed."

Dan came over to them, holding the beer bottle Chuck had pressed into his hand the second they arrived.

"Dan, meet Kingston, the last of the Ballards you hadn't met."

The two men shook hands.

"Good to finally meet you," Dan said.

"Likewise. Thanks for everything you did for the boys."

"I'm glad it worked out."

"And way to work yourself into the will," Kingston said with a teasing grin.

Dan laughed.

"Seriously, though, we appreciate what you did."

"It helped that they were innocent," Dan said, "which makes things easier. Not that it always turns out this way, but it helps to have the truth on our side."

Kara's siblings took turns thanking him, shaking his hand and expressing their appreciation.

"Very well done," Kelly said to Dan as her son, Connor, clung to her leg. "Thank you for everything you did."

"No problem."

Kelly started to say something else, but apparently thought better of it and moved on, taking Connor by the hand. Maybe she'd learned not to push her luck. Kara could only hope.

"I googled you," Luna said to Dan as she ran a chip through onion dip. "Impressive."

"Is that right?"

"Duh, like you don't already know that."

He laughed and gave her a playful bop on the head. "Don't believe everything you read."

"So you haven't helped to free tons of wrongly accused people, including two of my uncles?"

"That part is true. Some of the other stuff you might see about me is BS."

"Like what?"

"That I dated every actress in Hollywood. That's most defi-nitely false."

"It was more like half of them," Kara said.

"Hey! It was fewer than five."

Luna snorted with laughter. "Anyone I'd know?"

"Maybe?"

"Oh, this is going to be good."

"Luna, leave your uncle alone," Kendra said. "He's supposed to be celebrating."

"He was just going tell me which famous actresses he dated."

"I'll text you," Dan said with a wink for the girl, which made her smile broadly.

Kara was overwhelmed with gratitude to have had this time with her family and friends in Maine, for Dan to have gotten to meet many of them for the first time, to reconnect with her nieces and friends as well as Bertha and Buster, who were at Sea Swept for the first time in years.

She thought she was seeing things when Renata walked in with her father, Kara's uncle Henry, who hadn't been anywhere near their family in two decades. "What the hell?"

"Who's that?" Dan asked.

"My uncle Henry. My dad's brother."

"You don't say."

Chuck smiled when he saw his brother and went to shake his hand. "Welcome. I'm glad you could make it."

"Thanks for the invite. Happy to help celebrate the good news."

"What is happening?" Kara asked Renata.

In the years since she'd last seen her uncle, his dark hair had gone gray, and there were lines on his face that hadn't been there before.

"My dad texted your dad to say how relieved he was to hear the good news and that he knew Keith and Kirby were innocent from the start," Renata said. "Your dad wrote back, thanking him and saying it was nice to hear from him. They talked back and forth a bit, and your dad invited him to come to the party."

"Stop it. For real?"

"He's here, isn't he?"

"I can't believe it," Kara said as she watched her mother hug her brother-in-law. "We've wished for this for so long."

"It only took your brothers being charged with murder to get you home and to patch up a decades-long rift between our fathers."

"It's weird, isn't it, how good things can come from something so awful?"

"For sure." She glanced at Kara. "Does this mean you guys are leaving soon?"

"Probably, but we haven't made any plans yet."

"I know you're looking forward to getting back to your island, but I'll miss having you close by."

"I'm always just a text, a call, a FaceTime away."

"I know, but it's not the same."

Kara nudged her with her shoulder. "You're going to be so busy with your new man that you won't have time to miss me."

"Hush."

"I won't hush."

"I'll always miss you when you aren't here."

"I'll make sure I'm here much more often going forward. I promise."

"And I'll come there, too. I promise."

"I'd love that. We're looking forward to having the whole crew there next summer."

Renata rested her head on Kara's shoulder as they watched their fathers laugh together for the first time in forever. "Love you, cousin."

"Love you, too."

CHAPTER
Thirty-Two

CHUCK WHISTLED LOUDLY to get everyone's attention. "Mom and I are so delighted to have all of you home for dinner," he said when he had their attention. "I can't recall the last time that happened."

"Christmas, fifteen years ago," Kellen said.

"If Kell says it was that long ago, he's probably right," Chuck said. "At any rate, it's been far too long, and it took something awfully upsetting to make it happen. Keith and Kirby, we're beyond relieved to put this episode behind us and to have you back home where you belong. And we're deeply and forever thankful to Dan for everything he did to make it happen, and to both Dan and Kara, for dropping everything when we called to come running when we needed you. It's been so great to have you both home, and we hope you'll be back soon. We've missed you very much since you moved away, sweetheart, and we've loved this opportunity to be with you and to get to know Dan even better. Although we could've done without the whole arrested-and-charged-with-murder aspect."

"You and us both," Keith said with a small grin for Kirby.

Kirby raised his bottle of Sam Adams to Dan. "Thank you, brother. Thank you so much."

"I'm glad it worked out."

"It didn't just work out," Keith said. "You saw to it, and we'll be forever grateful for everything you did for us."

"Family takes care of family," Dan said.

"Goes both ways," Keith said. "If you ever need anything, anything at all... If a toilet backs up at your place, I'll be on the next flight."

Dan laughed. "I might just take you up on that, because according to my lovely wife, I can't fix shit."

"I'm your guy," Keith said. "Any time. Anywhere."

Judith served a delicious dinner that included grilled chicken and steak and what seemed like twenty different sides.

"How'd you pull this together so fast, Mom?" Kara asked her.

"Are you kidding? I used to feed thirteen people every day. This is nothing." Judith looked around at the gathered family and seemed pleased that everyone was there—and getting along. "Our family hasn't been close the way I hoped it would be."

"There's still time to turn that around. You've got us all here now."

"Yes, I do. In fact..." Judith pinged a knife against a glass to get everyone's attention. "I'd like to invite you all home for Christmas dinner this year. It would mean a lot to me to have everyone here."

Most of the siblings nodded in agreement.

Dan glanced at Kara, eyebrow raised to let her know it was up to her.

"We'd like that," Kara said. "I'll see how I feel after having the baby in November. We'll try to be here, though."

With Kara back in the fold, all eyes turned to Kingston, who was usually the main holdout on anything to do with the family.

After a long pause, he said, "Sure, Mom. That sounds great."

. . .

DAN AND KARA PLANNED TO FLY HOME TO GANSETT three days after the celebration dinner, having decided to give themselves a little more time in Maine before they left. They spent another day on the water with Bertha and Buster, took a hike in Acadia and went out for a fancy dinner for two in Bar Harbor. On their last night in town, they invited everyone to Bertha's for a lobster- and clambake, overseen by Buster, the expert.

He taught Dan how to dig the perfect hole and to use seaweed to flavor the food.

Standing at the kitchen window, Kara watched her husband, shirt off and glistening with sweat, working side by side with her beloved uncle, tears springing to her eyes.

Bertha came up behind her and squeezed her shoulders.

"Look at them," Kara said. "Dan's right in there with him."

"Only because Buster likes and respects him, or he'd tell him to get lost."

"That's true," Kara said with a laugh. "Oh, Bertha... I never should've stayed away from here so long. I can see now that I was only punishing myself."

"Sometimes you have to go back to find the way forward."

"I never would've known that until I experienced it."

"That's how life works. We're learning until we die."

"Can you believe my dad and Uncle Henry, picking back up like they weren't on the outs for close to twenty years?"

"I'm very happy for both of them. The power of forgiveness should never be underestimated."

"Does that mean I need to forgive Kelly and forget about what she did?"

"No, never. Some things can't be forgiven. That's one of them."

Kara laughed at the emphatic way that Bertha said that. "I

think, at some point, whether I should have or not, I forgave them because I simply don't care anymore. Their actions led me to the life I was meant for, and I suppose I should thank them for that."

"Don't you dare thank them for stabbing you in the back."

"Okay, I won't."

"I'm glad you don't care anymore. That's a good thing. And it's a good thing that you can be in the same room with them and not be upset or hurt. You can be cordial for the sake of your parents and your children—yours and hers—but don't you *ever* forget what they did."

"You're right." She turned to face her grandmother. "Do you think it's possible for people to change?"

"Yes, I do, and I see Kelly trying to be better. She was very sweet when I saw her at your mother's house, and her little guy is adorable. I'm glad I finally got to meet him. But, that said... The person who did what she did is still inside her, you know? I'd advise proceeding with caution there."

"Good point. We can be civil without being overly involved."

"That's probably the best approach."

Kara hugged Bertha again, because she could, because soon she'd be missing her again. "Thank you for everything, not just now but always."

"Aw, love, you've given me so much more than I could ever give you."

"No way."

"Yes way."

Smiling, Kara held on tight to the woman who'd been her rock, her best friend, her true north.

That's where Dan found them when he came inside to get drinks for himself and Buster.

"Everything all right in here?"

"Everything is perfect," Kara said as she released Bertha. "We're just getting it in while we can."

"I hope you'll come to Gansett any time you want," Dan said to Bertha. "Our friend Slim will pick you up and fly you over. He's the best pilot I've ever met, and he'd take very good care of you."

"I may take you up on that."

"Please do," Dan said. "My wife is so much happier when you're around, and so am I."

"I've been thinking about taking a few days off here and there."

Kara stared at her in shock.

"Don't look at me that way. I've worked hard all my life. I need to start enjoying myself more, and visiting this island that has you both so captivated is at the top of my to-do list."

"Any time," Dan said emphatically. "You call me, and I'll call Slim. We can surprise Kara."

"I'd love that. We'll do it for sure. I can leave Buster in charge here."

"He's welcome, too, of course."

Bertha laughed. "If you think it's tough getting me out of Maine, he's a whole other story."

"Truth," Kara said. "He's never left the state, and if he has his way, he never will."

"I'll work on him while we finish the dig."

"You do that," Kara said, smiling at Bertha, who rolled her eyes.

Buster wasn't going anywhere, and that was that.

THE LOBSTER- AND CLAMBAKE WAS A DELICIOUS HIT with the family and friends who joined them on Bertha's waterfront lawn.

Ellery's kids played with Kendra's girls, who chased the little ones, making them scream with laughter that added to the sounds of the gulls that flew overhead, looking for scraps.

Buster had strung lights over the yard that added to the glow of the bonfire he'd built from old traps and other scraps he'd been saving for such an occasion.

Full to the brim with seafood, potatoes and other yummy things, Kara sat next to Dan, holding hands as the sun set over the water.

"I love it here," he said. "We have to come all the time."

"We will. Considering the reason we came, I never expected this to be such a great trip."

"It's been great to see where you grew up and to meet all your people."

"They love you almost as much as I do."

"Check out the lovebirds over there," Dan said, using his chin to point to Renata and Myles, who were wrapped up in each other in a dark corner of the yard.

"They're too cute."

"They sure are. I have a feeling we'll be back here for a wedding before too much longer."

"You may be right about that. I'm so happy for her."

"Hey, I heard there was a party over here."

At the sound of Kirby's voice, Kara got up to greet him with a hug. "You made it."

"I did."

"Are you hungry? Buster outdid himself with the food."

"I could eat something."

Kara took him by the hand. "Right this way."

He was stopped no less than ten times by friends and family who wanted to hug him and express their relief that the charges had been dropped. "Sheesh," he said when they were finally inside. "They're treating me like a celebrity."

"Everyone is so thankful to see you and to have this awful stuff behind you."

"No one more so than me. I'm trying to get back to normal, but it hasn't been easy."

"I'm sure it hasn't. People are being nice to you, though, right?"

"Oh yeah. Everyone says they knew it was bullshit from the get-go. With me, anyway. They weren't so sure about Keith."

Kara smiled as she made a plate for Kirby. "That's sort of how I felt, but it makes me feel guilty now."

"Nah, don't feel guilty. He's been raising hell his whole life. No one knew what to think."

"It's a big leap from hell-raising to murder, and I shouldn't have let myself even wonder."

"Everyone wondered. Don't feel bad. Did you hear the ex-boyfriend was arrested in Connecticut?"

"No! When?"

"Earlier today."

They sat together at Bertha's kitchen table while he ate.

"I'm relieved for her family, but sad all over again. It's such a waste that ruins two young lives."

"Yeah, for sure. All because he couldn't deal with her breaking up with him."

"I'm sorry you got caught up in something you had nothing to do with."

"It's a little overwhelming to realize how quickly your whole life can be turned upside down when you're suspected of a heinous crime." He ran a clam through the melted butter she'd warmed for him and popped it into his mouth. "I'll tell you one thing... I have a whole new appreciation for the work Dan has done on behalf of unjustly incarcerated people."

"It's truly remarkable. And the people he's freed are so thankful. One of them shows up to cook for us any time we're in Malibu. Others do a wide variety of things for him throughout the year to show their gratitude, all of which he says is unnecessary, but you can't tell them that."

"He gave them their lives back. They see it as the least they can do."

"Exactly."

"I'm happy for you, K. You've found an amazing life for your-self on your island with a great guy who worships the ground you walk on. You deserve all the good things."

"So do you, Kirbs. I want you to have that, too."

"It'll happen if it's meant to." He shrugged. "I suppose online dating is out now that I pop up as an accused murderer on Google."

Kara didn't want to laugh at that, but the face he made sent her over the edge.

"It's ridiculous," he said. "The exoneration comes about twenty items below the charges."

"I wonder if Dan can do something about that."

Kirby shrugged. "Whatever. It's part of my story now, for better or worse. At least I won't need to worry about getting a job."

"That's true."

"Did you hear that Dad has put together a succession plan for the company that makes all eleven of us equal partners, with Kendra and Kellen as the managing partners?"

"When did that happen?"

"Earlier today. He sent a text."

"I haven't looked at my phone in hours. What do you think of that?"

"It makes sense to have them as the managing partners, since they're basically running the place now. I like that he gave a piece of it to all of us, and he put it in an irrevocable trust so no one can force anyone else out. There'd be no point in fighting over any of it."

"That sounds like a wise move in light of the family history."

"I agree. He said he's going to retire at the end of next year, and then the future is up to us to chart. Kingston immediately chimed in to say he'll have nothing to do with the company, even if he's an owner, to which Kellen replied that he can just cash the checks and not worry about it."

"Sounds like a reasonable response."

"King replied with a thumbs-up."

"That's good."

"Yep. It's all good."

Just as he said that, Buster shot off the first of the fireworks he'd procured for the occasion.

"Let's go watch," Kara said.

They went outside to join the others as the sky exploded in light and color.

Dan slipped an arm around Kara. "There you are."

"Here I am."

"How's Kirby?" Dan asked after her brother went to grab a beer from the cooler.

"He's doing okay." She filled him in on her dad's plan for the company.

"Sounds like a great plan that keeps the company in the family and ensures a smooth transition into the next generation."

"I agree."

Kara snuggled into his embrace to watch the fireworks as a feeling of true contentment settled over her. She'd come home, faced her demons and found they'd lost some of their claws in the years she'd been gone. Time had a way of marching forward and leaving the past and its many lessons behind, but those lessons had made her stronger and wiser, and they'd led her to the life she was meant to lead with the man of her dreams.

"Do you feel ready to go home?" Dan asked.

"I can't wait to get home—and I can't wait to come back here."

"I can't wait for all of it. Every single day with you and Dylan."

"Me either."

"Then what do you say we ask Slim to pick us up in the morning?"

"I'm with you, Counselor. All the way."

THANK YOU FOR READING HOMECOMING! I LOVED writing this book about Kara and Dan's trip to Maine and the chance to delve into the Ballard family dynamics while righting some past wrongs along the way. It was fun to showcase Dan's special talents for getting to the truth and finding the right people to help him.

As I've mentioned, Downeast is NOT going to become another series. I decided while writing this book that I cannot take on the commitment to another series right now with three others at various stages. I reserve the right to revisit this world in the future if inspiration strikes, but for now, there're no plans to continue this story, even if we may see some of these characters on Gansett Island in the future. I have a LOT on my plate already with the First Family, Wild Widows and Gansett Island Series still going strong and another series chomping at the bit to be written. Not to mention I'm planning a new Quantum book for 2025. I never want to promise more than I can deliver, thus the decision to keep Downeast to this book and the Dan & Kara Prequel novel.

Join the Homecoming Reader Group at *www.facebook.com/groups/homecomingreaders/* to discuss this new story with spoilers allowed and the Downeast Group at *www.facebook.com/groups/downeastreaders* for any future updates in this world.

Many thanks to the team that supports me behind the scenes: Julie Cupp, Lisa Cafferty, Jean Mello, Nikki Haley, Ashley Lopes, and Emily Force. Thank you to my editors Linda Ingmanson and Joyce Lamb, as well as my A Team Beta readers Anne Woodall and Kara Conrad. Thank you to my author friend and former attorney Sawyer Bennett, who helped with some legal details to keep that part of the story as authentic as possible.

I recruited some of Gansett Island readers as well as readers who live in Maine to help out with a few details and beta reads. Thank you to: Holly, Janet, Jennifer, Jen, Deb, Karen, Irene, Jean, Jill, Juliane, Marianne, Bethany and Amy.

I read and enjoyed "How to Catch a Lobster in Down East Maine" by Christina Lemieux Oragano, "Downeast" by Gigi Georges, which gave insight into the area as well as the lobstering tradition.

Thank you to my readers, who make all things possible. I'll never have the words to properly thank you for supporting me and my books the way you do.

Much love,

Marie

Also by Marie Force

Contemporary Romances Available from Marie Force

Downeast

Dan & Kara: A Downeast Prequel

Homecoming: A Downeast Novel

The Gansett Island Series

Book 1: Maid for Love *(Mac & Maddie)*

Book 2: Fool for Love *(Joe & Janey)*

Book 3: Ready for Love *(Luke & Sydney)*

Book 4: Falling for Love *(Grant & Stephanie)*

Book 5: Hoping for Love *(Evan & Grace)*

Book 6: Season for Love *(Owen & Laura)*

Book 7: Longing for Love *(Blaine & Tiffany)*

Book 8: Waiting for Love *(Adam & Abby)*

Book 9: Time for Love *(David & Daisy)*

Book 10: Meant for Love *(Jenny & Alex)*

Book 10.5: Chance for Love, *A Gansett Island Novella (Jared & Lizzie)*

Book 11: Gansett After Dark *(Owen & Laura)*

Book 12: Kisses After Dark *(Shane & Katie)*

Book 13: Love After Dark *(Paul & Hope)*

Book 14: Celebration After Dark *(Big Mac & Linda)*

Book 15: Desire After Dark *(Slim & Erin)*

Book 16: Light After Dark *(Mallory & Quinn)*

Book 17: Victoria & Shannon (Episode 1)

Book 18: Kevin & Chelsea (Episode 2)

A Gansett Island Christmas Novella *(Appears in Mine After Dark)*

Book 19: Mine After Dark *(Riley & Nikki)*

Book 20: Yours After Dark *(Finn & Chloe)*

Book 21: Trouble After Dark *(Deacon & Julia)*

Book 22: Rescue After Dark *(Mason & Jordan)*

Book 23: Blackout After Dark *(Full Cast)*

Book 24: Temptation After Dark *(Gigi & Cooper)*

Book 25: Resilience After Dark *(Jace & Cindy)*

Book 26: Hurricane After Dark *(Full Cast)*

Book 27: Renewal After Dark *(Duke & McKenzie)*

Book 28: Delivery After Dark *(2025)*

The Wild Widows Series—a Fatal Series Spin-Off

Book 1: Someone Like You *(Roni & Derek)*

Book 2: Someone to Hold *(Iris & Gage)*

Book 3: Someone to Love *(Winter & Adrian)*

Book 4: Someone to Watch Over Me *(Lexi & Tom)*

Book 5: Someone to Remember *(2025)*

*The Green Mountain Series**

Book 1: All You Need Is Love *(Will & Cameron)*

Book 2: I Want to Hold Your Hand *(Nolan & Hannah)*

Book 3: I Saw Her Standing There *(Colton & Lucy)*

Book 4: And I Love Her *(Hunter & Megan)*

Novella: You'll Be Mine *(Will & Cam's Wedding)*

Book 5: It's Only Love *(Gavin & Ella)*

Book 6: Ain't She Sweet *(Tyler & Charlotte)*

The Butler, Vermont Series*

(Continuation of Green Mountain)

Book 1: Every Little Thing *(Grayson & Emma)*

Book 2: Can't Buy Me Love *(Mary & Patrick)*

Book 3: Here Comes the Sun *(Wade & Mia)*

Book 4: Till There Was You *(Lucas & Dani)*

Book 5: All My Loving *(Landon & Amanda)*

Book 6: Let It Be *(Lincoln & Molly)*

Book 7: Come Together *(Noah & Brianna)*

Book 8: Here, There & Everywhere *(Izzy & Cabot)*

Book 9: The Long and Winding Road *(Max & Lexi)*

The Quantum Series*

Book 1: Virtuous *(Flynn & Natalie)*

Book 2: Valorous *(Flynn & Natalie)*

Book 3: Victorious *(Flynn & Natalie)*

Book 4: Rapturous *(Addie & Hayden)*

Book 5: Ravenous *(Jasper & Ellie)*

Book 6: Delirious *(Kristian & Aileen)*

Book 7: Outrageous *(Emmett & Leah)*

Book 8: Famous *(Marlowe & Sebastian)*

Book 9: Illustrious *(Max & Stella, 2025)*

The Miami Nights Series*

Book 1: How Much I Feel *(Carmen & Jason)*

Book 2: How Much I Care *(Maria & Austin)*

Book 3: How Much I Love *(Dee's story)*

Nochebuena, A Miami Nights Novella

Book 4: How Much I Want *(Nico & Sofia)*

Book 5: How Much I Need *(Milo & Gianna)*

*The Treading Water Series**

Book 1: Treading Water *(Jack & Andy)*

Book 2: Marking Time *(Clare & Aidan)*

Book 3: Starting Over *(Brandon & Daphne)*

Book 4: Coming Home *(Reid & Kate)*

Book 5: Finding Forever *(Maggie & Brayden)*

Single Titles

In the Air Tonight

Five Years Gone

One Year Home

Sex Machine

Sex God

Georgia on My Mind

True North

The Fall

The Wreck

Love at First Flight

Everyone Loves a Hero

Line of Scrimmage

Romantic Suspense Novels Available from Marie Force

The First Family Series

Book 1: State of Affairs

Book 2: State of Grace

Book 3: State of the Union

Book 4: State of Shock

Book 5: State of Denial

Book 6: State of Bliss

Book 7: State of Suspense

Book 8: State of Alert

Book 9: State of Retribution *(2025)*

Book 10: State of Preservation *(2025)*

Read Sam and Nick's earlier stories in the Fatal Series!

The Fatal Series*

One Night With You, *A Fatal Series Prequel Novella*

Book 1: Fatal Affair

Book 2: Fatal Justice

Book 3: Fatal Consequences

Book 3.5: Fatal Destiny, *the Wedding Novella*

Book 4: Fatal Flaw

Book 5: Fatal Deception

Book 6: Fatal Mistake

Book 7: Fatal Jeopardy

Book 8: Fatal Scandal

Book 9: Fatal Frenzy

Book 10: Fatal Identity

Book 11: Fatal Threat

Book 12: Fatal Chaos

Book 13: Fatal Invasion

Book 14: Fatal Reckoning

Book 15: Fatal Accusation

Book 16: Fatal Fraud

Historical Romance Available from Marie Force

About the Author

Marie Force is the #1 *Wall Street Journal* bestselling author of more than 100 contemporary romance, romantic suspense and erotic romance novels. Her series include Fatal, First Family, Gansett Island, Butler Vermont, Quantum, Treading Water, Miami Nights and Wild Widows.

Her books have sold more than 14 million copies worldwide, have been translated into more than a dozen languages and have appeared on the *New York Times* bestseller list more than 30 times. She is also a *USA Today* bestseller, as well as a Spiegel bestseller in Germany.

Her goals in life are simple—to spend as much time as she can with her "kids" who are now adults, to keep writing books for as long as she possibly can and to never be on a flight that makes the news.

Join Marie's mailing list on her website at *marieforce.com* for news about new books and upcoming appearances in your area. Follow her on Facebook, at *www.Facebook.com/MarieForceAuthor*, Instagram *@marieforceauthor* and TikTok *@marieforceauthor*. Contact Marie at *marie@marieforce.com*.

www.ingramcontent.com/pod-product-compliance
Ingram Content Group UK Ltd.
Pitfield, Milton Keynes, MK11 3LW, UK
UKHW041308200225
4682UKWH00021B/162